Finch Books by Carryn W. Kerr

Single Books
The Renascent World
The Renascent Effect

I0646146

THE RENASCENT EFFECT

CARRYN W. KERR

The Renascent Effect
ISBN # 978-1-83943-736-6
©Copyright Carryn W. Kerr 2021
Cover Art by Louisa Maggio ©Copyright August 2021
Interior text design by Claire Siemaszkiewicz
Finch Books

Published in 2021 by Finch Books, United Kingdom.

Finch Books is an imprint of Totally Entwined Group Limited.

THE
RENASCENT
EFFECT

Dedication

For Kai, Cindy and Daniel,
With all my love, I thank you for bearing with me
through it all.

To my most adored Peter, Liam and Cassidy,

Of all outcomes, I never thought I'd say goodbye to you like this. Should I apologize? I suppose you won't want that. Please understand that I face my next journey with peace. Nothing any of you did or didn't do caused my fate. This is on me alone. The world is full of danger.

Peter, my heart breaks to know I'll never again feel the warmth and safety of your loving embrace. I long for it, even now. You are my heart and soul. You always were, even in high school.

Liam and Cassidy, my heart explodes with pride when I think of you both. Continue with your studies. Forget all that has happened. Love and learn and grow into all you're meant to be. Don't be held back by this tragedy.

In the olden days, people who had committed treason died. Even if you blame Gina, it will not help bring you comfort or me back. I'm almost embarrassed that I denied involvement because someone discovered where I'd hidden the notes in my office – and, of course, they then alerted Gina.

Please know that it was never my intention to hurt the three of you – the people I love most in this world. So yes, in my own way, I am sorry.

Your ever-loving wife and mother,
Emily

Chapter One

I peered through my bedroom window at the dark, oppressive thunder clouds rolling across the sky. They seemed to mock me—a personalized manifestation of the cold vise gripping my heart. I slithered into the glossy black dress and smoothed the silky fabric. Ignoring the tingling sensation in my hands, I squinted into the dresser mirror, fingering bits of hair from my up-do and coaxing them into fine ringlets. When I lowered my vision to my face, an icy, haunted chill slid down my spine. But this wasn't Mom—not her oval face or her deep blue eyes. No, it was me. Red lines mapped the whites in the mirror, the blue irises shimmering like the glistening black fabric of my dress. Except phantom-liquid glossed the dress, not tears. And those fell thick and fast. No matter how I swiped at them, more fell. On top of that, I kept fixating on the sixteen silver sparkle bangles Mom and Dad had presented me with two years earlier, and on my other wrist where Grandma's wrap-around bracelet pen clung. Too many memories came with both, so I slipped them off and sealed them in my dresser drawer.

After composing myself enough, I left my room but halted on the stairs. Liam was waiting near the front door with Achilles and Yvon lying at his feet. My brother's sleek outfit glimmered on the polished dark wood floor. He flashed one upward glance but refused to look at me. As I descended the stairs and crossed the hall to him, new tears blurred my vision. "Please don't do this, Li."

His otherwise-bright-green eyes dulled, and like mine, red lines streaked the whites.

He didn't meet my pleading gaze, nor did he reply. I couldn't leave it at that. "How long are you going to carry on blaming Eric and me for Mom's murder?"

When I'd left the cage to face Gina, he'd said it wasn't our fault—only because he'd thought Gina had meant to kill me. Since she hadn't, he'd gone back to sticking Mom's murder on us.

He finally spoke, but his voice had turned to stone. "It's no different from how you blame Eric."

A few days ago—in fact, the day after Gina had murdered Mom—Eric had broken my heart. "But it *is* different. Eric *confessed* to making a deal with Gina."

Liam glanced upstairs and cleared his throat as Dad descended to join us. Dad wore a dazed expression, a black tie dangling around his neck.

I gulped a lump down my throat and gestured at the tie. "Can I help you with that, Dad?"

He managed one slow nod.

I approached him, raising his collar. "You're looking thin. When *did* you last get something into your stomach?"

He gaped at me as if I'd asked the strangest question, and after a long pause murmured a simple, "I ate."

My fingers trembled as I constructed the Windsor knot and patted it flat. I studied my father's troubled eyes—the same vivid green as Liam's. It brought a burning lump to my throat.

He touched my shoulder, his voice flat and neutral. "Mom would be so proud of you, Cassidy. Now please don't cry. It rips my heart out."

The pleading in his voice made me swallow the lump, but my harsh words burst out before I could stop them. "I don't want Mom's *approval*. I want her *here*."

Dad jerked back, a hoarse whisper grinding from his chest. "My girl, I didn't mean—"

Liam glared at me, his Adam's apple bouncing. His words gushed. "Don't snap at Dad, Cassidy! This is *your* fault."

Our father amplified his voice to a broken grate. "Liam!" He blinked. "Please, guys. We can't go on blaming each other. Gina took Mom from us, not Cassidy. In all fairness"—Dad directed his gentlest tone to me—"neither did Eric. Can either of you tell me in all honesty you'd have done something different in Eric's place?"

Liam's Adam's apple continued to bounce, but fury burned through me. "Eric made a pact with the devil. He betrayed us!"

Dad shook his head in slow repetition, as if he wasn't disagreeing, just sad *I* saw it that way. "Now, I think you know very well that he tried to protect you in the best way he knew how." He laid an arm around both Liam's and my shoulders. "We shouldn't entertain those thoughts. Rather, let's get through today, okay?" Then he let our tan-and-black Dobermans out through the back door.

I didn't want to fight with my father. He needed us to stand together. Sucking my disagreeing words back,

I nodded. Liam must have been thinking along the same lines, because an empathetic frown tugged at his forehead. After heading through the front door...he froze.

Mourners crowded the park over the curved walkway beneath waterproofed, Kaleidotonium umbrellas, which floated over their heads like a thousand black mushrooms. Kaleidotonium was Graham's discovery and the reason we were alive. The indestructible shell had protected Petriville while we'd lived in Earth's orbit. Regardless, I hated everything about this place and Gina. I was glad she wouldn't be here today. Susan Petri had imprisoned her mother for Mom's assassination, but even though she was imprisoned, I still loathed Gina.

I forced my mind to the present. Graham, the Winters and the Carter families waited on our front lawn. I found my attention flicking to the tall figure at the back of our party of friends. With gritted teeth, I swiveled away. This *wasn't* the same as Liam blaming me. Eric had betrayed us all. I wanted to head over to him and tell him he should leave right away — demand that he never return. *Not now, not in front of Dad*. I'd do it later.

Liam laid a palm over Dad's shoulder. He matched Dad's height now. His rapid-fire speech emerged only a tad slower than normal, but as soothing as a melody. "Dad, would you like to lead the procession? Are you up to it?"

A vacant expression glazed our father's features as he tilted his head at Liam, confused. "Do you think your mother would wish that?"

Liam didn't skip a beat. "I do, Dad. Mom would like that very much."

I smiled at Liam, grateful that he treated our father with such tenderness. He didn't return it. I hung back and trailed them along the walkway. Mom seeped into every memory, looping through my mind, like when we'd arrived home together after Gina had discovered my friendship with Eric, her warm smile whenever I'd walked through our front door, how her ankles had stuck out below the hem of her jeans. Yesterday I'd gripped her beige cashmere turtleneck to my face and recalled my absolute contentment when she'd cuddled me against her. The wool still smelled of her. It broke me.

The nearest transparent intersection footbridge glowed in its reflection of rainbow colors. Behind Dad and Liam, I made for the inbound of the dual conveyors. As we rode the gentle upward slope, I scanned our hometown. Every digital billboard dotted along the conveyor from here to the town square showed images of Mom. Etched beneath her photo were her name, date of birth and date of death — *of her murder, more like it.*

Even more black umbrellas lined the dual conveyor than filled the park. Their wards stood in clusters between lollipop trees and Victorian street lanterns, while the rain beat a steady rhythm against the Kaleidotonium shells.

From behind, our closest friends ushered us toward the town center — something like a date extending his hand to the small of one's back, offering support and encouragement. The rest of the funeral procession joined in after they passed.

We drifted beneath several glowing footbridges. The conveyor-ride left me alone with my thoughts for far too long, but finally the town square — or rather, circle — came into view. The large, shiny number two marked the end of the line. If I thought too many mourners had trailed us on conveyor two, even more poured into the town plaza. Thousands dismounted the twelve conveyor streets that, like the hands of a clock, cut wedge-shaped sectors into the area.

Crowds milled about the cobbled paving and the grassed areas, speckling the town center, only avoiding sitting on the wet park benches.

In silence, people cleared a path. We made our way to the far side of the square. I looked over my shoulder, landing on sector five—on Mom's old-style stone office building. We'd spent many hours together there when she'd taken me on as an intern. *Who will teach me now?*

As we neared the glossy number seven, I looked up and right toward Dad's office. Like with every building edging Petriville's central circle, old-style stone bedecked the walls. I couldn't recall the last time I'd visited him there.

Behind Dad, Liam rounded the large number and boarded the conveyor beyond. He didn't turn to see if I'd kept up—my brother who professed to love me so much. I wasn't sure which cut worse—me hating Eric or Liam hating me.

We sailed toward the graveyard on Petriville's outskirts. After what felt like forever, I exited the conveyor onto sodden grass. Until now, only a single grave had occupied it. One! It wasn't right that we were burying Mom in the second gaping wound, scarring Petriville's soil. The realization hurt as if someone had ripped my soul through my chest.

A bleak, gaunt and hunched-over version of Dad faced the world these days. No longer did he hold his tall, lean physique with calm, erect confidence. Lines of wretched agony raked his prominent forehead.

After we spread out around Mom's grave, Harriet moved beside Liam. She clung to him and offered me a heavy blink. At least my friend wasn't siding with my brother in hating me. Her blonde waves hung limp and tears gushed down her face.

A Taiwanese priest from sector four stepped from the crowd, then faced us. He directed his sermon to Dad, Liam and me, humming Mom's story in a gentle tone. Digital billboards around Petriville broadcast the sermon to those too far away to hear his words. "We gather here today to celebrate the life of Emily Jones, adored by her husband Peter and children, Liam and Cassidy."

I surveyed the mourners and found Susan Petri. She lingered beneath a tree with Amanda and Gregory, her teenage daughter and son. I scowled, but Susan averted her gaze. Although my reasoning lacked logic, I detested her too.

And because I loved him despite his betrayal, I searched for Eric. He stood with Graham in a clearing. As he trained his gaze on me, I angled away. But I couldn't keep from looking back. He shuffled his feet, dropped his chin to regard his shoes and wrung his hands. Black circles ringed his aquamarine eyes.

The priest continued. "The strength of an attachment formed over a hundred and thirteen years is incomprehensible. Our equestrian veterinarian, Marissa, can attest to bonds formed over fifty…uh…sixty years"—he surveyed the crowd for Marissa before going on—"having lost her husband, James." He frowned and fumbled with the sheets of paper in his hand.

Liam glanced at me for the first time in days, and my mouth dropped open. Not because I thought he'd forgiven me, but because none of us had known that

Marissa's *husband* was the man who'd died all those years ago. No wonder she always looked sour. Harriet and I had still been attending junior school when the rumors had circulated about how he'd died in a kitchen accident.

The priest pressed the microphone into Dad's hand.

With a long blink, Dad frowned, light creases raking his forehead. He looked so frail as he parted his lashes, skimming from person to person. "Emily," he murmured, "my wife, my soul, Liam and Cassidy's mother—gentle, kind, loving. Those words best describe the woman I adore." He spoke about her school-life, her energy and savvy, her many academic and sporting awards and how a room sparkled when she walked in. He added things about my mother I hadn't known. Had I neglected to learn about her life while I'd had the chance to discover who she'd been? Dad ignored the crowd and spoke to Mom in the softest croon. "I will love you forever, my most incredible and beautiful Emily."

Tears streamed down his face and mine. I filtered my attention through the haze. Streaks marked the faces of Liam, Harriet, Jonas, Roger, Megan, Joshua, Caroline, Samantha, Paul and…*Susan. Susan crying? It's probably from guilt.*

Dad handed the microphone back to the priest, who cleared his throat and gave Dad three roses—one red and two white. As the sermon concluded, Dad passed a white rose each to Liam and me. A soft whirring jerked the straps holding Mom's coffin into slow motion, lowering my mother into the ground.

We approached and Dad let the red rose fall, his expression impassive. Liam followed, letting the flower waft out of his fingers. It landed with its stem crossing Dad's, but when I freed mine, it set down several inches away. My head spun with something like vertigo, and before Liam had the chance to spin from me, I clasped his hand. Until that moment, I hadn't planned on defending Mom's honor.

My voice emerged thick, but my tone sounded resolute, giving me the courage to go on. "Our mother didn't deserve to die. She did nothing wrong!" I fixed on Susan, who never looked away this time. "I want to know why Gina killed my mother, and not the rubbish you fed me about Gina thinking my mom had led the rebellion. As much as I hate her, Gina is *not* that stupid. I want the real reason."

Susan's face reddened as she averted her gaze. Liam released my hand, tears rolling down his cheeks. I thought he'd abandon me to my own embarrassing declaration. He didn't. Instead, he hauled me to his chest, arms around my body and head, keeping me safe and warm. "Not now, Cass. Not now, little sister. Think of Dad."

I focused on the priest as he proceeded with his closing words. Numb sadness took hold of me. I never noticed people dispersing. Once more, Eric fixed me with a look. Then he returned his attention to Graham as Susan, Amanda and Gregory joined them.

Liam didn't pull away from me as we retraced our route along conveyor seven, though he opened a gap and encouraged Dad to fit in between us. I slipped my arm through my father's and looked up at his fair, sculptured features. My heart fractured. Yes, for Liam and yes, for me, but more for the wonderful man between us. "Dad, tell me you're going to be okay. Please tell me you'll get through this."

Dad blinked and angled his face toward me. "We must, my daughter. We have no choice."

Susan held Mom's wake in the town square. Although I didn't want to, I couldn't stop myself from scanning the thick flagpole rooted beside the wide Roman stairs. The tall spire rose toward the sky. At its pinnacle, the bright orange Petrician Enterprises flag wafted in the breeze.

I grimaced at the twisted morbidity, the memory slamming into me with the force of a wrecking ball — the scene of Mom's murder.

When Petriville's mourners finally dissipated, dusk settled. The antique-like stone of the municipal building which spanned sectors eight to ten awoke, the eerie glow of the amber lights growing brighter.

As Liam, Dad and I made our way home, wrapped in each other's arms, new tears surged down my face. Drawing a breath, I wiped them away and made myself a pact. From that moment forward, I'd save my tears — for Mom and the few others who mattered.

Chapter Two

The town of Petriville remained exactly where we'd crash-landed, nestled in an ocean bay, tipping the beach — and squashing the forest. A week after Mom's funeral, while dense waves of humidity shimmered over the town, Dad and Liam played backgammon at our rosewood dining table. I slouched beside them in a light summer dress and sandals, with *Jane Eyre* dominating the single firm, paper-like digipar before me.

I pressed my index finger to the lower right corner and flipped the virtual page to the next. Glancing up from the text and narrow cover-image heading, I tapped Dad's arm. "Please send for an extension on the books. I'd like to read them again."

Dad managed a subdued laugh. "Now come on, Cass. Don't you want to discover other stories?" He flipped over a few that were laying before me. "*Around the World in Eighty Days. Oliver Twist. Great Expectations.*"

"They're classics." I rotated to Dad. "Did you roll your eyes?"

An easy laugh burst from his lips—his first since Mom… I ripped my thoughts from the dark and mock-pouted at him, hands on my hips. "You did. You rolled your eyes at me."

Liam allowed a slow, appreciative smile to form on his lips.

A knock drew us from our moment of shared joy. Liam raised one dark blond brow. "It's your turn to collect the casserole, sis."

I fixed him with a teasing glare, sighed and stood. "Fine…I'll get the door."

All week, neighbors from near and far had dropped off food packages, flowers and condolences—kind gestures, but unnecessary. All Petriville's food outlets sold ready-meals, but I liked the flowers.

I pricked the door open and smiled around it. "Yes?"

In a reaction too instant to restrain, I jerked back. And yes, I erected my posture, glowering at my stupidity for wanting to impress him. Eric shifted from foot to foot on our front porch. Iridescent light danced off an hourglass Kaleidotonium vase filled with the most enormous mix of white roses, carnations and lilies. The prongs of a bright-silver trident stuck out between the flowers. It propped up two mini digipars.

"If you're here to give your sympathies, you shouldn't have bothered. Or is this more like a guilt tribute, since you haven't visited even once?"

He showed his palms. "Hey, you told me you never wanted to see me again. Shouldn't I have listened?"

I ignored his question and opened my mouth, intending to tell him to go. But that smoky vanilla scent assaulted me. My forehead tightened into a confused frown as pained lines raked his face. *Those damned eyes and his crevassed cheek dimples.* After all this, how was it I still wanted him to grip me in his muscled arms, sweep me off my feet and kiss me for all he was worth? At the same time, the allure of slapping the flowers from his hand and warning him to leave me alone almost made me smile. I peered at him through the more-closed-than-open door.

His familiar, faint Texas accent broke into my assessment. "Won't you talk to me, Cassidy? Let me in." Although the words implied a demand, his tone and pained voice made them a plea.

I gaped at the dark circles beneath his eyes. "You look worse than the last time I saw you."

Eric's swallow told me my jibe had gotten to him, since that had been at Mom's funeral. My stupid lips trembled. I squeezed them together to hide the quiver and managed a whispered hiss. "What is there to say, Eric?"

He didn't answer but steadied on me as he awaited my decision. I opened the door. "Okay. Well, you might as well come in."

Eric stepped through the door, greeting Liam and Dad.

My ever-polite father came over, but even he struggled to maintain his composure, and his handshake must have been hard because Eric winced. "I hope you're here to apologize, young man."

Eric moved his focus to me, and I almost felt sorry for him. *Almost.*

Liam didn't even bother to stand. Instead, he pretended to focus on his game and expelled a distracted grunt. Without encouraging Eric to follow, I stalked to the lounge-come-VE Room. He pursued me anyway. As I flopped into a leather recliner, he set the flowers on a side-table, gesturing at the chair to my right. "May I?"

I snorted. "Why are you being so ridiculously polite, Eric? Of course you can sit down."

He heeded my instructions, angled forward, braced his forearms on his knees and interlaced his fingers. "It's easy to see I'm not wanted around here and —"

I cut him off. "Really? You can see that?" I made it a question and glared. "Are you surprised, Eric? This is *your* fault."

He puffed an exasperated laugh. "Like I was trying to say… I know it's justified."

I changed the subject. "Are those new jeans?" As much as Eric deserved my cold shoulder, a pang of empathy gnawed at my stomach. Eric had worn old hand-me-downs from who-knew-where when I'd brought him to Petriville. Unlike us, he hadn't had access to designer stores. I looked away, leaned toward the vase and wriggled the mini digipars free from the prongs. Silver writing addressed one to *The Jones Family* and one to *Cassidy*.

"The clothes are good here." Eric's half-laugh, half-grimace seemed laden with uncertainty.

"They are good — not that you'll be here long enough to enjoy them." I cringed at my chilled tone, then buckled. "I know I'm the one who addressed the subject, but I'm sure you didn't come here to talk about clothes."

He wrung his hands and gulped. "You're never going to forgive me, are you? Do you want me to leave?"

I shrugged, wanting to fall into Eric's arms, give myself over to him and forget everything. But that would betray Mom's memory. I *couldn't* do it. "Please give me time?"

With a slow blink, the lines on his forehead smoothed. After a moment, he again met my gaze. "Take all the time you need, my"—he cleared his throat—"what I mean is…Cassidy." The way he said my name was like he needed to feel it sliding off his tongue. It made me warm inside—and cold.

I locked my gaze on my lap and fiddled with my sixteen silver sparkle bangles and, on the other wrist, with Grandma's wrap-around bracelet pen. After Mom's funeral, I'd taken to wearing them again—as if I needed to keep that connection to her. "I doubt you'll wait, though, Eric." When I looked up again, creases stretched across his forehead. I didn't waver. "The girls in Petriville are beautiful and not all of them have a DNA match."

Eric hooked me with a curious gaze. "Are you trying to get rid—?"

Another knock sounded and I lifted a hand to silence Eric while listening to Liam skid across the dark wood floor in socks. In a loud voice, I announced, "You're like a two-year-old, Liam. Do you know that?"

He ignored my taunt and must have gone outdoors because the conversation grew muffled. After a few minutes, the door shut and a moment later he skidded into the lounge, his words the usual rapid-fire. "So, it was Amanda at the door."

I squinted. "Amanda? As in Gina's granddaughter? What does *she* want?"

Liam set his palms up in a 'don't-shoot-the-messenger' gesture. "Gina wants to see you. She's in the east prison wing. Amanda says it sounds important because"—he shook his head—"she wants you to go now."

I shot up. "Now?"

Liam wore his fatherly face again. "You're not *going*, Cassidy. You must know she means to torment you."

I tilted my head away, fingers curling. "She can't hurt me from a prison cell."

Liam arched his brows in something like suppressed annoyance. "Not in the physical sense! But she doesn't need to. She's snake-enough with words."

I set the mini digipars beside the flowers. "Well, she might tell me why she murdered Mom."

Liam flattened his lips as Eric rose. I skirted them both as Eric faced Liam. "Should I go with your sister?"

I spun on him, but Liam beat me to the punch. "What is your plan, Eric? To make sure Gina doesn't tell Cassidy how long you worked for her?"

Dad called from the dining-room. "That's enough, Liam!"

Eric tried again. "Can I at least walk with you?"

"I need time to think, Eric." Without waiting for his reply, I raced for the front door with Dad yelling after me, "It's a bad idea," and Liam howling, "Wait, Cass—"

I followed neither's guidance.

Chapter Three

My mind raced as I sprinted over the intersection footbridge and hopped aboard the conveyor to the town square, slowing only enough to dodge the few mid-morning commuters. When a bobbing head of long dark hair came into view, I slowed beside her and did a double take. I hadn't acknowledged Amanda at Mom's funeral, through my blur of tears and haze of emotions. She looked different from the plain, plump girl I remembered. "It *is* you. Amanda! You've lost a ton of weight since the party. You look good. I heard your coach promoted you to Team Salamander's major league."

Amanda half leaned away as she glanced sideways at me. "Hello to you too, Cassidy."

"Oh, yes. Sorry. Hello, Amanda."

She widened her dark brown eyes. "I'm unsure how I should take that little speech of yours. Was there a compliment buried somewhere in there?"

A grimace dragged my mouth down and sweat beaded on my brow. "I mean, you're quite beautiful now. You look nothing like Susan or Gina."

Her enormous eyes grew even wider, and she raised her brows. "Why bring up Mother and Grandmother? You're not helping your case." She sighed. "But it is true that I'm more like my dad."

I found my lips stretching into a smile. "I'm guessing he was a handsome man."

"He was. My mom destroyed his photographs, but she missed one and I have it hidden away."

A touch of empathy rose, surprising me and making my brow tighten, but I ignored it. "Why *does* Gina want to see me? Do you know?"

Amanda shrugged. "She said it would be in your best interests to visit her. She may be fibbing, but she said she could help you."

When Gina had held Petriville's reins, she'd confined Dad in the east wing. Only two weeks ago, we'd helped him escape.

"I can get to the prisons from the tunnels, but how do you get there from street-level?"

"The stairway is inside the train station. When you're inside, head for the wall nearest sector five. You can't miss the stairs. Once you're down there" — Amanda fell into a mordant drawl — "you can follow her voice. She doesn't shut up for a second."

"Thanks." As we reached the glossy number two, marking the conveyor's end, I slipped around it and darted ahead.

A mix of Petrician Enterprises employees and students from the college fronting sector eight bustled about in the town square. I charged across the cobbled paving toward sector four and up the wide stone stairs. The one-way glass doors of the train station glided open, and I raced through, my attention skittering to the far side of the platform.

A minute later, I descended the silver stairs. Recognition only set in after three flights, where I arrived at the upper of the silver tunnels. An image of the lower tunnel and its dual conveyor system flashed through my mind. When rescuing Dad, we'd accessed the prison through this tunnel. I skimmed over the words 'East Wing' that was etched into both tunnel walls before I took the side tunnel and the final downward flight. The prison cells lay halfway down—midway between the upper and lower tunnel.

Amanda was right. The snake-like yet somehow rhythmical monotone of Gina's sneering voice echoed through the corridor. In the lowest tunnel, four soldiers sat around what looked like a kids' table. They were playing a virtual card game. Each man fanned the bright blue outlines and red-backed images of seven old-style cards. Wads of cotton wool stuck out of the men's ears. One looked up without removing the white fluff. I signaled toward the racket Gina was producing.

"Your funeral," he sang before refocusing on the game.

With fidgeting fingers, I turned into the tunnel as Gina continued yelling her insults. Luckily, she occupied the only cell—two or three away from where she had imprisoned Dad. A shiver ran through me, despite the hot weather.

Gina glared through the window, her familiar horn-rimmed spectacles fronting her parrot face. Although little of her stumpy body appeared, she was higher than I expected—not much below my line of sight.

I scoffed. "Well-planned viewing windows, Gina. Now you have to stand on your bed to see out. You probably never predicted you'd take up residency in one of these."

She ignored my taunt and slid the viewing window glass wider. "Oh, it is delightful to see how you still obey my every command."

She thrust her chin and gripped the bars like a caged monkey.

I rolled my eyes. "The look renders your attempt at arrogance a little inauthentic, don't you think, Gina?"

"Perhaps, but this is only me and you, and I've just proven I am still capable of summoning you at will."

A sneer twisted my mouth. Neither it nor the bitterness in my words were intentional, I didn't think. "You don't get to call the shots. Not anymore."

Gina delivered a disgusted snort. "And yet...here you are. Oh my... It appears you have learned nothing from your mother's death. Silly girl. As arrogant as ever."

I folded my arms, tilting away. "The difference is...I can leave."

Gina lengthened her neck, jutting her chin. "Yet you shall not. I, in fact, keep secret something you desperately desire—a carrot I dangle over your head. You shall keep returning until I decide to appease your curiosity. A real little dogs-body I could make of you."

I hated how true her words rang in my ears. "Am I here for your amusement, Gina—so you can gloat? Or do you plan on telling me anything worthwhile?"

"Mm-m. Perhaps I enjoy our brief chats. Or perhaps I shall offer you a thing or two of value."

My words sounded lethargic. "Well, what am I waiting for, Gina?" She'd played me for a fool long enough. I made to leave.

"Indulge an old woman for a moment, won't you, Miss Jones? Not much amusement comes my way."

The hairs on my neck bristled, as the last time she'd called me 'Miss Jones' replayed in my mind. It had been just after she'd murdered Mom. "I'm not here for your entertainment, you evil woman. You didn't summon me for my benefit."

She lifted a hand to her heart. Only the tips of her fingers showed through the viewing window. "Oh, you wound me."

I pivoted and started down the passage, but as Gina's singing words reached my ears, I froze. "Susan lied to you."

She paused. I cursed myself for sucking in a deep breath. Once again, I gave in to her and headed back. "About what—?" Though I already knew.

Gina confirmed my suspicions. "Your mother did not agree to take the fall as the rebellion leader."

I snarled at her. "Why are you telling me this?"

Sweet venom filled her smile. "Mm-m. I think I shall keep that tidbit of information for another visit."

A lump formed in my throat as I made an about-face, paced down the corridor and up the stairs. In the upper tunnel, I stopped and rested against the wall, breathing in ragged chokes. Numb anguish roiled through me and I gaped at the engraved words on the opposite wall—*East Wing*. The same word on this side scratched my back. The physical discomfort prepared me for another kind of pain I needed to face, and there was no time like the present.

Two stairs at a time, I ascended into the train station and out. My mind reeled as I crossed the cobbled town square and climbed the broad Roman stairs to the open-air lobby of the municipal building. My mind skidded over how to approach Susan. Only as I entered the elevator up to Susan's office did my awareness return. It surprised me that her office elevator doors opened.

But they did, and Susan was present. She barely looked up from the kingly, dark-wood desk where the bay windows framed her. Gina and Susan's photograph no longer took the focal point of the decorated wall. Susan, Amanda and Gregory had taken its place, though the pictures of Amanda and Gregory in different stages of growth remained.

As I stalked over the lavishly patterned carpet toward Susan, she stood and rounded the desk. She nodded to one of the plush, brown leather one- and two-seater armchairs around a coffee-table. I plopped into a single-seater and Susan sat opposite.

She kept her tone gentle. "What brings you here today, Miss Jones?"

I hesitated. "I…uh…just visited Gina."

She spoke in a drawn-out lilt. "Yes?"

Am I ready for this confrontation? I gritted my teeth. "You lied."

Her tone didn't change. "About what was that, my dear?"

I snarled my reply. "My mother never offered to take the fall!"

Susan drew a deep breath. "You're quite right. I shall not deny it, but frankly I'm surprised Mother delayed so long in telling you. Did she mention she knew this *before* murdering Emily?"

I leaped up, clenching my fists. "Before? What do you mean, *before*?"

"Now sit down, Miss Jones. Let us remain rational. This involves far more than you realize."

I didn't sit. My stomach knotted as I growled, "What more?"

"Mother never killed Emily for her involvement in the rebellion. When Mother told you Emily led the rebellion, I went along with her story. I had to give you *something* until I could establish her actual motives. Sadly, she still refuses to inform me what those were. My new title has kept me too busy appeasing townsfolk and council members to investigate the matter. However, I shall return to it as soon as I have a moment. In the meantime, I am quite certain that, considering you are Emily's daughter, you are the one person who shall find the truth." A wistful smile passed over her lips. "Your mother was a cross between a pit bull and a bloodhound when it came to fact-finding."

My nostrils flared. "What facts did she need to find?"

Susan clasped her knees and half looked away. "You're well aware of what she sought in her work. In this matter I cannot say I have any more knowledge than you, my dear. It was something Mother mentioned" — she squinted up and left — "'*Emily Jones is rather too unrelenting for her own good when she puts her mind to research.*' I think that was how she put it."

Susan seemed honest, candid even. My breath caught in my chest. "Why are you telling me this?"

She considered, then hoisted her chin. "Mm-m. Perhaps, Miss Jones, by learning the truth behind your mother's death, you may help us all."

I guessed she understood way more than she let on but was equally sure she'd tell me no more. My shoulders collapsed, and I spun, swishing my long, dark walnut ponytail.

Susan called me back. "Miss Jones?"

I didn't turn, however my frozen posture encouraged her to go on. "A MAC Challenge might raise morale. I shall let the coaches know."

I said nothing but stalked into the still-open elevator and pressed the 'descend' button.

Chapter Four

Achilles and Yvon raced to meet me at the door. While Achilles barged into my legs, Yvon skidded to a stop and peered up, observing as if in a question. I smoothed a hand over the bumps at the back-center of their otherwise sleek black heads. "What? Don't tell me you're hungry. You could both use a few more runs at the stables."

Liam and Dad still sat at the dining table, and Eric's vase of flowers stood at the center. My brother didn't lift his gaze as he spoke but slid a rook across the virtual squares of their battlefield. "Anyway, it's unlikely, since they've just eaten." As if knowing he spoke of them, the dogs pattered across the dark wood flooring and flopped down near his feet.

I gave in to my urge to check the lounge and my heart sank. Eric had gone. Only then did Liam call out. "Is this what you're looking for?"

I returned to the dining room. "You could have saved me the effort of looking in there."

Liam winked. "And miss this expression on your face?" He picked the miniature digipars up between his fingers, and when I grabbed at them, he jerked back, separated the two, studied the addressees and flicked one at me.

As soon as I caught it between my thumb and forefinger, glowing silver lettering popped up on a pale gray surface.

Dear Peter, Liam and Cassidy,
Please accept our deepest condolences for the tragic loss of Emily.
Graham, Eric, Ethan, Craig and Olivia

"Give me the other one! Did Eric say anything before he left?"

Liam didn't exactly answer my questions. "Look, Cass. Maybe you're being too harsh on him."

I did a double take. "Me? Are you kidding? You blamed him too!"

Liam shrugged and moved his bishop as Dad raised his bright green eyes from the shimmering chess board. "Now, Eric wanted you to read his message, and I suggest you do." With that he handed me the second mini digipar.

The moment I touched it, it granted me access. Again the glowing silver lettering appeared.

Dear Cassidy,
It's a cop-out to explain the reasoning behind my choice in a message. So, please talk to me when you're ready. Any question you ask, I swear to answer honestly. Anything at all.
Always and forever.
Eric

I puffed an irritated sigh but took the message, headed upstairs to my bedroom and closed the door. After shoving in earbuds, I lay on my bed and drowned out the world. As I kept the mini digipar between both thumbs and forefingers, I stroked the words until I fell asleep.

No surprise—I dreamed of Eric.

Chapter Five

Three weeks after my confrontation with Susan, the MAC Challenge day arrived.

I slipped the sparkle bangles and Grandma's wrap-around bracelet pen into my dresser drawer. My hands trembled with nerves as I flipped my hair forward and wove it into a braid, making it less easy for other teams to grasp. After taking my 'Team Paladin' cladding from my closet, I spread it across my bed and slithered into the mostly black leggings. Absently, I traced the color-band with my fingers, smoothing the bright red strip across the top of my buttocks and down my outer thighs. At the knee, the red line twisted toward the front, and I straightened the band down my shins to my feet. The familiarity of the breathable fabric granted a sense of comfort, as cool as a summer breeze. Along with the seamless inner-leg, the dense fabric protected our legs from chafing against the saddles.

I stretched the red priest's collar, then tugged the top over my head and fed my arms into the long sleeves before admiring the outfit in the mirror. The thick red stripes on either side of the front and back coaxed the black-based fabric into my waist. The men's outfits clung to their bodies in a somewhat less-flattering style.

After pushing my feet into the black-and-red fast-grip rubber footwear, I rose, rolling my ankles from side to side as the inner skin molded around each foot. Last of all, I tucked my high-tech grip gloves—black with a red stripe around the wrist and down each finger—into the waistband of my leggings.

Jonas and Harriet, who lived on the main conveyor street a few houses around the corner from ours, waited on the far side of the transparent intersection bridge.

After going over it and joining them, I high-fived Harriet and, as she launched herself at Liam, I hip-nudged Jonas. "I'm surprised to see you without Olivia attached to your side."

Jonas faked a laugh but didn't reply. He'd met the petite, dark-haired girl during our time at Graham's refuge.

Liam had wrapped Harriet in an embrace, hoisting her tiny, color-coordinated body off her feet. He pressed his face into her luxurious blonde hair, seeming to breathe in the scent. After a moment, she pulled back and took in his face, then addressed us in her mild Scottish exclaiming manner. "So, you guys better be ready, because I want to win this thing. No excuses."

Excitement was always in easy reach when around my best friend, and my laugh flowed naturally. "For sure, Harri. I for one refuse to sacrifice our untarnished record."

Smile lines fanned around Jonas' eyes. The familiar cadence of his Scottish accent was less intense than their parents' but stronger than Harriet's. "Here I thought you'd ditch us and get a team going with your boyfriend."

I hiked a brow. "Well, that means you don't know me very well."

The usual flecks of light brown in his irises seemed a fraction darker than normal. "Oh, I *do* know you, and anyway I'm teasing. Are you and Eric talking yet?"

Jonas was one of the few people I didn't need to hide my thoughts from, and they spewed out unbidden. "Not properly. I can't get past his betrayal." I heaved a breath. "And I really miss Mom."

Jonas grazed the backs of his knuckles down my cheek. "I know, Cass. There's still a long road ahead of you — even if you get back with him."

Harriet grabbed my wrist and spun me away, her bright blue eyes sparkling. "This game… It's exactly what you need, girlfriend. It will distract you for a while. Come." She took my hand and led me onto the bustling conveyor with Jonas and Liam trailing.

I sensed, rather than saw, Jonas laying a hand on Liam's shoulder. "Are you up to winning this year, then? We should scratch if you're not. I wouldn't hold it against you." It wasn't an accusation, just the warm offering of my brother's closest friend.

Other commuters, on observing our MAC cladding, found it fit to thump us on our backs and cheer us on with a collection of "make way for our sector two champions," and "go get 'em," and "make us proud."

As if adhering to their chants, the digital billboards came to life with loud emboldening music and scenes from our last match, interspersed with images of earlier years' fireworks and balloons floating toward Petriville's Kaleidotonium shell — in the days when it still protected us from the dangers of living in Earth's orbit.

Ten minutes later we reached the town square and crossed the cobbled paving three sectors to our right. The large number eleven wasn't the normal glossy black, but a thousand gleaming colors blinked in and out over the entirety of the digits. From each a *MAC Challenge* banner protruded — one black-on-gold and one gold-on-black.

Cheers ushered us along the conveyor toward its outer terminus. Here the normal number eleven lay flat — embedded in the lawn.

The familiar long pitch stretched away from us, ending at the rock-faced climbing wall, which rose higher than the municipal building flagpole. Both left and right, spectators filled the parallel grandstands. They too shrunk away toward the wall. Between the two, the gap more than accommodated our seventy-two restless horses. Music played and horns blared. As we entered, our images flared up on the digital displays that skirted the outer rim of the enormous arena. While throwing waves and kisses to the crowd, we strode forward. They roared their appreciation in a mix of cheers and hoots.

After we'd freed our horses upriver on our return trip from Graham's refuge, they'd somehow made their way back to the craft, bringing Eric's gelding, Warrior, with them. When they'd returned to Petriville, Marissa, our horse veterinarian, had gone easier on us than we'd expected, given that we'd lied to her. Maybe she'd empathized over us losing our mother.

At the starting line of the pitch, minor league players tried to calm our horses. Anticipation stirred the excited animals into a frenzy. Most ran in circles around their handlers. Erected before each horse was a row of three distantly spaced posts. Each post carried a cluster of three red reinforced balloons.

As I neared Zenobia, I wiped my sweating palms down my leggings, thrust my hands into my gloves and fastened the Velcro wrist bands. Adrenaline seeped into my veins and my heart thumped. To calm the nervous energy, I squatted into a series of stretches, withdrawing into myself. *Inhale…exhale…inhale… exhale.* From my senses, I cut out sounds, and behind my eyelids, I blocked out sights.

Jonas' voice brought me back. "What the hell is he doing here then?"

I followed his gaze and blew out a breath that rattled my lips. "What indeed?" Eric chewed on a blade of straw with the team three to our right. Team Salamander. He wore their colors of navy and silver — and not just their colors, their full MAC cladding.

Liam groaned, voicing what I thought. "He's with them. He's *competing.*"

As if aware we were speaking about him, Eric peeled away from his teammates — Aretha, Rick and Amanda — and walked over.

I stood beside Liam and dug my palms into my eyes. "Li…do you think I should forgive him?"

Liam laced an arm around my shoulder. "Cass, baby sister, everyone is responsible for themselves. You didn't *make* Eric consort with Gina. For your part, you'll either forgive him when you're ready or you won't — and you'll both move on."

I didn't like the idea of Eric…*moving*…anywhere but didn't tell Liam that, as I dipped into a deep side-stretch. Angled toward the ground, I watched Eric approach.

Liam nodded while Jonas extended a cold, curt handshake. Harriet didn't consider Eric's actions as a betrayal. She reached up, and as he bent to give her a peck on the cheek, she hugged him.

Gina had almost killed Jonas and me once before. She'd chained us to rocks and had intended to drop us into a lake. It had been Eric who'd planted the bolt-cutter that had saved our lives.

Eric turned to me as I continued stretching, trying my level best to ignore him.

He didn't let me. "Great arena you guys have here." I ignored his rhetoric, and he drew his brow into a pained frown, then flicked the straw away and changed the subject. "Did you get to thinking about what I asked, Cassidy?"

I looked up at him from my side stretch, one arm in the air. Everything about him made me want to forget it all and melt into his arms — from the way he lifted his long, lean muscled legs, to his dancing aquamarine eyes, his fissured cheek dimples, how he now clenched his teeth and how it emphasized the outline of his square jaw.

"Why are you dressed like you're competing with *them*, Eric? Do you take pleasure in torturing me?"

He lowered his gaze to his team footwear. "That would be a real foolish way of trying to win you back." He sighed. "Jason injured his knee and Amanda asked me to fill his spot for the tournament."

"Well, that was convenient."

He slumped. "Do you want me to withdraw? Say the word and I will."

"What do you care, anyway? You seem quite happy with your new little sector five gang."

"What was I supposed to do? Sit around on my own and wait in case you might one day speak to me again? If you'd bothered to come see me once since we've been here, you'd know that Susan assigned Graham a house in their area. Amanda said she kept seeing me moping around. She and her friends were kind enough to take me in."

"Oh, I'm sure that was *utterly* a matter of their unwavering *kindness*." Then I added. "Them taking you in or providing you a place on Team Salamander... They probably injured Jason on purpose."

Eric tightened his jaw. "Really! You think me such a MAC asset and them so callous that they'd intentionally hurt one of their own?"

I softened and swallowed. "No. Not really." Then the words blurted through my lips. "You might as well have thrown my mom from that platform yourself, and I can't deal with her loss. I wish you'd feel my pain." As soon as the words erupted, realization hit. I slammed my eyes shut. Eric had lost his parents at only seven years old and his twin brother — his only sibling — a few months before we'd met.

Eric neither raised his voice nor changed his tone, but his last word cracked. "And you think I never *have*?" Then he turned his back on me and jogged to his teammates. With a sinking feeling in the pit of my stomach, I watched him go. He'd had his dark blond hair cut shorter. He'd clearly visited one of the robot-barbers, and he looked so good. *Why am I so irrevocably, almost unnaturally drawn to him?*

Stupid! Stupid! Stupid! I gritted my teeth.

Chapter Six

The five-minute siren sounded.

Jonas hip-bumped me. "Can I give you a leg-up then, Cass?"

"I can jump."

He glanced sideways at me. "I know that, but Zenobia's tall and—"

"It's not up to you to try to make me feel better, Jonas."

Without giving him a chance, I leaped onto my mare's bare back and stroked her sleek liver-chestnut neck.

With a light-hearted chuckle, Jonas mounted Boudicca—a dark bay tobiano mare. Liam launched Harriet onto her palomino mare, Charity, before jumping onto Black Pearl.

A single, broad elasticized band in team colors encircled each mare's girth. Around midway, thinner elasticized lanyards extended toward the horses' mouths. At the end of each, a metal hook clipped onto their bits and kept the horses going straight. They probably didn't need them. They knew what to do.

Organizers permitted no coaches on the pitch, but a minor league player held Zenobia with a short red-and-black halter lead. The mare circled the girl, no less agitated with me on top as the girl handed up my nine-arrow quiver. After strapping it to my back, I took the bow and pulled back on the drawstring to check the tension.

The two-minute siren sounded… My handler led me to the starting line. One minute… Harriet rode to my left and Liam to hers.

To my right, Jonas clutched a bunch of Boudicca's mane in one hand for her initial speed-burst and readied his bow in the other while Boudicca spun around her handler. I did the same.

The siren sounded, and the watching crowd exploded.

Zenobia reared then leaped forward into a gallop. Her back muscles strained and flowed beneath me. My mind whirled through my mental checklist. *Arrow nocked. Head straight. Bow hand relaxed. Shoulders relaxed. Wrist steady. Center the bow string. Draw. Index finger to the corner of the mouth. Line up the elbow. Breathe.* I aimed for the first cluster of three red balloons on the post. *Wait for it…wait for it…wait for it. Now!* I let the arrow fly.

Without me thinking of reaching up and drawing another, I called it into my hand. I nocked and fired, barely having time to aim before we flew past the post. *How many did I hit? One? Two? Three?* I never usually hit two with one arrow. Back at the refuge, Eric had shot three true bursts, one after the other.

We neared the next bunch of balloons too fast. I nocked the arrow and let it fly, then slipped the next into place. Without time to aim, I trusted instinct and shot, inserted the next and fired. Zenobia zoomed past. *Too late.* I'd wasted an arrow. It had missed. Only one post remained before the ever-nearing rock-face. Again, I relied on instinct. My arrows flew. *One. Two. Three.* Then I bolted past, with no idea how many lay shredded. As we bore up on the rail, Zenobia sat back on her haunches in three halting strides.

She was still trotting when I leaped from her back and ran her into the next staging area. Loosening her girth and throat-lash, I hauled the lot over her head. Then I raced through the turnstile and tossed everything onto the scales. The next gate wasn't yet open. I twisted to my teammates just as Harriet dumped her load for weighing.

Then the turnstiles shot open and the four of us raced through, collecting at the bottom of the rock-face and tugging at ropes dangling from the top. As I jerked the first, it came loose, slithered down the face and piled up at my feet. The same happened with the second.

Liam, Jonas and Harriet reached halfway. I clutched another. It held. I stretched for a nook with one hand, wedged my foot into another and tugged, swapping hands and securing the rope around my wrist with each upward advance. If not for the gloves, the rope would have torn our skin to shreds.

Although I didn't have the time to assess how the other teams were progressing, in my peripheral vision I scanned the rock wall. Many were climbing, spread out at various heights across the face.

Liam crested first then Jonas. Harriet and I scrambled over the lip at the same time. I searched for others, and my gaze landed on Eric. Alone, he awaited the rest of his team. The rules prevented him from helping them or leaving the staging area before they all joined. Our gate for the next area flicked open just as Aretha, Team Salamander's next strongest player, summited.

Harriet looked at them, then Liam, Jonas and me. "Go left!" She sprinted forward across the plain, making a run for the closest zip-line.

Without a second's hesitation, I darted forward. But I didn't go left as she'd suggested. I glanced back as Team Salamander burst into the staging area not thirty seconds behind. Other teams were summitting every few seconds. They filtered through their turnstiles in groups of four and swarmed the plateau. With only one zip-line handle per team, missing the opportunity to steal the three extra lines from surrounding teams meant losing the game. Liam and Jonas veered left, following Harriet's suggestion. I couldn't second-guess my choice. The one on the right looked nearer. With my speed, no Team Salamander player would catch me, not even Eric. Two zip-lines lay between us and them. I sprinted for our neighboring zip-line, throwing my body into every stride.

Liam neared the farthest wire and Jonas the one beside him. Harriet ran slower than them, pushing her short legs for every stride. Her central placing, with no one on her tail, gave her the extra time she needed.

With every passing second, I closed the gap to mine. I passed the halfway mark. My confidence soared, and I pushed my legs harder. My muscles burned with the effort, but no-one would stop me. I was going to make it.

Footsteps thudded behind me. Impossible! I couldn't believe it. They gained on me. Before much longer, heavy, warm breaths feathered the nape of my neck. It was unthinkable! I ran faster than most male players.

"Aargh." The fall knocked the wind from my lungs, as powerful arms wrapped around my waist and knocked me forward. My attacker twisted me as we fell, and I never bore his full weight as we thudded to the ground. His vanilla aroma washed over me even before we skidded to a halt with me half on top of him. My back to him, I kicked and squirmed to escape. With every heaved breath, that scent assaulted me, distracting me from my purpose. My voice emerged as a growl. "Get *away* from me!"

I struggled as he grappled with me. "No. You're going…to get hurt. Will you…please stop…fighting?"

I did, but only for the second it took for him to loosen his grip. I took the opportunity, kicked back and charged forward, scrambling away from him. The zip-line lay right ahead. I sprinted, not listening for his footsteps, his breathing, only focusing on the zip-line as I stretched for the handle.

I locked one hand around the metal rod and clicked the release button with the other. A muscled arm grabbed my waist as Eric gripped the metal rod beside me. He took its whole remaining space. None was left for my other hand, and I'd caught the rod with the weaker of my two. Eric didn't release his arm from my waist. He could have let me tumble to the slope below. Instead, he clung onto me tighter as we moved. It seemed our combined weight increased our acceleration. My hand began slipping from the rod. Eric firmed his arm around my waist, gripping me to him.

I fixed on the bumper wall, pulsing against it and filled with air fluttered thousands and thousands of huge, multi-colored fingers. They enticed us to miss our drop into the pool — to get absorbed in the soft protection of a safe deceleration. That would get us disqualified.

My hand lost grip entirely, and Eric tightened his grip around my waist. A moment later we plunged.

I didn't notice my feet entering the pool, only the cold water closing over my head. We'd finished! I wasn't sure how well. Nothing in the rules said two people could not ride the zip-lines together. We always aimed to beat competitors and steal their zip-line handles. The run down the slope made it impossible for residual teams to reach the pool and guarantee a spot on the podium.

I shoved away from Eric and swam for the shallows. As I gained the chest-high water and stood, Eric again caught up. He wrapped his arms around my waist from behind, voice low. "This reminds me of a different time, when you still liked me."

His body-warmth filtered through our MAC cladding, seeping into me. My mind flashed back to the moment he spoke of — the day we'd made out after climbing from the rock pool in the cave near the refuge. *How did things go from that to this?*

Still, Eric didn't let go, but spun me toward him. I wanted to slap him away, but my hand wouldn't move. My effort to stop myself from tilting my head back failed as he lowered his. *Damn, damn, damn!* I wanted him to kiss me, wanted to feel his warm mouth against mine. A second before we touched, he stopped short, those full lips inches away. As I licked mine, a smile glimmered over his mouth. For a long moment, he searched my eyes. Heat warmed my cheeks, my chest, my body. Then he slammed his mouth to mine, moving against my lips and parting them with his tongue, flickering and tasting me as I absorbed him, inhaling his familiar dusky vanilla scent. The cheering crowd dragged my attention from Eric. I looked around as he weaved his fingers through mine. Then I snatched my hand away and swam for the edge of the pool. Without a backward glance, I heaved myself out and ran to Liam, Harriet and Jonas on the broad, semi-circular concrete paving. Olivia raced up and launched herself at Jonas, throwing her arms around his neck and knocking him a step backward.

Because of our scuffle on the plateau, Eric and I had gotten to the pool last for Team Paladin and first for Team Salamander. Individual player scores appeared on the enormous displays. Race officials calculated team results from those.

Liam's name came up at the top. He'd reached the pool first, his total time four hundred and twenty-nine seconds. Balloons, five, fifty seconds from his total score. Total score, three hundred and seventy-nine.

Jonas' score arose next. Total time, four hundred and thirty-three seconds. Balloons, four. Total score, three hundred and ninety-three.

Harriet's name surfaced. Total time, four hundred and forty seconds. Balloons, three. Total score, four hundred and ten.

Eric's and my scores popped up at the same time. Our total time was four hundred and forty-two seconds. My balloons, four. Total score four hundred and two. Eric's balloons, *nine*. Total score, three hundred and fifty-two. A new MAC record. I scowled at him.

On the right-hand side of the display, our team total popped up, Team Paladin average, three hundred and ninety-six. Other teams were still sliding down zip-lines and landing in the pool. A horde of competitors chased and rolled down the hill. All the while player scores appeared on the display in no particular team order. I watched for Team Salamander's results, clenching my fists at my sides.

Aretha hit five balloons with a total score of three hundred and ninety-five.

Rick's four ended him with four hundred and six.

A few other players came up before Amanda. I didn't even read their scores, fixed on the display and waiting for hers…and Team Salamander's.

Long seconds ticked by before it finally flickered onto the display. Amanda—four hundred and sixty seconds and three balloons, ending with four hundred and thirty.

Team Salamander, average score—three hundred and ninety-five point seven-five. My legs gave way beneath me and I sank to the concrete, sliding my arms up and over my head. We'd lost for the first time after three successive wins. But I wouldn't let them see me defeated, so I rose to my feet.

The crowds took in the results displayed across every screen in Petriville. Their cheers rose in a crescendo, vibrating the entire arena. I glared at Eric just as Amanda leaped up, threw her arms around his neck and kissed him on the lips. Eric flashed me a glance but squeezed Amanda around the waist. It didn't look like he returned her kiss, but at that moment two pale beanpoles with long, scraggly white hair and beards raced up. As usual, Ethan and Craig burst into the scene, shirtless and dressed in baggy shorts. They hauled Eric from Amanda and grabbed at his legs, raising him to their shoulders. Shaking her head, Amanda joined their teammates in patting him on the back. Liam slumped and he turned his back on the scene, while Jonas swiveled from Olivia and paced—as stunned at our loss as Amanda seemed about Eric's…what? Rebuff? Not really. Ethan and Craig *had* pulled him away. But he didn't look exactly disappointed, did he?

Jonas continued ignoring Olivia's calls, but she wasn't deterred as she followed him. Harriet didn't notice any of it. She looked drained and stood in a half-slouch with her hands on her hips and her mouth gaping.

She met my gaze. "*Quarter*! They won by a quarter of a point." Her rounded cheek dimples pressed in as she scowled. "Eric!"

An empty weakness dragged at my muscles. "And the worst thing is we beat our own record!"

I still glared at Eric while Amanda continued patting him on the back. Then she collapsed—literally crumpled to the hard concrete floor. As if in reaction, Aretha fell. Eyes stretching wide, I looked to Harriet. She wobbled. A moment later she, too, buckled to the floor. As if something tied Liam to her senses, he shot around and raced back, sweeping Harriet into his arms. At the same time, Rick lifted Amanda. Eric half-leaped from Ethan and Craig's shoulders while they lowered him to the ground. Then he lifted the small russet-skinned Aretha, cradling her head against his chest, her ponytail of black braids swinging loose around his muscled, sun-bronzed biceps.

I jumped up. "What is going on, Li? What's wrong with Harriet and the others? They looked fine a moment ago."

Liam didn't answer my question but growled. "Where are those damned medic robots?"

Over the next few minutes, MAC stragglers entered the pool. Also, in that time, four more players dropped. After what seemed like forever, the lifelike medic robots glided onto the scene dressed in white scrubs — *as if their dress code were even necessary.*

Chapter Seven

We raced after the four medic robots as they bore Harriet's small, inert form on a stretcher, heading for the medical facility which backed the municipal building.

Once inside, they disappeared with Harriet, making us wait in the reception. A short while later Roger, Megan and Dad rushed in. After an hour of us pacing, a robot in a lab-coat returned.

Since we formed a semi-circle around it, the medic couldn't decide who to address, so with a swivel, it spoke to us all. "Miss Winters is stable. You may follow me."

We pursued it through a long, slippery silver corridor, through a series of one-way glass doors that sailed open as we approached, and finally into a ward with a single cot.

I took in the sight of my frail, petite friend as she lay in the bed, looking confused. My heart ached for her. Liam seemed barely able to keep it together, though he hid it well. Still, he inhaled as he took Harriet's hand, stroking his other thumb across her forehead. Megan didn't hide her sob but clasped Harriet's free hand between both of hers as if she carried a fragile egg. At the head of the cot, Roger cupped her shoulder with a comforting hand. Through the blanket, Jonas put a hand on one foot and Dad on the other. I wedged in between Dad and Liam, clutching her ankle—all of us needing to touch some part of her.

Harriet and I had met when we had been four years old. Even at that young age, she was like the sister I never had. That had happened before Petriville had left Earth—before we'd escaped the nearing meteor. The memory of our first encounter struck me with physical force, and emotion tightened my throat.

Harriet ducked her blonde head beneath an older boy's elbow, forcing her way through a throng of five- and six-year-olds.

The kids yelled, "Fight! Fight!"

Pushing my way through after her, I caught up as she reached the inner edge. "What's going on?"

She didn't answer but stormed forward, planted both hands flat on a boy's back and shoved. He towered above her, standing nearly twice her height. His size didn't intimidate her—not Harriet.

She blurted in her mild Scottish accent. "You leave my brother alone! He's younger than you! Stupid bully!"

I later learned the bully had been fighting Jonas Winters. Her brother wasn't much younger than the bully himself, held his own and was two years older than Harriet. The older boy rotated his head toward his new quarry. His gaze found nothing until he lowered his focus on Harriet Winters' open face, and her fair, plump cheeks dimpled as she scowled up at him. He laughed and turned around. In that instant, Jonas grabbed the boy's wrist and spun it behind him. The fight ended with both tumbling to the ground and Jonas seizing the boy's arm in one hand and thrusting a knee into his back.

Four-year-old me clapped my hands to my cheeks and giggled – until little Harriet twisted to face me with a scowl. A moment later, appreciating her brother's victory, she broke into a cheeky grin.

All these years later, Harriet was still my best friend.

I came out of my reverie as a male-like medic robot bustled in, its white lab-coat billowing around it. My cheeks grew fiery hot as the humanoid ripped Harriet's hand from Liam. "Give me space. Give me space."

Jonas growled. "Do you see why I want to punch these things then?"

The robot was, in the emotional sense, entirely ignorant. But its programming clearly empowered it to not take insults lightly. "Would you not consider that rather unkind?"

Jonas didn't miss a beat. "To me, yeah. I'd probably break my hand if I punched you."

Megan shifted her tear-stained face to her son. "Well, we're focusing on Harriet now, and pointing out a robot's lack of courtesy won't help your sister." More tears flowed down her cheeks and Roger wrapped a thick forearm around her shoulder, softening his normally booming Scottish-accented voice. "Hey there, Meg. Our son is probably feeling helpless, I think. You cannot blame him for that."

Megan used one hand to hold a tissue to her nose and gave a small blow. "We all are. You cannot blame me for worrying about my daughter now, can you?"

Harriet fluttered her eyes open and a pained smile touched her lips. As slow and weak as her voice emerged, she still punctuated her sentences with exclamations. "Don't fight, guys! I'm fine! It's a bit of dehydration. You'll see!" She closed them again.

This was *not* dehydration, but I kept the thought to myself. Liam and I swapped glances, then he squinted at Dad before refocusing on Harriet.

The medic robot moved the lab coat aside and directed its focus to its torso, where it slid open a curved drawer to its interior. Then it stuck long fingers inside and got a shiny silver rod protruding from the center of a small metal disk. It placed the disk to the inside of Harriet's forearm. "That should do it. Ms. Petri will report our findings."

As the robot skated from the room, someone else peered around the door. Eric. He didn't enter but spoke in the gentlest voice. "How is she?"

Even now, I couldn't keep sarcasm from my tone. "Shouldn't you be with Amanda?"

Eric flinched, his shoulders drooping, and Dad interjected with an out-of-character sharp edge to his voice. "Now isn't the time, Cassidy."

He waved Eric in and Graham followed. The old man's warm mahogany skin sagged around his mouth while deep hoops of skin hung beneath his dark brown eyes. His springy salt-and-pepper curls were trimmed into a short afro.

A few minutes later, Susan Petri entered the room. "I'd like a word with the family."

I glimpsed Liam, knowing he wouldn't want to leave Harriet for a second.

Roger didn't hesitate. "Out with it, woman. We're all family here."

Susan blinked. "Very well. The news is not good, I'm afraid. These kids are aging."

Megan rolled her watery red eyes and snorted. "Well, we're all aging now, aren't we?"

"What I mean is, they're aging faster than they should." Susan drew a breath and shuddered. "I shall not beat around the bush. My daughter is the same way. They're aging ten times as fast."

Roger narrowed his eyes. "So instead of aging like the rest of us—at a tenth the speed of a normal human—they're aging at the rate that nature intended. Is that what you're saying?"

Susan flicked her attention to her black stilettos, then looked up again. "No...they are aging ten times faster than that, a hundred times faster than the rest of us."

Megan collapsed into Roger's embrace, her voice a wailing growl. "I'll bet my life this is Gina's doing. I'll kill that woman! Just let me get my hands on her."

"Now...now, Megan." Roger soothed. "Surely the old bat wouldn't do that to her own granddaughter" — his gaze drifted to Susan—"would she now?"

Susan didn't waver. "Mother may be many things, but she would not harm her own family. If we think about it, we should all have died of old age a long time ago if Mother had not acquired the longevity elixir. Since every living being within Petriville's Kaleidotonium shell was exposed to the airborne drug, it included every person, domestic animal and those in the zoo habitats. I think our primary focus now must be on finding a cure."

As she concluded, she flicked her gaze to the floor and smoothed her palms down her dress. *She doesn't entirely trust Gina.*

Harriet opened her eyes. "So, it's the same with Amanda." She again allowed them to close.

Susan nodded slowly. "Yes. My daughter is also suffering from this illness. Your bodies could not cope with the physical exertion of the MAC Challenge, and as the adrenaline wore off, you fainted. We do not know what is causing this, so we shall test everyone."

Without another word, Susan traveled her thumb and middle finger together over her eye-sockets, turned and left the room.

The medic robot swept back onto the scene, again demanding space to work. It stooped over Harriet and withdrew a small brown dripper-bottle from inside its torso. After depressing Harriet's chin, it squeezed three drops of a thick orange liquid onto her tongue. "There you are. You're good to go, young lady."

Then it settled an uncannily sympathetic expression on Megan. "This shall keep your daughter well for now. She may return for another dose if necessary, but as long as she doesn't exert herself, she ought to remain fine."

It propped the bottle back inside itself and re-extracted the silver device. Then it floated around the hospital room, proposing to conduct the skin test on each of us. Somehow the device knew who it tested, and the medic didn't pause from one to the next — it probably referenced our individual DNA sequences.

When it got to Eric, Graham hauled him back. "There is no need to test my son."

He didn't share the same concern when the medic aimed the silver disk at his own arm. Instead, he presented it for the test.

Eric rested a quizzical frown on him, but when Graham pursed his lips, Eric didn't object. He clearly trusted Graham's decision without question, understood the old man had his best interests at heart.

When I re-centered my focus on Harriet, she slipped from the bed in her hospital gown. "Hand me my clothes, won't you, Mom? I want to go home."

She looked fine. Her color had improved, and she sounded as energetic as normal. Liam flung his arms around her and yanked her to his chest. "Hey, babe. We'll fix this, okay?"

The look he pierced Eric with implied the responsibility was his, since his parents had created the longevity elixir. But his parents had died when he had been a young child, and he'd only learned about these drugs when we had. Graham and Gina had known, though—right from the beginning. For nine out of every ten years, they had dosed us with the annual memory wipe solution—Graham to those in the refuge and Gina to the citizens of Petriville. That meant, out of every ten years, we retained memories of only one. Eric's parents had supplied this drug, having advised that our lengthened lifespans could have serious psychological effects.

Eric swung around to his adoptive father. "Did they mention anything like this? Or did they supply treatments for side effects of the longevity elixir?"

With a dejected sigh, Graham spoke in his usual slow cadence. "They told me little, and you must remember that it happened a hundred and sixteen years ago."

"Maybe Gina recalls something." I countered.

Graham cocked a brow. "If my boys' parents hadn't mentioned the dangers to me, I doubt they'd have told her. Although"—Graham raised his knuckles to support his chin and contemplated—"they did leave notes."

A few of us chorused, "What notes?"

"Notes which I read a long, long time ago, though I'm sure they said nothing about this. Regardless, I planned on sending Ethan and Craig back to the refuge to get news from the families who stayed to care for the farmlands and animals. They can collect the notes and try to salvage unbroken vials of the neutralizer or any remaining annual memory wipe solution. I'm not sure if any of those will help, though."

At that moment, the humanoid medic robot reported in a cheery sing-song voice that the rest of us were in good health.

As we prepared to leave, I met Eric's gaze. For a few seconds, he kept mine before dipping his chin and gulping, his Adam's apple bouncing. Without another word, he stalked out after Graham.

Chapter Eight

The following day, Ethan and Craig left for the refuge. Craig itched to return to his crows and Ethan to his weapons—not that they were necessary, since the rebellion had petered out. Susan had entrusted Craig with the few carrier birds from Petriville's zoo, obviously hoping to expedite the delivery of advice or medicine if they found either.

In the meantime, Gina summoned me again—probably toying with me—but I wanted answers too.

As I got into the train station, Gregory, Gina's freckled grandson, walked out. His cropped dark hair peeled away from his head in curly tufts and he slumped his shoulders.

Only when I stopped in front of him did he raise his focus from his sneakers.

"Hi, Gregory. Are you okay?" I didn't wait for him to answer but frowned. "How's your sister?"

He squished his pudgy face at me, entirely ignoring my first question and skirting around the second. "What do you care? You're not her friend."

I warred against my rising temper but maintained a slow and clear voice. "I may not be Amanda's friend, but I *do* care if she's okay."

"Humph. Why don't you ask that boyfriend of yours? I'm sure he knows."

A vise gripped my chest, and I struggled to keep jealousy from my voice. "So, Eric and Amanda spend time together."

Gregory curled the edge of his lip. "They spend time together. Unlike you, they *are* friends." He appeared to force the sweetest smile. "I'll tell him you asked."

With nostrils flaring, I walked away. "Does it feel good to make people squirm?"

I didn't wait for his muttered reply.

Only after descending the stairs and stepping into the lower tunnel did the rage heating my cheeks subside. A different group of soldiers sat around the small table playing cards.

One guffawed. "More people use the station these days to visit this woman than to ride the train to the zoo."

Another chuckled. "The only difference between the two places is that the habitats are…well…habitats, not cages, so I guess everyone is in their right place."

They all roared at his obviously repeated and barely amusing joke. I ignored them and stalked past.

"Who's there?" Gina squawked in the familiar hateful voice.

I said nothing but slowed and softened my stride. She'd already opened the small face-high window. Although her arrogant voice and words invaded her surroundings, the posture of her shoulders seemed deflated.

"Oh. Now I wonder what brings you here, Miss Jones?" Gina heaved a sigh and proceeded in her slow monotone. "Well, I suppose my charm is such a draw." She gestured to my wrist. "Or did you decide to try to kill me with that thing again?"

I glanced down at Grandma's wrap-around biro pen that I'd coiled around my wrist again that morning. Somehow, it looked lonely without the sparkle bangles. To clear my head, I shook it then snorted. "Sadly, unlike your charm, there's no longer any venom in this. Anyway, since your granddaughter is sick, it's reasonable to assume you'd *want* to help."

"Mm-m, perhaps. On the other hand, it's possible I don't feel the need to care."

I rolled my eyes. "If that's the case, then why did I bother coming?" Then I glowered. "More importantly, why did you call for me?"

"I did?"

I ignored her sustained attempt to rile me. "Why them? Why did those few people get sick? Why not everyone?"

Gina threw a knowing glance and tapped the side of her nose. "Ah-h, yes, of course. It wouldn't affect you — nor your brother and the Winters boy. Oh, but his sister… Now that is a different story. Mm-m. It all fits quite perfectly into place."

I glared at her. "So, if you know who is sick, then it stands to reason you know *why*."

Gina shrugged, arching an eyebrow. "Perhaps I employed spies, or it is possible that I simply guessed. I should most certainly not have achieved my level of success without the occasional accurate prediction."

I scoffed. "So, you *predicted* landing up in jail and, by extension, intended to?"

Gina ignored my quip. "Let us get to the reason for your visit, Miss Jones—or were you merely missing my company?"

I didn't stop the fake smile from slipping onto my lips and didn't bother correcting her again, my words slow and measured. "Since I'm here... Did Eric's parents tell you this might happen?"

Gina couldn't help herself. "Did Eric's parents tell me *what* might happen, Miss Jones?"

I sighed. "Please stop with the games, Gina. Eleven adults and forty-one teenagers tested positive! If you have a shred of conscience left in you—" I broke off, my voice pleading, even to my own ears.

Her lack of surprise at my question implied she was aware of the numbers. She didn't answer. Instead, she shoved her chest out. "Very well. They did not."

I wrinkled my nose. "Surely they left you *some* information."

"They may have. Ask your questions and I shall answer if I deem fit and if they covered the topic."

With deliberate slowness, I blinked. "Why can't you supply *Ellen* to everyone"—then, in case she'd forgotten—"the neutralizer to the longevity elixir? It's not as if it would feel any different if we all lived a normal life, since you wiped nine out of every ten years from us, anyway. Plus, it might cure them."

She smirked at my dig. "I am well aware of what *Ellen* is. I told Matthew and Elena Morgan I would destroy my supply—and I did exactly that."

"I know what you said, Gina. You wanted Petriville's youth to"—I sneered the next word—"*breed* for as long as possible. But I don't believe you destroyed it."

Holding a hand to the small window, Gina gave two dismissive hand-waves. "Believe what you will. Besides, if I had kept it, I would certainly not hand it over. You are clearly unaware that the administration of *Ellen* would render the effects of the longevity elixir void, including any future use." She paused for a second. "You may ask your boyfriend's beloved father if you must. I assure you he shall confirm this."

My forehead tightened. "What does it matter, Gina? If *Ellen* stops them from aging so fast, then we *must* use it."

"I might have examined a sample of the neutralizer." She snickered. "While I cannot establish the exact formula, my preliminary studies found it shall not cure these people."

"Why didn't they get sick until now?"

"It seems the annual memory wipe solution delayed the onset, but—"

I cut her off. "Then why don't you give them that?"

She lengthened her neck and dipped her chin to the side then continued in her slow monotonous rhythm. "Now, Miss Jones, I am fairly certain you know we ran out of that a year prior to returning to Earth, which means no one has received it for the past two years."

"Are you going to give me any worthwhile information, Gina, anything at all?" I went on, not meaning to sound desperate, but I couldn't help it. "Don't let them suffer. Please."

"Mm-m." She hiked both eyebrows, pressing creases into her forehead. "I do not believe, from inside a prison cell, I shall offer anything of value. Perhaps you should instruct that pathetic daughter of mine to release me from this dungeon. If that were the case, I might help."

I turned to leave. "It's hardly a dungeon, Gina. But honestly…I don't care. I'm done with you." I walked away, intoning over my shoulder. "Don't ask me to come here again."

"Wait, Miss Jones. Wait a minute and I shall clarify." A tinge of something close to curiosity invaded her voice. "It rather surprised me that Caleb was not with his brother. I assumed that, considering their circumstances, they might have been closer."

I hadn't told Gina before, and I had no intention of telling her now that Caleb had died on a scouting mission to find the nearest of Graham's refuges.

Despite them being out of Gina's range of vision through her small window, I tapped the toes of one extended foot. "Is there a question somewhere in there?"

Without waiting for Gina to make an actual enquiry, I turned on my heels and strode down the tunnel.

Something niggled at the back of my mind.

I spun. "Why me, Gina? Why didn't you ask an adult to visit—or Eric?"

She puffed a laugh through her nose. "Now that is an interesting question. Perhaps it is that you might remind me just the tiniest bit of myself when I was your age."

My reactive response came as a growl. Spittle flew through my lips. "I'm *nothing* like you, Gina. *Nothing*!"

Rage burned through me all the way to the tips of my toes, and I stormed through the tunnel and up the stairs.

Chapter Nine

On my arrival home, Liam, Harriet, Jonas and Olivia walked down our front porch stairs.

Harriet was back to her bouncy and bubbly self. "So, guess what? There's a *party*. *Tonight*. Here's your invite." She sang the word 'party' and squealed the word 'tonight'.

I rolled my eyes but couldn't help the smile tugging at my lips at Harriet's obvious joy. "Tonight? Another date-n'-mate!" I phrased the next sentences half as exclamations and half as questions. "So, Susan still wants us to go through with Gina's plans, even after all this."

Obviously, Jonas would like the idea. These days, he barely spent a moment without Olivia. "I don't think that's what she's doing, Cass. The invite says it's a MAC afterparty, since we never got to celebrate Team Salamander's *victory*." He scoffed the last word.

Images of Eric with Amanda on his arm flashed through my mind. The thought had my heart clenching, and I grimaced. "I've got nothing to wear. Do you…Harriet?…Olivia?"

Harriet flashed Olivia a glance and shuffled her feet. "We went shopping at Madam Belle's earlier. Why don't you clean up before going there? They're staying open late, and they'll get you dressed and made up."

A flicker of unease tightened my forehead. "What…what are your plans? Won't you go with me?"

Harriet again flashed the tiniest glance at Olivia as Liam laid a palm over my shoulder. "Let me walk you inside, Cass." After heading up the stairs and walking through the front door, he spun and shut it, speaking in his gentle, hasty voice. "Cass, you need to do something for Jonas."

I jerked my head back, squishing my brows together. "For Jonas? Of course. But what does that have to do with the way you guys are treating" — I pressed a hand to my chest — "oh-h."

Liam nodded. "Olivia sees how Jonas looks at you, and it makes her uncomfortable."

"Jonas doesn't look at me that way anymore. He's into Olivia now." I gestured through the closed front door. "Isn't that obvious?"

Liam huffed a laugh. "Not to me." He gave my shoulders a squeeze. "Don't let their relationship make you feel like an outsider — especially now, while things between you and Eric are difficult. But give them a chance to get to know each other, okay?"

I blinked and swallowed to chase away the burning in my throat. "Are you saying you don't want me to sit with you guys at the party? I have no one else? Or mustn't I go at all? How's that fair?"

Liam sighed. "That's not it. Of course you must come, and you're definitely sitting with us. Shouldn't I have said anything?" He never awaited my answer. "But seeing you out there...I had to give you some explanation for how Harriet reacted. If you're aware of this, you might keep your distance from Jonas until Olivia is surer of him—you know?"

I gave another swallow. "Of course, Li. Don't worry about it. I'll meet up with you guys later."

Then I turned and jogged upstairs without looking back but stopped before going into my room, listening as the front door opened then clicked shut.

After a long bubble-bath soak, I dressed in sweats, T-shirt and flip-flops, then rode the conveyor to town. I did feel left out...and alone. Regardless of what Liam thought, Jonas *was* over me. Olivia was behaving ridiculously, but...Jonas was my friend, and I didn't want to be the subject of an argument between them.

I barely noticed walking to town or entering the square until I turned up sidewalk four. It bustled with party-goers—primped shoppers leaving and non-primped ones like me arriving. Like Petriville's last party, hundreds of glittering balloons hovered above street level. Sweet music serenaded the twirling mannequins. Glamorous evening dresses swirled around female legs. Sleek men's formals outlined and enhanced their muscled structures. Alone or together, they danced and skated from inside Madame Belle's display window. They glided an oval across both conveyors and the far sidewalk, then looped back— dexterously dodging commuters as they whirled.

Inside the store, lifelike humanoid assistants skipped around and beamed, helping shoppers choose the perfect dress. Deciding to have my makeup and hair done first, I supplied my voiceprint for payment, then followed an assistant to the salon. A humanoid stylist snaked strings of diamonds through my hair, twisting my braids into a soft, elegant up-style and leaving loose a few spiraling strands with interwoven diamonds. Another manicured my nails into a subtle point and dripped a shimmering metallic-silver overlay on each. I watched as the drops wriggled and flattened, taking the nail's shape before settling in an instant.

The assistant, after applying my makeup and mapping tiny pearls beaded along one cheek, led me into a cubicle. It brought a range of evening dresses, then cooed and ah-ed as I modeled each before it. When I slipped into a pale silver one, it paused. "Are you okay, dearie? Is that a tear I see?" It raised a hand and wiped the single wet drop from my eye, then looked at it with a tilted head.

Mom had helped me dress for our last party. She'd done my hair and makeup and had gushed over me. I gulped the tears back. Not that it mattered. Nothing smudged our high-tech makeup.

My dress contoured to every one of my feminine curves, glittering as though layered in diamonds. The slit up my exposed, sun-darkened leg was just shy of too revealing and hinted at what lay beyond. Like gleaming strands of mercury, silver patterns snaked up my open back, chest and arms, not attached to the fabric but reaching for my neckline and thinning out until stopping short of my collarbone and the nape of my neck. They made my skin tingle, as if anticipation crawled over me. Diamond strands slithered up from the stilettos, wrapping around my ankles with one lone thread snaking up and around each leg.

The assistant left and returned a moment later with diamond teardrop earrings and my favorite perfume.

With generous abandon, it puffed several sprays over me while I pivoted. "Ooh." It enthused. "You are spectacular. Who's the lucky young man?"

I wasn't sure why I bothered answering, but I did. "I'm…on my own tonight." Maybe it was to remind myself.

Normally I loathed the humanoids, but tonight I took comfort from its unnatural though seemingly sincere kindness. "Oh my. What a terrible shame."

I ignored it and, after the assistant's promise to have my casual clothes messengered to my house, I escaped the store into the fresh night air, retracing my steps to the now-empty town square. Digital displays showed couples arriving in the underground stadium. Instead of crossing to the municipal building, where the cobbled paving would have done its utmost to bring me to my knees, I walked along the square's smooth encircling edge. A soft breeze fluttered the light fabric of my dress and an amber glow lit up the municipal building's old-style stone walls. It was quiet as I mounted the stairs and thrust my shoulders back then walked into the glass elevator. As it sailed downward, a soft melody hummed. Soon a shimmering golden light radiated upward from the underground stadium. As I drew nearer, other details came into focus. Thousands of gold-and-black balloons hovered mid-air above the arena. While the elevator drifted past those, Petriville's fifty thousand youth came into view, seated around eight-seater tables with gold-and-black overlays. In a rainbow of colors, a glowing Kaleidotonium ball hovered above the center of each table.

As I descended toward the scene, I sought only one face, and only one looked upward — toward the elevator. He watched me, his mouth agape. My heart skipped a beat when he rose as if unconsciously. My breath caught as he moved toward the elevator bank. His body-hugging black formals glistened, shaping his muscled physique. Mercury epaulets flowed from his neckline over the edges of his shoulders, dripping down the fabric over his chest, back and arms. The elevator door opened, and I gasped.

Chapter Ten

No expression crept over Eric's face, hardened his jaw muscles or deepened the lines etched into his cheeks, but his eyes glinted, and he let out a single hoarse word. "Cassidy."

As much as I wanted to demand an explanation of Gregory's claim about Eric spending time with Amanda, I didn't. Instead, I drifted my gaze up his neck to his close-shaved chin, his full lips, his soft gaze. "Eric. I'm…I'm sorry for pushing you away."

"It's me who…" He swallowed. "Please let me explain."

As I locked on his gaze, my forehead tightened. "I will. I'm ready to listen. But can we just enjoy tonight? We'll talk later."

He didn't argue but closed me in an intense embrace, his relief palpable as he tugged me against his body. I reached up, sliding my arms around his neck and dragging him down. With a low moan, he touched his mouth to mine, slipped a hand inside the fabric of my low-cut back and pressed his palm to the arch. He glided the other hand up the silky fabric of my dress until he cupped the nape of my neck. I leaned into him, wanting more, and as I parted my lips he responded, urging his tongue through and teasing mine into a slow dance. I groaned, roving my way up the ridge of muscles along his spine. His warmth seeped through the body-hugging fabric like I was touching his bare skin.

Eric tilted back, combing his gaze over me. "You are so beautiful, Cassidy — so impossibly beautiful." With a shudder, he yanked me against him and emitted a low moan, relief tingeing his smooth voice. "Since I've already ravished you, how about we ditch this place?"

I half slapped him on the back. "That's not going to happen, Eric. You're the man of the hour."

"The credit holds no value to me. But" — he drawled the word — "I'm not averse to showing off my prize."

I glanced sideways at him. "You know it's a floating trophy, right?"

With his brow cocked, Eric quirked one edge of his lip. "Floating? I'd hope not" — he inched his lips to my ear — "since that prize is you."

My cheeks flushed, and a laugh made its way through my throat as Eric double-bounced his brows. Then he fed his fingers through mine and we entered the stadium.

I flashed a glance over the tables but couldn't see my friends from this low angle. "Do you know where Liam and Harriet are sitting?"

"Yup." He paused and glanced down at me, softening his voice. "Susan didn't seat us together."

It wasn't uncommon for teams to sit together at MAC after-parties, but it wasn't a hard-and-fast rule.

I squinted up at him. "Do you mean to say — "

He nodded. "Susan saw fit to put Gregory at your table and me with Amanda."

"And the rest of Team Salamander — are they with you?"

"They are, but what I mean is…she put me *next* to Amanda." He drew a deep breath. "*Right* next to her. It was *no* coincidence."

A reflexive shiver ran through me. "Not that I'm surprised, but why do you think she did it purposely?"

Eric led me toward my table. "It's no secret how I feel about you. Aretha told me Susan has ulterior motives and I shouldn't trust her because she still plays to her mother's tune."

Despite the seriousness of Eric's declaration, I couldn't help but smile. "I really like Aretha. I should hang out with her more."

Eric threw his head back with a laugh, then met my gaze and bit his lower lip. "That's the girl I know. That's my Cassidy."

As we reached the table, he extracted the only remaining chair for me — which happened to be beside Gregory. I lowered to it and Eric pulled Gregory's chair back, tipping the boy forward. "Scoot. Go sit with your sister."

Gregory grunted, but wordlessly stalked away.

Liam shifted his focus between Eric and me with his head cocked and a half-amused frown across his high forehead. Harriet beamed, flashing her straight, very white teeth. However, I fixed on Olivia. A smile twitched her mouth, and she dropped her gaze to her fidgeting hands. Jonas closed his large hand over hers.

Harriet, meanwhile, swiveled a forefinger between Eric and me. "Well, assuming this is what I think it is, I for one am glad you guys have sorted through your...rubbish."

Eric puffed a laugh. "Well, you're sounding better, Harriet... Are you?"

"I am better. Much better. It's like nothing ever happened."

Eric dropped into Gregory's chair and smiled at Olivia, who sucked in her pink lip. "It's been a while, Eric." Then she giggled at her own joke, and another warm smile rose on Eric's lips. She was like a sister to him—orphaned young and raised under Graham's care, both in the refuge and now here in Petriville. The old man seemed to have a penchant for taking less fortunate children under his wing.

Eric appeared eager to gain Liam and Jonas' approval. "Sorry about the match the other day." He shifted his focus between them. "You guys played well, and we were lucky."

Liam scoffed. "That wasn't luck, Eric. You're a skillful player. I told you that before." Then he pressed a hand to his mouth, changing the subject. "Normally I'd have hauled you aside for this, bro. But we're all friends here, so I'm going to say this once." With a sharp inhale, his pupils contracted as he locked on Eric. "Don't hurt my sister again, okay?"

Eric nodded, but I gulped. Not 'don't hurt us' or 'don't betray us' but 'don't hurt my sister'. My brother still loved me. Warmth flooded my veins as Liam flicked his bright green gaze to me, soft and warm.

Jonas said nothing but turned in his seat and chatted to Olivia.

I gestured to the other two members of our table. "Oh, Eric, this is Samantha and Paul. They're Joshua and Caroline Carter's kids. I've told you about them before. Remember… Joshua is the astrophysicist who discovered the asteroid — Graham's friend."

I'd barely seen Samantha and Paul's family since Mom's funeral, but she and Olivia got on well. The girls almost looked like sisters as they bantered across the table.

Paul's blue eyes contrasted with his pale brown skin and springy hair. Samantha's bush of long black hair and smooth russet skin accented her huge brown eyes, long eyelashes and high cheekbones.

Eric rose and leaned over me, shaking Paul's hand. "Now your dad's is a name I know well, thanks to mine."

Samantha booted her brother under the table. "Stand *up* during introductions." Then she followed her own advice.

Eric smiled and lifted Samantha's long, elegant fingers, then gave her a nod and released them. "Not to worry, Samantha. Paul's young. It's great to meet you guys."

Robot waitrons served entrees of black mushrooms, sautéed in a fusion of sherry and garlic, then a honey-balsamic glazed duck main and a strawberry soufflé desert. The bounty of food choices in Petriville still never ceased to amaze me. Although I wasn't sure what part Jaya had played in the production of this concoction, the guilt slithered over me every time I had eaten since meeting the slaves beneath the streets of Petriville. Gina had treated them so poorly. At least Susan had moved them into town and now compensated them for their labor.

With a click of his fingers, Eric summoned a robot-waitron and flashed me a glance before taking a second plate of glazed duck. I gave him a sidelong glance. "You're abnormally hungry."

He grimaced, but Liam laughed. "Are you telling me you've never noticed, sis? Eric normally eats much more than this."

"He doesn't" — I swiveled to Eric — "do you?"

Liam flashed a glance at Eric but spoke to me. "Maybe not around you. No doubt he's trying to be polite. On a normal day, he'd be on his fourth helping by now." Liam chuckled again. "What, bro? Did you double up on your last meal? When was that — like an hour ago?"

Eric laughed, but red crept up his neck and face. "Hey, okay. These portions are small. And...yes...I have a good metabolism."

Jonas joined in their mirth with a rhetorical question. "*Good*? You reckon it's simply a...*good*...metabolism, do you then?"

As before, robot waitrons cleared our table. Beneath their frilly white aprons, they slid open the doors around their slender torsos and placed dirty plates onto dishwasher racks inside.

After they bustled away, the central stage lit up, the middle shrouded in pitch dark. The stadium went silent as a robot in a formal suit cleared its throat behind the podium. "We are here to celebrate the first new team's victory after three years."

In the darkened area, a light shot down from above and illuminated a glass case in which rested an enormous trophy.

"Team Salamander!" The announcer amplified its voice over the din of the crowd. Across the top of the stage, 'Team Salamander' flashed in their blue and silver colors.

I pushed Eric to his feet, but surprise made my mouth fall open when Liam rose, moved around the table and hoisted Eric's arm. "Enjoy the moment, bro. You deserve it."

Then Amanda, Aretha and Rick pulled Eric away and dragged him to the stage, a beam of light tracking their movements as a mix of roars and boos rippled through the crowd.

On the stage, more lights came on, revealing virtual musicians dressed in clichéd rock-band attire and sitting or standing behind instruments. With all the enthusiasm the celebrating crowd encouraged, they played and harmonized — strange, considering theirs wasn't an emotional response.

Liam rose, holding a hand out to Harriet. "Are you up to dancing, babe?"

Liam's sleek body-hugging pants and shirt emphasized his muscled body, the glossy black pants ending inside leather ankle-boots. His shirt was neither gold nor transparent but both, and a glossy black, molded epaulet tipped over the edges of his shoulders.

Harriet took his hand. "For sure, Li. I feel amazing."

She got to her feet, and I did a double take. "You look spectacular, Harri."

Her dress glistened the same bright green as Liam's eyes. The long, light fabric flowed behind her in an airy train and greeted her curvy body at the lowest rib, driving upwards and enhancing her ample breasts. Shimmery gold threads snaked patterns up her hands, arms and the exposed part of her chest, flowing up toward her refined neckline. Like Liam's shirt, the fine straps of her stilettos and heels as well as her countered collar were an ethereal combination of gold and transparent.

For a second, I found Jonas' green gaze. He darted a glance at Olivia and shoved a hand through his hair. She gave me an uncertain look.

Like Liam had said, it was up to me to ease her discomfort. I forced a smile. "Aren't you going to ask your girlfriend to dance, Jonas?"

"Uh…uh, yeah…of course. Would you, Olivia?"

They stood. Olivia was younger than us, sixteen like Samantha…and pretty. She and Jonas wore a theme to match Olivia's name. The warm olive and gold brought out Jonas' green and her dark hazel eyes.

Eric returned, and Amanda followed, as if in tow. She sat in Jonas' vacated chair and drooped across the table toward Eric. "Why did you sit here?"

Eric squeezed his eyebrows together. "Don't get funny, Amanda. It's obvious, I'd think." He lifted my hand, cradling it between both of his.

"I thought she dumped you. Besides, Mother would like us to discuss something, so will you come sit with me?"

Eric burst into a laugh. "Seriously, Amanda. At some point you'll get used to the fact that I'm with Cassidy and talk in front of her."

Amanda rolled her eyes. "Well, Mother thinks Graham is lying. She thinks he'll hide what he has left of his formulae and his notes. All three drugs" — Amanda listed them on her fingers — "*Ellie*, the longevity elixir. *Ellen*, the longevity neutralizer. And the annual wipe formula. She thinks he'll want to keep them for his people in case they get sick too."

I touched my hand to my mouth. *Doesn't Amanda know better than to attack Eric's adopted father and only living relative?*

His face reddened, and he inhaled a long breath. He spoke in a measured seethe. "It's not lost on you that these drugs could save your life, right?"

Amanda tilted her head back in exasperation and folded her arms. "Obviously."

Eric still didn't change his tone. "And you know that even the *annual memory wipe* solution could halt your illness while you're taking it."

"That would suck, because when we have kids, somebody would have to reintroduce them to us at the beginning of each year."

"It's still better than you guys dying in five or six years' time — of old age! It's a solution until they come up with something better. More than that, *Amanda*. If you think, for one minute, Graham would risk *anyone's* life, you know nothing about him."

"Mm-m. Perhaps."

"Listen, Amanda. I'll make your mother a deal. If in the event Ethan and Craig come up empty, I'll find my old home and see if my parents left anything — if, of course, our house hasn't transformed to dust."

Amanda scoffed. "After over a hundred years! I doubt anything remains."

"Regardless…it's worth a try. My parents weren't idiots. If they left anything, they sure as punch stashed it safely — safely enough to keep for a long time, at least."

"Well, Grandmother wants to get *Ellie* so I'll live as long as you. She won't let Mother give me anything else."

Eric all but growled the entire conversation, while Amanda seemed obliviously nonchalant.

Finally, I added my five cents' worth. "Has no one stopped to wonder why this has only affected you guys? Why not everyone? I think your grandmother knows."

Amanda darted to her feet, her fist on her hip. "Well, if she did, she wouldn't tell me." Then she strutted back to her table, where Gregory sat with three full strawberry soufflés in front of him and three more empty ones. Amanda slapped the spoon from his hand and muttered something unfathomable beneath her breath — scathing, judging by the wince forming on Gregory's face.

Chapter Eleven

After the argument with Amanda, Eric took a few minutes to slow his breathing. Then he stood and held out his hand, palm up. Placing mine in his, I followed, not to the dance floor but to a distant centerfield barrier. The thumping beat and quick electronic chords had couples near the stage dancing in wild disarray. Not Eric and me. He spun me toward him, then slipped an arm around my waist, pulling me close and dipping his chin to rest his cheek against my temple. He raised our hands and rested them between the soft curve of my shoulder and his hard chest. In slow, delicate rhythm, Eric swayed us to our own music.

For a few songs we danced in silence, before he tipped his mouth to my ear, his low voice barely audible over the music. "This is a dream come true for me, Cassidy. Do you remember when I told you you're my world?" Without expecting an answer, he proceeded. "Well, over the past weeks I felt as if that world was crashing down. But you need to understand something—as much as you might hate me for it—because faced with the same situation, I'd do it again."

I stiffened, but Eric firmed his grip. "You said you'd listen, Cassidy. Please give me that."

I glanced up into his beautiful aquamarines, shimmering with a soft glow, his forehead furrowing in a plea.

With a swallow, I nodded. "I'll listen, Eric."

He met my gaze and threaded his fingers between mine. "Then let's get out of here, okay?"

After taking an elevator from the stadium, we left the municipal building. The large digital billboards showed images of earlier couples arriving at the party, the bright orange Petrician Enterprises banner heading each.

Eric guided me through the square to the central fountain, where cherubs spewed into the swirling water, making the submerged green lights appear to ripple across the surface. As we sat on its edge, Eric wrapped an arm around my shoulder. I leaned into him and waited.

He didn't make me wait long. "It doesn't matter how I approach this subject. It isn't going to be easy on either of us." He turned his face down to me and drew a deep breath. "When I lost you, my heart snapped. But like I said, even if you won't forgive me, the alternative would have been worse."

I grimaced, but I *had* said I'd hear him out, so I shut myself behind my eyes and my words behind my lips.

Eric went on. "Your mom would have agreed with me on this. Trust me. You may recall me leaving the refuge to collect uniforms from my soldier friends. Well, Gina caught me. She'd already tried to kill you and Jonas. So, when she told me she would eventually find and murder all four of you plus everyone from the refuge, I didn't doubt her capability."

I opened my eyes. "We escaped the prison, so that proves it's not impossible. And we were safe in Graham's refuge."

Eric closed his free hand over mine. "The thing is, Cassidy, her soldiers were scouring the area, and it was only a matter of time before they stumbled on us."

"So, you *brought* us downriver to her! You manipulated us."

Eric's eyelids drooped for a moment, his voice a whisper. "Yes."

I nearly exploded, but Eric proceeded in the same quiet voice. "She killed my friends."

"She what? Your soldier friends?"

"She killed them. All four. They were young, Cassidy. Our age. She shot them right there in front of me." His voice cracked.

"Why didn't you tell me, Eric? At least we'd have known what to expect and planned our next move together."

"Cassidy, not to offend you, but you're as impulsive as Caleb was — although he jumped to insane conclusions a whole lot. Anyway, I hardly thought you'd agree. Graham said if we told you, you'd run off and get yourself killed like my brother did. You thought your parents were only safe as long as you didn't return, especially since Gina got a thrill out of humiliating and shocking people then watching them suffer."

My voice emerged dry and hoarse. "But my assumption was right."

"Yes, you were right, but Gina swore if you returned, she wouldn't harm any of you or our people from the refuge."

"Were those her words — *any of you*?"

"Yes. I never considered that could exclude your families."

I scowled as a tear leaked from my eye. "She has a taste for messing with the truth. If Graham knew this, why did he follow us downriver?"

"He insisted. As much as I told him not to, he wanted to make sure Gina kept her word."

Eric laid his fingers beneath my chin, his gesture tender. "That wasn't how I meant things to play out and" — he dropped his gaze to his hand — "you can't imagine how sorry I am for what she did to you...what I did to you...to your mother." He paused and fixed on my gaze. "That's everything, Cassidy. All of it. There's no reason for you to trust or want anything to do with me, but I hope you will find it in your heart to at least forgive my actions. For what it's worth, I swear she'd have made things worse for you if we'd handled it differently. Gina would still have killed your mother, but she'd also have killed you, your father, Liam and everyone else you care about. Then she'd have come after Graham and everyone at the refuge."

Eric had clearly tormented himself enough over this — and I'd gone and tossed him aside. "I'm sorry for pushing you away, Eric. More than that, I regret implying you don't know the pain of losing someone you love."

"Don't be sorry, my Cassidy. It was my risk to take — making you hate me — because the alternative was unthinkable." He released my hand and stroked a thumb down my cheek. "I don't mind the rejection, but

I wish I had been there to console you when you needed me most. As for your implication, I guessed you didn't mean it."

I never replied as Eric gripped me against his chest and pressed kisses to the top of my head.

As he exhaled, the breeze fluttered my hair. "There is something else I need to tell you. It may have relevance to Harriet, and it's the reason I'd like to return to our old home. The other day, Graham told me our parents didn't give Caleb or me *Ellie*, the normal longevity elixir. They gave us something they called *Livvie*, an irreversible formula. The bottom line is that *Ellen*, the neutralizer, will have no effect on us. Our parents meant us to live ten times the natural life-span." His voice cracked. "Caleb wasn't meant to die. The rest of my extended life, I face without my brother. No matter how incorrigible he was, he was still my twin." He wiped a single tear from his cheek and hugged himself. "I loved him so much, Cassidy. Sometimes the fierceness of that love for him and Graham doubles me over with physical pain. It did, even before he died. But losing Caleb—" He broke off, swiping at his eyes.

"I know, Eric." I looked up at him. "Thank you for opening up." I inhaled a shuddering breath, melting at the intensity of Eric's emotions. "Did you already tell Liam and my dad? Because the other day, Liam had a change of heart."

With a slow nod, he murmured a tentative "Yes."

"I have another question." I found his gaze. "Why did Graham stop you from having the test? Did you ask him?"

Eric rubbed his chin. "He couldn't give me an answer. He said he just reacted—that the idea of that thing touching me made the hairs on the back of his neck stand up, but he didn't know why."

"Don't you *want* to know, though, Eric? Don't you want them to tell you if you're sick?"

He cast me a sidelong glance, a cheeky grin spreading across his face. "The way my heart raced during the MAC Challenge, if I didn't collapse then, trust me, I'm fine." He nudged his arm against my shoulder. "And I'm *not* talking about the physical exertion. You get my pulse speeding up faster than any sporting event."

I shivered at the memory of skidding down the zip-line in Eric's arms—a warm, excited shiver—and bit at the smile tugging my mouth.

Eric took in my expression. He slid his teeth over his lower lip then crushed them to mine, his kiss tender, deep and *hot*—as hot and electric as the fire and ice skating over my skin.

Chapter Twelve

The next day, Harriet and I made our way across the town square to sector eight and trudged up the broad staircase of the old stone college building. When a hand grasped my wrist from behind, I snatched it away while Harriet and I both jerked around. My gaze landed on Amanda and I barked a laugh. "What do *you* want?"

Amanda darted her dark brown eyes around as if nervous. "Can I talk to you, Cassidy?"

I couldn't help it, and the sarcasm slipped off my tongue. "Might I point out you already are?"

With an eye-roll of pure exasperation, Amanda flattened her lips. "Obviously...I *mean*...can I talk to you...*alone*?"

Amanda wasn't much shorter than me, but that never deterred Harriet, who glared up at her, fluttering her long eyelashes — a curtain over her bright blue eyes. "You don't get to make Cassidy miss her lecture — not for some random gripe. If that's the case, you can talk to her later."

With that, Harriet linked her arm through mine and turned toward the lecture hall. I hesitated. She'd clearly missed what I'd seen—how ashen Amanda appeared. *Is Amanda sick again? Surely, she followed medic orders to not over-exert herself.*

I frowned, unlinking our arms. "It's okay, Harri. I'll be right in."

Harriet cocked her head and thrust a small fist to her hip. "Don't be long. This lecture's important."

I twisted to Amanda. "What's so earth-shattering that you can't wait to tell me?"

Amanda scowled. "This is something you'll want to know." Then she glanced around. "I shouldn't tell you. Don't use it against me, okay?"

"You can't expect me to agree to something without knowing what it is."

"Fine. Well, I'll tell you anyway because it's the right thing to do."

When she paused, I drew out a single "Yes-s…?"

"I was on my way to visit Grandmother, but I got distracted and didn't go all the way downstairs. I ended up one corridor too high. You've seen the floor above the cells, right?"

"I'd have to be an idiot to have missed it. What's your point?" I omitted telling her we'd used that tunnel when rescuing Joshua, Roger and Dad.

Amanda continued. "Well, as I turned around, I heard voices coming through a vent."

"Someone was visiting Gina…" I surmised.

"Yes. My mother."

Again, Amanda waited for my prompt. This time I revolved my hand like the reel of a film to encourage her onward.

"They were discussing my illness, and I expected them to talk more openly if they thought I wasn't around, so I listened."

I angled toward her. "And…?"

"But they didn't…or at least they kind of changed the subject."

I slumped my shoulders. "So, what *did* they talk about?"

"Your mom."

I took a step back. "My mom? What about my mom?" After shooting a glance around, I hauled Amanda into an alcove.

She spoke while still walking. "Mother told Grandmother to give the real reason she had Emily killed."

My temper flared. "Gina didn't *have* my mother killed. She murdered her herself!"

Now Amanda looked around. "Yes, yes. I know that. But listen, will you?" She puffed out a frustrated breath. "Grandmother said Emily discovered something best *kept a secret*"—she air-quoted and ground out the last three words—"and apparently Emily told Grandmother she couldn't withhold whatever it was, that the people deserved to learn the truth. Apparently, Emily threatened to tell everyone if Grandmother didn't."

"So, didn't your mother ask Gina what she was talking about?"

Amanda rolled her eyes. "Naturally, she did. Mother isn't an idiot! Grandmother told her the information would come at a higher price than the few hours of sunlight a day she got."

I paced the alcove. "So, what was it?"

"The price? Grandmother said she'd think about what she wanted and that Mother should return this afternoon."

As if involuntarily, my feet slowed and stilled. "So, she never told your mother what mine discovered?"

"No. Anyway, that's all."

I cupped her shoulder, leaning in to convey the urgency of my question, but Amanda started so I stepped back before adding, "Do you think it's possible they were talking about Gina's stash of the neutralizer, the one they call *Ellen*? Do you think she still has it?"

"That's what I wondered."

I squinted. "Why are you telling me this, Amanda? Did somebody put you up to it?"

Her mouth fell slack as sarcasm filled her tone. "Not everyone is out to get you, Cassidy. I thought you'd want to know about your mother, and like I said, it was the right thing to do."

"Well, thanks. If I find out this is a bluff, I *swear*—"

Amanda raised both brows. "Well, if you tell *anyone* what I said, then *I* swear—"

With that, she stepped from the alcove and strode down the passage toward the exit.

I slunk into the lecture hall and looked around for Harriet. She waved from the top row, and I ran up the stairs two at a time, dumped my books on the desk and dropped beside her.

With a side-glance, Harriet grimaced. "What was that about?"

I snorted. "To be honest, I'm not sure. You'll be the first to know when I figure it out."

Regardless of missing only the introduction, I never took in a thing the virtual lecturer discussed. My mind drifted. *Is this the real reason Gina killed Mom?* It sounded…plausible.

Come afternoon, Eric had lectures until late and Harriet ditched me to spend the afternoon with Liam. I wasn't complaining because my afternoon was, for all intents and purposes, free.

I grabbed a cheese and tomato sandwich from the college cafeteria, crossed the square to sector four and arrived at the train station. No one saw me going down to the prison cells, but to make sure, I checked again before ducking into the upper tunnel. I didn't need to guess where along the tunnel Gina's cell was. As I walked, her voice grew louder and louder. From the sound of it, she was remonstrating with the guards in her snake-like monotone. "My useless daughter promised me three hours of sunlight a day. Since you dullards allowed me only two and a half, I demand you take me up for another half an hour. In case you boys are too stupid to work out what three hours is, it is a…hundred…and…eighty…minutes!"

Then she griped about the food quality, the state of their uniforms, her cell needed cleaning, her bed linen gave her hives, she needed better toiletries… Her ability to find things not to her liking astounded me. *How many things are there?* Every time I thought she'd ceased her tirade, she came up with something new.

I shook my head and settled into an offshoot beside the vent. For two hours I listened to her complaining and to various sets of boots trudging up and down the stairs. Finally, the soft *tink* of stilettos on the metal stairs echoed in the tunnel. I sat bolt upright, shifting nearer the vent. Only when Susan arrived at Gina's cell did

Gina's voice grow quiet. Still, the women's soft words carried through the vent. Although their voices shared similar timbres, Gina's bore a greater measure of arrogance.

Susan didn't bother with formalities but dived straight into the negotiations. "Have you reached your decision, Mother? You need to, because our birds returned. Apparently, the notes in Graham's refuge mentioned nothing about this illness. Also, no drugs remained but *Ellen*, of which Ethan and Craig found only crushed vials with no trace of residue."

Gina ignored Susan's information about Craig and Ethan's findings but answered her question. "Mm-m. Perhaps. Or rather, the decision will be yours to make. I studied these formulae extensively and have gained a fair amount of information that may well help cure your daughter."

"And *your* granddaughter," Susan reminded her with restrained coldness.

"No matter. You shall receive nothing if you do not agree to my terms."

"Oh, I can only imagine what those terms are, Mother."

"Regardless, you need the information I am able to offer."

Susan's voice wearied. "Please stop beating around the bush, Mother. Tell me what information you have and state your terms."

"I am able to cure everyone for no other reason than I know what is wrong with them."

"Are you a hundred percent certain of your facts, Mother?"

"Mm-m. You doubt me? Regardless, I shall tell you nothing without a signed pardon. Release me and I might offer to assist."

Susan's voice trembled. "I can't simply release you from prison after you murdered Emily. What will the people say? I'm shocked you wouldn't *want* to help Amanda, if no one else. Tell me something in good faith. Does *Ellen*, the neutralizer, have anything to do with the cure and do you still carry our supply?"

Gina's low voice held all the arrogance of our very first meeting. "I help *myself* first." She thrust her shoulders back. "Whether *Ellen* is part of the cure, I shall inform you after you release me. As to whether I still carry my supply? I told you I had destroyed it and have little reason to lie about that. Irrespective, you will need to locate all three formulae or the drugs themselves." She gave a low snicker. "Another thing you ought to be aware of... You might want to keep that young man close and secured. To be safe, I should be inclined to locate that twin of his."

"He has a twin?"

So, if Eric had told Amanda that Caleb had died, Amanda hadn't mentioned it to Susan. The knowledge didn't stop my blood from turning to ice in my veins or the prickly sensation clawing at my skin. I closed my eyes, awaiting Gina's confirmation, but I already knew the answer.

I didn't hear it though, because at that moment a fiery breath stung the back of my neck and a deep voice whispered stale air into my ear. "Ah-ha! Eavesdropping, are we?"

I spun around, only just suppressing a squeal. I faced one of the card-playing soldiers.

His mouth stretched into a toothy grin, and dark shadows edged his teeth and gums. I gritted mine. "You don't understand…"

Still, he kept his voice in a whisper, his hot stale breath sticky against my cheek. "Rat you out, I should. But…" He dragged out the single word.

Is he going to blackmail me, or worse, report me to Susan?

After a long pause, he went on in the same whisper, "…that would be assuming I didn't loathe the subjects of your entertainment. Off with you now. Not all would be so lenient on your transgressions."

I didn't hesitate and tiptoed my retreat toward and up the stairs. At least I'd learned what I'd come for. Gina knew what caused the illness, and she'd identified the cure—at least she'd said she had. The cold alternative… She was using this to manipulate her way out of prison.

Chapter Thirteen

Susan released Gina from prison the next day. The news spread across town faster than the silver bullet train took to reach Petriville's encircling zoo habitats. Dad's soul seemed to crack a little more, and Liam raged about the injustice of it. But me…? Well, silent guilt burned through me — worse, since I hadn't told them what I'd discovered. But raising Liam and Harriet's hopes — telling them Gina could cure her — wasn't an option. Too many variables came into play. *For one, what if Eric's old home no longer exists? And two, what if Gina hasn't discovered the cure?* This whole thing was too Gina. She wouldn't pass up the perfect opportunity to escape her prison sentence. She'd packaged it so neatly. A gift to unwrap.

Whatever came next, finding the truth mattered most. That list included finding the cure and the reason Gina had murdered Mom. I'd somehow fix this. Fix *them.*

Liam eyed me across the dining table over our breakfast of croissants, muffins, honey and cheese, not exactly with suspicion.

He knows I'm hiding something.

His soothing voice emerged soft and uncharacteristically slow, almost pained. "If there is no cure for this thing, Cass, I don't want to live when Harriet—" He couldn't finish his sentence. Couldn't say the word *dies.*

His agony landed on me with a crushing blow. "How could you say that? What about Dad and me?" I picked at the hem of my coolest summer dress, which was now stifling enough to make me want to tear at the fabric. I dropped my gaze. "We'll cure Harriet, Li. We will. And the others. Eric thinks his parents might have left notes at their old home. If nothing else, Gina's an excellent genetic engineer. Not in the same field as Eric's parents, but she's the one who found matches in our DNA, and most of those were a success. Plus, she has outstanding scientists. Along with the Morgans' notes, I'm sure they'll figure something out."

At least I'm not offering him false hope in case Gina hadn't established a cure, but any measure of hope, however vague, is more realistic.

He stiffened. "Excuse my lack of confidence, Cass, but I wouldn't trust Gina to hand out anything but a death sentence."

I covered his hand with mine. "We might not have a choice. Gina might be our only hope. I swear we'll find a cure. On everything I am, I swear it."

He ignored my over-optimistic promises but held my gaze, his shoulders slumping. "If given the choice, Cass, I wouldn't hesitate to take her place."

"I know, Li. I know how you love Harriet."

"I'd do the same for you."

My throat caught. "That's because you're a good person." I wanted to say 'better than me,' but not for wanting to trade places. I'd also do that—for Harriet, for Liam, for Eric, for Jonas. But no, his principled nature made him better than me. He'd never withhold what I'd overheard.

An urgent knock on our front door jerked me from my musing. In a second, I leaped to my feet, racing across the hallway and ripping it open.

Amanda waited outside, her dark eyes bugging. "Come quickly. It's Eric! Mother is arresting him!"

Liam leaped from the table. "What the hell is going on in this place?"

I leered at Amanda. "How is it *you're* the one to tell me this?"

Amanda tapped her foot. "It isn't like that, Cassidy. Eric is so in love with you that he wouldn't notice if a girl threw herself at his feet."

"Like you've been doing, you mean."

Amanda snorted. "I overheard Mother and Grandmother talking at home this morning. Grandmother said there is no better place to secure Eric than the prison. Then they left."

"Are you sure of Gina's phrasing?"

"I wrote every word down, see." Amanda shoved a digipar toward my face.

"So, you didn't find out if she has already arrested him or is still going to?"

"No. But I thought telling you was the—"

"Yes, yes, Amanda. I get it"—I scoffed—"…the right thing to do." Then I blasted past her. "Well, don't stand there. Let's go."

"I'm not going with you," Amanda called. "Don't dare mention *who* told you about Eric."

Liam was right on my tail, his voice a growl. "Well, I *am* coming. *Somebody* had better give us answers."

At as near a sprint as I could manage in my brown leather sandals, I took off ahead of Liam along the curved walkway, over the intersection bridge and onto the inbound conveyor, where he caught up. Even then, we kept up a fast jog and slowed only to a puffing walk as we reached the town square. We arrived as four soldiers, who'd surrounded Eric, led him into the train station with his hands cuffed behind his back.

Liam shook his head as we cut across the circular square at a run. "Why is she doing this?"

Everything happened too fast. The color drained from my face, my sentiments bursting through my lips. "It feels like this is a repeat of everything she did to us before."

As we entered the station, Liam wound his arm around my shoulder. Judging by his words and the way he frowned, he wasn't trying to appease me. "How does this woman always get the upper hand? How can we stop her?"

Although his questions were rhetorical, they were ones I wanted—no, *needed*—answers to. We aimed for the staircase at the far side of the silver bullet train, and with sudden certainty and clarity the answer slammed into me. "Knowledge is our ally. We must learn everything she knows and more. That's how we'll stop her."

Liam fixed his curious gaze on me. "You probably have a point, Cass. Your determination is admirable."

I smiled up at him and puffed an embarrassed laugh. As we descended the stairs, my stomach clenched for Eric. "He's going to be all on his own in here."

Liam nudged me with his elbow, trying to ease my tension. "That has to be better than getting Gina as a cellmate."

As we turned into the passage, a guard slammed a cell door — the one farthest from the stairs, away from where the guards usually sat around their little table.

I was wrong. Eric wasn't alone. Not now, at least. Susan and Gina stood outside, their arms folded. Ramrod straight, Gina thrust her shoulders back, her chin high.

After hesitating for a second, Liam and I strode toward them, but Susan looked down and away.

Gina, on the other hand, faced us head on without adjusting her posture. She projected her voice. "My, my... Fancy seeing you two here. I do wonder *how* you learned of Eric's arrest so soon." She flashed a glance at Susan. "Tell them, *daughter*. Let them understand why you have arrested Eric." Gina never allowed Susan a chance to speak. "No, no. I shall inform them. Although...let me savor the moment a little longer. I take such delight in doing so."

I ignored both women and broke into a beeline run for the cell door, gripping the bars to the small window with both hands. "Eric, why are they doing this?" From what I'd overheard and what Amanda had confirmed, Gina considered Eric a threat. But *why*?

He slid open the small window and closed his fingers around the bars and mine.

Gina squawked, "Well, that's rather obvious, I should think. It was Eric who caused this malady among our citizens."

A frown ripped across Liam's forehead as he cast a glance from Susan past me to Eric, his face full of uncertainty. "Is any of what she's saying true, Cassidy? Did Eric have a part in making Harriet sick?"

My forehead tightened as I met his gaze. "Of course not, Liam. You've seen how she twists everything. You know Eric has nothing to do with this."

From the cell, Eric's voice emerged, soft and defeated. "Cassidy's right, Liam. On the lives of every remaining person I love, I swear it." He slid me a glance, then again fixed on Liam. "You know what your sister means to me. I'd do anything to keep her safe."

Liam narrowed his bright green eyes, squinting. He shoved a hand into his wavy blond hair. "I should. But so much has gone wrong since you entered the picture."

Eric withdrew his hands from mine and flinched away from the door, as if his proximity might somehow contaminate me. "Liam's right, Cassidy. Everyone is best served with me in here." His voice softened to a pained whisper. "Even you. Everyone I'm close to gets hurt."

Susan spoke for the first time and did not look at me, but she glared at Gina, voice trembling. "Mr. Morgan is right about this, Miss Jones."

"Yes," Gina agreed, thrusting her chest out. "You would be most wise to listen to him. Needless to say, Miss Jones, it shall be your responsibility to sort out this mess, since it was you who allowed this vagabond to enter the safety of our world." She made a dismissive wave at the cell.

I scowled, but Liam changed the subject. "Has anyone heard if those damned birds have returned from the refuge?"

About to nod, I caught myself, gritting my teeth instead. Any reaction would warn Susan and Gina that I'd overheard their conversation.

Susan's voice sounded tired. "Sadly, they found nothing worthwhile in the refuge. I haven't yet informed Mr. Porter but shall later today."

Although I'd already guessed the answer, I growled, "So, what do you want me to do? How am I supposed to sort this out?"

Gina confirmed my suspicions. "You'll need to locate the formulae for the drugs. *All the drugs.*" She emphasized the last three words, then added in a cold, even flatter tone, "And that brother of his."

I gulped and found Eric's gaze through the small window. He wrapped his arms around himself and expelled a puff of air. The right to talk about Caleb's death lay with Eric. I took a step back.

Eric lowered his voice more, his words cracking and the last softer still. "My…brother died."

"What was that?" Gina mustered no sympathy in her tone. "Did you say he's dead?" Still, her voice conveyed no compassion. She continued in her train of thought. "Well, that is not marvelous, but in truth, I suspected as much." She paused for a few seconds. "Mm-m, perhaps…yes…well, no matter."

I growled at her. "You suspected nothing! I'd think you're a callous reptilian bitch if I didn't know better! More kindness lies in the heart of a snake than in yours."

Eric and Liam both gave small laughs.

Gina, however, didn't raise her voice or change her calm monotone. "Regardless…it's not me who wants these people saved. I care not one way or the other."

Susan winced. "Not even for your own granddaughter?"

Gina thrust out her chin and brows. "Everyone dies."

Eric spoke up. "Let me go with Cassidy. She'll never find what you're looking for. As young as we were when they died, our parents taught me and Caleb how to think like them. Even if the house is still standing, Cassidy won't know what to look for."

"Well then, Mr. Morgan, I suggest you coach her well." Gina focused her pale blue eyes on me. "You leave tomorrow. Perhaps, Miss Jones, I shall release your dear young *sweetheart* upon your successful return. The thought of his impending death, should you fail, might sufficiently motivate you to meet your objective."

Eric reached for my fingers as Liam wrapped an arm around my shoulders. Liam spoke first. "Jonas and I will go with you, Cass. I want to do this for Harriet." He ground his teeth. "Frankly, sitting around here waiting for someone to come up with a solution is killing us both."

Eric cocked his head. "Well, let's get Jonas in here. With my parents in the mix, an element of problem solving is inevitable, and three heads are better than one. They won't have left vials of the drugs in case they'd be compromised, so you'll be looking for notes on their formulae."

Hating leaving Eric to Gina or Susan's mercy, I raised a loaded question. "Susan, why stop Eric from going with us? He'd improve our chances of finding what you're looking for *and* you'd have him out of Petriville."

Susan swallowed and glanced at Gina, who answered my question in her stead. "Insurance, shall we call it? A tiny incentive for you to return."

Liam scoffed, his words even faster than normal. "Bah! As if Harriet and the others being ill isn't incentive enough."

I batted my eyelashes at Susan. "And since when did you relinquish your leadership and serve it on a platter to your *mother*?"

Not that I expected her to, but Susan didn't reply. Instead, the two women turned and left.

After a long moment, Liam sighed and softened his voice. "Why don't I give you two a moment while I fetch Jonas?"

I swallowed and nodded. Then Liam retraced his route down the long corridor and turned the corner as he ascended the stairs.

Chapter Fourteen

I swiveled to Eric, who stared at our touching hands, his expression resigned. "So, she's parting us again. It makes little sense why she insists on trying to create a rift between us."

As I tapped a finger to my temple, I pursed my lips. "It cannot be her sole intention to divide us."

Eric peered through his thick, dark-blond lashes. "You're probably right. Although she'd do anything for the power to control her subjects." He clenched his teeth, the muscles bunching along his jawline. "And stuck in here, I can't do a thing to help."

He flattened his fingers and eased them between the parallel metal rods, cupping my cheeks as I reached up on my toes. I angled into his touch and he drew my face as near as was possible, touching his mouth to mine—warm, soft, moist. It wasn't enough—not nearly.

With a frown, Eric pulled back, withdrew his hands and seized the bars, rattling them as though to dislodge them from the frame. "I can't even kiss you properly through these goddamn things."

I fed my hand through to him. "Please don't, Eric. Don't waste our limited time on anger."

Eric pressed his mouth to my knuckles and exhaled a heavy sigh. As he returned to gripping the bars, I propped my forehead between two of them. He followed suit, laying his forehead on mine. His warmth seeped into me as if soothing energy flowed between us.

Eric gasped a soft whisper. "You're going out there and I've got no way to keep you safe. It's this helplessness! It's making me crazy."

I managed a soft smile. "I'll be fine. Gina isn't after me this time."

"You'll face other dangers. Don't take unnecessary risks. Please, Cassidy. Promise me that. You're strong. You're tough. I get that…" His voice cracked "But…get back to me, okay?"

My voice sounded thin, even to my own ears. "The risk thing you're talking about… It goes both ways. Don't get yourself into hot water with that woman. She's not normal."

"No matter what, babe, don't forget you're my world and" — his swallow made the muscles in his forehead contract and shift against my head — "I love you, Cassidy Jones. Don't you forget that. Okay?"

"You say that as if I won't find what we need — like I won't save Harriet or stop that woman from murdering you. Please tell me I'll make it, Eric. Give me hope."

He nodded against my forehead. "The truth is, if my parents left notes and their work is safe, you're as likely to find them as me. Don't doubt yourself, okay? Because I don't."

My eyelids drooped, and I tried to hide the uncertainty from my voice. "Thank you for that, Eric."

For some time, we rested against each other, our foreheads touching as we caressed fingers. My heart squeezed with yearning to tell Eric how I cared. But that was exactly the point. I wanted to *know* I hadn't — to *remember* it. If I ran into a losing battle and needed mental strength, I meant for that knowledge to spur me on. A silent tear trickled down my cheek and Eric caught it with a finger. He misinterpreted the reason for my sadness, his voice quiet. "It's not going to go down like last time. You'll see."

Not that I planned on correcting him, but Liam and Jonas ensured I didn't need to as their footsteps sounded on the metal stairway. While they turned into the passage, I allowed every part of Eric to filter into me through our connected fingers and foreheads. Then I extracted my long, olive-toned hands — Mom's hands — from beneath his and half-turned to face them.

Liam wasted no time. He whipped out the small cylinder — Mom's digipar — from his trousers pocket — the one with her letter to us. Dad had given it to Liam. I trembled as he held it before him, thumb-tapped the center and released it in midair. As if magic suspended it, it unfurled and stretched out beneath his hand. He picked up the digipen and instructed, "New," then spoke to Eric. "Right. Let's get to it. The location of your house."

Eric flashed me a glance, narrowing on Jonas, who cleared his throat. "For what it's worth, I'm sorry the old bat's put you in here."

Eric tensed his stance. "Don't worry about it. When we figure out her play, she'll lose the power she's gotten over us."

Eric relayed the Ponte Vedra Beach address to Liam, who scratched it into the digipar and watched as it converted the scrawled text to a map and co-ordinates. "What else should we know?"

Eric peeked at me, a smile growing on his soft, full lips. "Do you remember the rhyme, Cassidy?"

For a second, I bowed my head, then looked up. "The one you chanted in the refuge? Yes."

"Well, they told us we should always remember it. So, if anything has relevance, I'm guessing that will be it."

Liam mustered no warmth in his voice. "So, all you're handing us is some stupid rhyme. How's that supposed to help Harriet?"

Jonas cupped Liam's shoulder. "We can't really blame Eric for this, can we then, bro?"

Liam raised his brows. "You didn't hear what Gina said."

As Jonas studied him, he bent away. "No. Normally, I'd take your side. But it's common knowledge how she manipulates situations to her advantage. Also, I think your anger has more to do with my sister than Eric."

I cottoned on to Jonas' thread, my voice gentle. "Why don't you stay and take care of Harriet, Li?"

He hiked a brow. "I think you of all people should know that answer."

I did, of course. "Jonas and I will be fine."

He steeled. "Like the last time? No matter how I hate leaving Harriet, considering the two of you out there is worse. I don't want to discuss this again." He delivered his last sentence with resolute finality.

He fixed on Eric, sounding less cold, almost resigned. "Okay. Carry on."

Without hesitation, Eric began.

If a song and the wind and the rain tell six,
The ocean, a lake and the tree are nine,
Then where would you meet with your nearest and dearest?
Why? Where the sun and the moon misalign.

Liam smirked. "That's so remote." But he wrote it verbatim into Mom's hovering digipar, then looked up. "What does it mean?"

Eric sighed. "That's the part I don't know. Neither does Graham. Too much time has passed since we learned it. It feels like it's on the tip of my tongue — like if I walked through the door, all those memories would come flooding back. Hell, it's even hard to recall the fine details of my parents' faces" — he shook his head slowly — "and I have a photograph of them."

Liam cocked his head, but Jonas grimaced. "Is there nothing else you can tell us then? Nothing at all?"

Eric rubbed at the back of his neck, eyes on Liam and Jonas. "Graham and I have gone over this for days — ever since I considered the trip home. Nothing else comes to mind. Honestly, unless I'm at that house, it's doubtful anything else will." He inhaled and glanced at me. "Please take care out there, guys." He flashed between Liam and Jonas. "Keep my...keep Cassidy safe. Please bring her home, okay?" His voice cracked at the end.

Jonas fist-bumped Eric and spun to leave. As Liam too gave Eric the casual greeting, his posture relaxed. "Cassidy would tell you she's quite capable of looking after herself" — his face straightened — "and honestly, I believe she is. Still, rest assured. We'll do whatever it takes to bring her home. Until then, Harriet will check in with you."

Jonas flashed me a glance. "I think you know where I stand. My loyalty to Cass will never waver."

As they retreated toward the stairs, Liam spoke over his shoulder. "We'll wait outside." They stopped where four guards sat around the kid's table. I couldn't hear their words, but as they rounded the corner to mount the stairs, the guards stood and stalked down the passage toward me.

Each placed a thumb to different, random spots on the door. "We'll let you in for five minutes, but don't you go blabbing about it." The door un-clicked and, as if Eric would attempt to escape, they blocked it while I entered. As it shut behind me, one soldier clucked, "Five minutes." Then they retreated.

Stepping toward me, Eric slipped one muscled forearm around my waist, reached the other hand to my face and stroked my cheek with his thumb. "Oh-h, my Cassidy. It's not sitting well with me, this thing of you going out there with Jonas. Don't go falling in love with him, okay?"

I slid my arms up his hard chest and around his neck, absorbing his shimmering gaze. "Eric, that won't happen. I…I" — his brows squished together, expectant. I went on — "if that were going to happen, it would have long ago. You don't realize how I care for you."

"Then tell me. Tell me what you feel."

I hauled myself closer. "We don't have time. Just kiss me. Please?"

Eric closed his eyes and shuddered. Then, clamping his teeth together, his jawline hardened as he wove his fingers into my hair. For a moment he searched my gaze. Then he brought his mouth down on mine. Hard, hungry pants escaped him as he kissed me, urgency rising as he pushed his tongue between my lips. He groaned a deep, ravenous, "Cassidy," and tugged me against his firm body. I twisted my fingers in his coarse blond hair, leaning into him, my voice catching between a moan and a soft cry.

"Oh, Cassidy." He broke the kiss and clutched me tight, his palms firm and warm. I lay against him, listening to his heartbeat as his chest rose and sank in ragged, tormented breaths.

He tilted back, his words a plea as he stroked my cheek. "Say the words, Cassidy — if you feel the same."

At that moment, the door jerked open. "Okay, you two. Break it up."

Hard grips yanked me from the cell.

Eric growled the words, "Don't you touch her," and ran at the door, but they slammed it against him.

Eric gaped at me through the iron bars, swallowing hard. He dropped his gaze, and when he looked up, his frown pleaded and he kept gulping. "Just go, Cassidy. I can't" — his voice cracked — "I can't bear this."

I couldn't steady my voice, and it quivered. "I will come back to you, Eric." With that, I swung away, my throat tight with emotion.

I hated Gina for doing this — for once again ripping me from Eric. Hated her with every bone in my body. But I wasn't going out there for Gina. This was for Harriet. Tears blurred my vision. Barely noticing my legs moving, I mounted the stairs and drifted through the train station. True to their word, Liam and Jonas waited outside the one-way glass doors. I joined them and Liam wrapped me in a hug while Jonas kept a warm hand to my back.

But we had work to do, so I steeled myself and pulled away. "I'm okay. Let's get this thing done."

Despite my bravado, as we crossed the town square a dull ache spread across my chest, vomit clawing up my throat. I thrust my shoulders back and forced a steady gait. For Harriet and for Eric, I could do this. Hell, I'd even do it for the Salamander team members — Amanda and Aretha, plus every other sick Petrivillian.

Once again, Gina had hurt me, but she wouldn't break me. Not this time. I'd grown stronger. Harder. Tougher. *Does this mean my compassion has waned?*

If it meant survival, as much as I hated the thought I might turn into Gina, I didn't care. This was her fault — not mine.

Chapter Fifteen

The morning awoke me—deceptive in that bright sunlight peeked around my curtains, and birds' chirping sounds drifted through my open window, trying to trick me into cheerfulness. My stomach knotted so tight that it had me hugging my knees to my chest. The weight of foreboding pressed against me. I was once more leaving home. This time, Mom wasn't sitting beside my bed and handing me a cup of tea, comforting me. No. I was alone. Never again would she soothe away my fears. I contemplated putting on my silver sparkle bangles beside Grandma's wrap-around pen, but I didn't. Harriet had once commented on how, when they tinkled together, they'd have given our location away. I wished I'd had time to refill the pen with venom, though Ethan had probably taken his with him.

My old backpack most likely lay where I'd left it—beneath the dome assembled near the pod—but the new one, a soft pink color, lay beside my door. To its side, I'd strapped my bow and a quiver loaded with arrows. Everything inside was new — from my lace bras and panties to jeans, tops, shoes, socks, jacket and even a headlamp. I'd also crammed in a few old things like my brown leather sandals, since they fit so snug and soft against my skin. I'd also stuffed in a few coiled digipars from the municipal building library. Because we were traveling with no horses to carry our luggage, I'd limited my toiletries to essentials. Finally, into a narrow side pocket, I wedged a small brown-paper package I'd wrapped for Eric the previous evening.

Susan sent a message for us to meet her at the northernmost train station — on the line trimming the inner circumference of Petriville's encircling Kaleidotonium habitats.

I dressed in jeans, a loose-fitting top and trainers, then twirled my hair and clamped it beneath a peak-cap.

While I descended the stairs, Liam propped his enormous black pack beside the front door. Against its side, he'd also strapped his bow and arrows.

I reached the hallway and Liam held out his hand, but as I hung my backpack over his palm, he feigned dropping it. "Have you packed your entire wardrobe in here?" Then he chuckled and lowered it beside his.

It had been weeks since Liam had tried to lift my spirits, and my heart warmed. He'd done it so often and so easily when Mom had still been alive.

Fast asleep and snoring, Achilles and Yvon lay sprawled out on the dark wood flooring of our hallway, while Dad sat at our dining table with Graham. Fine red lines crisscrossed the whites of the old man's dark-brown eyes.

His voice quivered as he spoke in his familiar slow, gentle voice. "Morning, young lady. Tell me why they're doing this to my boy?"

I moved to Graham. "Gina won't harm Eric." *What am I saying? This isn't my claim to make.*

"If only that were guaranteed." He passed his gaze between us, his voice a plea. "Don't fail my son." He breathed a deep sigh. "Please don't fail...anyone."

I touched the back of his hand. "We won't, Graham. We're all invested in this."

Graham nodded, still visibly unappeased. He shuffled in his chair and tapped a heel beneath the table. Blatant discomfort rolled from him in waves. "Susan informed me that Ethan and Craig found nothing at the refuge."

Liam blinked once and pulled out a chair. "We heard."

As he sat, Graham met his, then my gaze. "Eric surely told you about the other refuge."

I took the chair beside Liam. "Are you talking about the refuge Caleb aimed for when his group—" I broke off, not wanting to regurgitate Caleb's death on top of everything else.

Graham pursed his lips. "I am. But it is possible—if they survived—that they may still have drug supplies there." He paused, seeming to think we needed more motivation. "It's a distance from here, but nearer than the Morgan home."

Dad interjected, his words measured and heavy. "Graham will supply co-ordinates for this refuge. As you're aware, Susan needs all three drugs. *Ellie*, *Ellen* and the annual wipe formula. This means if they don't have them all, you must find the Morgan home."

Graham slid a sealed digipar to Liam, then clasped his hands under his chin. "This letter is for their leader, a Mr. Thomas Rodrigues. It explains our situation, in the event they don't trust you. It will unseal at his touch and contains our codeword so he'll realize it's from me."

At the center of the table, Dad had heaped toast on a plate. Beside it, he had set a jar of strawberry jam, marmalade, a dish of curled butter and a flask of coffee. The last time we'd left, Mom had prepared scrambled eggs. My stomach twisted as I filled two mugs and handed one to Liam, then picked up a plate, a knife and two slices of toast. Despite my best intentions, I couldn't bring myself to take a single bite.

After a while, Liam touched my hand. I examined his expression and dipped my chin, pushing away from the table. Dad followed as we made for the door, but Graham remained seated. For a moment he covered his face in his palms, then returned them to the table. He fidgeted with his fingers. "For everyone's sake, please get what Ms. Petri demands."

Dad inhaled and released a slow breath, squishing his mouth into a line. "Again, I find myself in a place where my children are embarking on a likely dangerous journey that adults should undertake." He scoured a hand into his hair. "And the last trip resulted in the death of my —" He cut off and fixed on his shoes, his voice a croaked whisper. "Please don't misunderstand me, Liam and Cassidy. I blame myself, not you."

I embraced him around the shoulders, then heaved up my backpack and threaded my arms through the straps. "It's Gina who we should blame, Dad. Besides, we're fitter, stronger, better trained and better prepared than any of you." I forced a smile. "And who, at over a hundred years old, is a kid, anyway? In the greater scheme, we're not much younger than you."

Liam lifted his black backpack and slipped an arm through one strap. "Cassidy's right, Dad." Then he smiled at Achilles and Yvon as they yawned and stretched. "Oh, hey, dobes. So, you've decided to see us off."

Half asleep, they padded toward him. Liam stroked the tops of their black heads while I bent to a knee. As I scratched behind their ears, they leaned into my hands and I succumbed to the natural smile stretching my lips.

I stood. "See, Dad? How could we *not* return to these beautiful faces?"

With a distracted smile, Dad shook his head as if lost in thought. "Yes…yes. How could you not?"

After clicking the strap around my waist, I shifted the backpack's weight until it felt comfortable.

Then, for what must have been the ten thousandth time, we walked through our front door. Liam shut it behind us, and I took in its large decorative white rectangles. "This could be the last time we turn our backs on it."

Liam's voice emerged hard, a turnabout from the gentle persona he'd left Dad with. "Don't you even consider that likelihood! We *are* coming back, because I will move heaven and hell to save Harriet. And I'd like to believe you'd do the same for her…and Eric. If it's not like that, Cassidy, then don't bother coming."

My forehead tightened as I peered up at him. *When did my brother grow so bitter?* I swallowed. "You know where I stand, Liam. Plus, I'm physically strong."

He drew in a deep, shuddering breath. "I get that, Cass. Emotionally too, since Mom —" He didn't finish his sentence.

I latched on to his gaze. "Not stronger, Li — harder. There's a difference. Don't confuse bitterness with strength and don't confuse compassion with weakness. Our parents taught us both — strength and compassion — because no matter what, we always knew they loved us. This bitterness and near lack of compassion we've allowed to creep in is Gina's fault. Don't let her control who we are." At that moment, I decided I wasn't becoming Gina, because I could choose which person my circumstances turned me into.

Liam sucked in his lips, a smile flattening them as he looked down at me. "Profound."

I gave him a light punch on the shoulder, surprised by the laugh bursting from my chest.

Chapter Sixteen

Liam and I waited on our side of the intersection footbridge, watching Jonas and Harriet as they left home. While they walked, Jonas threaded himself into his backpack straps, bouncing it onto both shoulders. His bow and quiver, also attached to the side, stuck out above him.

Liam no longer smiled. When Harriet reached him, he lifted her from her feet and gripped her against his chest as she flung her arms around his neck. "Don't go, Liam. Find another way to fix this. You can't leave me here. Please."

Liam shuffled his feet and shifted his focus from Jonas to me and back to Harriet, as if torn. He cleared his throat. "If only you knew how this is breaking my heart, babe. But I need to help find your cure. Your Mom and Dad will keep you safe while we're out there. And when you're better —" He cut off.

I knew my brother didn't want to give Harriet false hope, and despite my encouragement the previous day, I hadn't convinced him Gina had perfected the cure.

Harriet pulled away from Liam and wiped her shimmering bright blue eyes. As I wrapped her slight frame in a hug, she stretched up to her tiptoes. Her chest heaved, and she drew slow, deep breaths. "You get your skinny ass back home, Cass. Don't you dare pull a stunt like last time. And bring these stupid asses with you. Okay?"

As if I'd planned anyone locking us up in the fort.

I ignored how her comment affected me. "You too, Harriet. Don't get up to too much mischief while we're away." I rolled my eyes. "My brother will be impossible if anything happens to you." Then I pulled the small package from my backpack and handed it to her. "Give this to Eric, please?"

A playful smile quirked her lips, her cheeks denting as she fluttered the package between her fingers. "It's so light. What is it?"

My cheeks heated, and I pressed one eye closed as I grimaced. "Pieces of straw to keep him company."

Harriet guffawed. "I'll be sure to report back on his expression."

Then she spun away and dove into Jonas' thick forearms. His face softened. "Hey, Harri. You're squeezing me like this is our last goodbye. Can't you put a little faith in me then?" He measured a fraction between his thumb and forefinger but, with his arms around her body, Harriet didn't see that.

After Jonas released her, he linked an arm through mine. "Let's go, Cass. Give them some space."

We crossed the glowing transparent intersection footbridge. "Where's Olivia? Isn't she coming to see you off?"

"She's meeting us at the train station."

As we stepped onto the conveyor, I cast a backward glimpse at Harriet and Liam. They clung to each other. Tears trickled down Harriet's face while Liam shut himself away behind his eyelids.

Before we reached the town square, I startled at the activity.

Jonas frowned. "It looks like the entire town's here."

The crowds faced conveyor two, and as we neared, they clapped and cheered. Jonas groaned. "Is nothing in this place private, then?"

Somehow, word must have leaked about our departure to seek a cure for their ailing family and friends. The digital displays came alive with Petrician Enterprises' bright orange banner at their center. The live feed then followed Jonas and me as we ambled from behind the glossy black number two and cut a chord through the town square. Footsteps sounded behind us and Liam jogged up beside us, his face now composed.

I linked my free arm through his. "You okay, Li?"

He grated out, "Let's do this thing and get home."

"Yup." Jonas hummed. "The three musketeers are at work again."

After linking arms, we strode toward the train station and paced up the wide staircase amid a roar from the crowds. The one-way-glass doors glided open. As they shut behind us, they cut off the outside noise.

When Jonas withdrew his arm from me, my gaze landed on the reason. Alone on the platform beside the silver-bullet train, Olivia's lip trembled, pink against her dark olive skin. She blinked her deep brown eyes and her petite frame quivered.

It was Jonas' turn for goodbyes. After quick hugs with Olivia, Liam and I hopped aboard the train, making our way to the back of the carriage. We dumped our packs on the floor against a central pole. Tightness assailed my throat. Eric was so nearby. I yearned to hold him, touch him one last time. My reasoning for not telling him my feelings grew fuzzy, slamming into my chest. *"Am I wrong, Mom?"*

Mom's imagined answer whispered in my head. *"Cassidy, my daughter, whatever gives you the strength to return home is the right decision."*

Liam studied me, tilting his head to the side and twitching his eyebrows. "Jonas and I will get you back to him, Cass."

Although I didn't tell him about my invented conversation with Mom, as he held my stare without removing the tilt from his head, I wondered if he knew.

After a few minutes, Jonas joined us. He peered at Olivia once as the doors shut, but as he made his way to the back, he seemed to blink away emotion. He *did* care for her. That was good.

Jonas bounced his backpack from his shoulder and propped it against ours, then plopped onto a nearby bench and cleared his throat. "That was…unpleasant."

We drifted into silence as the train made its slow, whooshing descent past Petriville's outskirts and automated ecological factories. Not that these were manned, but they still made me think of how Gina had enslaved Jaya's people. The thought continued as we swept through the crop-farming and domestic animal rings. These, the men and women still worked. Susan now credited them for their labor, and they lived in Petriville—in proper homes.

The otherwise-empty train stopped at no stations. Scorching sun shimmered over the grassland paddocks surrounding the stables. Some mares grazed beneath a nearby willow, others in the copse on the far side of the field. Yet others rested a leg and dozed beneath the scatterings of trees throughout. I couldn't make out Zenobia, hidden among their numbers.

Before long the train took the familiar gentle curve south and continued its route alongside the Kaleidotonium-encased zoo habitats—an invisible moat-like, opalescent donut around Petriville. We sailed past the undulating changes in the environment of each species' home. From deserts to grasslands, snowy peaks to jungles and lakes to solid ice-scapes. After completing the entire trip around Petriville's habitats, we arrived at the northernmost station. The train slowed and eased to a silent stop.

Susan and Gina awaited us on the platform with Austin, Susan's boyfriend—the gorilla-like soldier I had once thought tried to kill me.

After collecting our bags, we disembarked. I didn't give Gina the tiniest acknowledgment. "Morning, Susan, Austin."

Susan responded. "Good morning, Mr. Winters, Mr. and Miss Jones. Thank you for meeting with us. My apologies for the roundabout journey. Austin's technician coded the long route in error."

Gina stepped ahead of her daughter. "Now, now, Miss Jones, is there a particular reason you find it necessary to avoid greeting me? Especially since this will most likely be the last opportunity you have."

I cocked my head and raised my brows. "Tell me, Gina, why would I bother? Whatever happens out there can't be worse than showing you civility, even if it's false."

She tittered, her mouth forming a knowing grin. "Ah-h, yes. We shall see about that."

Despite the fanfare, my insides pitched and churned at her implication that we'd probably die. I wanted to growl at her — tell her she was evil. But I refused to give her the satisfaction of knowing she could still rile me, so I shrugged. "Maybe."

Gina continued. "If you fail to return, that boyfriend of yours shall meet a similar fate to that of your" — she dripped syrupy sweetness over the next word — "*darling* mother. Don't go supposing my daughter won't cede Petriville's control to me — even if behind the scenes. I have a lot more hanging over her head than you realize."

Susan shook her head, whirling on Gina. "Oh, Mother...must you tantalize the girl?" Then to me, "Ignore her, Miss Jones. You have a way of getting under Mother's skin."

Liam and Jonas remained quiet, their arms folded — mildly more polite.

Austin stood at attention, looking as if about to salute. "I've stocked your transport with food and supplies. The captain has set co-ordinates to both destinations. He'll show you what to do once you're inside. Now" — he aimed toward a descending bright silver spiral staircase — "let's get you to the capsule."

As we went after him, Gina's hateful, slow monotone pursued. "Do you think you shall miss me, Miss Jones?"

With a calming breath, I stopped mid-stride but didn't turn. "I might spare you a thought when you hang for what you've done."

"Mm-m." She didn't come up with a 'Gina' retort.

"Be safe, you three. Best of luck out there." Susan sighed. "I hope you return with good news."

I nodded, and Jonas replied for us all. "We'll be quite fine as long as that one" — he gestured at Gina with his forehead — "has no influence on the outcome."

Liam added in his familiar rushed way, voice as smooth as a melody, her name a question, "Susan? Keep Harriet safe while we're away. Please?"

She dipped her chin. Then both women boarded the train. Austin cleared his throat to catch our attention and tramped down the winding stairs. After sharing a quick glance, Liam, Jonas and I followed.

Down, down, down the stairway we spiraled — deeper than we'd ever gone before, stadium aside. When we finally emerged, I gasped.

Chapter Seventeen

As we entered an enormous bright silver chamber, my gaze fell on virtual monitors, keyboards and control panels edging the room. However, that wasn't what had me freezing in place. In the center lay a giant Kaleidotonium ball, its lights glimmering off the iridescent rainbow of colors.

I shrunk back and hugged myself, my voice a squeak. "That isn't what we're traveling in...is it?"

Jonas reacted entirely differently. His mouth dropped open. With slow steps, he walked as if gliding toward the giant ball, his eyes wide as they roved over every inch. "Wow!"

Liam stopped, scrutinizing with neither fear nor awe. In slow, clearly unthinking movements, he cupped an elbow with one hand and, raising the other to cup his chin, he nodded in deliberation. "Well, this is better than walking."

"And probably faster than riding," Jonas agreed.

The sphere didn't thrill me nearly as much. "We don't even know what it does."

Jonas walked around the base-support, his head back as he peered upward at the shimmering Kaleidotonium. "Nope...but I'm getting an idea."

Jonas turned to Austin. "It's some kind of waterball-boat thing, isn't it then?"

Austin stood with his legs wide and fists on his hips. He smiled. "Good guess. As it happens, that's exactly what it is." He spaced his thumb and forefinger a bit apart. "Bigger than a mere boat though — outside *and* in."

A vertical opening pierced the ball from the quarter line up to midway, a little taller than Eric and a tad wider than Austin. From the lower rim of the opening, a long ramp bowed to the floor, identical to the gap in both size and shape.

"How does it work?" My question wasn't so much from curiosity as a need to establish how safe we'd be inside.

Austin didn't seem to notice my unease and launched into an animated explanation. "Well, it comprises two waterproofed Kaleidotonium balls — an inner and an outer. A stern and bow will protrude from the ball once you're on the water, but you won't get to see them — and they disappear in rough water. For now, when you're sealed inside, air passes through the shell in the same way it did in space, though some modifications to this one make it impervious to water. Air flows in and out of both compound layers — similar to breathing. This means your oxygen supply won't run out. Along with ball-bearings, high-density air maintains the gap between the two balls. Of course, in the event of extreme turbulence, you'll want to strap yourselves in. The Kaleidotonium will tint over to prevent dizziness and nausea. Besides, it won't be bad because the base of the inner ball is weighted so Earth's gravity keeps it mostly upright. Well" — he raised his brows and hands, palms out—"that's how I understand it, anyway."

Liam observed with a more objective than subjective expression. "What about waste?"

Austin answered without pause. "It gets processed into fuel, like in Petriville."

I squinted and cocked my head, still unappeased. "How will you get this thing out there?"

"Oh, yeah...that part... We have a chute. It comes out deep in the ocean, under water. Be sure to get yourselves strapped in, because the inner ball won't be staying upright for the launch." He boomed a laugh. "Oh, right! Make sure you seal your belongings inside the lockers in the bedrooms. Pack them tight if you don't want the contents to get damaged. Now let's get you loaded. You should reach your first destination in around three days."

As soon as he concluded, he herded me toward the opening. Jonas needed no encouragement but bounded to the top and peered inside. From behind, his head bobbed left and right and up and down.

A laugh burst through my lips. "Do you...know how...funny that looks?"

Jonas turned back to me and cocked a brow. "Overreaction, Cass." Then he held his palms out. "You'll want to see this before mocking me."

With my hands on his back, I pushed. "Well, I can't see anything if you carry on blocking my view."

It never drew me in nearly as much as it had Jonas, but I still scanned the unusual room. Four black leather recliners encircled a silver column that stood at the center. I pursued Jonas past the column, taking in its bright blue virtual protrusions—keypads, knobs, sliders and buttons.

As Jonas darted through an inner doorway, I spoke to his back. "I hope they don't expect us to navigate this thing?"

He smirked. "That's funny. I hoped for the exact opposite."

As Liam entered, he stared around the control room with the same weightless gaze he'd adopted before, his arms loose at his sides and him commenting as if to himself. "It looks safe enough."

I followed Jonas through the doorway, but he scurried through another—a bedroom on the left of a long, broad area which ended in a kitchenette. Instead of setting my bag in the one on the right, I headed past, aiming for the glossy silver central dining table, where I smoothed a finger along its length.

Jonas exited the bedroom and plopped onto one of the long silver bench chairs, his back to the table. He bounced up and down on the soft orange cushions and shrugged. "Not bad. I think we'll probably find this journey more comfortable than the last."

Then he leaped up and darted to the only bathroom while I made my way around a shoulder-high partition that separated the kitchenette and dining area. My attention landed on the counter, its back against the low wall. "Ooh-h, coffee," I crooned while touching one of the virtual buttons. The wall-mounted beverage machine sprang into action and, attempting to cancel the order, I jabbed at every other blue delineation.

Jonas probably never heard my running commentary. "Too late." The dispenser had already produced and filled a disposable cup with a steaming drink. As the aroma of rich dark chocolate permeated the room, I pressed a foot-pedal marked, '*dispose*' and the cup and contents disappeared into some inner working.

Turning to the back wall, I slid open an opalescent Kaleidotonium door. Cold air rushed out, and I scanned the rows of pigeon-hole-type shelves. Each gap held a line of pre-packaged meals. I read some labels inside three out of the four fridges. "Bacon, eggs and tomato. Croissants. Cheese and tomato sandwich. Beef, mustard and salad sandwich. Spaghetti Bolognese. Chicken a la king." The list went on and on. I pulled open the fourth door. Secured inside were bottles of water and assortments of sodas and fruit juices.

"Clinical," I observed.

Jonas finally added to my one-way conversation-slash-observation.

He thrust his head through the door and chuckled. "It's the same in the bathroom." Then he read his own list. "Shampoo. Conditioner. Body soap. Hand soap. Body cream. Towels. Tissues. Loo paper. Toothpaste. Toothbrushes."

When Liam walked through the control room door, I headed into the bedroom opposite the one Jonas had taken. "You'll have to share with your buddy, though I don't know if he's taken the top or bottom bunk."

Liam shrugged. "Does it matter? If he's taken the top, I'll kick him off. No way am I sleeping below someone who drools in their sleep — especially one who sleeps on his stomach with his head off the mattress."

The bedroom cupboards were — for all intents and purposes — the Kaleidotonium lockers Austin had mentioned. I slipped my backpack inside one and twisted a handle to seal it.

As I returned to the control chamber, the outside door rose. Liam sat corded in a recliner and it strapped his head, arms and legs to the chair.

One final hissing sigh escaped the outer door as it vacuumed shut. Beside Liam, rigid cords slithered over Jonas' body, legs and forehead like a hundred snakes binding him to the recliner.

He hiked a brow. "Would it be an inconvenience to ask you to get yourself strapped in before we go then, Cass?"

With a shudder, I recalled my previous encounter of a snake near the refuge, but that wasn't what made my eyes stretch wide. "You mean we're leaving now!"

Since the straps allowed no other part of Liam's body to move, he rolled his eyes toward me. "Yes. Once the air-levels regulate." He followed his comment with a sigh. "But by all means, take your time."

I dived onto the recliner between them. "Uh-h. Does this thing come with operating instructions?"

Liam gave an impatient snort. "Well, while you two analyzed our upcoming lifestyle, Austin delivered those in person. You're lucky, though" — he added even faster than normal — "because everything's automated."

A second later, the firm cords slithered over me and tightened around my body, securing me in place. Not constricting — but cold, like *snakes*.

The recliners adjusted and whirred into a lying position. Six masks fell from a panel above — two over each of us. They slowly descended until one clamped over my mouth and the other over my nose and eyes. Panic shot through me and I jerked against the restraints. I made no headway. Liam murmured something beside me, but only garbled echoes found my ears. I inhaled a sharp breath through my nose. Clear, fresh air filled my lungs. I exhaled through my mouth. The mask misted up, then cleared. I repeated the action before relaxing.

A second later, the sensation of moving had my stomach clenching. I thrashed against my bonds, but the straps limited my range. Our housing shivered, but gravity still carried us right-side-up. In almost indiscernible increments, the shivering grew to vibrations and the floor shifted. As the whispering sound of metal on metal reached my ears, the vibrations became shudders, increasing the noise to a low grind. A low warmth seeped into my body from the notion of tremendous speed. My skin tingled.

As the shuddering intensified, I slammed my eyes shut. The noise became a deafening screech. My chest tightened and heat burned through me. My fingers and toes tingled and my insides roiled. Again, and again and again, the sensation of rolling faster and faster surely flung my organs around. Dizziness engulfed me and I groaned, vomit clawing its way up my throat, scalding my mouth as it flew into the tube, which thankfully sucked it away. The waterball threw me left and right, upside down and right-side up in constrained movements. The dizziness grew until my head wanted to explode.

A pop. Then a hard thump and a few dissipating bounces then all motion stopped. Time ceased. My organs settled, but my head pounded, and I heaved and heaved. The world felt smoother—the rocking of floating on water. But the sense of spinning still dizzied me. I groaned, and wretched choking sounds made their way through my stomach and chest. A buzzing silence rang in my ears. After long minutes, the masks released their suction. Finally, both they and the straps retracted.

I took deep, gasping breaths, afraid to make the slightest change to the position of my head. Jonas, however, launched up and looked around. "Well, that's that then."

Without adjusting my head, I glided my view along my periphery as he threw a hand over his mouth and raced through the living-area door.

Liam remained prone in the recliner beside me. "If you knew to expect that, Cass, would you have come?"

I settled on the overhead panel, not wanting to bang on the bathroom door with the need to take Jonas' place. "That's not a fair question right now...but I'd have opted for the horses."

He laughed.

Over the next few minutes, the tint of the Kaleidotonium above us faded, revealing a bright blue sunny sky. Also in fractions, the recliners moved upright until finally we sat.

I slid my legs over the edge toward Liam. "The only thing I can liken that to is sitting in a dentist's chair with a drill flying uncontrolled around the room."

Liam puffed a laugh, pitching and dropping both eyebrows. Then, resting his forearms on his knees, he loosely interlaced his fingers, gaze on the floor.

For a few seconds he sat in silence, then he swiveled toward me and lifted his bright green gaze to meet mine. "It's not a laughing matter...I mean, with what lies ahead. Is it, Cass." He didn't so much make it a question as exhale it as a resigned statement.

I reached for and squeezed his hand, but we didn't speak. My brother always carried the safety of those he loved on his shoulders. Harriet and me more than anyone else. As I released his hand, I beamed a heartfelt smile. "I'm glad you came with us, Li."

The silver deck glistened in the sunlight. Liam sighed and squeezed my shoulder. "And me, Cass. And me. But thank you. I needed to hear you say you wanted me to be with you on this journey."

Chapter Eighteen

After what felt like an age, Liam and I started for the living quarters. An even longer time later, Jonas escaped the bathroom and thrust a thumb over his shoulder at the closed door. "That's now a dead zone."

Liam pitched a brow. "Thanks for the heads-up, but the fact that you're green around the gills makes your attempt at humor seem out of place."

Jonas straddled the soft orange bench, elbow on the table and head braced in his palm. "We should have taken the horses."

I walked to the fridge and grabbed three bottles of water, handing one to Liam and one to Jonas before unscrewing the cap of the third. A grating laugh made its way through my throat. "Here I thought this thing intrigued you."

Jonas ignored my quip, uncapped the bottle and took a drink.

A memory tugged at my mind, and I held my hand up. "Wait with that, Jonas. My mom's remedy for queasy stomachs is renowned — to our family, anyway." I shrugged.

I cast a glance at Liam as he pressed his mouth into a reminiscent smile.

After returning to the kitchen counter, I placed an order on the virtual display panel.

With barely a sound, the machine lowered a four-cup holder to the counter and propped three filled disposable cups inside. I carried them to the table and drew in the sweet scent of chamomile tea. After putting one in front of Liam and one before Jonas, I withdrew the water bottle from his hand, replaced the cap and set it down. A pang of empathy rose in my throat and I grazed his cheek with my knuckles. "This will help, Jonas. Try it."

He lifted his green eyes to meet mine and the cup to his thick boyish lips. "You're wrong, you know?"

My forehead crumpled. "About the tea?"

He sighed and shook his head. "Not the tea. You're a smart girl. Figure it out for yourself."

I knew what he was referring to. Of course, I did. I'd convinced myself he no longer had feelings for me, and he'd guessed as much.

Liam watched our exchange with an unfathomable expression, and when he met my gaze, he gave the tiniest shake of his head. No anger touched his handsome features, only compassion.

I half-nodded, but Jonas didn't miss a beat and elevated his gaze from the cup, his voice bored. "Stop with the silent conversation, guys. I can feel when you're doing it."

I ignored his comment and glimpsed into his half-empty cup. "Is the tea helping?"

He shrugged, then picked it up. "Even if it is, it's taking too long. I'm going to lie down." Tea in hand, he made for the bedroom, the door gliding shut behind him.

Liam put his cup on the table and sat, so I slid onto the opposite bench, cupping the tea between my hands. He rested on his elbows, steepling his fingers to his mouth and staring down at the shiny silver surface. Thankfully, he didn't revisit my interaction with Jonas.

I finally broke his silent contemplation. "What did you mean, Liam? The part you said to Harriet about when she's better. You stopped mid-sentence."

Liam swallowed, then frowned before leveling his bright green eyes on mine. His soothing words emerged slower than usual. "When Harriet is better...and she will damned get better...when she does, I'm going to ask her to marry me."

"But you're both so young."

"That may be—physically. But we're not really, are we? None of us are young in the ways that count. And I've thought about it a lot. I don't want anyone else...not ever. Besides, don't you think, after what we've been through, we have the right to decide things like this?"

A thought popped into my head, and I grimaced. As much as I hated the idea, Liam needed to consider this possibility. I measured my words, voice low. "What if there is no cure?"

As if he already had considered the idea, Liam didn't hesitate. Still, his voice cracked. "I'll still marry Harriet. And I'll love her for the rest of her days. Even when she's gray and wrinkled, she'll be the love of my life."

"Oh, Li." With a gulp, I reached for his hand. "I get it, I think."

He didn't shove me away as I might have expected, but squeezed my fingers then stood with his tea. "I'm going to lie down too."

With nothing else to do, as soon as I'd finished the soothing drink and disposed of the empty cup, I too made for my bedroom. For a long while, I lay on top of the strapped-in blankets before finally drifting off.

Eric firms his embrace around my body as I lie against his chest. With my fingers I trace the curve of his muscles, slide them up over his collarbones and around his neck. A shudder grips him and he arches back, pulling me closer. As I tilt my head and take in his unfathomable eyes, he darts them toward mine. They sparkle in the glowing firelight, and for a moment, I watch them before again lying against his chest and listening to the rhythm of his heart. His breathing speeds, his voice low. "Join me, my Cassidy. Dance through life at my side." Then he shifts his feet, leading me in slow circles. We drift from the world, swaying to an unheard beat – the music of our souls. My heart shudders and Eric pulls me closer, a moan rasping through his throat.

The world grows dark. Eric's movement slows. His heartbeat fades and his arms slacken, then they fall away. I shake him and scream, but my voice has no sound, Eric's body no weight – a puff of smoke in my arms. Prison bars slam down between us. Then...nothing.

My eyes shot open, and my throat burned with emotion. The room tilted. It had nothing to do with my dream. I launched from bed. A motion-sensor light came on. "Liam! Jonas!"

Seconds later footsteps sounded, and my door flew open. "Are you okay then, Cass?"

I glared at Jonas. "Can't you feel the floor's moving?"

"Uh, yeah. There's a bit of a storm. The weighted base is keeping us still, though."

My voice rose in pitch. "This isn't *still*."

Liam poked his head into my room. "Would you rather strap up in the recliner?"

I grunted. "No. I was in the middle of—" Not wanting to tell them about my dream, I cut off.

The floor rose and fell, but not with its earlier violence.

The scent of warm food wafted in from the living area. "Are you guys *eating*? Isn't it the middle of the night?"

Liam went back to the kitchenette and called over the counter wall. "There's a great selection of food. And no, it's almost dawn."

He fetched a container labeled 'bacon, eggs, tomato and buttered toast'. After squishing the self-heating pads at the center of each long side, he took it to the table, which was laid with disposable cutlery and plates. Liam flipped the already-heated food onto a plate and handed it to Jonas, then warmed one for himself.

The smallest tidbit would probably tip my stomach scales from 'maybe, maybe not' into 'okay, now you've done it'. "Is there bread?"

Jonas responded with a question. "Slices or rolls?"

"Slices. White. Dry."

He chuckled. "Tea?"

"Funny, ha-ha...but yes, please. Chamomile with honey."

I slumped onto the bench chair and laid my cheek on the table, hiding my face behind strands of dark walnut hair. "How is it you're so okay, Jonas? You were as sick as a dog a few hours back."

He snorted a laugh. "And now it's your turn."

I didn't lift my cheek from the table but peered through my hair. "Despite your penchant for insults, I miss this…easy banter."

Liam warned, "Cassidy…"

Jonas ignored him. "And despite yours, me too. More than you'll know."

He set a cup of tea on the table before me and tucked a strand of hair behind my ear. Then he dropped to the bench, leaving a gap between us. He set a digipar book on the table and read the static, stylized title. "*Around the World in a Hundred and Eighty Days* by Jules Verne."

I leaned in and exhaled a deep sigh. "Oh, are you going to read to me? Please. I love bedtime stories."

Liam squinted as he watched, not hiding his disapproval. But why should I lie? I *had* missed spending time with Jonas…and Liam. Plus, Jonas had gone through so much with me. Surely I didn't have to hide how I cared for him. Still, Liam had a point. I hunched my shoulders and one edge of Liam's lips kicked up into a smile.

"I still hate it when you guys do that," Jonas sang, not removing his gaze from the digipar book. Then he answered my first question. "And no, not that it's bedtime. I'm not reading to you. Get one of your own books out. You brought enough of them."

Over the next few hours, the ocean calmed, and for the following two days we reminisced, played games or read. At least the time passed without Liam needing to impart any further silent reprimands.

As much as I adored my brother, I *did* love Jonas and Harriet nearly as much. We'd grown up on the same small corner of Petriville, attended the same school, played for the same MAC team, ridden the horses for joy and the challenge, shared secrets, hopes, happy times and heartaches. I found Jonas and me sharing jokes once more and me again in Liam's embrace.

Late on the third morning, the gentle rocking of the waterball we'd grown used to changed to something different—harder.

As the siren wailed, Liam jerked away from the silver table and slipped the small cylinder with Mom's digipar into his jeans pocket. "Move."

Chapter Nineteen

Liam launched from the table and raced to the control room, where the overhead tint slowly darkened until blackness shut out the blue sky.

Like the two boys, I plopped into the same recliner as before and the straps slithered over me. My heart lurched. "Do we really have to do this again?"

"It won't be as bad—" was all Liam got out before the dual masks clamped down on our mouths, noses and eyes. The rest of his sentence came as nothing more than a muffled garble.

After a deep breath, I examined the panel above. I could only move my toes and fingers, which I curled into fists, digging my nails into my palms.

This time, the waterball didn't toss my organs around so much as bounce me like a ping-pong ball. Although the spring chair slowed and softened it, my brain still rattled around in my head. In a short time, we came to a pulverizing halt. Grating and a sense of rocking took over, and I braced myself for another round of shuddering, but that didn't happen. After some minutes, the rough movements settled and ceased. Then the masks retracted, seats inclined and safety straps wriggled loose.

A nervous laugh burst from my chest. "Are you telling me we're already there?"

Liam heaved a breath. "You two should have stayed and listened to Austin's rundown. This is the beach nearest the refuge, though we have a hike ahead of us before we get there."

I rocked my head in a slow, deep nod. "Aha... Is there anything else you neglected to tell us?"

Liam shook his head and laughed. "Shall I slap you now or later?"

I shrugged. "Both...if that makes you happy."

He caught me around the shoulders, knowing how it would incapacitate me as he assaulted my ribs with unrelenting tickling fingers. With desperate squeals, I squirmed and thrashed about until he let me drop through his arm to the floor.

A few seconds later the waterball sighed and the door yawned. Then the opening glided away in a downward arc. Although it had beached on sand, that wasn't what caught my attention as my gaze traveled up to the sight beyond—to a towering forest-covered mountain.

Jonas pored over it with a concentrated stare. "And I'm guessing that's the hike you're talking about, then?"

Liam never answered because his mouth hung open and he gulped.

Jonas clapped him on the back. "I'm guessing you didn't know every detail after all. You should have paid more attention."

A snorting laugh burst from my throat as I headed to the bedroom to retrieve my backpack. We packed food for a few days and water for one — since more than that weighed too much. Plus, Liam said his map showed a few safe water sources en route. Once ready, we went down the stairs to the beach. The scents of salt and fish washed over me as waves lapped on the sand. A gull squawked and dove into the ocean as another caught a wind current and spiraled up, up, up. Others flew with the side-wind, gaining speed and soaring in a near-straight line.

As I rested my gaze on Liam, he slid his palm over a nondescript area beside the doorway. A moment later, a bright blue virtual keypad lit up. He punched in PQ316T.

I rolled my eyes. "That's the pod number Eric and I used to communicate through."

"That's because Austin altered it to make it the same, so we'd remember it under pressure." As Liam spoke, the door rose in its silent arc and suctioned into place. Then the virtual keypad faded away.

Liam extracted a familiar small cylinder from his jean's pocket — Mom's digipar. He thumb-tapped it and let it go. Like before, it uncoiled and flattened in midair. Then he stated, "Show me Rodrigues' refuge." A map swapped spots with Mom's writing and he tapped the X, then raised his gaze toward the summit of the steep slope. "Yup. That's it. Straight up there and some way farther." He tapped it again, and the digipar curled up before he popped it back inside his jeans' pocket.

Something stirred deep inside me and I wheeled on him. "Why don't you ever let me read Mom's letter? You're always looking at it and keep it so close. It's like you don't think I have any right to it."

Guilt raked lines across his forehead. "Oh. Oh, Cassidy, I'm sorry. Of course, you have *every* right to it. I didn't think you wanted the reminder of Mom's murder."

I met his bright green eyes, my words soft. "I'm tougher than you think. You can keep it safe for now, but I want to read it when we get back, okay?"

Liam nodded then looked up at the sun, which baked down in shimmering swirls across the sand. With a sincere smile, he turned and moved off. I hitched my backpack higher on my hips, clipped in the belt and continued. As we trudged up the grainy beach sand, my booted feet sunk in and I gave the waterball a backward glance. My eyes met only the vast ocean beyond—a mirror of the waterball's opposite side.

Then I followed Liam and Jonas into the shadow of the forest, where bright green ferns covered the damp soil. Innumerous tall trees made overhead canopies. Some plants exposed narrow leaves of pale green, and on others hand-sized, dark green leaves wafted. Most came in every shape, size and color between. Bright flowering plants grew in clumps. Shrubs of every hue of green and brown emerged between and beside rocks. Despite the canopy of trees, heat, humidity and a cacophony of chirrups filled the forest air. Of the many broken branches scattered on the forest floor around us, we selected three fairly straight ones.

Liam and Jonas lowered to a boulder. From beside their bows and quivers, they pulled out hunting knives and leather straps.

I thrust out my chin. "What about my dagger?"

While strapping his hunting knife to the end of his branch, Liam darted an unwavering gaze to my indignant one. "You don't need one. Any powerful male will disarm you and before you know it, he'll turn the weapon on you. If you want to arm yourself, ready your bow and arrow."

Jonas wedged the branch between his hip and muscled thigh, strapping his dagger to the end. "I doubt any other males are out here. And if there were, they wouldn't so easily disarm Cass."

I dipped my chin in a smug nod. "Precisely."

Liam offered no acknowledgment to either of our responses. With his dagger fixed to the end of his staff, he stood and thrashed against the thick undergrowth. In seconds, the razor-sharp blade had cleared a path. "If you want to lead, you can take mine."

"No, thanks. But it would have been nice to have the option." I glared. "More than that, why this sudden doubt in my abilities?"

Liam tilted his head back and puffed a blast of air. "I don't doubt what you can do. It just concerns me that you're both being so cavalier. Of all people, you guys should know this isn't a game." Jonas rose to his feet, his eyes bulging, but Liam whirled on him. "This is about your *sister*" — then on me — "and your *best* friend!"

Jonas slumped, voice soft and calm. "I get your anxiety, bro. But whether we face this task with anger or calmness, it won't change the outcome — or Harriet's fate." His voice sounded choked. "But don't go thinking I love my sister any less than you love yours."

With no challenge or anger left in his posture, Liam fell silent. He swiveled and started clearing an uphill path, his shoulders curved forward. Jonas said nothing more but tracked Liam while I picked up the rear.

Insects buzzed around as we trudged through the forest. Although I'd dressed in jeans, a T-shirt and boots, even with the repellant I splatted more than a few mosquitos that were *vampiring* my arms and neck.

As morning became afternoon, I drained my second water bottle. And when Liam's stomach gurgled, he stared down at it as if it were a foreign object. Then he slipped the straps off his shoulders and dropped his pack to the earth. "I was hoping to stop for lunch at a water source where we could fill our bottles, but it doesn't look like that's going to happen."

Sitting on a large boulder, we ate sandwiches and washed them down with the remaining water. When we again braved the mountain, my legs ached. The slope towered above us, seeming to bend back on itself. In an attempt to relieve my bruised hips, I loosened the belt and adjusted the weight of the pack, loading more onto my shoulders. Still, we climbed. When a clear stream finally burbled across our path, we all but dove into it and drank our fill of the sweet, cool liquid before topping off the bottles.

The afternoon heat mounted as it wore on. With it, my mood soured. We stopped speaking and took shifts in the front, thrashing at the thickest of the brush. Somehow, we ended up on an actual footpath — surely animal-formed. The climb was easier after that. While Liam and Jonas untied their daggers and returned them to their packs, I opted to lead. As I snaked higher and higher, I rapped my stick on the ground to ward off snakes and kept my gaze on my foot placement. I'd pulled ahead of the boys when a tall rock and sharp V-bend made a switchback on the path. As I rounded the bend, something rock-solid halted my forward motion when I slammed into it — something descending the path. No, not something…someone. In slow motion, I trailed my vision from the leather boots and up the long jean-clad legs. I studied the shape. Too familiar. When I reached his torso, I stepped back, my eyes widening as a gasp flew from my lips. "You escaped!"

Chapter Twenty

I rephrased my observation into a question. "How *did* you escape?"

Then I dropped my pack to the earth and leaped, barely reaching Eric on the higher ground. As I threw my arms around his neck, he caught me around the waist—his embrace strong and warm.

He seemed unable to reply as he embraced me. "Uh-uh."

I leaned back and cupped his cheek, taking in his hair, his eyes, his mouth. He gaped, even more dumbstruck than me. With a long blink, I drew in a deep breath, then crushed my mouth against his. For a moment he hesitated before groaning and pressing up against me as he reciprocated with a breathless, all-encompassing kiss. The straw in his hand tickled the nape of my neck. Something was wrong. I pulled back, frowning.

Reality dawned, and I gasped. "You're not—" I broke off. A thousand thoughts raked through my mind, and so many contrasting emotions sent tingles flooding through my veins. Joy. Sadness. Pain. Warmth. Anger. Ecstasy. And a hurt so deep, it made my chest ache—though it wasn't mine. No. These sentiments belonged to another.

I laid my hands on the chest of the boy before me and shoved—hard. Jerking from his embrace, I wiped my mouth, staring up at him. "How could you?"

He chuckled and propped the straw between his teeth. "Hey, who am I to walk away from some beauty who turns up out of the blue and kisses me?"

I wasn't sure why—maybe for the pain in Eric's expression when he'd spoken of his brother, probably because I'd kissed the boy and definitely because he'd kissed me back. Without thinking, I raised my hand and, with every bit of strength I could muster, slapped him. The power of my strike thrust his face to the side— a face too similar to the one I loved, from the bright aquamarine eyes to those deep clefts marking his cheeks as he grimaced and his tall, lean, muscled body as I slid my gaze down to the straw he rolled between his fingers. Caleb was *alive!*

He rubbed his cheek and spoke with the same faint Texan accent as Eric. His shoulders gave him an air, not exactly of pride, but definitely oozing with confidence. While he spoke louder, the timbre of his voice sounded the tiniest touch deeper. "Ouch. What was that for? You're the one who kissed me."

He was like Eric yet…different. Not yet to me in distinct, identifiable ways, but in something more subtle. I suspected that if I got to know him, though, I'd find he wasn't at all the same.

The slap didn't seem to worry Caleb, who grinned down at me before shifting his gaze to Liam and Jonas.

My brother growled. "Do you normally go around kissing strange girls?"

Caleb shrugged, his free palm out toward me. "Like I said, I'm hardly likely to turn down the girl's advances."

At that moment, six older boys with huge muscles stepped up behind him.

The nearest spoke in a gruff voice. "Well, well. What's going on here?"

Caleb flicked the straw away and folded his arms, the smile not leaving his lips. "It seems we have visitors. Who knows where they're coming—?" He cut himself short, hardening his glower. His smile turned tight. "Where *are* you from?"

Without a second pause, the six boys leaped on Liam and Jonas, snatching the branch-come-walking sticks from their hands.

I whirled around, a squeal bursting through my throat. "Stop!"

The boys ignored me, but three of them slammed Liam with his face to the dirt while three dove on Jonas. One pushed a knee on my friend's backpack while another bound his wrists above his head. I jumped to Jonas' side — nearest his arrows — and fought the boy on his back. Being as surreptitious as possible, I eased the sheathed dagger from beside his quiver and tucked it inside my T-shirt. All the better if they decided the bulge meant a belly.

Then I leaped on the boy for real and wailed. "Please don't hurt them? Please!"

He tossed me off as if I were a rag doll. I leaped on again. This time another grabbed my wrists in one hand. I kicked again and again until he swept my feet from beneath me.

Liam thrashed, his mouth covered in dirt as he scrambled to keep his arms free. It took only seconds for the three boys to overpower him.

I wrenched at my captor so I could attack the boys fighting Liam and Jonas. The entire time, Caleb hadn't moved an inch. He stayed in exactly the same place, his arms knitted over his chest and a sneer twisting his mouth. I struggled after sharing so many intimate moments with his identical twin to see him as an enemy. "Why are you doing this?"

He answered with his own question, his voice a growl. "Since you kissed me, it's reasonable to assume you thought I was someone else. I know of only one person who looks enough like me to warrant that. So, I'm going to ask you once. Where is my brother?"

I gave him an innocent half-smile. "Who is your brother?"

"It's not like I never expected that answer." He held out his hand. "You can give me those." The boys handed Caleb our bows and quivers, and he tossed them over one shoulder. Liam's dagger *wasn't* among them.

"He's...he's..." I slumped. Telling Caleb that Gina had imprisoned Eric struck me as the worst idea. He definitely wouldn't trust us in that case. "Who's your brother?"

Caleb clenched his fists at his side, jaw as hard as stone as he grated his teeth together. He pivoted. "Take the girl too. Let's go."

I ripped at the iron-fast hand gripping my wrists. "I'm not...*the girl*."

The boy didn't let go but lifted my backpack in his free hand and snorted. "Feisty."

Jonas hip-nudged me but addressed Caleb, his voice nonchalant. "Where are you taking us then?"

"And why?" Liam added. "I assume you're not a total dunce and can see that three of us couldn't overpower you. So, please explain the threat."

Caleb didn't glance back. "Not you. But that woman has an entire army at her disposal, so we hear."

"What woman?" I feigned ignorance.

Now Caleb half rotated back while he walked. "Don't play me for a fool, *girl*." He emphasized the last word, already facing forward.

Caleb was nothing like Eric. Had he always been this cruel? Did something happen after he'd left Graham's refuge — something that had brought out his dark side? Although Eric had said Caleb jumped to conclusions.

He carried on talking without looking back. "If that woman has harmed a hair on my brother's head, you can be sure I'll avenge him."

My temper flared. "That's noble of you, especially since…" I slammed my mouth closed, sealing away the words swirling in my mind. *Especially since you had no misgivings about letting Eric think you were dead!*

Caleb wheeled around and glared at me, his eyes glacial. "Especially since what, *girl*?"

My throat closed, and I pinched my lips. If I didn't stop going the rounds with him, it wouldn't be long before I tripped up.

A small bulge protruded at the front of Liam's T-shirt too. I almost laughed. Liam's abs were as flat as an ironing-board. My legs ached from the long uphill climb, so I silenced myself and let my captor half-drag me onward. No one spoke again, though Caleb occasionally crossed his arms or muttered in some internal debate.

During mid-afternoon, we finally summited. Caleb called a halt. "Have water while you wait."

He darted off along the ridge. For ten minutes, our captors grumbled as we rested. When we asked them where 'the other one' had gone, they ignored us. Liam and Jonas must have come to a similar conclusion as me, because they didn't confess to knowing Eric either.

When Caleb returned, he again toyed with a piece of straw, and he wore a sneer to challenge any of mine during a particularly tense moment with Gina.

Hard sarcasm tainted his voice. "So…from the lookout, a person can view the entire stretch of beach below. And what do you know?" The sarcasm died and his voice caught before changing to bitter steel. "That thing you arrived in got me curious. If a person didn't know what to look for, they'd surely miss it—what with it being almost invisible and all. Kaleidotonium! Did you think we wouldn't recognize it?" He gestured down the slope toward the beach and aimed his glare at me. "You lied when you said you weren't with that woman. It makes me wonder what else you lied about."

I feigned a dramatic eye-roll and snickered. "I never lied. Without a name, how would we guess who 'that woman' is?" Then I chanced a blatant lie. "And I can't fathom where you're getting your information from, because there's no army in Petriville."

Liam flashed me a glance but kept silent.

Caleb caught our shared look and squinted. He shook his head several slow times. "We'll see about that." He turned to the boys. "Let's get them back to the refuge."

A seething madness seemed to take hold of Caleb—enough for him to kill us with his bare hands. Did he honestly think we'd harmed Eric? He'd mentioned the refuge. A light switched on in my head. *Of course!* Graham's letter to Mr. Thomas Rodrigues. Once Caleb learned the truth, he'd have to believe us. I'd keep silent until then and make him eat his words. Our freedom approached.

Chapter Twenty-One

We remained quiet during the hike across the plateau. Given the anger radiating in waves off Caleb, I expected him to fly into a rage at one wrong word. He kept chewing on a blade of straw, then crushing it in his hand before tossing it aside and plucking another. Mom had once said I should stop and think of consequences before blurting out my thoughts, and now I was. As night settled over the forest, the chirrups of crickets and beetles rang through the trees. Only when I begged Caleb did he finally allow me to take out our headlamps and prop one each on Jonas, Liam and myself.

Eventually, we emerged through a copse of trees to overlook a high cliff with blackness concealing its depths. Caleb led us along the top, but a short distance farther, the path dipped and veered closer to the edge. Then it sank below the summit. On one side of us the cliff rose, while on the other a coal-black drop plunged away. The farther down we walked, the higher and higher the cliff beside us towered. Finally, the path leveled, confining us on the only route. As we continued, the ledge gradually widened until three men could walk abreast—not that anyone did. In the dark of night, we all stayed well away from the edge.

Finally, Caleb halted at what could only have been a Kaleidotonium door. The light of our headlamps danced off it in brilliant opalescence. Still, as we stepped through, I hugged the rock wall. Even if the Kaleidotonium protected the open side, I wasn't taking chances. A short way ahead, light shone out from the cliff face, brightening as we neared. My stomach tightened. As we followed Caleb toward it, I forced one foot in front of the other. People hung around on the shelf, leaning against the rock wall or dangling legs over the edge. Some straightened. Some leaped up. However, the dim light didn't hide how every adult and every teen narrowed their eyes and folded their arms.

An older man walked forward, flashing a light in our eyes. "What is this? Tell me, young man. Why did you bind them?"

Caleb gritted out his reply as if barely containing his rage, but something else snuck into his voice. It cracked with hurt. "They're no visitors, Dan." He tossed a glance over his shoulder, speaking to the boys. "We'll take them to lockup."

At that moment, his voice sounded so like Eric's. No matter how I should have feared him, his pain ripped a hole in my heart.

The group backed up then disappeared into the light that was emanating from a large cave entrance. They made space as the boys shoved us toward a tunnel. Like in Graham's refuge, a duct of lights ran along the ceiling. Their glow shimmered off the Kaleidotonium coating of every surface. Our captors propelled us forward along a downward-sloping tunnel floor. For ten minutes, we walked in silence. The farther we moved from the entrance, the dimmer the overhead lights became — as if Caleb were herding us to a less-used section of the caves. The distant sound of water caught my attention. Rushing water. The noise grew until it drowned the echoes of our footsteps. Our captors pushed us on and on, closer to the source, until its roar drowned every other sound. Did Caleb plan on having us thrown into this underground river — for it to sweep us away? Panic-induced goosebumps pricked up on my skin. Still, the boys nudged us on.

We split off at a Y-bend — a narrower and even darker passage. As minutes passed, the roar of water decreased. Our guards stopped beside bars which separated the tunnel from a small, rough cave, its door ajar. Déjà vu rocked me backward as memories of Jonas' and my imprisonment flooded back. Jonas' face contorted, and he kicked and thrashed at his bonds. His strength was nothing against so many captors.

None too gently, they unbound us then hustled us through the cell door. I slammed into the cold stone floor and the rough rock surface scraped into my face, my body. The pack my captor had carried slammed into my back so hard that I cried out. As their bodies thudded to either side of me, Liam grated out a moan and Jonas grunted. Then the door clanged shut and a key rattled in the lock.

Cowering to the rear wall, I tugged my knees to my chest. Jonas took only the seconds he needed to throw off his pack before he huddled beside me. He drew up his knees and embraced his legs like he couldn't get them close enough. Our time in Gina's fort had left us with deep scars.

Liam inhaled and got to his feet. As if in slow motion, he rotated, studying the nooks and crannies of the small cave. In equal consideration, he lowered his pack to the ground. As he observed our hunched bodies, he gave several pained shakes of his head.

Only after the guards' footsteps dulled beneath the rushing river did Liam growl his response. "Graham had no need for a lockup in *his* refuge. What caused this place to be different?"

The reason didn't matter to me. I hunched over and moaned, fully aware of Jonas rocking back and forth beside me.

Liam squeezed in between us and threaded his arms around our shoulders. His voice rippled through his throat—a low, broken growl. "It's beyond heartbreaking to see you two like this. It renders me wild with a rage so great I could rip someone to shreds. What you went through—" He broke off, his voice catching.

It took the longest time before I convinced myself that the courage of lions ran through my veins. I forced my shoulders to straighten and slowed my whimpers and my breaths. Then I stood, barely recognizing the tears running down my cheeks—at least until I wiped at them and my hands came away moist. I slid my palms down my T-shirt, but they hit resistance above my belt as I placed them over…Jonas' dagger!

I intended to voice this when the echo of nearing footsteps made my heart again crumble. After so long—too long—their wielders arrived at the cell. Two teen boys flanked Caleb. He could probably have rested his elbows on their heads without raising his arms at all. One clung a bedroll to his chest, his straight hair as black as pitch and skin the color of warm ochre. The second bore a large pitcher of water and what looked like maple leaves. In stark contrast to the first, his pale ivory skin and white brush crown made him appear weaker. Caleb held two extra mattress rolls with bedding curled up inside, and a piece of straw sticking out from between his lips. After dropping them to the floor, he unlocked the door. He tossed all three beds against the side wall, his face a mass of hard lines. The pale boy slipped the pitcher and leaves inside before ducking back out, as though we'd attempt to escape. Or worse…hurt him. Then Caleb re-locked the door.

Chess pieces. That was what the boys reminded me of. I barely contained a — possibly hysterical — chuckle.

Apparently, I wasn't the only one, because Jonas pouted his thick lips between his fingers, then voiced his opinion behind a cough. "Fifteen more pair and we'd have a game."

Caleb shot Jonas a glare, then watched the boys retreating down the tunnel. He didn't move, but his rage seemed to have leached from him. Now he looked drained.

Chapter Twenty-Two

For a while Caleb stood outside our cell — silent, as if lost in contemplation. At various moments, he rested his familiar gaze on each of us. Finally, he breathed out slow, measured words. "Honestly, I can't decide what to do with you. However, I do need answers." He dipped his chin and ran a sun-bronzed hand through his thick, dark-blond hair. He looked up and pointed the straw toward the far corner of the cell. "You can use the runoff for ablutions. The urn is to wash it away…and the maple leaves? Well, I'll leave that to your imagination. The boys'll bring food."

This was too much pain, too much heartache. Eric would go crazy with rage if he saw how Caleb was treating us, especially after what Jonas and I had gone through. But revealing my feelings for Eric wasn't an option. Caleb would consider my words a lie. Although sitting here before Eric's near exact double…

I nearly gave in to Caleb when Liam beat me to bat. "I'm assuming your friends deliberately avoided using your name during the hike up here? If you want answers, tell us who you and your supposed brother are."

Caleb had tried to catch us in a lie—a trap—one I'd have fallen headlong into. He cocked his head, pursing his lips and narrowing his eyes. "That's something I'm guessing you don't need me to answer. Like I said, don't play me for a fool."

Liam raised his chin. "Are you the leader in this place?"

My brother was good at this…*thing*.

Caleb snorted. "Bah! You know I'm not." He put the straw between his teeth and clapped his hands three times—slow and deliberate. "Bravo on the act."

Liam didn't relent. "Then may we *speak* with your leader?"

Caleb considered before extracting the piece of straw and responding, clearly assessing if this was information he needed to guard. He tilted his head to one side, steeling his expression. "The leader is dead. Now, those who remain defer to Dan."

Although Liam controlled how the air deflated from his chest, Caleb caught me unprepared. Before I considered stopping it, my gasp erupted. He snapped his head to me and I feigned blending the traitorous puff of air into my voice, though I intended my question as a trap. "When?"

"Just after they opened—" Caleb almost fell for my ruse. He spied me through slitted eyes. "Nice try…*girl*."

Like me, Caleb *was* impulsive. Eric had told me as much. That was why Caleb had almost slipped. But I guessed the hasty words he'd cut off 'the refuge'. I flashed glances first at Liam, then Jonas. The tiniest light flickered in their gazes. They also realized what Caleb had stopped himself saying.

It meant Graham's digipar was useless. We'd have to find another way to prove ourselves — to convince Caleb that Eric was safe. Not even Graham or Dad had considered this possibility.

I weighed Caleb's need for proof. If he loved Eric as much as Eric loved him, he *needed* that evidence. "You can start by telling us your name if you want us to respond to your questions."

Caleb's jawline bunched into hard ridges. "Your continuous evasion attempts can mean only one thing." He choked, turning his face as if steeling for a blow. "Instinct tells me what that is." His voice shattered. "Tell me the truth. She killed my family, didn't she?"

He fell back against the tunnel wall, sliding to the dirt, doubling over and wrapping his arms around his knees, the straw loose between his fingers. He heaved a racked, broken cry. "Did she torture them? Is that how you learned of this place? Tell me the truth. Please. I already sensed something was wrong with him. How can you just sit there? Can't you see this is cutting me to shreds?"

I shuddered, my throat burning as tears threatened to spill. I wanted to run to him, to hold him, to tell him Eric was fine. More than fine…he was safe. At that moment, the reality slammed into me of what Eric would experience if he discovered Caleb wasn't dead. A scene flitted through my mind. Eric discovering this news. How joy would brighten his face. How happiness would spread a smile onto his soft, full lips and drag those crevassed dimples down his cheeks. How elation would twinkle in his aquamarine eyes.

Beside me, Liam blinked, pulled me against his chest and spoke close to the top of my head, his voice an indistinct murmur — a demand, not a request. "Don't."

Although I wasn't sure of the right thing to do, Liam was better than me with social subtleties. I considered the thoughts swirling around in Caleb's head right now. Of course, that did nothing to expunge the icy chill spreading through my veins. If we wanted to get out of here alive, then letting Caleb know Eric was in Petriville—in prison—was a sure way to send him into a violent rage. Our task...our way out of here...was to convince Caleb we knew nothing.

He lifted his tormented stare. "Did you see them die? Did you watch when she killed my brother and my father?"

My voice croaked but sounded sincere, even to my ears. An overwhelming amount of compassion washed over me. "We don't know what you're talking about—" I cut myself short. I'd been so caught up in Caleb's devastation that I'd nearly blurted his name.

I tried to conceal my blunder. "Do you consider us so callous that we'd hide something like that when you're so obviously heartbroken? Do you think we'd feel nothing?"

"What you feel"—he closed his eyelids—"I wouldn't know. It's likely you kissed me as a ploy to gain my trust. Who knows what you people are capable of!" It wasn't a question, but an agonized statement of fact.

To justify kissing him, I replayed the scene in my head. My gaze had started on his feet, then drifted up his legs. Had I reached his face? He'd been uphill—so much higher than his normally tall self. I softened my voice to just above a whisper. "You looked like someone else."

Caleb frowned and his chest caved. While his voice still trembled with grief, it also sounded resigned. His accusation emerged as tired understanding. "Well, now I know you're lying. While we hiked up here, that scene kept going around and around in my head. There's no way this makes sense. You may not have seen my face before you launched at me and stuck your tongue down my throat." Caleb followed his logic with wild speculations. "Who's to say what that waterball of yours does? It might identify people climbing down the slope, then glean information about them. On *us*. The entire operation could be a ploy to gain access to this refuge."

I considered the first question I'd asked him—when I'd thought he was Eric. I'd asked, *"How did you escape?"*

He pre-empted my observation. "You're going over what you said, but I've got a thought about that too. It makes me wonder who you expected needed escaping. And what did that person need to flee? I figure that was part of the ruse—like the kiss. It makes sense. Confuse your enemy to hide your real motivation." He popped the straw between his teeth and folded his arms in some kind of self-satisfied triumph.

My eyes shot wide. "Wow. You have an answer for every—"

"Aha!" Caleb cut me off, plucking the blade of straw from between his lips and using it to point at me. "My guess was spot on."

I slammed my eyes shut. All the emotions filling the day clouded my thoughts. Now, when I needed it, my mind lacked clarity. I shook my head. Nothing came. No ideas. No possibilities.

A low Scots-accented voice cut into my thoughts. "Cassidy's boyfriend is back in Petriville. His mother is super-protective, if you get my meaning." Jonas scoffed with a mixture of amusement and irritation. I wanted to pat him on the back with a *'good acting, Jonas'* as he went on, "His mother didn't want him joining us on this out-of-town vac."

Caleb gritted his teeth and flew to his feet, crushing the straw as he sneered. "That's it. You lot have an answer for every question, don't you? But you're lying. Do you seriously think you can keep fooling me? Trust me on one thing. The truth *will* find a way out."

Caleb looked back up the tunnel as the two teenagers returned carrying metal trays. One held three bowls and the other steaming mugs. The scent of stew wafted into the cell. Caleb strode between the boys, flattening a palm beneath each tray and slapping upward. They flew into the air, stayed suspended for a moment, then clattered to the dust, spraying food and liquid across the floor, as the plastic dishes and cutlery clattered on the stone. "Go hungry for all I care."

With that, Caleb stalked away. The boys gaped at his back, wide-eyed. Turning their focus to us, the black-haired boy gasped. "What did you lot do?"

They didn't wait for an answer as they bent and scraped the leftover bits back into the bowls. Without another word, they stacked the dishes on the trays and scurried away.

Their footsteps soon died amid the rush of water and I crossed my arms, my posture drooping. "Well, that couldn't have gone any worse. Should we have told him the truth?"

Neither Jonas nor Liam hesitated, voices forceful but not loud. "No."

In a resigned whisper, Liam added, "He wouldn't have believed us, no matter what we said. You heard him. He sensed something wasn't right with his brother. Twins can sometimes have a connection like that. And think about it. Something *isn't* right with Eric.

He's stuck in prison and probably out of his mind with worry about you coming out here."

Jonas leaned around Liam. "Isn't it possible Caleb *wants* to believe Gina murdered Eric, then? He already knows she abandoned Graham on Earth. Don't get me wrong. She *is* evil—the epitome of it. Only, it's also *all* Caleb knows about her."

Liam nodded. "Jonas is right, Cass. Look at Eric when you first met him. He thought you took Gina's side just because you lived in Petriville."

I swept my palms down my face. "But Eric isn't cruel, guys. What made Caleb turn so hard?"

Compassion filled Jonas' gaze. "He's grieving, Cass. Or at least he thinks he is. Given this situation, Eric would react the same way. Anyone worth their salt would."

The question blurted through my lips. "Will he kill us?"

As if I'd asked about something mundane like the weather forecast, Liam shrugged. "Time will tell."

No one returned with food or drinks. We pulled out the remaining sandwiches and the last of the water from the stream. I poured a bottle and a half down my gullet before un-packaging a sandwich. But my stomach flipped. I couldn't force even a single bite down my throat.

Liam met my gaze. "Please eat, Cass."

I shook my head. "I'll throw up if I do."

He retrieved the contents of my hands and slipped the sandwiches back inside the package. "I'll leave them next to your bed. You might wake up hungry in the night."

At the back of the cell, I rolled out a mattress, placing the head against the backward-sloping wall—farthest from the cell door and the runoff. They'd included no pillows with the bedrolls, but I made one from a throw blanket I'd brought.

As luck would have it, my bladder wanted to pop. I stood and retreated to the alcove, passing instructions as I walked—"Turn around." I glanced over my shoulder. They'd already turned away. I issued another command. "And hum. This won't work with you listening."

They hooted, and Jonas spoke. "I'm not sure the associated noise is the greatest problem."

"Don't be gross, Jonas." I groaned, thankful it was only my bladder that ached.

Mission accomplished, I flopped to the mattress. Either the physical exhaustion, the emotional weariness or the mental fatigue got my eyes fluttering as my thoughts drifted between Eric and Caleb.

The brothers do share some bond. Their heartache rang true and their love strong. As I continued pondering, the lullaby of the rushing water sent me sliding into a deep sleep.

Chapter Twenty-Three

Eric is running beside me through a field of long, billowing grass and myriad white daisies. He slips his strong fingers between mine and firms the pressure of his hand, warmth seeping into me. As I inhale, my airways fill with the sweetest floral scent. A brook crosses our path, bubbling over pebbles and stones. When we stop before it, Eric presses a kiss to my knuckles, then his gaze probes mine. A cheeky smile warms his face, dragging fissures down his cheeks. Releasing my hand, he faces the brook, testing his foot on a steppingstone, then his weight. He moves to another...and another. Before I know it, he's on the far bank. I want to follow but I stop. The water between us is no longer clear, no longer fresh. It is languid, bubbling molten lava. Heat rises from deep within the earth. The molten rock boils and pops. Steam escapes small pores and fire bursts from the flow. Higher and higher, flames reach for the sky. I meet the pain in Eric's gaze as the fiery river widens, forcing us to step back. It is no longer a field of grass and daisies that Eric stands in but a terrible and blackened wasteland. It engulfs him – pulling him farther and farther from me. Lava laps at

my feet, burning, scalding, melting my shoes. The smoke of
the raging fire slides razor blades through my lungs. I take
another step back, and when I set my foot down, it rests on
burned ashes. Another. Another. No color touches this land,
this sky, these waters. Not anymore.

I awoke with a gasp, whimpering over the remnants
of my dream. Liam and Jonas slept on. The dull light of
the tunnel left me with a strange sense of security, and
when my heart finally slowed, I drifted off again. No
further dreams disturbed my sleep.

The next time I awoke, Jonas was pacing back and
forth, reminding me of a similar morning in Gina's fort.
Liam sat on his mattress, lying against the sloping wall.
A faraway stare seized his features, and he tapped a
digipen on his knee before pressing it to Mom's digipar.

I angled toward him. "What are you writing?"

He offered a typical Liam half-answer. "A journal.
With no wireless infrastructure, there's no way to
transmit it, but if we don't make it out of here..." He
trailed off, floating back into his own thoughts. I didn't
push the matter. I didn't need to. He was leaving notes
of our last days in the unlikely event Mom's digipar
ever found its way into Dad's hands.

The soft tread of arriving footsteps infused the
distant rushing water. My stomach knotted...or
probably it growled. I hadn't eaten since lunch the day
before. "I hope that's not Caleb."

Just noticing I'd awoken, Jonas cocked his head and
frowned. "Aha! Morning, Cass. I doubt it...unless he
comes bearing gifts, because that's definitely bacon and
eggs I smell...and coffee too, I expect."

Liam sniggered. "You're like a bloodhound when it
comes to scenting out food."

Jonas was right. It wasn't Caleb who came into view, but the teenage boys from the previous evening. After darting glances over their shoulders, they placed two trays on the floor. While the fair youth opened the door, the dark-haired teen slipped the trays through and ducked back. As if we'd bolt for it, they slammed and locked the door. The trays bore three sets of cutlery, three steaming mugs and three plates of bacon, eggs and toast.

These kids carried an air of innocence. I managed a smile. "We don't bite, you know. Is that what you're worried about?"

The black-haired boy displayed the top of his head. "We're not so much worried *about* you as worried *for* you. The chef said we could bring your breakfast."

The white-haired boy shrugged one shoulder. "We kind of felt guilty when Caleb left you hungry last night."

Liam snatched at the thread, phrasing it as a question. "So that's his name...Caleb?"

"Oh" — realizing his mistake, the black-haired boy shot his dark eyes wide — "oh! You tricked us. He didn't want us to say his *name*." He dragged out the last word.

Turning, they scurried away.

Jonas called after them. "Can you at least tell us *your* names then?"

They didn't, but raced away, their footsteps soon dissolving into the rushing water.

I set my coffee on the stone floor and leaned against the wall.

Jonas chewed like he was mimicking a robot and seemed to disappear into a different place.

My brows twitched together. "What's got you so deep in contemplation?"

He turned to face me, and after some time opened his mouth. But he never got to answer because when heavy footsteps neared, his jaw fell slack.

My stomach gnarled as Caleb strode into view, a rigid scowl twisting his face. It turned mine cold, as if all my color had drained away.

Every bit as bleak as before, he listed against the tunnel wall. Black circled his eyes. Now, instead of sounding enraged, his voice lacked vigor—deflated. "So…the boys leaked my name."

I didn't respond to his statement. "Have you even slept…Caleb?"

Caleb's defiance returned in full force. He balled his hands, his nostrils flaring. Although a blade of grass still protruded from the end of his fisted hand, it was as if he was unaware of it—in the same way we wouldn't think of each hair on our heads—like it was an extension of himself he couldn't discard. An icy chill entered his voice. "You assume using it will build some kind of affinity between us?" He made it a question.

The way he skewered me with his aquamarine gaze made him look so different from Eric. I flinched. In no memory had Eric ever glared at me like that.

For the longest time he stared, saying nothing. Eventually he shook his head. "The reason I came down here was to make sure *you* lot hear me out."

Liam folded his arms over his chest. Jonas fixed on his shuffling feet, shifting his weight from side to side.

Caleb wasn't seeking our acknowledgment, but he softened his tone. "The thing I keep turning over in my head is this. It's clear you're not telling the truth. That part, I'm sure of—as sure as I am that there's no boyfriend waiting back home with his possessive mother." He flashed a glare at Jonas, then back at me. "It makes me wonder what you're trying to hide. Now, either it *was* my brother who you thought you kissed, and you do care for him — which, considering where you're from, I'm finding it hard to believe. Or like I said yesterday, you came out here looking for me. But why the facade?" He dropped his gaze to his shoes, then looked up at Liam and Jonas. "The obvious explanation is that you — or that devil you work for — needs something from us, most likely information. So, I got to figuring, you found out I headed to this refuge. That begs the question, how? And the logical answer is — you *tortured* them." His voice cracked on the offending word. "So that's my conclusion. You're out here on some kind of scouting mission to take information or *something* or *someone* back to that — "

I rolled my eyes, cutting him off. "Seriously, Caleb? Do you know what I think? You're brandishing wild speculations and hoping to get one of them right. If what you're saying *was* true, why, pray tell, would Gina send us — two boys and a girl? Surely if she wanted to attack you, then sending seasoned soldiers would be a more prudent tactic." I softened my voice. "You see that, don't you?"

Caleb didn't back down. "It's likely you intended to win our trust and in the process gauge numbers and fighting capability. It's a shrewder strategy to send three youths that seem unlikely suspects." He growled his next sentence. "And we all know she's that. She left my dad to die, even after all he did for her. She abandoned him on Earth. Now I'm wondering if her military isn't far behind you lot."

He'd gone off on a tangent. I drew a deep breath and flashed a glance at Jonas, then Liam. Jonas gave no impression that he was listening, his attention glued to his shoes. But Liam rotated his head a minuscule amount. In fact, such a tiny bit that I nearly missed it.

Caleb did not. He glowered at Liam. "What was that about?"

Liam stared him down. "You've already made your mind up and I dislike you interrogating my sister. I don't see any reason she should engage with your insanity."

"Sister? You don't look like siblings. And that one?" Caleb flashed a glance at Jonas, who finally looked up.

Jonas gritted his teeth, clenching his fists at his sides. He shook his head at Liam, then me, then Caleb. "Enough of this damned stupidity!" He held his palm toward Caleb, studying first Liam, then me. "Don't you see the man's in agony?" He didn't wait for our reply but directed his conversation to Caleb. "Do you want the truth then? Well, here it is. I don't much like your brother, because Cassidy *is* in love with him. Despite my feelings, *he* at least has my respect."

Liam scraped his palms down his face, leaving his eyes closed.

Caleb narrowed his. "That leads me to the other thing. My brother is too honorable. He has an insane need to protect. If he loved this *girl*, he'd never have let her come out here without him."

Because he'd addressed me as 'girl,' I glared at him. "But that's not always the case, is it, Caleb?"

He squished his brows together—one quick pinch before relaxing them—curious about my reference, as if he already knew. He didn't ask. I considered raising the point. He'd left Eric and Graham to presume he'd died.

Not yet, I told myself and instead softened my tone. "What if Eric had no choice?"

Caleb met my gaze. The steel in it softened along with his voice. "That's exactly my point. Why didn't he have a choice? There's only one reason for that."

I closed my eyes and sighed. "Well, it doesn't matter, because I'm done talking. You refuse to see anything past your prejudice."

Caleb swallowed. "Tell me what she did to them. I beg of you." His voice quivered with the choked plea.

Liam barred his teeth. His words tumbled out in that gentle tone of his. "Why are you insisting she's done something to your brother and Graham? Are you so stubborn that you don't *want* to listen to what my sister's saying?"

Caleb hardened at Liam's soothing accusation. "Well, you still haven't told me why my brother isn't here, and you're giving me no reason to believe you."

I considered his words, observing the uneven rocks of our ceiling. Then, giving an exhausted shake of my head, I slowed my voice—as if speaking to a child. "I already told you, Caleb. And why is it so hard to suppose I have feelings for him?"

"Because he's my identical twin, and the way you look at *me* is with nothing less than contempt, so I doubt you harbor kinder sentiments for him."

My temper flared. "*Contempt*? Have you tried tacking the word 'compassion' to my expression, to see if it's a better fit? Besides, you shouldn't talk! If you cared so much for your brother, you'd never have left him thinking you'd died. Instead, you sent him a bird to tell him you were *done for*! Who does that?"

The color drained from his face, as something like pain and anguish flashed across his brow. His anger flared hotter, and he hurled the words at me. "You know nothing about our relationship. Furthermore—"

I cut him off. "What I know is you're a selfish pig."

Jonas laid a hand over my shoulder. "This isn't helping, Cass."

Caleb slumped, his anger dissolving into soft words. "I sent that bird because I *was* dying. After getting that message off, I released the rest. It wasn't fair to let them die of starvation or thirst in a cage. And I *was* on my way out."

Now it was me who slumped, losing steam from my voice. All I managed was a quiet "Oh."

Caleb threaded the straw between his fingers and locked an icy gaze on me, his voice low. "I want to believe you, but every time I try to understand, you evade my questions. On top of this unbearable knot in my stomach, I *know* you're hiding something."

More footsteps sounded in the tunnel, and the chess pieces arrived. Between them, they held the handles of four steaming mugs of coffee.

Caleb took his with a distracted "Thanks."

The boys lowered the remaining three through the bars to the rock floor.

Cocking his head, Caleb considered. "Wait with that, boys." He focused on the mugs on the floor. "Get one of those back."

The black-haired boy frowned but extracted a single mug, then righted himself. They didn't leave but waited for Caleb's next instruction.

Caleb nodded, then swallowed and returned to addressing us. "So, I'll tell you what… You're going to chat with me individually. I'm guessing one of you *will* slip the truth."

He tossed his chin at me. "You first." Glancing at the chess pieces, he murmured, "Stay here. Make sure these two" — he gestured with a tap of the straw at Liam then Jonas — "don't speak to each other. I don't want them matching stories."

Liam launched forward, voice a hard growl. "You're taking my sister nowhere, Caleb. I don't care who you are."

Caleb squinted and matched Liam's tone. "You're in no position to bargain...*brother*. Do you want to challenge me on that?"

Liam was tall and strong, but Eric and Caleb were more of both. Plus, Eric had always said Caleb was the tougher of the two. Still, Liam would have taken up the challenge, so I darted in front of him. Facing away from Caleb, I slid a subtle downward glance at the small bulge in my T-shirt. "It's okay, Li. He won't hurt me." I wasn't sure I was right, but at least I was carrying a weapon.

I didn't know whether Liam believed Caleb to have similar moral fiber to Eric, if he respected my right to choose, or thought that with the dagger I stood a chance against Caleb. Either way, he relented. Caleb opened the door only wide enough for me, and I stepped through.

Chapter Twenty-Four

As soon as the teen had handed me a mug, Caleb twisted my free arm behind me. He shot out his other forearm with lightning speed and gripped my throat in a chokehold. Then, wrenching me against him, he hauled me backward to the far tunnel wall.

With vicious bellows, Liam and Jonas launched at and rattled the cage irons, but Caleb ignored their cries, bent low and spoke into my ear, his fiery breath feathering my collarbone. "Drop it."

I feigned a sweet, innocent voice. "Drop what?"

Caleb ignored my act and jerked at my neck. Instead of clarifying, he growled a low "Now!"

A hoarse choke slid through my throat. "Okay. Okay."

As I extracted the hem of my T-shirt from my jeans, Jonas' dagger fell to the dusty floor with a dull thud, where Caleb kicked it to the teens. They didn't move but gaped at it wide-eyed and as still as statues.

Caleb breathed a heavy sigh. "Don't stand there looking at it as if it's a snake. Pick it up."

As though thinking Caleb would strike him, the fair boy squatted and lifted the sheathed blade between his thumb and forefinger. Then Caleb spoke at the cell. "Now you...*brother*. If you value your sister's neck, that is."

Liam didn't wait for Caleb to jerk my neck again but raised one hand in surrender. With the other, he removed the dagger from his shirt then skidded it over the stone floor, beneath the grating and out of the cell.

After the dark-haired teen picked up that dagger and retreated to the wall with his friend, Caleb released his hold around my neck. He spoke to the chess pieces. "Be sure not to let those two manipulate you into handing them the blades."

Without another word, he jabbed me forward the way we'd come. As we walked along the echoing tunnel, the water grew louder. When we reached the fork, Caleb turned me not toward the entrance but away. The instant we rounded the corner, the volume doubled, continuing to grow louder and louder the farther we traveled. Over the next few minutes, I sensed the tension leaving Caleb's body while the tension in mine escalated.

Then we came upon a rocky cavern. Judging by the noise, I'd expected a waterfall similar to the one we'd come upon along the river near Graham's refuge. It was not. This was little more than a gushing series of descending rapids, the cavern amplifying the sound. Still, it ran fast enough to offer a watery grave to anyone who slipped in—or got shoved.

Although blood pounded in my ears, I feigned nonchalance and spoke over my shoulder. "You can't blame us for trying." I faced forward again. "I mean, keeping the daggers."

Caleb cleared his throat. "Nope. And I don't. That's not why we're here."

I tried again. "Has anyone fallen into this river?"

Caleb snorted a chuckle. "It sounds like you're trying to give me a suggestion — as if I haven't already thought of it. Anyway, if you're hoping to escape that way, rest assured you won't make it out."

Caleb didn't take me to the waters' edge but ushered me to a rocky chair-like outcrop, where he gestured for me to sit. After dusting the rock with one hand, I did. Then I set the warm mug on my knee. "Why did you bring me here, Caleb? *Are* you planning to throw me in?"

Caleb didn't bother cleaning the rock as he dropped beside me, his leg brushing mine. He replied to my second question. "That would be a real foolish way of trying to get information from a person."

I gulped. His phrasing was almost exactly the same as something Eric had said before we'd left Petriville. I turned my face away.

Caleb held the mug and straw, leaned forward and rested his toned forearms on his thighs. When he continued, he kind of answered my first question. "In all honesty, I like it here. It's peaceful."

I glanced sideways at him. "That's not *really* what I meant."

He puffed a laugh. "Obviously...but—" He broke off.

I got to the point, no longer beating around the bush. "How can I convince you we're innocent?"

He didn't hesitate. "If, in fact, you have feelings for Eric, you'd recognize things about him that most people wouldn't. I'm thinking you'd rather not share those things in front of Jonas since you have a *history*" —

he phrased the word as a tentative question—"or at least, he's in love with you."

I rolled my eyes. "Our *history*, as you put it, is a lifelong friendship. Jonas isn't in love with me. He has a girlfriend."

Caleb scoffed at that. "Bah. His expression when I singled you out for questioning tells me otherwise. He was ready to punch me right through those bars."

I bit my cheek. "He's protective."

"Mm-m." Caleb agreed, the smile in his voice making him sound no more convinced. "Your brother is *protective*. But Jonas—? Anyway, we're getting off the point. You're great at this diversion thing. Were you a lawyer in a past life?"

His sudden calmness did nothing to help me relax. "Can we get to it?"

Caleb nodded, set the mug on the rock beside him and threaded the straw around and between his fingers then back again. "As long as you give me direct answers, I'll keep it simple."

If I closed my eyes and listened to his voice, it was almost like Eric sat beside me. I wanted to lean into him, feel the warmth of his arms closing around me. It took all my self-control not to fling myself into his embrace and kiss him. But some subtle differences between the two crept into my senses. I couldn't put my finger on the exact characteristics. Not yet. So, I gave him a simple "Okay."

Instead of letting me settle into easier questions like I thought he might, he slammed me with the one I'd hoped to avoid, his voice steady and cool. "Where are my dad and Eric?"

"Can't you start with something simpler? You told me you wanted proof of my feelings for Eric."

"Honestly…Cassidy, is it?" He didn't wait for my reply. "I don't care what you *say* you feel for him. I want to know if he's okay."

I smoothed my tone. "If I tell you he's safe, will you leave it at that?"

He hardened. "What the hell are you hiding?"

I slumped. *Can I tell Caleb? Will he believe me?* "Nothing, Caleb. But can I tell it in my own way? Please?"

With a single nod, Caleb lay back against the rock, folding his arms over his chest. "I'm listening."

So, I told him about the longevity drugs their parents had created. That he and Eric would never age normally because of *Livvie*, the irreversible longevity elixir. I explained how Graham had given us a digipar for Mr. Rodrigues, telling him we needed the formulae. Then I covered how in each refuge Graham had supplied the annual memory wipe solution on an automatic timer, how they'd lived for a hundred and ten years in the refuge and us in space. But I didn't tell him *why* we needed these formulae — that Harriet was sick and we needed a cure.

Caleb huffed several times but listened without interruption. It didn't matter what I said, though. The way he crossed his arms and tightened his grip on the blade of grass told me he was waiting — listening for a slip. Although he didn't contest my revelation of his extreme old age, I sensed he believed none of it.

I ignored his skeptical body posture and went on, telling him how his parents had created *Ellen* to neutralize the longevity elixir, but a rockslide had destroyed Graham's stash.

I asked if he recalled how sometimes people vanished at the refuge, how it always happened over the new year, how a new grave accompanied each disappearance, how Graham never explained why but diverted questions until people came to accept it as part of refuge life.

Throughout my monologue, Caleb's body posture stiffened more and more. When I concluded, he jutted his chin, tone soft, slow and singsong. "You must think me an idiot."

With a slow inhale, I met his extraordinary eyes. "I don't, Caleb." A shiver ran down my spine. "Do you know how similar you and Eric are? Yet…you're so…*different*. But I swear I'm not lying to you. Send someone to the refuge if you don't trust me."

He dismissed my statement with a puff of air. "Already done, but that hardly helps. The round trip is at least two months—and that's assuming they all make it. Everything you're telling me might be an elaborate lie intended to gain my trust. She could have tortured my dad and brother for the other intelligence." He narrowed his eyes. "And you've told me nothing about my brother—nothing that a person who cares about him would share."

My eyelids drooped in a long blink. "Fine. First, I want to know something about *you*." As I cocked my head, I checked his expression. "What happened out there?"

Although I never clarified what 'out there' meant, Caleb understood. He responded without hesitation. "Malaria. One by one it took them, until it was only me. I couldn't get food down my throat by the time this lot found me. I was on my last, but they brought me here and nursed me to health. Only of late has my full strength returned." With his gaze on the rocky ground between his feet, he lowered his voice, seeming to speak to himself. "If I'm to believe you, then my dad and Eric think I'm dead."

I confirmed his thoughts. "Eric searched for months before they found the remains of scavenged bodies. That, together with the bird's note, convinced them you *must* have died."

He rotated his head, regarding me. It felt strange staring into those eyes, that face. I scanned the familiar toned body, the way he carried himself as he straightened, how a frown raked his prominent forehead at my observation. He wore so many of the expressions that I loved. It only made it more at odds with this stranger's personality.

"In answer to your question" — I let my eyes drift shut, a soft smile pulling at my lips. "What I can tell you about Eric is that he's super-defensive of Graham, though you know that. Something you wouldn't be aware of is how he risked his life to rescue Jonas and me. He's brave enough to wrestle a venomous snake and keeps a flick-knife in his right front jeans pocket. He's compassionate and he thinks before he speaks. He doesn't hesitate to put his heart on the line in the face of rejection." My smile widened. "Oh, and he's a brilliant MAC player! He burst nine balloons in the last challenge." I swiveled and met his gaze. "Do you realize his love for Graham and you is so fierce it causes him physical pain? And he always chews on random pieces of straw. He says it reminds him of you."

Caleb's Adam's apple bounced. He unfolded his arms, placing his palms over the edge of the rock. His voice emerged as a hoarse plea, his gaze fixed ahead of him. "Then I beg of you... tell me where he is now."

I looked at Caleb and lay my hand over his, surprised he didn't pull away. "Please hear me out before you say anything. There is a reason Eric isn't here—"

Abrupt shouts echoing down the tunnel cut me off. Caleb pulled his hand free of mine and cleared his throat.

The two boys ran into the cavern. As the black-haired boy spoke, the volume of his voice increased in bursts. "Come, Caleb. Someone else arrived. Dan says you'll want to hear what they have to say."

He bowed down to Caleb's ear, words impossible to make out above the roar of the water. Whatever it was, though, it made Caleb again turn his glare to the coldest ice and his face contort in mistrust.

Chapter Twenty-Five

Caleb crushed the blade of straw in his hand and tossed it aside as he leaped up, grasped my upper arm and hauled me to my feet, dragging me with him as he ran. He pressed his fingers down with such force that my muscles ached. Behind me, pounding footsteps told me the chess pieces were keeping pace.

"Ow." I jerked at his grip, trying to pull my arm free. "I'll run on my own."

My effort had Caleb gripping harder, making my biceps numb. Never mind that I'd spent the last hour pouring out my soul to coax him, to gain his trust, Caleb's voice once again turned as hard as stone. "Oh, no, you won't. You're going straight back to lockup. We'll deal with you later."

He raced me up the tunnel to the y-bend, slowing only enough to turn us into the narrower passage where he shoved me ahead of him. Every few paces he slammed a hand into my back to make me run faster, yet I was already surging into every stride. When we got to the cell, he grabbed my arm and yanked me to a stop.

"What the hell is going on now then?" Jonas stood with Liam. They clutched the bars in both hands. They must have heard us running—or more like Caleb chasing me.

Caleb growled. "You'll find out soon enough." Then one-handed, he unlocked the door.

He thrust me inside with such sharp and violent force that I stumbled into my awaiting brother. While Caleb slammed and locked the cell door, Liam threw protective arms around my shoulders. I shot Caleb a backward glance, but only caught his booted heels as he raced past the chess pieces.

The boys were about to follow Caleb. I called them back. "Wait! What's going on? Who's here? Please tell us." My last sentence came out as a plea.

It didn't help. They both shrugged and spun. As they sprinted after Caleb, the white-haired boy hollered over his shoulder. "Dunno. Dan told us to get Caleb up there real quick."

Their earlier whispered conversation with Caleb told me he was lying, but I didn't pursue the truth. He probably wouldn't tell me.

Left on our own, we stewed over possibilities. Liam and Jonas paced back and forth across the small cave, spouting their conjectures.

Jonas fixed on me and launched a verbal attack. "Did you tell him the truth then?"

"Some of it," I confessed. "I didn't tell him about Harriet, or Eric being in prison, or that Graham is in Petriville."

He aimed a palm toward the tunnel. "So, you told him nothing."

"He didn't know about the elixir, but this was more about me proving I"—after hesitating, I chose a noncommittal word—"*know* Eric."

Jonas lifted a brow, as if interpreting what I'd actually meant, then continued with his enquiry. "So, what is this about then? The boy looks like he's in agony. Why do you insist on keeping secrets from him?"

Liam narrowed his eyes. "Don't go taking this out on my sister. She has a better understanding of how Eric would react, given this situation. And since they're brothers…" He trailed off, leaving the rest to Jonas' imagination.

I met Liam and Jonas' frowns with a sigh. "You're both right. But Caleb won't believe she'd keep him alive." I looked at Liam. "You just said how suspicious Eric became when he found out I lived in Petriville."

For a while we continued to bat and ball our opinions, but that drove the knot in my stomach into gripping harder. I retreated to my mattress, reached into my backpack and extracted the library's digipars. After picking out *Great Expectations*, I leaned back against the wall and tapped the front. Across the top, the static, stylized heading came to life amid its bright cover-image landscape. The first line lit up below 'Chapter One'. *'My father's family name being Pirrip, and my Christian name Philip, my infant tongue could make of both names nothing longer or more explicit than Pip.'*

At times, while I silently read, voices echoed down the tunnel, forcing Liam and Jonas to fall still. I found my eyes and ears reaching for those voices—sounding them out. Jonas mostly dove at the jail exit, shouting some random retort, but no one responded.

After what felt like an eternity, approaching footsteps seeped into the rush of water. I slanted my ear toward the sound, counting the pairs of booted feet. It was not Caleb. His steps tended to hit the floor with heavier and louder echoes than the boys' smaller shoes.

Liam beat me to voice the observation. "It's the chess pieces."

A moment later they came into view, sidling up against the far wall of the tunnel, each bearing a lunch-tray — sandwiches packed in cellophane, glasses, a jug of water and three mugs of coffee. Again, one opened the door while the other slipped the trays through.

Jonas didn't seem to notice the fear radiating off them — the way they bowed their heads and averted their gazes, how they backed against the opposite tunnel wall, the tightening of their postures at the sound of his voice. He *did* observe something, though. He grunted his statement to them. "Something has changed here and you boys are going to tell us what the hell is going on!"

I gentled my tone, making it more curious. "Wait, Jonas." I observed the boys. "What's got you so scared?"

The black-haired teen spoke this time, as if urging bewilderment into his trembling voice. "We're not scared." Once again, they swiveled and raced back along the tunnel.

Liam watched them go before shaking his head and collecting the sandwiches. He glanced at the contents with a shrug and tossed Jonas and me a pack.

I caught mine in both hands with a hurried "Thanks." Setting it on the stone floor, I got up and fetched water. While I filled and distributed the three glasses, Jonas placed a mug of coffee at each mattress.

The boys didn't use the wall as a backrest but straddled their beds.

I sipped my coffee and turned the wrapped cheese and onion sandwich over in my hand. It looked good enough, but my stomach rolled and pitched. I pushed it aside. "How can you guys sit there eating?"

They both looked at me and slowed their chewing. Liam tilted his head. "They won't kill us, Cassidy."

"Are you sure about that? Because I'm not. You didn't see what happened at the river."

Jonas gulped, and they both packed their half-chewed sandwiches back in the cellophane.

When Caleb's faraway voice finally made my ears perk up, a chill slithered down my spine. I cocked my ear toward the sound, holding up my palm.

Chapter Twenty-Six

Two angry baritones accompanied Caleb's voice—one in broken English. The men wearing these boots pounded the floor with deliberate footfalls.

Caleb came into view ahead of his companions—Dan and another older, dark-haired man I hadn't seen before. Caleb's scowl rivaled an attack dog's, and the men too wore murderous expressions—their nostrils flaring, hands quivering and forearm muscles straining against their skin.

I leaped up. Instinct had me launching to the back wall and turning to face our attackers. Jonas clambered beside me. This felt too familiar—too much like our ordeal in the fort. Like before, he threw his arms around my shoulders and head. I hesitated only a moment before clasping mine around his waist. A sweat broke out across my skin. My palms grew clammy. My body pulsed, but Jonas shivered too, clutching me hard—too hard. Genuine fear dug its claws into my throat.

Until that moment, I'd never believed we were in real danger. *How naïve!*

Liam captured our expressions, his fists clenched and forehead furrowed. "They won't hurt you, guys — not while I'm alive." He stood in front of Jonas and me, facing the door with his back to us — a shield. I squinted around him at Caleb and the men outside the cell.

Dan pressed his eyebrows together before loosening his grip. Swiveling to Caleb and their companion, Dan made a tossing gesture with his head and all three wandered out of our sight-line — and earshot. For a long while, they argued in whispered voices. I could make out nothing of what they said. Then two sets of footsteps reached my awareness. But they drifted away. I relaxed my grip around Jonas the tiniest bit — knowing only one of them had stayed. Before long, the departing steps intermingled and faded beneath the underground river.

Caleb reappeared and Liam widened his stance — a valiant but useless attempt to protect Jonas and me. I peeked around him and sucked in a breath.

A glacial glare tempered Caleb's eyes. "Your fear makes me wonder what you're so scared of. No worries. Logic is screaming the answer. Your secret is out, and you know what's going to happen. And you" — he switched to addressing Liam — "are such a *hero*. You don't even care that you're going to die. Regardless, your reckless bravado won't save *their* lives." He aimed both forefingers past Liam toward Jonas and me.

Liam gave an audible swallow. He maintained a calm voice, a touch slower than his usual bullet train speed. "Hear us out, Cal —"

Caleb cut him off. "Enough with your attempts to manipulate me! I'm done with your deceit."

Despite how Caleb loathed us, I struggled to stay afraid of him—however absurd. I unwrapped Jonas' embrace and stalked around Liam.

Jonas grabbed my wrist. "Wait, Cass."

I swung around, steadying on his concerned green gaze. He locked on mine for a moment, released my wrist and took my lead, skirting Liam's far side.

I took a step nearer the bars, my voice soft. "We really *don't* know what this is about, Caleb. We're not lying."

"Well, this name might jog your memory. What do you know of the *Cordova* family?" He hurled the name like a weapon.

I gasped. My reaction surely sealed our doom. But I couldn't help it and clamped my eyes against the memory—against the image.

Caleb noticed the recognition on my face. "Ha-a! You know *exactly* who I'm talking about. Soldiers executed that innocent family on the beach, right below that accursed place-machine-whatever-thing. They were farmers, for heaven's sake—farmers eager to get home after Graham unsealed the refuge. But they weren't the only family to leave us! Did you *not* consider when killing them that these families kept in touch—traded? One of them found the bodies on the beach. He followed the boot impressions to a camp full of soldiers. And you said she had none. Another lie. When that man returned with help to retrieve and bury their friends, someone had removed their bodies—or hidden them, or something worse!" Caleb's voice cracked. Like Eric, Caleb had known the Cordovas, and he'd just heard the news.

Raw pain seeped into his stance. He took a step back, wrapping his arms around himself and shaking his head over and over in slow repetition. Not only was he reconciling the death of the Cordovas, but he was also being drawn back into his pre-conceived idea.

His voice emerged in rough, clipped tones. "Is there no limit to her cruelty? Everything you said was a lie, Cassidy. You'll never convince me she didn't murder my dad and my brother." He swiped at his cheeks.

I met that beautiful, pained face, and in a last vain attempt, smoothed out my voice. "That's not the complete story, Caleb. Eric was—"

Caleb cut me off, sharpening his voice. "Don't dare bring my brother into this. You don't have the right to tell me he and my dad were with the Cordovas when those soldiers gunned them down." His voice cracked, and he scraped a hand down his face, wiping away tears as they flowed. He dropped his gaze to his boots, voice stony. "Now you'll suffer the same fate."

Without waiting for any response, he turned and strode down the tunnel.

Jonas yelled after him, "Are you completely insane?"

Liam looked gobsmacked.

Nothing we'd spoken of at the river would make any difference. But I couldn't bring myself to hate Caleb, no matter how stubborn his refusal to believe our claims. Part of me cheered his love for Eric—celebrated it. No one could destroy that shared sentiment. At least, not while we *both* lived.

Liam set his jaw into hardened steel and, like a traumatized animal, he paced back and forth. Jonas' mouth twisted into a vicious snarl. He gripped his hand, bearing it as if he intended to slam it into the rock wall.

With my softest touch, I caught his arm. "Don't, Jonas." I gestured at the hand. "We may need those yet."

He ripped his arm from me. After a moment, he frowned and brought his fist in front of him. For a long moment, he observed the appendage as if it were a foreign object. Then he lifted the other and appeared to compare the two. "What…these?"

Unable to help myself, I imitated Jonas' reaction and a *definitely* hysterical cackle burst through my lips. "He's going…to kill…us, and you…look like you're deciding…which hand to punch him with."

That transported Jonas from his trance. He looked up at me and rubbed his forehead, but Liam did a double take. "How can you laugh at a time like this?"

That urged me from my mirth. My laughter floated away under the dark umbrella of our reality.

Liam voiced his thoughts. "Eric is going to kill him for this."

As we shared glances, none of my laughter remained — neither from hysteria nor joy. Solemn dread penetrated my gut like the blade of a dagger.

Liam and I no longer have those. But I still have Grandma's wrap-around pen — that no longer contains venom. Even if it did, and I got the opportunity to stab Caleb, could I? Could I kill him? For Liam and Jonas?

Caleb never came back to our cell once over the next week. The chess pieces delivered food and drinks, but their expressions never changed from wary, even suspicious.

When Caleb finally arrived, my heart sank. Not because of the thunder in his heavy stride or even from the steel in his expression. What sparked my adrenaline was the coiled rope in his hand.

I opened my mouth. "Caleb, wha —?"

With a hiss, he cut me off. "Your lies fall on deaf ears."

Chapter Twenty-Seven

He pressed his lips together and glanced between us, then back up the tunnel — *conflicted*. From the little I knew of him, this wasn't an emotion familiar to Caleb. Before I got to voice my observation, his internal battle seemed to vanish. Once more, he steeled himself. His jaw ticked as he planted his feet and steadied his gaze. He fingered no straw now.

Caleb confirmed my thoughts, speaking as if emerging from a week-old argument. "Can you believe Dan and Carlos felt *sorry* for you two cowering there against the back? They fell for your ruse — told me to give you the benefit of the doubt. Just so you know — I have none. It's me you lot are playing." A disgusted sneer twisted his mouth. "And you're using my dad and brother as your weapons. Not anymore." He lifted his chin, widening his stance. "Give me your hands."

I jammed them behind my back. "Don't we even get a trial?"

He crossed his arms. "You did — and now it's over."

Jonas snapped. "What kind of trial is this then, when the accused cannot defend themselves?"

Caleb raised both brows. "And spout more lies? I don't think so."

"We're not laying our lives on a platter at your say-so, Caleb," — and as if my subconscious mind decided on my behalf — "no matter how confident you pretend to be about your decision."

Liam followed with "Why bother giving us a trial at all? In your mind we've already been convicted."

Jonas rehashed Liam's earlier comment. "Your brother is going to destroy you for this. Maybe not over Liam and me, but if you murder Cassidy…" He trailed off, shaking his head. "Do you *want* him to hate you then?"

Caleb took half a step back, running a hand through his hair, his eyes flickering with uncertainty. As quickly, he gritted his teeth, darted forward and straightened. "These attempts to manipulate me won't work. You're wasting your energy."

The words burst through my throat. "You're so *frustrating*! Do you know that?"

Caleb spat on the rocky ground. "That may well be…but it's not your observation to make."

He jerked open the cell. Before Liam or Jonas could react, Caleb snatched my wrist and twisted, spinning me around. Again, he wrapped his muscled forearm around my neck and pulled me against his chest. This time he clamped harder — steel-like. I clawed at his arm. Not even my nails made him flinch as I dug them into his flesh. He hauled me from the cell.

Even in this compromised position, his warm body against my back reminded me so much of Eric. My real undoing was his scent. Smoky vanilla. It bombarded my senses from every direction—so close to Eric's that it hurt. My forehead tightened, chin trembling as moisture blurred my vision. *Keep it together, Cassidy. Be brave. With Caleb at his side, Eric won't need you as much. He'll be okay.* The thoughts skimmed my mind, but I knew they weren't true. I was lying to myself. Caleb thrust his other arm around my waist and pulled me back from the door, opening a path to the exit of the refuge.

He growled at Liam and Jonas. "Now. Get out of there and start walking. You can go ahead of me, but you'd better make it slow or I swear I'll end her right here...right now."

I choked the words through my constricted throat. "Stay inside the cell, Liam! Jonas! *Please*! It won't change anything."

Liam wasn't listening to me. As he walked from the cell, his voice cracked. "Don't even *consider* hurting my sister."

Jonas had heard me but walked only a step behind Liam, his voice soft. "How then, Cass? Do you think we could stick our heads in the sand—let you suffer whatever his sick mind deems fair punishment on your own?"

Caleb repositioned me and threw me over his shoulder with the ease of carrying a small child. His arm around my waist, he locked me in place. My range of vision included the tunnel floor, Caleb's leather boots, his jeans, a thick metal belt-buckle and his gray T-shirt—flat against his rock-hard abdomen. Even from this perspective, he was Eric...and he wasn't Eric.

"Caleb?" I made his name a question, though my voice wheezed. As much as I hated passing on this message through Caleb, if it was the only way I could, then I'd put my pride in my pocket. "When you see Eric" — because I guessed even Gina would let Eric search for us if we didn't return — "please tell him I'm sorry…and tell him…I love him."

The revelation slammed into me, and my breath caught in my throat. Because I *did* love Eric. Of course I did. With every beat of my heart, I loved him. What had I thought to gain by refusing this admission before? More than that, how arrogant had I been to presume I'd return to tell him? I shut out the truth, locked away my pig-headed pride. My heart ached for Eric — and he might never know.

Caleb faltered, his footsteps slowing as he stiffened his body against me. After a brief hesitation he continued with renewed determination, his strides even bigger, his voice a snarl. "There is no end to your mind-game inventions, is there? You still insist on trying to manipulate me into believing you."

Too quickly, we neared the exit. Light seeped into the tunnel and Caleb dropped me to my feet. Instead of walking, I slowed then halted, but Caleb dragged me forward. "Move, *girl*!" Liam and Jonas had also stopped, and Caleb kicked past Jonas' guard at the back of my friend's knees with a growl. "Did I tell you to stop?"

Even facing down as we arrived at the ledge, I blinked against the sunlight. After our semi-dark days in the cell, I blinked against the dazzling brightness. Caleb grabbed both my wrists in one hand and released my neck. My throat scratched and my neck burned. After I freed my hands, I rubbed it up and down, and a choking sound made its way from my throat. Caleb gave me no time to regroup, but I did. As he threw his arm around my lower ribcage, I winced at his extreme pressure, but I would *not* give him the satisfaction of witnessing my pain. I kicked my heel back against his shin, causing him to grunt and curse. Then I threw a sharp backward head-butt. My head rang as it bounced off his rock-hard chest. Caleb firmed his hold around my wrists and I thought they'd break under his grip. I slumped. I couldn't get a hold of grandma's wrap-around pen if I tried. *What does it matter anyway? The pain will soon be over.*

At least thirty large men milled about on the ledge, their attention on Liam and Jonas, then Caleb and me as we passed. A few wore frowns of sympathy. In silent vigil, those clasped their hands before them. Others scowled, their chins high and arms folded over their chests, hatred written in every hard line of their faces. The chess pieces weren't here. No teens were. Half the group walked ahead of us toward the Kaleidotonium entrance and half walked behind.

"Move!" Caleb again kicked out at the back of Jonas' knees, but I shoved back against him. His kick still landed, but not as hard as it might have. As Jonas buckled, Liam kept him up with a steadying hand. I wasn't sorry for the attempt, though it didn't help my case. Caleb steeled his grip more as he prodded me forward.

Too soon, we exited the Kaleidotonium shell — the same way we'd entered these caves. The men walked on a short distance and halted as if to block our escape. If my heart wasn't pounding so hard that blood roared in my ears, I'd have hurled some sarcastic remark at Caleb. As it was, we had no escape in any direction except down, which was no escape at all.

I took in our surroundings — the vast, plummeting cliff before us, a blue line threading through the center of a valley far below, the land rising, the opposite peak higher than where we awaited our sentencing. A lone bird-call resounded, bouncing back and forth between the mountains in a mournful echo.

Dan stepped from behind Caleb and moved toward the far group. My heart plummeted as he turned and observed us. As an air of unease appeared to wash over the older man, I appraised him. He brushed a hand through his thinning dark hair and clasped them before him. Caleb thrust me forward between Jonas and Liam. I rubbed at my wrists and neck but forced myself to stand straight and clutched their hands.

Dan didn't look at us. I followed his gaze back and up — to Caleb's unreadable countenance. In a low measured tone, he addressed Caleb. "Are you sure you want this, son?"

Caleb rested his gaze on his boots, then looked up again, swiping at his glistening eyes. "They watched my dad and brother get murdered. It's not right to let them live — or anyone from that place, if it comes to it." He waved his arm across the general direction of the ocean and south.

So much hatred. Such prejudice. All he knew of Petriville was that Gina had saved us and abandoned them. I tried to understand Caleb's feelings. Tried…and failed. Eric had heard me out when I'd explained it to him. He'd listened. Even Graham had afforded us the benefit of the doubt. But Caleb…? He refused to contemplate even a possibility of what we said.

Six men assembled behind us, shoulder-to-shoulder. Two hands clamped around each of my wrists. I ripped at them, throwing my body weight into each thrash.

Almost tugging free, I back-kicked at legs with wild ferocity. But, keeping out of reach, they gripped tighter.

Someone booted the backs of my knees, and I collapsed. As the men switched over behind me, pain shot through my shoulders and I cried out.

That was when Jonas got an arm free. He punched the second man in the face. With a crack, the man's blood spurted and a pained grunt tore from his throat as he shot his palms to his nose. Jonas was free. That lasted for exactly one second. Six others dived on top of him, their combined weight forcing him to the ground. The men scuffled in the dust for long, breathless moments, finally getting hold of Jonas' wrists. They raised him to his feet, bridging his arms behind his back. As my restrainers yanked me up, my shoulders screamed in pain as if ripping from their sockets.

A further three men clustered behind us, holding thick black hoods and ropes. *They're hooding us!*

As soon as the fabric touched, I whipped my head out of reach. Again, they jerked my arms backward and up. I recoiled, crying out in pain, but the heavy cover still came down over my face, a curtain of blackness descending over the world—stifling, hot, suffocating blackness.

Beside me, Liam and Jonas bellowed with what sounded like fury more than fear. A drawstring tightened around my neck, rope binding my wrists. The footsteps retreated. The trial was over. Our execution was upon us. They meant to throw us to the wolves—literally. Or to whatever other creatures out there would obliterate any trace of our broken bodies.

It was better that we couldn't see. Better that Liam and Jonas couldn't witness the horror wrenching my face. Better that I couldn't glimpse my expression mirrored on theirs. Falling would be the first thing we noticed. My heart stuttered as the three men waited behind us. I braced myself, anticipating the end. Was one of them Caleb? I inhaled a lungful of air. Yes. His scent would always give him away—at least, it would to me. That was almost over now as he stood behind me in utter silence.

I lowered my voice. "I hope Eric never forgives you, Caleb. And I hope you have nightmares for the rest of your miserable life."

Caleb didn't respond, but I guessed I heard him swallow.

Despite my bravado, ice washed over my skin. I was engulfed me in a violent fit of tremors. To calm myself, I sucked in the deepest breath and stilled. I wanted to reach out for them—impossible, with ropes binding our wrists. Instead, I spoke in a soft whisper. "Come closer, guys. Liam…Jonas. Stand closer to me. Please?"

They responded without question or comment, crowding me.

Tears slid down my cheeks. "I love you, Liam. And, Jonas, I love you too. You guys and Harriet made my world a brighter place."

Liam's voice lowered and constricted. "I failed you. Both of you. I failed Harriet."

Jonas remained silent but couldn't conceal his hard swallow as he leaned his shoulder against mine. We were together in that moment, together for our end. With the surrounding throng, we had no escape. My fight disappeared, and Liam and Jonas no longer battled our captors. They'd accepted our fate too.

With a gentle hold, Caleb pushed me a step forward. Not harsh and not angry. Gentle, but not conflicted. He urged me another step. And another. Gravel slithered away beneath my feet and trickled down the cliff face. I gripped my fists so tight that my fingernails cut into my palms, and I trembled so violently that my teeth clattered. In an abrupt reaction, I pushed back against Caleb, one name bursting through my lips. "Eric! I love you. I always have. And I never stopped, not for one minute." At the same time, Liam whispered Harriet's name and his declaration of undying love. Jonas remained silent.

I screamed — alone in my torment. No other shrieks joined mine. My echo reverberated through the ravine. Liam and Jonas inclined against me, and my knees buckled. I almost missed the collective gasp of the surrounding crowd. However, I never missed the cheerful shout, ringing out in such stark contrast to the prevailing mood, as it echoed across the valley.

"Hel-lo-o there."

Chapter Twenty-Eight

Behind us, our captors' feet shuffled. My knees weakened, and I stumbled back against Caleb, my trembling increasing. He didn't seem to notice—as if something had distracted him. Neither did he try heaving me away, like he'd lost awareness of my presence.

Liam and Jonas pressed harder against my shoulders. They also thrust back against their assailants—one step, two steps. No one pushed back.

Caleb's feet scuffed the ground, and he freed my arm as if half turning away. I never expected him to drop the other. But a moment later he did. A gasp climbed through my chest and throat. Three pairs of footsteps crunched away. I needed no more encouragement, but we were walking blind. Still, no one stopped me as I slid my feet back, inches at a time, Liam and Jonas right beside me every step of the way. Their warmth comforted me, and they never left my side. After long agonizing minutes, my heel struck something solid. A moment later the rear cliff face touched my buttocks and back. With another gasp, I shoved against it. A low grunt came from Jonas and a choke from Liam. This wasn't over — merely a reprieve, worse because all too soon we'd face our terror again.

We couldn't escape, not until we got the masks from our faces and ropes from our wrists. As I hoped the group was fixating on whatever was happening, I half-twisted my back to Jonas. From our time in the fort, he might have guessed to do the same. A deep sigh burst through my chest as he responded. Grazing his fingers over my wrists, he felt for the knots. He fiddled and yanked and finally pried the rope loose. As soon as it slithered away, I worked at his bindings. Then he was free. I rotated my back to Liam, ready to bump him if he didn't know to turn. He was already in position. In half a minute, his ropes slipped off. I reached behind my neck and fumbled at the drawstring fastening the hood.

From the front, rough hands jerked mine down. "No, you don't." The voice wasn't Caleb's, nor was it familiar. He didn't rebind our wrists.

Still, the chatter and shuffling of the surrounding crowd continued. The near joy of them conflicted with our fear — like a raging fire right beside solid, un-melting ice. My emotions reeled. My head spun. The overlapping babble made their words unclear, their shouts competing for dominance.

Footsteps approached. A familiar voice raised goosebumps on my skin. "Well, who've we got here? This lot must have murdered someone real important to deserve this punishment." He sucked in a strangled gasp.

Caleb replied with a voice as cold as ice. "They did."

Another spoke—definitely familiar. "Who did you say they killed?" I needed more than his few words for any chance of identifying him.

Distracting me from the attempt, Caleb spoke. "I didn't say." He took a long pause then said, "My brother!"

The first voice again. "What? Eric was fine yesterday. Who are they?"

Hands tugged at the drawstring and snatched the hood up. Sunlight flared, and my vision blurred with moisture. I couldn't make out the figures standing before me. Then I knew. The voices—the blurred beanpoles—the long pale hair.

Before they came into focus, Ethan and Craig gasped. As my vision finally cleared, Craig backed up, his mouth agape while Ethan's eyes bugged. "What the hell, dude? Are you freaking insane?"

Craig's laugh quavered. "Back there you said you were about to kill them. Is that *true*? If it is, your brother would have totally strung you up—"

Ethan completed Craig's sentence in a slow, hoarse whisper. "If he didn't think you were already dead. I'm kind of thinking we arrived in the nick of time…to save their lives and *yours*."

Caleb slumped, but I flung my arms around both their long necks. Their stringy white-blond hair and beards feathered my skin, the tickle reminding me I was alive. "I don't think I've been so happy to see anyone in my entire life."

Ethan spoke to Craig as they closed me in a hug. "Can you believe he meant to kill them?"

He didn't seem to expect an answer, though, and Craig didn't give one. He turned to Liam and Jonas as the four clapped each other on the back.

Jonas' voice scraped out. "What the hell are you doing here then?"

A tear trickled down my cheek, and I wiped at it, moving back from Ethan and Craig. From my chest broke a hysterical laugh that continued through my words. "You...sound disappointed, Jonas."

Liam hauled me to his chest. "You're okay, baby sister." With a long blink, he stepped back. "And it's no thanks to my being here."

I cocked my head at him, knowing exactly what was trickling through his mind. "You're finally grasping how little control Jonas had over what happened in the fort."

A muscle in Liam's jaw ticked, then he shook his head and swallowed.

As the adrenaline in my veins dissipated, relief flowed through. Goosebumps tingled my skin. Then came the *rage*—sheer and burning and ravenous. I whipped upright and around, fixing on Caleb.

As if struck, he stumbled back, his arms slack at his sides. He cast his attention from Ethan to Craig to Liam to Jonas before he finally rested on me. He held my gaze and gulped. A guilt-ridden frown lowered his brow and he hunched his shoulders forward.

A halting murmur came through his lips. "Why didn't you try harder? You could have convinced me. You should have—" He cut off with a frown.

I dived at him and slapped him across the face even harder than the first time we'd met. "You're blaming *us*!" The last word sounded like a murderous hiss—even to my own ears.

Ethan clearly underestimated the violence surging through me, having no idea of how incapacitated I'd felt. He chuckled. "Seriously, Caleb. Did anyone ever convince you of anything once you'd made your mind up? Like *ever*?"

Caleb shuddered, not answering Ethan but as if he were speaking to himself. "They're innocent! I'd have murdered them if— Are you guys serious? Eric's okay?"

Caleb advanced toward us so fast that I flinched back and stepped on Ethan's considerably narrow foot.

Ethan steadied me with his long, pale arm around my shoulders. In a burst of speed, Jonas launched at Caleb. He slammed his broad fist into Caleb's face with a *thwack*.

Caleb took a single backward step. He lifted three fingers to his mouth but displayed no other sign he'd taken the blow at all. Even his facial features drooped as he inspected the red coating the tips of his fingers. "I guess I deserved—"

Jonas spat on the sandy rock flooring. "You *deserve* a hell of a lot more than that, you piece of trash!"

I stumbled when Liam intervened—not to admonish Caleb, but quite the opposite. He laid a hand over Jonas' shoulder. "What if it were you, bro? What if you were sure someone had killed Harriet or one of us?" He left the question dangling in the air before addressing Caleb, his machine gun voice calm. "Regardless, you will have some explaining to do."

Caleb nodded, his voice soft. "Well, best we go inside the ref—"

Just as quietly, Liam cut him off. "I'm not talking about explaining to us, you jerk. You've cost my...my girlfriend precious time. Your brother thinks you're dead. And you didn't bother to let him know you're not. Worse than that, when he finds out you tried to kill my sister, maybe you'll wish you were. Hell, he probably will. No matter how happy he is to see you're alive, he'll flatten you."

With no fanfare, the crowd left us and filtered through the Kaleidotonium entrance. All except Dan. He strode to Caleb, setting a hand on the boy's shoulder. His hold, however, offered no comfort. As Dan squeezed the muscle beside Caleb's neck, he flinched. Fueling the flames, the older man stared Caleb down. "We saved your life, took you into our community, respected your decisions, and hell," — Dan gritted his teeth — "we even valued them. But regardless of how highly we value your contribution here, *never* put us in that situation again. Is that clear?"

Dan sharpened the pressure and Caleb winced once more, but the older man didn't await Caleb's reply. Dan released his hand and passed through the entrance. With his gaze on the dusty rock path, Caleb trailed at a distance.

As I watched him go, my anger receded. His slouched shoulders and dejected walk told me he regretted acting on such a cruel impulse. Now that my shock had subsided, it surprised me that compassion bubbled up. That became the dominant emotion running through me. As much as he deserved it, I couldn't hate Caleb.

As we headed to the entrance, I latched onto Ethan. "How is it you got to come here?"

He puffed a laugh. "Susan thought you might need some help. Austin told us your waterball had landed a week before and hadn't changed since."

My eyes stretched wide, and I spoke to the sky. "Well, thank you, Austin. Wherever you are right now. You just saved our lives…again."

Chapter Twenty-Nine

Dan waited at the cave entrance, his voice still rattled, though a measure of confidence warmed the edges. "Shall we try this again? I'm Daniel Parker. Welcome to our refuge. In the unlikely chance you're keen on joining our little community, I should tell you we'd appreciate your help, since most of the original crowd have gone off on their own and we still have farmlands to work."

One by one he clasped our hands in both of his, unable to conceal their clammy warmth. "Somehow, young lady, any apology would be inadequate, deplorable and insulting. Despite that, I find myself grateful you looked at Caleb with kindness. He's been through a lot in his young life. Regardless, I'll think twice before trusting his choices. Now, if in any *humane* way you want him punished, I'll comply."

I didn't miss his emphasis of 'humane' as one of Liam's warm, veiny hands landed on my shoulder, his long, strong fingers curling forward onto my collar bone. On my other one, I didn't need to look to know it was Jonas who'd settled his broad, powerful hand. Nor did I need to see their confirming nods as I answered. "Thanks, but we'll pass. Honestly, what would it achieve? Caleb believes us now."

Dan chuckled a relieved sigh. "You're better than me, you three. I'd have wanted retribution."

I regarded him. "Not really! I'm curious, though... Why the lockup? Have you had need of it before? Worse than that, did you subject someone else to your *inhumane* punishment?"

Dan averted his gaze. "Not me personally, but Mr. Rodrigues. Somehow a serial killer ended up in the refuge. He'd killed three of our young women before we suspected who it was. And we had ten thousand people here to protect. He was like any normal young man, and that got us over-suspicious of everyone. Caleb only heard the story though, so I can't see what made *him* so untrusting."

Then Dan turned and waved a hand for us to follow — not toward the prison cells, but in the opposite direction. "Come on. Let me show you to a dormitory. Most rooms are vacant now, so you can pretty much pick."

He led us along another, much broader, Kaleidotonium-lined tunnel. A long central duct illuminated the walls in bright white light — unlike the normal rainbow colors of Kaleidotonium.

A little way in, a rough doorway cut into a large cave. I threw a quick glance inside. Semi-flat machined walls surrounded at least a hundred scattered tables with extractor fans whirring overhead. On a countertop against the far wall lay platters of sandwiches, salad and a large glass urn brimming with juice. Beyond that, another door led into what I assumed was the kitchen, containing washing and refrigeration chambers – if I went by the layout in Graham's refuge.

At more or less a quarter of the tables, people sat and most looked up from their meals to stare at us. Not Caleb – he sat at a table with the chess pieces and the man with the foreign accent. He seemed oblivious to our presence, his gaze locked on the plate before him as he toyed at lettuce leaves with a fork, then picked up a sandwich.

Dan popped his head through the doorway. "Okay, okay" – he clapped his palms together three times – "the show's over, ladies and gentlemen. You can get back to what you were doing." Then to us, he murmured, "There's plenty of time for introductions later."

Farther down the tunnel, the same dazzling glow I recalled from Graham's refuge seeped in. It grew brighter and brighter until we came upon the entrance to one farmland – a Kaleidotonium-lined 'outdoor' cavern. We peeked inside.

Dan glanced over his shoulder, opened his mouth, shut it and opened it again in a mellow crow. "It looks to me like you've seen something similar to this before."

With an absent nod, I took in the half-grown plants stretching away toward a distant cavern wall. This field was home to a sugarcane plantation. The scents of earth and greenery filled the air. Far overhead, the Kaleidotonium shell reflected light in bright sky-blue – like in Graham's refuge. Shifting graphics sprinkled fluffy clouds that drifted in languid splendor across the sky, forming and reforming. Other graphic displays spread distant mountain ranges along the rock-faces.

The 'sun' arched bright and orange overhead, casting glorious, seemingly natural light on the plants. I knew that in the evenings, the 'moon' relieved the sun and took up the task of sliding along the track, arching across the high roof. Above the Kaleidotonium shell, water from unseen irrigation pipes filtered through in the form of rain.

Back in Graham's refuge, Eric and I had walked hand in hand through a similar cavern. The recollection summoned a smile, though my heart pinched.

Dan brought me back. "Come along, then. Let's get you to your rooms."

A minute later he led us into an offshoot where, beneath another sunlit sky, an enormous botanical garden spread away. The nearby red brick dormitory seemed relatively small in the enormous space. Several cobbled pathways wound between flowers in colorful bloom. Trees blossomed with young fruit—apricots, peaches, plums, pears. Around the myriad flowers, butterflies flitted and bees buzzed, collecting pollen. A soft breeze fluttered leaves and varied rich scents seeped into the air. We took the main path toward the building's solid double-wood doors. Dan yanked and kept one open while we stepped through. Glossy flooring made up the broad passage. The sense of déjà vu slammed into me. It looked exactly like the dormitory in Graham's refuge. The same hundred-bedroom entrances led off each side, and I walked straight for a particular door.

As I pressed the handle down, Dan laid a hand on my arm. "You might want to reconsider going in there."

I peered up at him, a frown wrenching my forehead. He offered a smile. "That's Caleb's room."

"Oh…no! I wouldn't want that. But it makes sense. He and Eric shared the same room in Graham's refuge."

Dan puffed a laugh and gestured at an open door farther down the passage. "Why don't you try that one? A young woman about the same age as you lived there."

I twisted Grandma's wrap-bracelet around my wrist. "What…happened to her?"

Dan laughed. "Oh" — he cocked his head — "*oh*! No, she's fine. Amber moved away with her family. We often trade with them."

Like me, Amber favored pastels, and I walked inside with a smile, then turned back to Dan. "We must collect —" I cut off, pausing at the pink backpack propped against the wall. "Thank you." I met the older man's smiling dark eyes. "When?"

He winked. "After the first group of men returned, Blake and Ivan collected your luggage from lockdown. They were mightily pleased, let me tell you. When I reached the entrance, they raced past — told me what rooms they'd prepared for you."

I skimmed a hand over the number seventy-eight on the door and phrased my question tentatively, not sure he'd find our description of the boys amusing. "Are Blake and Ivan the 'chess pieces'?" I grimaced while air-quoting the reference.

Dan roared. "Well, that's the first time I've heard that one! It's a pretty darn apt description, though."

A second later Liam, Jonas, Ethan and Craig materialized beside Dan.

Jonas lifted a palm and motioned his fingers toward himself. "Come on. Share the joke."

"Chess pieces," Dan and I chorused, leaving Ethan and Craig passing quizzical frowns between each other.

"Later." Dan laughed then added, "Well, now we've got your rooms sorted, let's get you lot something to eat."

As exhausted as our emotional roller-coaster had made me, my stomach growled in agreement with Dan.

Liam cast a sideways glance at my grumbling tummy. "Good to see not everything has changed."

"Bah." Jonas snorted. "Like you're any different. Your gut discharged quite the roar back there." He tossed his head toward the entrance.

Craig focused on Ethan then Dan. "Listen, dude. We'd rather go exploring your caves, if that's okay?"

Dan flashed two rows of straight teeth. "Be my guests."

I touched Craig's arm. "Before you go… Please tell me if you saw Harriet and Eric? Are they okay?"

Ethan sucked in a less than convincing breath. "They're both okay. Everyone is…for now. But—"

Craig broke off, and I squinted at him. "But *what*?"

"Susan or Gina or Amanda—I'm not sure which— but they keep trying to convince Eric to put that silver disk thing on his arm."

I crossed my arms and tapped my foot. "Graham told him not to let them."

Craig held up a palm. "And he hasn't. He told us to let you know."

"Thank you." I sagged against the wall. "I'm not sure why it's important, but I think Graham is right about that disk. Not for us in Petriville, but if I were you guys, I wouldn't trust Gina—especially since she was once intent on killing you all."

Another thought tickled my mind. "You traveled out here on a waterball…right? Was it Gina or Susan who asked you to come?"

Ethan took this one with a nod. "It was Susan. She begged us to find you. She looked seriously worried. Oh-h, by the way, those waterball things are so-o super cool—especially the launch. It's a pity about that Austin-dude insisting on the machine strapping us in."

The launch was the part I hated most. I groaned. "Why am I surprised?"

Craig's eyes brightened. "But what a ride."

With that, the two risk-seekers raced away.

Chapter Thirty

Few lingered in the cafeteria when we returned — Blake, Ivan, Caleb and the boys who'd overpowered us on the mountain path. Although Caleb was on another round of sandwiches, he chewed mechanically while resting an elbow on the table, head in hand.

Only a scattering of lettuce leaves remained on the counter-top sandwich platter, and the juice urn stood empty.

Noticing my gaze, Dan chortled. "No matter. The chef will whip up a few in a minute." Then he called to the kitchen.

Caleb looked up, got to his feet and pushed his chair back.

"No, you don't, young man. You'll stay right here." Dan leveled on the chess pieces. "You two can get back to school." Dan amplified his voice and slowly rotated, addressing the entire cafeteria. "That goes for you lot, too. Lunch is over. Clear off."

In an instant, chairs scraped across the stone flooring and the people shuffled out. Blake and Ivan observed us, their lips in flat lines as they shifted from side to side.

I eased their tension. "So, who's Blake and who's Ivan? Let me guess. Black hair for Blake and Ivory hair for Iv—"

As if they weren't confusing enough, their cackles cut me off. The dark-haired boy spoke. "The other way around."

I had to force myself not to laugh. "Well, Ivan and Blake, this is Liam, Jonas and I'm Cassidy. Thanks for hauling our luggage to our rooms."

They both shrugged while Ivan seemed to swell "No problem." With that, they spun and raced from the cafeteria.

A moment later the chef burst from the kitchen like a bubble popping from a blower. He held a jug of juice in one hand and a smaller platter of sandwiches in the other.

Dan waved him over. "You can bring those right over here. Thanks, Chef."

Jonas groaned. "Did you know they do the same at Graham's refuge, then? I mean, they call their own chef, too!"

Dan squeezed his forehead into an obviously faked frown and winked. "Ah-h well. In our case, that's his proper name." He chuckled at his attempt at humor.

Caleb reacted entirely differently. He wheeled on Jonas. The frown lines between his brow penetrated with such intensity they looked permanent. "You *knew* that? And you didn't think to mention it?"

Not expecting Jonas to defend himself, I flared. "Excuse us for not thinking clearly about how we'd evade the judgment and death you were so desperate to impart."

Caleb slumped to his seat, his brows down and pulling together.

At the center of the table, Chef placed the sandwiches and pitcher. A minute later he came back with three glasses, plates and sets of cutlery. When Chef lifted Caleb's empty plate, Caleb reacted with lightning speed. Between vise-like fingers, he clamped the plate. "I'm not done."

Clearly used to Caleb, Chef shrugged, folded his arms and took a step back.

Dan gestured at the table. "Well, I'm pretty sure you have a lot to talk about, so I'll leave you lot to it." Then he left the cafeteria.

Honestly, I wanted to talk to Caleb—to understand him. As similar as he was to Eric, he started *looking* different—as if his personality had seeped into his appearance. I took the opposite chair. With an unforgiving sigh, Liam turned the backrest to the table and straddled the seat. Jonas did the same. Without acknowledging Caleb, they loaded their plates. After helping myself to sandwiches, I filled our glasses.

The enormous chef moved with stealth-like agility and, as if waiting for the central platter and jug, sped them away. "I'll get you more."

Caleb stared at the mountain on his plate. "That would be great. Thanks, Chef. I've barely eaten in days."

A disgusted snort burst through my throat. "Oh, spare us! We've had much more reason to lose our appetites than you. You deserve to starve for what you did."

Jonas ignored my retort, taking his gaze from his plate only long enough to glare at Caleb. "Out with it. Get explaining! What exactly made you think it a good idea to kill us, then?"

Caleb didn't give Jonas a direct answer, and his voice squeaked. "How..." He cleared his throat and began again. "How do I justify what I put you through? Or rather...why would you accept any apology I make? Would it make you feel better if you hurt me? I'd take whatever you handed out." He passed his gaze over Jonas, Liam then me, his tone imploring — "anything."

I rolled my eyes. "Oh...the *self-reproach*."

Jonas again ignored my need to deride Caleb and gritted his teeth. "So, telling you we'd met Chef would have done it then?"

"Probably not," Caleb admitted, glancing at his lap.

Liam's voice was quiet but no slower than normal and definitely not as gentle. "Caleb, you'd made your mind up. You'd have countered whatever we said."

Caleb bit his lip. "Maybe."

Simultaneously, Liam and Jonas slid backward off their chairs and got up.

Liam's cheeks twitched, jaw ticking. "You don't deserve our forgiveness, Caleb. And you most definitely don't deserve your brother's." He frowned at me, then jerked his head in a 'come with us' motion.

I didn't move but fidgeted with my fingers before me.

Jonas fixed on the stone roof. "He's not Eric, Cass. Let him stew in his guilt."

My stomach roiled, my temper flaring. Without a thought, I launched to my feet. As the back of my knees struck the light chair, it crashed over backward. I gave Caleb my most ferocious glare. "Do you know what,

Caleb? You can't imagine how I want to hurt you right now. And this" — I circled my finger around the table — "isn't happening. Not with knowing — " I broke off and stormed between Liam and Jonas, knocking into them as I passed. I rocketed from the cafeteria with the conclusion of my sentence thrumming through my skull — *'not with knowing Eric and Harriet's lives are on the line'*.

Chapter Thirty-One

I sped through the broad tunnel toward the dormitories, my eyes burning and throat closed.

Footsteps sounded behind me and Liam yelled, "Wait, Cassidy." He grasped my arm and spun me around. "We're not your enemies."

"Neither is Caleb!" I jerked away, my voice a choked moan. "With all my heart, I want to cause him pain, but I can't... I can't separate him from Eric."

I raced on until darting into the dormitory offshoot. When I emerged into the botanical gardens, I started on the main path toward the red brick building then peeled off onto a narrow side path that headed deeper into the gardens.

Liam's footsteps still tracked me, and his concern brought a faint smile to my mouth. Drawing a deep breath, I filled my lungs with the fresh scents of plants, flowers, birds, insects and water, absorbing their serenity. I crossed a small arching bridge over a narrow brook and continued along the winding path. Beneath an enormous willow tree, I stopped at a picnic table. The brook looped back beside the tree, bubbling over stones. I sidled into a bench affixed to the table and dropped my head to my palms. Liam slowed — tentative and without a word — and straddled the bench beside me.

We sat in silence for a time before Jonas joined us with a tray of food and drinks, which he set on the table. As if an explanation was necessary, he cleared his throat. "Chef wouldn't let us leave with 'empty stomachs'." He air-quoted the last two words, then sat opposite and set plates of sandwiches and glasses of juice before each of us.

With a smile, I looked up and raised the glass in a half-toast. "Thanks." Then I took a sip of juice but didn't put the glass down. "As much as I want to let Caleb stew for what he did, I also *want* to talk to him."

Jonas gave a hard, bitter laugh. "He tried to murder us, Cass. What could you possibly want to say to him then?"

Liam nodded. "I get that he's Eric's brother and you might find it difficult to see past that. But right now…" He trailed off.

Jonas completed what he thought Liam had implied. "I want to rip his head from his shoulders" — he threw a derisive laugh — "irrespective of Cassidy's devotion to his *brother*. In all honesty, that's the only thing keeping me back." He shook his head and directed his glare on me. "Do you really want to involve yourself with the identical twin of someone willing to murder people on a whim?"

"Eric is *nothing* like Caleb! You never once bothered to get to know him. And he's been nothing but kind to you…Jonas."

The edge of Jonas' nose curled up. "Well, he has no reason not to be, does he then? He's the one who got the—" He cut off.

The always-rational Liam interjected in his smooth, speedy tone. "What is up with you two? You're supposed to be friends. Stop ripping at each other."

Jonas stared at the too-close-to-real sky and moved his jaw as if trying to relax the muscles. I glared at him.

After the longest time, he sighed and reached a hand across the table to me. "Liam's right, Cass. We shouldn't be fighting. And you're right, too...about Eric. When we're back, I'll get to know him. For your sake, I'll do that."

I gave his hand a quick squeeze before withdrawing mine. "No, we shouldn't...fight, I mean. And it would mean the world to me if you'd do that—become friends with Eric."

Jonas screwed up his mouth, peeked at his hand, then up again, his tone gentle. "Is that it then, Cass? A quick squeeze and you're gone?" His voice rose at the end in a question.

I loosed a deep, frustrated breath, my voice tired. "What do you want from me?"

Liam rubbed the back of his neck and pressed his lips together. "Seriously, guys, should I leave?"

"No," Jonas and I chorused, and Jonas added, "I don't care if you hear this, bro." While he continued talking, he swiveled his gaze to me. "Give me a kiss."

"What?" Liam shot, but I laughed.

"I'm sure Liam would gladly give you a kiss. Only, I think he's in love with your sister," I said.

Jonas snorted, but Liam didn't see the humor in my attempt at diversion. Instead, he grabbed his plate and juice. "Tell me when you guys are done with this

Carryn W. Kerr

conversation." Without another word, he left the way we'd come.

After we watched him go, Jonas turned back to me and continued where he'd left off. "So that's what I want. One kiss."

I hiked a brow. "Then you'll stop this? All of it?"

He considered his hands again before shifting his soft green gaze to mine, his tone quiet. "Yes. I'll stop." After a moment, he laughed — "if, in the unlikely event, you still want me to."

I rolled my eyes. "What about Olivia?"

"Ah, Olivia." As if he'd forgotten, he shrugged. "What she doesn't know won't hurt her."

"But I will, Jonas. And she'll sense it. I'm sure I would if—" I cut off, not wanting to imagine Eric kissing someone else.

Jonas curled the edge of his boyish lips into a mischievous smile. "How about I handle Olivia, hey?"

I examined him and huffed a blast of air. "Are you sure this is what you want?"

He didn't miss a beat. "More than anything in the world."

"But you know what I feel for Eric."

"And if Eric never came into the picture, I'm convinced you'd feel that way about me. You care, Cass. I see it in your expression."

I inhaled as Jonas cupped my cheek. "I've always loved you. In my own way, I always will. But I'll step back. I swear I will if you give me this. We nearly died today, and do you know what was running through my head? I'm going to leave this world without getting to kiss the girl I love."

Jonas took both my hands and got up, edging around the table and helping me from the bench. After

227

slipping his thick forearms around my waist, he pulled me against him.

I blinked, unsure, but threaded mine around his neck, my words a soft whisper. "I didn't think of it that way."

Then his mouth touched mine, and he firmed his hold around my waist. In a gentle caress of his tongue, he parted my lips. This kiss felt so different from Eric's. It bore no urgency or need, only tenderness and caring. I settled into his embrace, enjoying the sensation of his touch—not the hot wildfire that surged through my body when Eric held me but a place of safety. Jonas had been right. I didn't experience a need to escape. In fact, it wasn't me who broke the kiss. Finally, Jonas leaned back, his face solemn, his soft green gaze on mine. He kept his hand at my cheek—cupping it. "Thank you." Then he went back to his teasing self, biting his lip and bouncing his eyebrows. "If I live a thousand years, I won't forget that."

He stepped back and sidled to the far side of the table. As I sat opposite, I met his gaze and a silent tear made its way down his cheek. He gulped. "Eric is one lucky boy."

Then he cleared his throat, picked up a sandwich and bit into it. We sat in comfortable silence. I opened a quarter sandwich—chicken and fresh mayonnaise. After slapping shredded lettuce leaves between the bread, I closed it and took a bite.

It hit the pleasure-senses of my tongue in all the right spots. A moan seeped up my throat. "I'm really going to enjoy Chef's food."

Jonas chuckled. "Here I thought my kiss would have gotten a sound like that from you."

I reached over and slapped his shoulder with a laugh. I silenced it a moment later. "You'd better keep this to yourself, okay?"

He lifted two fingers in a mock salute. "Scouts' honor."

"Hah. Like you were ever a scout. That's more a sector nine thing, anyway."

We continued our light banter while eating the sandwiches and drinking the juice. As we finished, Liam arrived with Ethan and Craig.

Craig protruded his chin. "Ah, Cassidy. Just the girl we were looking for."

Liam clipped his words. "Are you two done with your *business*?"

I understood his irritation a moment later when he sat beside me and, none too gently, wrapped his arm around my head. He pulled my ear to his mouth before whispering, "You're going to hurt him again, Cassidy. Does he deserve that?"

Liam was right, as usual. I turned my mouth to his ear. "Was I supposed to say no?"

He said nothing but released his grip and fixed me one of those lined-forehead fatherly looks, implying it was *exactly* what I should have said. It didn't make me feel any better.

As he again stepped over the bench, I inspected my lap and fidgeting fingers.

Liam waved Jonas to 'come'. With a shrug, Jonas threw me a skewed glance, as if curious about our exchange. Without waiting for my response, though — which I wouldn't have offered anyway — he left with my brother, probably for the *friendly* advice Liam intended to impart.

With a wry smile, I watched them go, then turned back to Ethan and Craig as they sank down opposite me. Their solemn faces made my stomach tighten.

Craig clasped his long pale hands before him on the table. "So, we're heading back in a day or two. Your dad, Jonas' parents and Graham will want news that you guys are okay. Plus, Eric is pacing back and forth in there like a caged wild animal. Graham isn't aware of Mr. Rodrigues' death, obviously — but he mentioned something about refrigeration chambers to us. Anyway" — he did a whirling motion with his finger — "Dan's got a bunch of boys out in the caves scouring for areas where they might be. Mr. Rodrigues mentioned nothing to Dan about the formulae…but when Graham had us holed up in his refuge, he didn't tell us either. So, no surprise there."

Ethan lowered his voice as if about to deliver a blow. "There's something else we should tell you. We're not sure how well you know that girl, Amanda…" He let the unspoken question hang in the air, his mouth open as he took in my grimace.

I twisted Grandma's wrap-bracelet. "A bit, but not *well*. What's this about?"

Craig frowned. "She's been visiting Eric, like all the time."

The sharp growl in my voice surprised me. "What's 'all the time'? Did you ask Eric about it?"

Ethan shrunk down on the bench despite his tall frame. "Like twice a day at least. And sorry, but no…guys don't talk about stuff like that."

A thousand expressions must have passed over my face. Ethan and Craig flashed each other uncomfortable looks. They rose and Ethan murmured, "Anyway, we thought you should know. Oh, and Harriet's been checking up on Eric too—but I expect you asked her to."

My heart pounded against my chest and my stomach flipped double somersaults. I didn't have any right to complain. I'd kissed Jonas. *Kissed* him! What had I been thinking? He wasn't Eric. The thought of Eric kissing Amanda made me want to hurl my guts into the plants. Amanda had never hidden her feelings for Eric. He was probably falling in love with her right at that moment. And here I was, trying to find something to make her well. Another wave of nausea washed over me. If I could have replayed the past half hour, I'd never have agreed to kiss my friend, because the thought of Eric kissing Amanda—kissing anyone other than me—tore through my heart.

Chapter Thirty-Two

The rich aromas of bacon and eggs wafted into the passage when Liam, Jonas and I headed to the already-crowded mess hall the next morning.

People amplified their voices to drown out the clatter of plates and cutlery, the bustle of feet, a breaking glass, chairs scraping across the floor. Groups of men and women wearing old jeans, T-shirts and trainers sat at tables, chatting and laughing while they ate.

Making our way through them, we aimed for the serving counter. When a hand tapped my shoulder, I whirled with a scowl fierce enough to scare the devil. Blake seemed to agree with that thought, because he took a huge backward leap. "Sorry. I forgot."

Jonas chuckled. "Still a little jumpy, are we then, Cass?"

I ignored him, but Ivan sucked his lips between his teeth, failing to hide his smile while Blake handed out warm plates.

Despite my pounding heart, I broke into a smile. "Oh, never mind. What are you boys up to today?"

Blake slouched his shoulders and drawled a single forlorn word. "School." He gestured at pushed-together tables where a group of teens sat. Before two vacant chairs lay small stacks of books. Not digipars, but books made of actual paper and bound in real hard-board covers. I gaped at them, not only appreciating their authenticity, but because they reminded me of the books Eric had taken along when we'd left Graham's refuge.

Like the adults, most teens wore jeans and T-shirts. Some girls, however, featured sexy little skirts and skimpy tops—albeit obvious hand-me-downs, like in Graham's refuge. With something like my fascination with the books, these teens watched Ivan and Blake, their expressions ranging from stunned to horrified. Occasionally they flicked their attention to Liam, Jonas or me before again settling on the boys.

I bent toward the chess pieces in a conspiratorial way and softened my voice. "Why are they looking at you like that?"

The boys tittered before Ivan responded. "They're like super impressed we know you. You know…since you're like celebrities and all."

Not missing a beat, Jonas wriggled his eyebrows. "Nearly being murdered wasn't exactly on my list of how to replace our MAC fans, bu-u-ut—" Drawing out the last word, he stopped with a shrug.

Liam produced an uncharacteristic snorting laugh through his nose. That made me guffaw, and I nearly dropped my plate as I dished French toast and bacon and twirled maple syrup over the top. After Blake and

Ivan served their own breakfast, they rejoined the group of teens.

Despite how full the cafeteria was, Caleb sat alone at a table near the far corner, his back to the door.

While Liam passed an impassive gaze over him, Jonas grated a laugh. "Is that dude seriously going to maintain that sad-puppy face until we forgive him?"

A twang of unexpected sympathy rose in my throat. "He's eating breakfast, Jonas. How's that expecting our forgiveness? And he's probably alone because no one wants to be around him."

Jonas targeted an emptying table against the far wall and scoffed. "After what he did, I'm not surprised."

For a moment I followed him and Liam. Then I paused and changed my mind. "I want to speak to him."

With that, I spun. They didn't stop me, but neither did they follow.

Caleb didn't notice as I stood behind the opposite chair and observed his glistening aquamarines. After a long pause, I said a simple, "Hello."

Slowly and seemingly dazed, he floated his gaze up to me then jerked his head back, surprised. "What are you doing here? I'd have figured you'd rather torture than *greet* me."

"I'm not here to persecute you, Caleb. I mean, I probably should"—I shrugged—"but it looks like you're doing a good job of that on your own."

His thick, dark-blond lashes lowered, transferring the tears to them. "But you must hate me." Was he trying to convince me I should?

I took my time replying, but when I did, I explained truthfully. "I can't, Caleb. Not when you remind me so much of Eric."

He studied his food. "You ought to. Your brother and *boyfriend* justifiably do." He air-quoted the word 'boyfriend'.

I plastered a wry smile on my mouth. "If you insist on referring to Jonas as my boyfriend then I might conform to their sentiments." I pulled out the chair and sat opposite him. "Give them time. They're angry."

Caleb swallowed, rubbing the back of his neck, voice low. "Are you not...angry?"

I peered down at my hands, then up at Caleb. The steel in my voice surprised me. "Oh, I'm angry enough. In fact, I'm furious — even more so because I can see the whole thing playing out through Eric's eyes. He'd be heartbroken. Do you realize that? Absolutely shattered. And I'm not even sure you care."

His jaw twitched. "You don't get to tell me if I care about my brother. You know nothing about our relationship."

"Yet *you* let him think you were *dead*." I glanced around at the faces that were now attentive to our heated voices.

Caleb did too. He forced his tone down — even lower than his creased brows. "I never meant for him to... I figured he'd know I was okay — like I sense when he's not."

"But that's exactly it, Caleb. He realized you were *not* okay. In his mind, the scavenged bodies simply proved it. But" — I scrutinized him — "I want to understand why you told Eric to stay with your dad? I don't believe it was because you thought Graham relied more on Eric — and that's the story Eric gave me."

I closed my eyes for a second then met his.

Caleb steepled his fingers and tapped his lips, his voice quieter than normal, as if his upcoming admission humbled him. "No, it wasn't. I mean, it is what I told Eric, and it's probably true. In all honesty, I was sick of being stuck there. I craved the adventure. What was it you called me? A selfish pig, right?" His voice trembled. "Well, you were right. That's exactly what I am."

Caleb stared at me, his voice even softer. "If any man deserves the love of a beautiful girl, it's Eric. He has a mountain of admirable qualities."

My smile seemed to fill my voice. "He does. And he's surprising. Even when I'm mean, he's kind and forgiving. When I demand answers, he replies with no judgment. And when I want retribution, he's accepting." My cheeks warmed. "Plus" — I ground my palms into my eye-sockets, grimacing at my shallowness — "he's really, really hot."

Caleb threw his head back and laughed.

"Oh." I pressed my face into my palms. I'd pretty much told him he was hot too…and he was, just not in the same way as Eric. "I…oh," I repeated, then silenced myself before I put my other foot in it.

Caleb didn't tease me, at least. Instead, he again grew serious. "So, you really do love Eric."

Sudden moisture clouded my vision. I blinked my eyes clear, surprised at the stoniness infusing my voice. "Why's that so hard to believe? I'm out here for him, Caleb. For Eric and Harriet, which is why I'm so mad with you for delaying us! Their lives are on the line." My voice cracked on the last bit and I waited, gauging Caleb's expression.

He curled his lip and growled. "What do you mean Eric's life is on the line?"

I breathed in. "Do you remember how you kept asking why he wasn't with us?" His chin dipped and I went on. "Well...you were right about something. Eric wouldn't have let me come out here without him." I steeled myself for the revelation. "The truth is Susan...or more likely Gina...put him in prison."

Caleb's neck corded, his nostrils flaring. "What the *hell*? You're telling me my brother's in *prison*! Why? Do Ethan and Craig know?"

My voice sounded tired even to my own ears. "I am. Insurance. And yes, they do."

"Insurance for what? And who is this *Harriet*? Is she in prison too? What does any of this have to do with Eric?"

I hurled a snort at him. "What do you think? You can't possibly be so naïve! It was Gina's way of making sure we'd return." I shook my head. "Not that we needed the motivation. Harriet is Jonas' sister, the love of Liam's life and my best friend. No, she's not in prison. She's sick."

With a long, blank stare, Caleb hung his mouth open then whistled. "I'm getting the idea my parents' formula somehow has something to do with whatever is wrong with this girl?" he lilted in a question.

"Yes...and no." I considered what I'd already told him. "So, I told you about the formulae. Something happened that caused fifty-two people to age a hundred times faster than us. They were fine until the annual memory wipe solution ran out two years ago. Now, if we don't find the drugs here, we have to locate your parents' house to find something that might help them. Then, even if we find the house, we don't know what we're looking for."

He tapped his fingers on the table. "You think our parents *predicted* this." Caleb jabbed a finger at me.

"And you didn't consider informing me of it when I spoke to you before?"

I wrinkled my nose. "First, I told you *some* of it. If I'd said Eric was in prison—in *Petriville*...how do you expect you would have handled that, huh?"

He sighed, his anger diffusing. "So, let's say I believe you that my parents supplied this longevity formula—and I'm not saying I do—but, for argument's sake. Maybe your friend developed some kind of allergy to it. But didn't the *Ellen* drug neutralize that?"

I spread out the first word. "Oh-h, Caleb. Finally, you're asking the right questions. I told you Graham's stash got crushed beneath a rockfall. Well, Gina says she destroyed hers, so the truth is she never distributed it to any of us. Plus, in all honesty, I don't want to get old and die while Eric is still a young man."

He gave a few slowing nods. "And you don't want your brother and friends to age while you're young." He focused on the ceiling. "Is it an allergy they have, though, or is something else making them sick?" He cocked his head. "What you're saying implies my parents had a connection with Graham and worse...that *woman*!"

A huge, slow exhale seeped from my lungs. "If you only knew the half of it."

Chapter Thirty-Three

Caleb jerked his head back. "Explain."

"It's a long story."

"I'm not going anywhere."

I answered with a small nod. "Okay. But be warned. You're going to challenge the things I tell you."

He sniggered. "Do you mean more than the things you've already told me?"

With a snorted laugh, I dragged out, "Well...probably not. But when Graham told Eric the story, he got pretty angry."

Caleb gave several slow half-nod-half-head shakes. Then, with deliberate movements, he revolved his hand for me to continue.

I looked up, pressing my tongue to the roof of my mouth and gathering my thoughts. "Well, for one thing, Eric didn't know your parents had once studied under Graham."

He stiffened. "Well now, that's impossible! We only *met* Graham on holiday."

An exasperated sigh accompanied my eye-roll. "Do you see —?"

Caleb held up a hand, cutting me off with a chuckle. "Okay, okay."

He didn't see what that did to me, how his dimples made my senses tingle, how his glinting eyes sparked a familiar yearning deep in my core. *No, Cassidy*, I chided internally, *this isn't Eric*. I looked away and blinked.

Caleb awaited the conclusion of my internal conflict with a half-smile.

My face heated, and I pulled the hem of my T-shirt down over my jeans.

He made to inspect the ceiling and tapped his toe. "Is there a reason we're waiting?"

A spontaneous laugh burst from my chest. Caleb reacted to my smile with an unmistakable expression passing over his face — milder, fleeting, but so similar to Eric's. The steady eye-contact... How he leaned in and faced me square on... The way he parted his lips then slid the bottom one between his teeth...

After clasping his hands together on the table around the plate of sandwiches, Caleb gave an audible swallow then cleared his throat.

My voice croaked. "Everything I'm telling you is in that digipar no one can open, so you're going to have to believe what I say."

Caleb raised his palms toward me. "How about you talk and I listen?"

I rolled my eyes. "Now there's a great idea."

After cutting his guffaw short, I explained how his parents had had associations with Graham and Gina...how Gina had meant for Eric and Caleb to be in Petriville with their parents...how she'd betrayed them and Graham by leaving them on Earth. I told him how

Harriet and the others had collapsed at the MAC Challenge...the reason we hoped their supply of the annual memory wipe solution hadn't run out...how we hoped to cure Harriet and the others. What seemed like a thousand times during my explanation, Caleb looked side-to-side in rapid succession—as if he were processing the information, reconciling it in his mind.

Finally, he steadied his gaze on me. "If my parents were friends of Graham, then it stands to reason they'd learned the meteor was heading on a collision path with Earth. If they understood that, why in hell did they leave Graham's refuge that night?"

I slumped, because I'd deliberately left out the bit about how their parents had died and how Gina had murdered my mother. I phrased my next sentences tentatively. "Listen, Caleb... Your parents never died in a car accident. And yes, they knew about the meteor. It was no fluke you were with Graham." I reached a hand over my plate and placed it on his interlaced fingers. "Before you even went there, they were exposed to a lethal dose of radiation. They didn't want to torment your childhood memories with images of their failing bodies and ultimate deaths. Graham agreed to raise you."

Caleb swallowed. "So, the holiday was no holiday! Does Eric know all this?"

I nodded.

Caleb squinted. "Me feeling like something was wrong with him... Was that about him being in prison? It's been going on for weeks."

I leveled on him. "He was sad before then. We all were. On top of that, Eric felt guilty. Plus, I refused to see him. Could you have picked up on his mood?"

"It's possible." Caleb retracted his hands and sat upright. "I'm getting the sense that this sadness you're talking of wasn't only about your friend?" He tilted his head.

I watched my hands as I flattened them on the table. "It happened before we learned about Harriet." I sucked in a shuddering breath. "This was about my mom." The moment the words burst out, tears blurred my vision. I palmed them. "It's…it's difficult to talk about."

Caleb inched a hand past his plate, tipping his fingers to mine. "Your mom?" Two vertical creases marked the center of his forehead, his voice the soft river of sound Eric so often spoke in. "What happened?"

Moisture seeped out with my words. "If you think you hate that woman, Caleb, trust me when I tell you I hate her more. When Eric and I met, she did everything to stop us. Then she planned to murder Jonas and me. The last straw was when she conned Eric into deceiving me, and that's what got my mother killed." The last word came with a choke.

"Eric? My brother? Colluded with *her*?" Caleb sat back, inspecting me warily.

A resigned breath slipped from my chest. "Eric tried to keep me safe — or he intended to. But that's another long story for another time."

Caleb's shoulders drooped. "I'm a real ass. Without getting to know you at all — find out what you've been through — I assumed the worst."

"You are that," I agreed with a puff of air.

He grimaced. "For what it's worth, I'm sorry. It was easy to think of you as being on the same side as her."

He brushed his fingers over mine.

I considered his gaze and laughed through my emotion. "Did you just go from prisoner to comforter — from enemy to friend?"

I'd shunned Eric when he'd tried. And here I was, laying bare my grief to Caleb?

Caleb glanced over his shoulder to the far side of the cafeteria, tossing his chin toward Liam and Jonas. "I thought I could feel daggers in my back. It looks like your brother and boy...uh, friend are ready to come over and kill me."

After unraveling a cutlery serviette, I dabbed my eyes. When I lowered it, Caleb half-opened his palms as if to let me place my hands in his. It wasn't a demand, nor even a request. It was an offer.

I didn't, but let my fists fall to my lap. "Eric told me you were impulsive and jumped to insane conclusions. He said if I'd met you at the same time—" I broke off, clamping my teeth.

Caleb chuckled, again tracking those damned lines down his cheeks. "You can't stop halfway through a declaration like that. Tell me what my brother said. Give me his secrets."

"Oh"—I lied, angling my face down to hide the heat creeping into my cheeks—"he said I'd have hated you."

Caleb wriggled his eyebrows, the smile filling his entire face. "Ah-ha."

I cleared my throat and changed the subject. "Okay. Let's get back to business. You could still come in handy—if Dan doesn't find the drugs here."

His eyes twinkled. "You want me to take you home."

I arched a brow. "Oh...I wouldn't put it like that."

He laughed.

"Show us where it is—your old home. Help us find the formulae."

Caleb greeted my gaze head on. "Will you do something in return?"

I thrust a fist to my hip. "As it is, you're hardly in a position to bargain."

He tugged his brows together in such a puppy-dog way that I sighed, first commenting to myself, "Maybe Jonas was right. Tell me what you want, anyway. We'll decide if it's something we're willing to give."

Caleb ignored my quip. "Take me to my brother. Afterward, I mean." He steadied on my gaze. "When this is all over. Take me to Eric. Please."

"Fine." With that I rose, lifted my plate and took a seat with Liam and Jonas.

Jonas scoffed. "Fraternizing with the enemy, I see."

I stared Jonas down. "As it turns out, I got him to agree to help us. So, my"—I used Jonas' words with a sarcastic twist to my voice—"*'fraternizing with the enemy'* wasn't a complete waste of time."

Liam steadied on me. "Speaking of which…while you *chatted* with Caleb, Dan told us the boys found the refrigeration chambers."

"And?" But I'd already guessed.

"There's nothing," Liam confirmed, blowing a heavy breath. "They found three labeled fridges in some hidden chambers. *Ellie*, the annual memory wipe solution and *Ellen*. But they were empty."

"So, I was right to ask Caleb for help."

Jonas rubbed his legs. "Don't bluster, Cassidy. It doesn't become you." He emphasized the old-fashioned word with a teasingly unctuous air.

I threw him a wry glance, then relayed our full conversation—well, most of it anyway.

Chapter Thirty-Four

Background music fills the air as Eric weaves his fingers through the bars. I press my body to the cell door and reach for him, resting my forehead on his. A blast of wind dissolves the metal between us and Eric is against me, feeding an arm around my waist and wrenching me to him, his body so warm. He lifts my chin and I stretch up, lacing my hands around his neck and pulling closer. As I press my mouth to his lips, I savor their warmth and bury mine in their softness and moisture. A sudden downpour of rain drenches us, but an explosion of heat burns through me. I taste him, inhale his smoky vanilla scent. "Eric," I moan. He responds with a low groan. "Amanda."

"No-o." My resounding wail jerked me from sleep. A moment later, I leaped to my feet. *Why hadn't I considered it before?* I tugged on jeans and a T-shirt, passed a brush through my hair and gave my teeth a quick brush. Not bothering about shoes, I raced from my room and bee-lined for a particular door.

After one knock, I rattled the handle. "Caleb. Wake up."

A yawn sounded through the closed door. "What…time…is it? Wait a minute."

Eventually his door swung in. "Not that I should complain about a beautiful girl waking me up in the middle of the night…but what exactly are you doing here?"

I ignored his weak attempt at—*Well…I'm not exactly sure what.* I deadpanned. "Can I come in?"

He looked up and down the corridor. "Well, you're going to wake the entire dormitory if you don't."

While he kept the door wide, I darted beneath his arm. After shutting the door, he leaned back against it.

I spun to face him. "Eric recited a poem. A rhyme. He's under the impression it might have some bearing on the antidote."

Caleb rubbed his forehead. "Can't this wait until morning?" As if thinking better of it, he loosed an exasperated breath. "Ah well, I'm sure not going to sleep after this. And judging by how wired you are, I'm pretty sure you're not either. Let me grab a jacket. You might want to put some shoes on those pretty little feet of yours. This is a cave."

I crossed my arms, curious. "Are we going to the cafeteria? At this hour?"

He glided his tongue over his teeth. "No, but it's hardly judicious to entertain someone like you"—he gestured down then up my body—"in my bedroom."

"Oh, please! What could possibly happen?" I rolled my eyes in emphasis.

Caleb ignored my question and ducked into the bathroom, shutting the door.

After some minutes he emerged and yanked a jacket from the back of a chair, and finally answered my question. "If you have to ask, then you're slow on the uptake—which I figure you're not."

I ignored him as he shoved his muscled arms through the sleeves and opened the door. With an outstretched hand, he signaled for me to lead the way.

Caleb waited outside my bedroom while I slipped on shoes and a jacket. We strolled to the path leading to the gardens—where he scooted off, plucked a blade of straw grass from beside a duck pond, and returned. Afterward, we continued on the path over the stream and toward the familiar picnic table.

I dropped to the same place as before and Caleb sat in Jonas' place.

He clasped his hands on the table. "This poem or rhyme you mentioned… It's one you'll never find in any story or fairy-tale books, isn't it?"

I nodded, and as I opened my mouth and recited it, Caleb spoke alongside me.

If a song and the wind and the rain, tell six,
The ocean, a lake and the tree are nine,
Then where would you meet with your nearest and
dearest?
Why? Where the sun and the moon misalign.

When we finished, Caleb's mouth slackened, voice soft. "Wow… Damn…that brings back memories." He blinked back emotion, then straightened. "Why didn't you tell me that rhyme when we met? That would have proved a good connection with Eric—if not his lover, at least a good friend. He would never have told that rhyme to an enemy."

A defensive note came through in my tone. "Eric and I are *not* lovers...but...we're not just *friends* either."

Caleb chuckled and threw his hands up in surrender. "Okay, okay. Now I know what offends you..." He broke off in another laugh.

I glared at him. "Not that it's any of your business."

He double-bounced his eyebrows, his first word teasing. "Mm-m. Well, regardless, my brother is one lucky slug. What did he do to land you?"

I stepped into his personal space. "*Slug*? And *land*? Really?"

He raised both palms. "Okay, I concede. Not the best choice of words."

"You're every bit as incorrigible as Eric said."

Caleb laid a hand over his heart, feigning wounded. "Eric said that?"

"Can you be serious for one minute, Caleb? You are nothing like your brother."

He composed his face and cleared his throat. "Okay. Back to business. Why did you say Eric reckons this rhyme has relevance?"

"I didn't say. Eric believes it's a key to where your parents concealed the formula."

Caleb sat back. "If, as you say, my parents did all this, why didn't they tell Eric and me? Why didn't they tell Graham? I ran over in my mind what you said yesterday and I'm kind of struggling to fit everything in place."

I scowled. "I can't make you take my word."

"You don't have to... I don't think you're lying. How about we go over it again to see if something pops out?"

Together, we repeated the rhyme several times. In the end, he tilted his head sideways and tapped his finger to his mouth. "It's right there, like it's on the tip of my tongue."

I puffed a laugh.

Caleb frowned. "That's a bit out of place, don't you think?"

I laughed my response between breaths. "It's exactly…what Eric said…about the rhyme."

He gave a wide grin. "Seriously? He said the same thing?"

I held up two fingers in a weird salute. "Almost verbatim, I swear it."

When he laughed too, the fissures in his cheeks deepened, and my smile fell away.

So did Caleb's. "What? Are you okay? Did I say something wrong?"

"No, Caleb. It's some things you do."

He cocked his brows. "I remind you of Eric."

"No…I mean, yes. Not everything. In so many ways, you're as different as chalk and cheese. It's just sometimes, you know? A look. A smile. It makes me miss him so much."

He connected with my gaze. "Me too. Eric is the better twin in every way." He sighed. "How about…since I can't replace my brother…we get you back to him, okay?"

A tear trickled down my cheek. "I didn't tell him, Caleb. I didn't tell him I love him. When you were about to kill us, I wished I had." As fast as I wiped at my tears, more replaced them.

Caleb propped a finger beneath my chin. "That's not something you need to worry about, Cassidy. Listen to me. I'll bet my bottom dollar Eric knows. You don't have to say the words to show it."

"Do you think so?"

Caleb shrugged a shoulder. "Nope" — a twinkle sparkled in his tropical-ocean eyes — "rather, I'm pretty sure I know it."

Silence descended for a long time before we headed back to our respective bedrooms. Caleb's words had soothed me for the time being. Eric knew how I felt. That knowledge — that simple understanding — somehow eased the longing ache deep in my heart.

Chapter Thirty-Five

When I returned to the dormitory the following morning after breakfast, the laundry I'd used over the past few days lay in a neat pile on my bed. After repacking it and my toiletries into the backpack, I threw it over my shoulders and clipped in the waist belt. With one last glance around the room, I stretched to open the door when a soft rap sounded.

Ivan peeked up at me with his deep brown eyes. "Dan told us you're already leaving. Is that true?" he lilted in a question but didn't wait for my reply. "Anyway, we wanted to say goodbye before school."

Without so much as a pause, Blake raised his concern as if continuing Ivan's sentence. "And is it true Caleb's going with you? Is that a good idea? I mean…after—"

His question got me smiling. I dipped my chin. "He won't give us any more trouble, and he'll help us find what we need."

Ivan looked down, fidgeting with his hands. "Well, at least he can help with the heavy stuff. He's really strong."

The boys shuffled their feet, and Blake cleared his throat. "Sorry we listened to him before." Then, as if I wouldn't know what he meant by 'before' he added, "You know…in lockup."

I swiveled my head between the two. "It wasn't as if Caleb allowed you a choice."

They dropped their gazes, then Ivan looked up. "Anyway, we hope you'll visit again someday." Without awaiting my response, they high-fived and raced off down the corridor. I smiled as I walked after them. I liked knowing that while I was here, I'd at least gotten the friendship of those two young boys.

Dan lingered outside the cafeteria with Liam, Jonas, Caleb, Ethan and Craig, and we walked to the exit together.

Dan stopped inside. "I'm thinking that Caleb ought to spend the better part of his life compensating for his misconduct. But" — he cast a downward glance — "the rest of us can't in all good conscience claim innocence in the matter. Our debt will never be fully paid. Truthfully, Caleb isn't the only one who loathes Ms. Petri. It was common knowledge what she'd done to Graham." He laid his dark gaze on Liam and me. "I understand you have a personal reason to hate her. Let's hope that daughter of hers hauls her back to prison. Now go save that friend of yours."

He heaved me into a light hug before patting Jonas and Liam on their backs. With a weak punch to Caleb's chest and a nod at Ethan and Craig, he spun and stalked back in the cafeteria's direction.

After an uneventful hike over the plateau, while snaking down the steep slope, I stumbled and nearly crashed to the path, if not for Ethan's quick reactions. Grabbing my upper arm, he steadied me. Regardless, we arrived at the beach in one piece around mid-afternoon.

Side by side on the beach lay the two enormous translucent Kaleidotonium waterballs. Ethan and Craig raced for the new one.

Before keying in the unlock code, Liam peered over his shoulder and signaled Caleb to join him.

I directed my glare at Jonas. "Why is Liam showing Caleb when he can punch the code in himself?"

"Don't ask me." Jonas held out his palms as if to ward off his involvement.

Liam was either caught up in his task or pretended to be. My face heated as he brought the keypad to life, then keyed in PQ316T. With a suctioning swoosh, the upper seam of the door formed a bright blue outline, which expanded as it peeled away from the shell. While it lowered to the beach, its upper base transformed from flat into several protruding stairs.

Caleb stepped back, crossing his forearms and fixing me with a squint. "You want me to get inside that thing?"

"Oh please, Caleb!" I puffed a mocking laugh and dripped sarcasm into my voice. "Don't tell me there's a coward hiding beneath all those muscles."

Jonas flashed me a 'what the hell are you doing?' glance, but Caleb ignored it and offered me a nonchalant shrug. "Oh, I'm a total coward. You should have thought before asking me to join your *quest*." He added a teasing tone into the last word.

Jonas flattened his thick, boyish lips at Liam. "Great. Do you see what I'm going to have to —" He broke off and flashed me a glance.

I glowered, knowing they were hiding something. "Okay, is somebody going to tell me what's going on here?"

Jonas and Caleb ignored me and escaped up the stairs into the control chamber. Then Liam rested a palm on my shoulder. "There's something I must tell you, Cass." From his jean's pocket, he extracted the cylinder with Mom's digipar.

When looking at it, everything became clear. I managed a strained whisper — a statement of fact. "You're not going with us!" I gaped at him and managed a croaked "Why, Liam?"

He cupped both hands over my shoulders. "I've gone over and over this, Cass. I shouldn't have come out here when — irrespective of how everyone hoped we'd find a cure — the girl I love may not have many years left."

My voice trembled. "I get that, Liam. I do. But I need you too. Doesn't that count for anything?"

Liam leveled on me. "I'll stay if you ask me to, Cass, but honestly, all that happened in there" — he gestured in the general direction of Dan's refuge with a toss of his forehead — "was that I finally understood how little I could have helped when Gina's soldiers captured you guys."

I swallowed. "That doesn't mean I need you any less." My breaths constricted and I rubbed my arms. After a long moment, I sagged. "No. It's okay. I'm being selfish. You *should* be with Harriet."

Liam didn't disagree with me. "Caleb will prove more of an asset, anyway."

"No one is more of an asset than you, Li. Not to me." I hid a smile behind my fingers. "Okay…maybe Eric is."

Liam crooned, "I don't think the word 'maybe' quite encompasses the scope of that fact. On a serious note…you have to know this wasn't a decision I came to lightly. If I didn't truly believe you'd be in excellent hands, I wouldn't go. But they'll keep you safe—Jonas *and* Caleb."

I scoffed. "How strange is it that the boy who tried to kill us is the one we're putting our trust in?" My laugh erupted. "Go back to Harriet, Li." I paused. "You'll be a spare wheel, anyway."

I didn't believe it for a minute, but compelling him to feel guilty wouldn't help anything.

Liam yanked me into a silent hug and handed me Mom's digipar, which I popped into my jeans pocket.

As we mounted the stairs, he kept his voice quiet and questioning. "Take notes, Cass…of everything."

My stomach churned over the idea of not having Liam with us, for Jonas and me. But Liam needed to see me smile. So, I did.

As we entered the control chamber, the reality of our *quest*—as Caleb had put it—slammed into me. I scanned the black leather recliners surrounding the low silver column. Liam explained the workings to Jonas and Caleb—how to activate the waterball into beginning its next route. Afterward, he led the way through the door to the living quarters.

In the same bedroom as before, I slotted my over-full bag into the locker. When I emerged, Caleb exited the one opposite.

I sniggered. "Oh boy. This looks like a disaster about to happen. You two had better play nice since you're sharing sleeping quarters."

Liam stood behind the shoulder-high wall at the kitchen counter. I strode past the central bright silver table and soft orange benches and cocked my head. "Are you joining us for coffee before you go?"

Liam appeared deep in concentration. He never answered but continued his task. He wasn't at the coffee machine but to its left, fidgeting beneath the lip of the kitchen counter. With a click and a swoosh, a thin drawer drifted out. An almost-flush Morse Code tapper lay beside a digipen and digipar, which displayed a list of alpha-numeric codes.

These codes, I recognized. "They're pod numbers." I jabbed my finger on a familiar one. "Look, there's the infamous PQ316T again."

"Yes" — Liam agreed — "but in this case, they're the waterball numbers."

Caleb seemed stuck on my comment, eyebrows squishing together. "Infamous?"

I bit my lower lip. "It was where, or how, I first met Eric."

"Okay-y." Caleb drew out. "Let's save those sordid details for later. How do we operate — ?" He stopped short as Liam lifted the digipen and scrolled to the right of the digipar, writing RH742A. The small tapper made a series of clicks and beeps. After a pause a ping and a message appeared on the digipar *RH742A...copy PQ316T.*

Beneath the reply Liam wrote, *Is it that simple?* More clicks and beeps.

A few seconds later another message flashed beneath his. *RH742A... Yes, now let's get out of here.*

As Liam slid the drawer shut and stepped away, I shook my head. "Why didn't Austin tell us about this communicator before?" I lilted in a question.

"Apparently" — he clucked his tongue — "it wasn't working. Anyway, now we'll have you on tap. We'll let you know when we reach Petriville."

He turned to Caleb. "Craig and Ethan decided not to tell Graham and Eric you're alive."

Caleb jerked his head back and stared at Liam with narrowed eyes. Then he sighed and tilted his head back, looking at the clear blue sky above the Kaleidotonium shell. "Because if I don't get back, they'll have to deal with my death all over again."

Liam nodded. "They don't deserve that kind of torment. And" — he shrugged one shoulder — "that will give you an extra incentive to make sure my sister and Jonas return in one piece."

Caleb agreed, with a simple "Good."

When Liam approached me, I flung my arms around his waist as he wrapped me in his. "Eric is probably going to lambast me for doing this."

With a cheeky laugh, I shoved him in the abdomen. "He might. You should go anyway. Your presence is no longer wanted."

"Ouch." Liam threw his head back and laughed. "You're going to be okay, Cass. You really are."

He and Jonas shared a shoulder bump and a clap on the back.

Jonas never made promises about bringing me home but gave Liam a confident nod. It seemed to give my brother some kind of male assurance. Without a backward glance, he turned and traipsed from the living area. Despite my bravado, my brother's departure left a Liam-sized hole in my heart.

Jonas cleared his throat. "How about we escape this place then?" He winked. "And let's give old Caleb here the *authentic* experience."

Caleb tapped his foot. "Stop talking as if I'm not here." He lengthened his next sentence in a faint Texan sing-song. "Let's get this *thing* onto the ocean."

As Caleb and I took our chairs, Jonas touched the virtual display above the central silver column before joining us.

Overhead, the Kaleidotonium darkened.

Caleb squirmed within the confining hold of the cords. "You guys are too comfortable with the strangest things."

Jonas chuckled. "Brace yourself. It gets worse."

With that, the masks came down and sucked onto our faces as the grinding, rocking and shifting started. Before long, the spring chairs began their slow bounce. The movement still rattled my brain but grew smoother and smoother until, as before, the masks retracted, the safety straps slithered loose and our seats inclined.

Then we headed to the living quarters, where Jonas would give Caleb the run-down.

Chapter Thirty-Six

The next part of our journey, Austin had expected to take around a week. As the waterball stabilized on the ocean, I made for the shower. Jonas sank to an orange bench at the silver table with a digipar novel while Caleb attempted to make coffee. He fidgeted behind the…in his case…diaphragm-high wall.

Jonas straightened, issuing instructions. "You can make me mocha. Unsweetened. Use the virtual keypad to—" Mid-command, Jonas stopped and offered, "Hey, Cass. Do you want some coffee then?"

I looked from him to Caleb, then back to Jonas, and snorted. "No thanks. I like mine hot." Then I entered and closed the bathroom door.

When I emerged with my hair damp and skin tingly clean, Caleb sat opposite Jonas, both of them with empty paper cups. Caleb threaded a piece of straw between and around his fingers. I considered asking him where he'd plucked this one, but something caught me off-guard—their conversation was…*amiable*.

I felt suddenly defensive of Eric and shook my head. "How is it, *Jonas*, that you never bothered to get to know Eric, and yet here you are entirely comfortable with someone who was seconds away from murdering you just days ago?"

Jonas completely ignored my outburst. "You should listen to him for a sec, Cass. He established an interesting point." He directed a palm to Caleb. "Tell Cassidy what you told me."

Caleb absorbed my less-than-friendly demeanor with his head tilted to the side, his voice tentative. "We can do this later if you'd prefer."

I tossed my laundry into the washer beside the back-wall fridge. With a series of clicks and thuds, it separated the clothes then started cleaning the divided contents. Turning, I placed a coffee order on the beverage machine's virtual display. "Okay, so spill." I glimpsed over the wall at Caleb. "Go on… I'm not talking to the coffee machine."

Caleb snickered but didn't speak as I sidled onto the bench beside Jonas and set the coffee before me.

Then he cleared his throat, twirling the straw between two fingers. "Jonas says no one at Graham's refuge is sick. It's strange to me that people in Petriville are, when we've had the same drugs—or at least everyone besides Eric and me have."

"Are you saying your parents gave Gina something different to Graham that induced this? If that's the case, then why aren't we all sick?" My voice amplified with sudden and increasing irritation.

Caleb lifted his empty hand. "No, no. That's not what I'm implying. Possibly at seven years old, I didn't know my parents well, but one thing's for sure. They were humanitarian. They wouldn't have done something like that out of spite." He locked on my eyes, replying to my second question. "Exactly."

I blew on the coffee and took a sip. "So, am I right you think Gina made this happen?"

"I'm not saying that either, simply raising a question is all."

Picking up his thread, I nodded. "So, what's different about the people in Petriville?"

Caleb and Jonas exchanged glances while I presented another assessment. "Gina knows. I don't think Susan does. But *Gi-ina*" — I drew out her name — "definitely knows what's causing this."

"Okay." Jonas rubbed his chin. "So, it's something she created for her own manipulation purposes."

I hesitated. "That might be reasonable. But why Harriet — and more than that, why Gina's own granddaughter? I don't buy it."

Jonas considered. "What better way to cast suspicion from her?"

I puffed a cynical breath. "Every time we turn this thing over, we're providing more questions than receiving answers."

Jonas swung his legs over the bench and rose to his feet. "More things to stew over." He tossed his coffee cup into the disposal unit. "Anyway, I'm off to clean up. If I'm lucky, I'll have one of those *shower-moment* insights."

As Jonas disappeared behind the bathroom door, Caleb stood. After refilling his coffee, he returned and straddled his seat, forearms on the table and tapping the straw at nothing. "Tell me something. The last time you saw my dad and Eric, how were they?"

I hedged my answer. "Safe. I'm dying to see the looks on their faces when they see you alive." I

The Renascent Effect

swallowed, emotion washing over me. "So, you'd better make sure you get back in one piece."

Caleb reached over the table and wiped a thumb down my cheek. I hadn't even realized a tear had slipped from my eye and slapped his hand away. "Don't do that. You don't get to comfort me."

Caleb accepted my rebuke, displaying no emotion. Then he crushed up the straw and dropped it to the table, lacing his fingers before him. "I get it. You don't want me stealing Eric's role. Strong, reliable Eric." Despite his hard words, and like when Eric had spoken about Caleb, no jealousy snuck into his voice. Instead, he spoke with affection and respect.

I looked up at him. "Eric always said you were the tougher one."

Caleb breathed out through his nose, a faint smile forming on his lips. "Tougher probably...but Eric is physically stronger. I'm only tougher in the sense that I get myself into scrapes. Even when we were young, I always hurt myself. Eventually it didn't bother me. Eric was more cautious, you know? But in strength, as in when the world looks bleak, Eric can shoulder anyone's burden."

As I took in Caleb's expression, warmth embraced my heart. "Eric also smiles when he talks about you."

Caleb's lip twitched. "I was smiling?"

"You were."

He cocked his head. "Tell me something."

I crowed. "You mean something else."

"Yeah...that. What was it you stopped saying in the cafeteria—something about my impulsive nature?" He took a sip of his drink.

My cheeks grew hot, and I tried to pass the comment off as insignificant. "That was it — that you're impulsive and irresponsible."

A mischievous smile stole over his face, tugging the deep lines into his cheeks. "Nope...that wasn't it. You told me Eric said that if you'd met us at the same time, you'd have hated me. So, either you forgot what you told me or you're diverting. Either way, it confirms my thinking there's something else. *That's* the part I want to know." He tapped the straw as he spoke.

"Oh, it was nothing, Caleb." I fixed on my hands, my voice as soft and fast as Liam's. "He thought I'd have been off on some wild adventure with you instead of staying with him." I elevated my voice and gaze, greeting the cheeky glint in his eyes dead on. "But it's not true."

Caleb chuckled. "Now that, I don't doubt." His smile waned. "Honestly, Eric is the better choice, but I can see why he's attracted to you. You're quite — " He broke off and cleared his throat. "Anyway, what I think doesn't matter." He hoisted both palms in surrender. "But why he would want to get himself tied down before enjoying the pleasures of life, who knows?"

I stuck my hands on my hips. "You are nothing like Eric. You're so cavalier about...everything...whereas he takes things more..."

"Seriously," Caleb concluded.

"Yes," I agreed.

Caleb grinned, wriggling his brows. "Would you like to spend some time with someone more fun?"

With a scoff, I tapped the side of my cheek. "Oh, please!"

As we fell silent, Caleb's smile evaporated. He scrutinized my expression.

Then I added softly. "Like I said, I love — "

Neither of us heard Jonas leave the bathroom, but his single growled word cut through the air. "Eric?"

He caught me unaware, and I snapped my response. "Well, *yes*. Not that it's your business, Jonas. Plus, I doubt Eric is holding his breath waiting for me."

Caleb sang his opinion. "I'll bet he's holding *every* breath waiting for you."

"No, he's not. He's probably having more than enough entertainment with Amanda."

"O-oh. The beauty is jealous."

I thrust out my chin with dramatic flair. "I'm not jealous. Besides, you haven't seen Amanda. If you had, you'd see I have a thousand reasons to be...*uncomfortable*."

"Well, she'd have to be a veritable goddess to outshine you."

"You're not making me feel better, Caleb."

"I'm not trying to. But don't worry. If in the unlikely event he's moving on, I'll be there." With a wide grin, he shrugged. "Hell, by the sounds of it, I'd take his dregs either way, since he's in such high demand."

Jonas landed his broad palms on his waist. "Are you done then, Caleb? Have you no respect for your brother?"

Caleb launched to his feet and squared up with Jonas — at least a head taller. "Don't presume to know anything about Eric and me. I'd have said the same things were he here. If you'd let me finish, I intended on telling Cassidy I *admire* her loyalty to Eric, because he deserves that."

Jonas flashed me a glance. I knew he was questioning the *loyalty* bit since I'd kissed him, but I got to my feet and flared. "Besides, Jonas, you're talking about me as if I'm property. If I'm with Eric, it's *not* because he owns me. You'd both be wise to remember that for your future — and present — relationships."

With that, I prepared a cup of cocoa and shut myself in my bedroom with Mom's digipar. I read her letter again, over and over, before settling down to sleep with the small cylinder clutched in my palm.

I'd learned some things about Caleb. For one, he wasn't so unlike Eric, not at the core. Yes, they handled life differently, but their mutual trust and respect seemed unshakeable. I missed Eric more than ever and couldn't wait to take Caleb home to him. The inevitable self-doubt crept in too. What if he had fallen in love with Amanda? Despite it being nothing less than I deserved, my heart ached at the idea.

Chapter Thirty-Seven

A day later, Liam got Austin to send us a morse message telling us they'd arrived. The sender was 'Ground-0'.

Three days after that, in the middle of the night, a high-pitched siren ripped me from my sleep. Completely at odds with that came a calm accompanying voice. "Please consider making your way to the control room."

The bunk moved in slow, swinging arcs — back and forth and side to side. My stomach roiled. Rough seas may have caused the swaying, but the shuddering and soft, accompanying grind got me shivering and sweat beading on my forehead, reminding me of another time.

"Jonas!" I shrieked, launching from my bed. Without throwing a robe over my shift, I dove toward the door. Everything around me slanted and lurched. My legs gave way. I stumbled before collapsing to the floor.

The door shot open and Jonas charged in. He clung on the frame, trying to steady himself as he stretched a hand to me. "Come, Cass. Let's get to the control room."

In something of a Viking handshake, Jonas extended his large hand past mine and clasped my inner forearm. An anchor. I clutched on to his broad wrist, words bursting from my shaking chest. "What's going on, Jonas? Where's Caleb? Please tell me this thing's not breaking apart?"

Jonas' widened green gaze carried all the tension tingling through my body. "I can't do that, Cass. We don't know what's happening."

His fear should have been greater than mine. His home had crashed down before him. But he kept it together as he hoisted me to my feet. "Up you get. We need to get to those—" He cut off as a violent surge of movement threw the waterball sideways.

As the siren began an unrelenting wail, we slammed into the far passage wall. I grunted, pain lancing through my shoulder. Jonas gave a low moan as we slid down and landed in a heap on the floor.

Without wasting a second, he staggered to his feet and hauled me to mine. "Get up, Cassidy! Move!"

Finally, he responded to at least one of my questions. "Caleb's in the control room. The pillar…thing is lighting up like a Christmas tree!"

After clambering along the short corridor, we burst through the door. Overhead, the Kaleidotonium dimmed the stars and the moon. A moment later it went black. Caleb clung to the backrest of a recliner, his face contorted as he raked a hand through his short dark-blond hair. He seemed more puzzled than afraid, his gaze on the bright blue outlines of the lazily revolving control pillar. The glowing virtual delineations of sliders, shift sticks and buttons protruded. Red flashes pulsed and beeped across several points of the low tower — the signals more meaningless to us than I cared to admit.

Caleb never removed his gaze from the pillar but amplified his voice so we'd hear him over the siren. "Do *either* of you have any idea what to do with this thing?"

Blood pounded in my ears, and my voice quivered. "Why would — ?" I gasped as my body lifted from the floor and flew against a chair with Jonas on top of me. Caleb clung to the recliner. As Jonas clawed his way to another chair, I adjusted my body to sit properly.

Jonas gestured to the recliner that Caleb had clenched his hands around. Jonas gritted out, "If you think you'd like to survive whatever *is* going on…please, would you *sit!*" He snarled the last word.

Only then did Caleb react and dive into the chair. Beneath me, mine rocked in slowed movements — like the dulled violence of a raging ocean.

The vibrations intensified, trouncing the siren. With it, a loud clattering entered the fray. As the violence of juddering and reeling surged, I clung to both edges of the chair. Jonas' knuckles paled as he gripped his.

He pressed his lips together and phrased the sentence as a question. "Why didn't Austin bother to prepare us for *this* emergency?"

I didn't try answering above the mounting roar. Finally, the recliners sprang into action, slithering their hundreds of cold cords over our legs, bodies, chins, foreheads. They secured — no, *locked* — us in place, reclining as the dual masks clamped down over our faces.

At that moment, the waterball lost all control of its automatic gravity. I slammed my eyes shut. The room tipped. The blaring siren was a whisper against the deafening roar, grind and clatter. My stomach heaved. Bile swelled in my throat, my world whirling and gyrating. The earth-shattering clatters and roars drowned out my shrieks. A *thump*, *thump*, *thump* grated into my head. My stomach gnarled and cramped as dizziness assumed control. Vomit clawed up my throat and into my mouth, burning as I forced it down. My temples throbbed with increased pressure. The inside of my skull thrummed, and pain pulsed in my ears. My brain would surely explode.

With no warning, the trembling ceased. Unease washed over me at the abruptness of it. The swaying dwindled. The severe roar, clatter and grind stopped. From the control pillar, the beeping subsided until only the siren wailed on.

A gasp burst my arrested breath. I tried a slow, tentative inhale, waiting for the next onslaught, dread seeping into my veins. Unmoving, the chair bound me in place. A wave of claustrophobia clung to me. My murmured words didn't leave the confines of the mask. "What if the recliners stopped working? What if they *can't* let us go?"

Neither Jonas nor Caleb even tried to decipher my garbled sentence. They remained silent. Still, the chairs provided no signs of awaking. Only the air flowed through the mask, in and out, in and out. The siren grew softer — as though it had run out of power. Like a weighted blanket, quiet descended. Everything turned silent and pitch dark. None of us spoke. My ears rang. The blackness. The hush. Both seemed unrelenting.

Caleb finally cleared his throat and made more garbled noises I couldn't make out. The whirr of systems cut his sentence into my own relieved sigh.

The masks retracted and the recliners rose to a seated position. Then the straps loosened and glided away while the overhead tint faded, revealing a starlit sky and a bright, almost-full moon.

Jonas and I knew better than to leap up...but Caleb— A moment after rising, he raced to the bathroom.

Jonas chuckled. "Better him than me."

My giggle rang guilty. "That wasn't kind. We could have warned him."

Jonas didn't miss a beat. "I'm not kind."

I rolled my eyes—because that wasn't true—and changed the subject. "What do you think happened?"

Jonas slowly lowered his legs to the floor on either side of the recliner. "It's hard to tell, but I'm thinking along the lines of a magnetic disturbance."

I crunched my face up. "Um...magnetic disturbance?"

Jonas sat away from the backrest and swiveled to face me. "Think about where we are."

"Uh-h. In the middle of the ocean."

"More specifically."

"Stop being cryptic, Jonas. What are you"— realization dawned—"ah-h...the Bermuda Triangle? That's fiction. Those stories were surely made up."

"Maybe. But maybe not...or at least...I can't think of a better reason." He stood and sniggered. "Shall we make the man some of your mother's tea, then?"

In slow motion, I followed Jonas to the living area. At the silver table, I plopped onto the soft orange bench, straddling it and propping my head on my palm. "Make me some too, please."

Jonas shrugged and ambled behind the shoulder-high wall. "It's coming right up, your majesty."

"I did say *please*."

He spoke with buttery sweetness. "And it sounded so sincere."

Still, two minutes later I sipped the warm, albeit too-sweet, liquid with images of Mom playing in my mind. Jonas set down two more mugs and sat across from me. He reached up and wiped my cheek with the back of his finger.

I started. "Sorry. I didn't realize—" I didn't add the words 'I was crying.' Jonas knew. I took in his worried frown. "I can't get used to her not being here anymore. Every time somebody does something that reminds me of her, it makes me sad, you know?"

Jonas nodded as a pale Caleb slunk from the bathroom. He closed the door and slumped to the bench beside Jonas. "It might have been nice of you guys to warn me."

Jonas quirked one side of his lip, ignoring the jibe, and pushed a mug toward Caleb. "Drink this. It will help."

I didn't ignore Caleb's remark but extracted a page from Jonas' book. "Well, we're not nice."

Jonas guffawed, but Caleb raised a brow before blowing on the tea and attempting a tentative sip. Jonas fired into his Bermuda Triangle theory, which Caleb absorbed without comment.

Chapter Thirty-Eight

Around noon the next day, the rocking again hardened. This time, we didn't hesitate and got to the control room before the tint darkened.

My heart thumped against my chest, but it wasn't only me who dived into the recliner. As the cords locked us in place and the masks came down, I yo-yoed between retaining my breath and gulping in fresh air. For a while, the spring chair bounced before an abrupt jerk ended in grating and shifting motions. Then the waterball silenced, the masks and cords retracted and the seats inclined. The tint faded to reveal a gray sky with raindrops splattering on the Kaleidotonium shell.

As we took a moment to acclimate, Jonas cleared his throat. "So, are you ready for this then, bro — being here in your hometown?"

I moved my attention to Caleb as he breathed out a deep sigh. "To be dead honest, I'm dreading walking out there and discovering the house has been razed to the ground."

Jonas sat and swiveled toward Caleb. "Oh...believe me when I tell you I get that."

As Caleb straddled his chair, he gave a distorted laugh. "How can you possibly understand? It sounds to me like you've been protected your entire damned lives!"

Jonas leaped up and squared his shoulders to Caleb. "You're a fool to make assumptions you know nothing about! Our family home disintegrated right before us."

Caleb inhaled in a sharp breath. "Oh. Wow. So that place isn't all grand. How did it happen?"

Jonas flashed me a glance. "When our *planet*" — he air-quoted the word — "returned to Earth, it didn't have a great landing." He continued as if talking to himself. "Not my proudest moment."

I jerked my head back. "Not your proudest moment?" I questioned.

Jonas shrugged. "I let my guard down."

"Against what?"

"Oh, Cassidy. You can be so damned naïve sometimes."

"I was being nothing but your friend. Like always."

"Precisely."

"We're not doing this again, Jonas."

A suction cut into our argument as light trimmed the opening hatch. The top peeled away from the Kaleidotonium inner and lowered toward the beach.

Caleb cleared his throat. "Are you two done with your lovers' spat?"

Almost simultaneously, Jonas and I launched our verbal defense. "We're not *lovers*."

For emphasis, I added, "And we never were."

Caleb tapped a foot, then strode for the exit. As he approached the top stair he stopped, his arms hanging limp at his sides.

Since he blocked the entire doorway, I leaped to peer over his shoulder. Each jump revealed snippets of a scene through the rain, but I couldn't pick out specifics. Caleb seemed to sense my failed attempts and glanced back over his shoulder, then walked down the ramp into the warm rain.

Many of the beach-front homes remained…more or less. Around half had collapsed. Left were mostly outbuildings, porches, skylights and balconies — plants overgrowing their crumbled skeletons. Creeping vegetation had long since grown up and over every building. A tree grew through the middle of one house, protruding tall and majestic out of the top. Vines and plants blocked most doorways. If any fences or walls had ever separated the properties, those were long gone.

Below us, Caleb waited on the beach sand with his fists on his hips, his hair soaked through. Raindrops slithered down his neck and bare bronzed arms.

Behind me, Jonas cleared his throat — seeming to realize at the same time as me that he'd seized my waist. He let go as I called out to Caleb. "Come back inside. Get yourself dry before we go out there."

He glanced up over his shoulder, then back to his home before finally trudging up the stairs. Inside, he shook his head like a dog, showering Jonas and me. I gave him a dramatic eye-roll, but he just shrugged and bit his lip.

Ten minutes later, he was wearing dry clothes. Also, we all donned rain gear and wet-boots — too big, in my case. I tucked Mom's digipar into my jeans pocket. Then we braved the rain.

Even with the heavy rubber boots, it was probably easier walking on the rain-soaked beach-sand than if it were dry. Soon we came to the fringing brush, squelching between wet bushes and through mud that sucked at my feet. Twice I got stuck and had to clutch the top of the oversized boot through the rain pants, then haul it free. Finally, we arrived at the over-grown porch of Caleb's once-grand double-story white house. Only the stairs held fast. The deck lay broken and half-submerged in overgrown grass. Plus, the plant-infested doorway exited more than six feet above us.

Jonas shrugged a shoulder. "Leg up then, Cass?"

I threw him a withering stare. "Sure. I'll give you a leg up." Though I knew he'd meant me to do the climbing.

"The back door might be easier," Caleb decided with a teasing lilt.

So, we pursued him through the mud around the side of the house and into a large courtyard. This wall had lasted. A single concrete step led up to the door. The rotten wood drooped on a single hinge and less overgrowth buried this entrance. Caleb tried to push it open, but it came free from its last hold and crashed to the concrete. We tiptoed over the broken wood and crossed the threshold to enter the home where Eric had once found joy and happiness—full of life with his parents' laughter and his brother's teasing, youthful voice. Now only a lost, forlorn shell existed.

I wiped water from my face and peered around. We'd entered what could only have been the scullery. Beneath cracked granite countertops, white cupboard doors dangled or were crunched up on the dust-encrusted, once-white floor tiles. The cupboards were bare. A robot cleaner lay on its side with half its innards ripped out — probably by people who'd survived the initial impact. Circuit boards were slung over its torso from tangled wires. A home dry-cleaning machine now graced the center — wrenched free from the wall. Its man-sized oval door lay open and the hanger area was gone.

After skirting the debris, we edged from the pantry into the kitchen. Neither looked in any better shape. A fridge door swung loose, clearly having been long-since ransacked.

An arched entrance led us into the hallway. A vision of a young Eric and Caleb played in my mind. Two near-identical, seven-year-old blond boys chased each other through the long passage, both tall for their ages. I barely noticed the soft smile forming on my mouth, but Caleb did. "What are you thinking?"

I peeked up at him. "How do you know I'm thinking?"

"You're smiling. My best assumption is that it has something to do with my brother."

I half-laughed, half-snorted a "Maybe." My focus dipped to the piece of straw he twirled between two fingers. "A million things you do remind me of Eric. He's always fiddling with some piece of grass he's picked up in the most unlikely places."

Caleb chuckled. "Decide, will you? You're exactly like Eric. You're not at all like Eric. Which one is it?"

I rolled my eyes and spun away, but not before noticing the smile forming on Caleb's mouth — an unusual mix of contentment and teasing.

The huge dining area stepped down into an enormous lounge. I swept a finger over what must have once been a grand suite. Thick dust coated my finger and the smearing of cream leather emerged beneath its dark gray coat. I wiped it off on my still-wet rain suit.

A dark wood bookshelf took up an entire wall and was filled with cobwebbed books. Dust covered every visible surface of three lampstands, shades, side-tables and an oval coffee table. Grey fluff encrusted a lopsided, three-legged ornament display cabinet. One glass and wood door flopped, the other crushed on the pine-wood flooring. Cobwebs laced every ceiling corner and formed strings from the lampshades to their bases, as well as beneath the coffee and side-tables. Paintings and photos lay crushed to the ground.

The only lingering wall-decor—and they only speckled a single inner wall—were seven clocks. They formed the shape of a hexagon around a central timepiece. No glass protected their faces, and a thick layer of dust obscured whatever colors or numbers had once adorned them. Their silver hands lay still, but I blinked a few times and gaped. They'd endured—fully *intact*!

For a long while Caleb stared at the clocks, the end of the straw between his lips. Then he flicked it aside and crooned a soft, familiar chant.

Chapter Thirty-Nine

If a song and the wind and the rain, tell six,
The ocean, a lake and the tree are nine,
Then where would you meet with your nearest and
dearest?
Why? Where the sun and the moon misalign.

I slid my gaze up to his. "So, this…rhyme…*is* a riddle."

Caleb smoothed his fingers over the top of the center one, then absently studied, then wiped the grime on his rain-suit. "My parents collected these clocks from around the world. Each symbolized the city of its source. I have this memory of our mother rehearsing with us, over and over for what felt like months. She never talked about the clocks. Or at least, not at the same time. Don't get me wrong. She talked about them…a *lot*! Just not while we recited." He gulped. "Eric once asked why it was important. Our father sat right over there" —Caleb turned and signaled toward a single-seater—"reading a newspaper. He laughed, saying it was nothing more than an old family rhyme they hoped we'd teach our kids one day."

I wiped my finger lightly over a small spot on the central face. When I lifted it, not merely dust came away. In its wake, only the shiny silver backing loomed. I squinted. "Has the original image turned to dust?"

Jonas went to the far side of Caleb. "Do you think we can clean it without touching the surface?" He lilted the last bit as if uncertain of the fact but concluded with a soft blow.

Since I stood on the far side of the clock from Jonas, loose dust billowed into my face and he chuckled.

I choked over my retort. "Seriously? That's not funny! And"—I glared at him—"your blowing dust at me hasn't helped at all!"

The gray coat still clung fast—as if embedded into the image.

I still coughed when Caleb clapped a hand on my back, the corner of his mouth quirking up. I shied away from the result of that smile, as it highlighted the lines in his cheeks, and I barely caught his next comments. "It is a *little* funny. Your skin is still damp. You should see what you look like."

When I wiped at my face, they both burst into roaring laughter.

"Now you've made it worse. Come on. Let me help you with that." Caleb pulled up the arm of his rain-jacket. With one hand at the nape of my neck, he wrapped the sleeve of his navy hoodie over the fingers of his other.

I peeked up at him before averting my gaze. But it was long enough for those accursed slits in his cheeks and surreal eyes to tingle my senses! I let myself drift into my imagination, where it was Eric laying one warm hand on my neck and pressing his sleeve-covered fingers to my face. With the softest touch, he brushed at my skin. I yearned to lean into his chest, wanted him to wrap himself around my body. But this wasn't Eric, not his chest, not his arms or his hands.

Caleb seemed to sense my discomfort, because he cleared his throat. When I looked, he again concentrated on the clocks. "Okay. So, trying to clean them won't help. And that's assuming they *do* in fact correlate to the rhyme. Even if the images were visible, I'm not sure I could decipher their meanings. Why didn't she just tell us?" His last question was clearly rhetorical.

Jonas observed the clocks, patting his chin. After a long while, he rebalanced his weight but continued gaping. Finally, he offered Caleb a questioning gaze. "Do you remember the image on each clock? Also, did your parents ever change the order?"

Caleb flattened his mouth and folded his arms. "I was seven" — he emphasized the last word and repeated even slower — "seven. Did *you* remember details with any clarity when *you* were that age?" A fine spray of spittle flew out with the question.

Jonas held up his palms in surrender. "Okay, dude. I'm not suggesting you should, only if you did, we could match the lines of the rhyme to specific clocks."

I followed Jonas' pattern of thought. "Let's go through it one line at a time."

Caleb recited the first phrase again.

It got me musing — albeit aloud. "The *'tell six'* part" — I air quoted — "makes sense now that the stage is set. It refers to the time."

Caleb gestured a hand over the display. "Yup. But which one of these?"

Jonas began pacing. "Do you recall if any alluded to music or the weather? Let's start with music."

Jonas halted beside Caleb, facing the clocks square on. He steepled his fingers in front of his chest as I bit my lip — my breath arresting.

Caleb exhaled a deep sigh, face slackening. Finally, he reopened them. "If I'm right, one was from Vienna, Austria. It depicted nothing about the weather but had music notes and photos of some ancient composers."

Jonas paced again. "Okay, so do you remember which of these it was, then?" Without slowing, he waved a hand between the seven clocks.

Caleb shut himself away behind his eyelids. A long moment later, he dipped his chin in a nod and seemed to absorb the timepieces into his mind. "It could be the upper right-hand one. Mm-m…I'm not sure."

Jonas didn't hesitate. "What about weather — wind or rain?"

Neither did Caleb. "One featured an abstract kind of wind. Commonwealth Bay, Antarctica." He jabbed his finger toward the bottom left clock. "That one."

I grimaced, my posture collapsing. "Antarctica? Why would you even go there?"

"Not us. Our parents. Research, I'm guessing. Many of their trips excluded Eric and me. We stayed home with our nanny since we had to go to school while they went off on their adventures."

I snorted, "Adventures!" and smirked. "Anyway, what about the rain part?"

Caleb shook his head. "It doesn't ring a bell. Let's come back to that one later."

Jonas suggested, "Since we're looking at cities with distinguishing traits, if it refers to highest rainfall, I know this one." He continued tentatively. "Did your parents ever visit Māwsynrām, India?"

Caleb skittered his gaze left and right so fast, he made me think of a computer accessing memory banks for information. After a moment, they relaxed. "Extreme right."

"So that's line one!" I concluded and reached for 'rain', while Caleb selected 'music' and Jonas moved a hand to 'wind'.

Caleb stopped us with a raised hand. "Wait! Knowing my parents, we should set them in sequence."

My forehead tightened, and my mouth pulled into a contemplative pout. "As in, like the rhyme?"

"Yes. Me first, then you, Jonas and Cassidy, you move last." As he spoke, Caleb turned the short hand of his clock to six and the long hand to twelve. He transferred his attention to Jonas and finally to me.

Then he went on to line two. "I'm guessing the ocean in the second line refers to an island, so that would be this one — Zanzibar Island." He shoved a finger at the left-most face.

Jonas tapped his lips with an index finger. "If the first two lines cover six images, aren't we missing some, then? Or do the last two lines refer to only one clock?"

Caleb looked up and to the right. "Yup," he agreed in a whisper. "Now I think about it, I recall that one clearly. It's at the top left — a family photo taken during a total eclipse. Or rather, it was taken just after the eclipse. Two minutes past noon."

I blew an exasperated huff. "Okay, Caleb. So, let's get this straight. You struggle to recall the layout of the clocks, but *that* little detail, you remember with ease?"

Caleb didn't hesitate. "Eric often teased me about him being the eclipse and me just the photo because I was born two minutes after him...and...I was pretty much always late for...*everything*." Caleb glanced down at his shoes and shrugged, his voice sheepish and even softer. "Strange what you remember."

Jonas cleared his throat. "Well, that means, besides the eclipse one, which we should do last, we must set the ocean one and the other two to nine o'clock."

"Except..." My words came slow and uncertain. "We still need the order. So, we have to figure out at least one of those two."

Caleb stared at the timepieces on the wall, shifting his gaze from left to right in slow repetition. "Between the middle clock and bottom right, one must be about trees and the other about a lake, but for the life of me, I can't conjure up any images in my head."

Jonas shrugged a shoulder. "What about trying the order out, first one way then the other?"

Caleb settled his gaze on Jonas—not contemplative, deadpan. "And trigger a failsafe that destroys everything we're hoping to find? If there's one thing I know about my parents, there's no room for failure— which means it has to be exact."

I distracted them from their testosterone-fueled glare. "So, if we're talking about trees...what about the Amazon jungle? Did your parents ever go there?"

"Do you honestly think I didn't consider that?" Caleb seemed to measure his next sentence. "Yes, they spent half a year in Leticia, Amazonas. But I can't remember if any of these came from there or even depicted or referenced the town or its surroundings."

Jonas tried a different tactic. "What about the lake? Loch Ness, perhaps?"

Caleb's stare dissolved into a meditative glaze. For a long while he remained silent, before giving a sluggish, focused nod, his words unsure. "Bottom right."

Although he'd spoken as if groping, I didn't doubt his conclusion. "I assume we must set the family photo one to the time it was taken — twelve-o-two."

Jonas cocked his head and frowned, seemingly analyzing my statement.

Caleb didn't hesitate for a second. "Yes. So, the sequence is…"

Jonas selected the left-most clock, Caleb the center, and I aimed for the lower-right one. Caleb continued. "…Jonas…Cassidy…okay, now me."

We had set three to six o'clock, and three to nine. Only the top left clock to finish. Jonas nodded at it. "That one is yours, bro."

In slow-motion, Caleb reached his hand toward it. He pushed the short hand to twelve and began altering the long hand, but jerked away. "It's not right. This was too easy."

My eyes flew wide. "Too *easy*!"

He didn't take his focus from the clocks. "Yes. Imagine the images *were* intact. It would have been straightforward for anyone who knew the rhyme. And yes, before you say it, I know what you're thinking…only Eric and I knew it. But my parents didn't think like that." He paused, rubbing his chin. "Do you think we should be considering the time zones of each location?"

"As you pointed out before, bro, you were *seven*." Jonas stretched out the number like Caleb had done before. "Surely your parents *wanted* you guys to get this right. If so, why further complicate it? You'd be messing with time zones that fluctuated in summer and winter." He placed his hands on his hips. "Where was the photograph taken, by the way?"

"Right here in our back garden." Without tilting his head back, Caleb peered at the ceiling, rocking his head from side to side as if weighing the possibilities. "Okay. You have a point. But just so you know…we have one shot at this. One. Get it? So, if we're wrong—" He broke off, allowing us to draw our own conclusions.

I sucked in a breath. Everything lay in the balance with this single action. Jonas flashed me a glance, his gaze tight and brow furrowed.

Neither of us said a thing as Caleb coughed. "Well, here goes." He stretched out a hand and slowly inched the long hand around the clock face. It landed on twelve-o-two with a clunk.

Chapter Forty

A mechanical noise rose from behind the clocks. The wall didn't change shape, but it vibrated. We stayed rooted, our gazes bolted on the hexagon before us, as the quaking intensified. Something deep within the wall clicked and ground — as if multiple cogs had awakened, crunching together after too long. The sheer violence of it threatened to bring down the entire wall. Plaster crumbled away. Huge clumps crashed to the floor. Each vacant patch exposed a shiny silver background. Overhead, the ceiling buckled, then parted. I ducked away, scanning upward, and rested on the same dazzling metal. From ceiling to floor, a crack formed between the clocks, interlocking, squared-off teeth pulling away from each other. The center timepiece settled right of the divide. Then the noise stopped. Nothing remained of that portion of the wall but the parting silver doors, which revealed a small, empty chamber. Silence descended. I gaped into the vacant room, stunned.

It didn't stay quiet for long before cogs started crunching. This time the noise came from above the rear wall of the chamber. *Click, click, whirr. Click, click, whirr.* In slow motion, a dust-covered silver staircase glided lower and lower until it met the floor with a thud. Silence fell once more.

Caleb wore a soft smile, his head tilted to the side. "Like I said...nothing they ever did was straightforward."

With a smirk, Jonas hiked his eyebrows. "It's pretty impressive though." He gestured a hand toward the stairs. "Well, don't keep us in suspense, bro. The honor is yours."

Caleb chanced a tentative step onto the first dusty stair, then tested his weight. "It's solid enough." He shrugged and tried the second.

I followed, with Jonas behind me. The stairway led into a small room. A large safe filled the far wall—a large, very locked safe.

"So, did you bring the dynamite then?" Jonas snorted at his joke.

As we gawped, the blue outlines of a virtual keypad took shape, protruding toward us.

Jonas turned to Caleb. "So, let me guess...You know exactly what the combination of that thing is."

"Oh yeah, of course. Look! It's written all over my forehead." Caleb thrust his face toward Jonas, one side of his mouth in a smile. "As it happens, that one is easier."

He wavered for so long, I wondered if he planned on announcing it at all. My voice came out slow and cynical as I displayed my palms. "And the answer to that is...?"

"Our home security code." He stopped again, and I arched my brows. Before I could add another snide remark, he continued. "E0521C0523."

Jonas grimaced. "That seems complicated. So, I'm guessing, like with the family photograph, there's some random reason you remember it," he lilted as if asking a question.

Caleb puffed a tiny smile. "The first five digits are Eric's time of birth and the second" — he bounced a one-shouldered shrug and a quick tilt of his head — "mine. Plus, we used it all the time."

Jonas nodded. "Ah-ha. That's because your parents left you guys here while they were off gallivanting."

I cut in before Caleb could return Jonas' serve, signaling with my palm to the safe. "Can we get this show on the road already?"

Caleb looked at Jonas, then me, before striding to the safe. On the glowing blue virtual keyboard, he entered the code.

The safe clicked and opened, the surrounding walls lighting up in the same blue outlines. Inside the safe, on a dusty glass shelf, lay a fusion power cell and a small triangular virtual experience cube.

In slow motion, Caleb reached inside, fingers trembling as he lifted the VE cube and power cell. He turned and handed me both. "Won't you do this, Cassidy? My damned hands won't keep still."

The surrounding blue lights danced off the VE cube as I turned it over in my palm. Using my nails, I pried open the back of the triangular device as Jonas got the fusion cell from Caleb. When I held it out to him, he slotted the cell in place with a click. After resealing the VE, I handed it back to Caleb. He moved to the general center of the room and set it on the floor, right-side-up.

Jonas chuckled. "It makes no sense they call this a cube when it's a triangle."

Caleb pulled back. "You know *why* that is, right?"

Jonas scrutinized the ceiling. "It's not something I took to studying in any great depth, but I take it you did."

Either Caleb missed the sarcasm in Jonas' voice or he didn't care. Either way, he appeared to enjoy sharing his understanding of the device. "The core is a cube. With this one, the triangular shape is its refraction shell. The exteriors of some VE cubes are also rectangular with the refraction mirrors inside."

"Right." Jonas dragged out the word. "Thanks for the science lesson. I'm guessing you know this because—" He cut off at the familiar whirring of the VE cube. Light shot up from its center, then opened like a blossoming flower as it sucked us into its virtual world.

A man and woman in jeans, sneakers and T-shirts appeared, as real as if they'd showed up in front of us. He towered—as tall as Eric and Caleb, with the same distinct dimples and short, wavy, dark-blond hair. A head shorter, she'd tied her long, sleek dark hair in a high ponytail. With their backs to the safe, they clutched hands, their expressions bleak. Her enormous eyes shone the familiar, unusual aquamarine. They were both so...real.

In milliseconds, I gleaned those details before Caleb's gasp overshadowed my thoughts. He withdrew a step—no, several steps back—almost stumbling.

I reached for his hand, but Jonas got to him first, catching his upper arm and steadying him. Caleb seemed unaware—frozen in a trance.

His father spoke — his quivering voice not masking the Texan accent. "Caleb." He cleared his throat, shaking his head slowly. "We hope beyond hope Eric is with you and it is merely your DNA activating the virtual experience. If that's the case, restart the VE once you've both touched it. Regardless, we're creating scenarios with each possibility in mind." He hesitated.

A tear slid over the woman's lower eyelid, her voice feminine and light, her Texan accent pronounced. "I guess we must be grateful if either of you makes it. The odds are so tiny." Tears slipped down her cheeks.

The man inhaled a deep breath and continued. "Caleb, take notes, son. We'll be supplying a heap of information." He paused, waiting for Caleb to ready himself.

I extracted Mom's digipar from my pocket. As I thumb-tapped its center, it unfurled and wriggled flat in mid-air before me. I picked up the digipen lying atop it.

Caleb frowned, semi-aware. He closed his fingers around the shaft of the digipen.

I kept my voice slow and gentle. "Enjoy this moment with your parents, Caleb. I'll take notes."

He fired me a glance of more confusion than defiance. But without a word, he released the digipen and again focused on his parents.

He gulped back emotions, his Adam's apple bouncing. "I know we'll take the VE for Eric, but he should have been here with me." He cleared his throat and went silent, slumping his normally confidence-bearing shoulders.

Caleb's father flashed his wife a glance before returning his gaze to the VE recorder — to us. The scene shifted ever so slightly, as if the angle, the lighting or the time of day had changed.

Caleb's mother spoke now, seeming unable to consider that only one of her boys would make it. "My beautiful sons. You'll get to watch this after we're long gone. I'm so sorry we won't be there to raise you, to see you grow into young men. Graham is the one man we trust to love and care for you, though. We're certain he'll forever remain an important part of your lives. Of what he knows, we're not sure how much he'll tell you or what you'll establish on your own." She cast a loving glance at her husband, then went on. "We developed a longevity drug which slows natural aging by ten times.

Although our intention is for everyone with Graham and Gina to live and see the planet recover from the meteorite strike, we won't witness it. Gina promised to take our family into Petriville, but after Dad and I got ourselves exposed to radiation, she refused. Some time ago we supplied her and Graham the longevity formula, along with two other drugs. An annual memory wipe solution erases exactly a single year of memories. We intended for her and Graham to administer it annually for nine out of every ten years. The reason we created this is that we're concerned about the psychological effects of an unnaturally long life. They should use the neutralizer once Earth is ready to repopulate—a counter to the longevity drug. We mean for most everyone to age naturally from that time forward."

She paid too much attention to her very white sneakers before wiping at her eyes and hugging herself with one arm. Caleb's father took over. "That is…everyone besides our sons. We hope we're doing right by you in wanting you to live as long as humanly possible." Uncertainty flickered in his gaze, as if he were second-guessing the morality of their decision. After a long moment, he opened them. "We gave you each slightly different variants of an irreversible longevity drug—*Livvie*." He swallowed and blinked. "Your DNA now carries unique abilities. But we'll get to that later."

He peered at his wife, who pressed her palms to her cheeks. Then he continued. "If a person gets resuscitated—something which has over past years become increasingly common in a growing list of circumstances—the longevity drug has a negative side-effect. During our research we found it causes rapid aging. In fact, the increase is ten times the norm. The good news is, we created a cure that results in subjects aging at the same rate as you boys. It is *important* to note something. Nearly instant death will occur if these subjects receive *Ellie* or *Ellen* alone *or* in any combination. One of them, however, is part of the cure. We'll walk you through the correct recipe. It is with some luck that the annual memory wipe solution halts the onset of this ailment, however, only if administered for at least nine out of every ten years. More than a year passing between doses voids the effect and speeds up the resuscitated subject's aging process. We'll deliver the chemical formulae for *Ellie*, the longevity drug, then *Ellen*, the neutralizer—and finally the cure."

Chapter Forty-One

The focus of the VE changed, landing on a large white board with a string of entirely unfamiliar black writing.

Mr. Morgan went on, calling it out as I copied the text into Mom's digipar, with Caleb and Jonas double-checking. He repeated the *Ellie* formula a further three times to be sure we'd gotten it right.

Caleb's mom spoke up. "Now we will give you the *Ellen* formula, then the remedy for the people who" — Caleb's parents grew fuzzy then came back into focus — "st…ar…t… a…ge…ing—"

They froze in place, as unmoving as statues — steady and lifeless. I gasped as a second later, they disappeared entirely.

We remained silent, as if sound or movement might stop them from reappearing. It didn't help. A muted, fuzzy blur appeared then blinked away. Over the next few minutes, the pattern repeated several times. Then that too stopped. We halted, stunned. A quarter hour passed before we finally conceded. The footage was faulty. Numb horror washed over me as Jonas murmured a one-word question…one name. "Harriet?"

The impact ran through my mind. Caleb and even Jonas gawked at the spot the twins' parents had left bare.

Gulping back emotion, I tiptoed into the topic. "It makes no sense. Harriet was never resuscitated! We'd have known—" I cut off as the possibility dawned. The result burst from my throat in a gasp. "Oh…"

In a daze, Jonas turned to me, managing a soft murmur as tears poured in rivers down his cheeks. "The nine wiped years?" He phrased it as a question, but it came as more of a realization.

He drifted his gaze back to the vacated spot. Caleb still stared ahead of him, far removed from our torment.

As true comprehension awakened of Harriet's future, my heart shredded, my voice a whimper. "Oh, Jonas."

If, somehow, that had happened to Harriet…if Gina had resuscitated her…we couldn't save her. Only the annual memory wipe solution offered any salvation. But with Gina's stash exhausted and no recipe, how?

I didn't realize I was shivering or that tears were sliding down my cheeks. Not until Caleb laid one steady hand on Jonas' shoulder and the other on mine.

Caleb understood the reality of the situation. "We could still get the recipe—if Gina's technicians can repair the footage." He sounded as doubtful as I felt.

A racked sob burst from my chest. "Harriet!" I wailed the word and Jonas hunched over, crossing his arms over his stomach as if hugging himself— heartbroken in the way this knowledge would destroy his parents, would shatter Liam. Just as Gina had caused our father to live an extended lifespan without our mother, so would Liam face the same fate without Harriet at his side. A fresh wave of anguish erupted. "Liam," I whispered, as if he could somehow hear me over the distance.

For a long while, Caleb stood aside before his soft voice of reason broke the silence. "It looks like there's nothing more to do here. How about we get this thing back to Petriville?" He released his hands from our shoulders, picked up the VE cube and slipped it into his jeans pocket.

A light made its way through my heartbreak. I was going home to Eric. A wave of guilt chased, rushing over me. How could we break this to Harriet?

Caleb guided us from the small room, down the dusty silver stairs, through the gaping wall, to the kitchen and outside. Rain no longer showered the land, but sunshine peeked through the clouds. The clean scent of satiated plants filled the air. Insects chirruped in the surrounding small trees, bushes and grass. Few birds chirped, though — a reminder of their near total decimation after the meteorite strike. As we moved around the house, Caleb snatched up a fresh piece of straw-like grass.

On the beach, the vaguely visible, giant waterball glinted in the rainbow-colored light bouncing off the wet Kaleidotonium surface.

Numbness blurred our walk across the sand. While mounting the stairs, Caleb turned. I observed his gaze deviate to his old home one last time. A soft, sad smile played on his lips. I closed my fingers around his and squeezed. "Come. Eric's waiting for you."

Caleb met my gaze, puffing a smile. "Not that he knows I'm coming…unless your brother spilled." He let out a slow breath.

Dropping his hand, I stalked after Jonas through the entrance. "Trust me, Caleb. Liam didn't tell Eric."

Inside the control chamber, Jonas poured over the low silver column and virtual control panel. He pulled back one of the blue outlines in the shape of a lever. With a *whirr*, the entrance-stairs slowly flattened and the doorway glided up, quickly sucking into place.

We were going home. My stomach clenched with a mixture of excitement and dread as, after Jonas and Caleb, I sank onto a recliner.

Jonas cleared his throat. "I don't want to believe this. I'd rather think they're going to fix the VE cube, and we'll have Harriet back to her old self...fit and well."

I shook my head, floating to an entirely different headspace. "I'm glad Liam isn't here."

We fell silent while the cords pinned us down and the masks clamped over our faces.

The now familiar grinding, rocking and shifting preceded the expected slow bounce of the chairs. My brain didn't rattle as much in my head. *Or my numb mind is making the launch appear smoother.* But before long, the straps and masks withdrew, and the seats inclined.

In enormous contrast to our first trip, Jonas leaped up, cleared his throat and shoved his shoulders back. "Right! Who's hungry then?"

Without comment, Caleb followed. I decided to encourage Jonas' positive frame of mind, however forced. "At least no one's running to the bathroom this time."

Chapter Forty-Two

Our return journey took eight days. When we morse-messaged the control center, we told Austin about retrieving the VE cube but that it was faulty. A few messages bounced back and forth, but we kept Mr. and Mrs. Morgan's revelations to ourselves. Austin seemed confident that Gina's technicians could repair the device. I silently asserted Austin's encouragement to myself, playing the mantra over and over in my mind. *We can stop this. We can save Harriet.* In my heart, though, I wasn't sure.

Caleb seemed less like himself now — less cavalier — and more responsible and perceptive, like Eric. It felt unnerving, but also sort of comforting.

On the seventh night, after a self-heating roast beef dinner, Jonas retired with a headache.

For a while, Caleb and I sat in comfortable silence, him reading a paper novel and me re-reading Mom's letter. When I glanced up, he was watching me.

I found his gaze and cocked my head, drawing out the word, "What?"

His mouth formed a fake smile. "I've been going over something."

"Ah-ha?"

"What's going to stop that woman from throwing me in prison right beside Eric and murdering us both like she did to your mother?"

I froze and gulped. "I honestly didn't consider that!" My jaw tightened. "It starts me wishing I'd killed her when I had the chance! I swear, if she touches a hair on Eric's head…" I trailed off. A memory surfaced of when Susan had spoken to Gina in prison. "I got the impression she doesn't intend to harm Eric. Also, she told Susan we should find you. I might be wrong, but I don't think she means to hurt you, either."

Caleb averted his narrowing eyes. "Well, if she does, then rather me than Eric."

Although Eric would do the same, Caleb's words warmed me. Emotion rushed through my body as our gazes locked.

An insane desire clutched me, the yearning to launch over the table, to throw my arms around his neck as he gripped me around my back, to kiss him, slide my hands beneath his shirt and over his warm, smooth skin.

As heat flooded my cheeks, I dropped my head into my hand, then returned to Mom's digipar—to her letter.

Caleb didn't let me disappear into my shame but cleared his throat. "Would you read it to me? Well, you don't have to…but you got to hear our parents' message to us, and—" he cut off.

I looked up at him. "Why?"

"It would be nice to get a sense of who she was."

"It's not pleasant."

Caleb shrugged. "Has anything been lately?"

So, I read.

To my most adored Peter, Liam and Cassidy,

Of all outcomes, I never thought I'd say goodbye to you like this. Should I apologize? I suppose you won't want that. Please understand that I face my next journey with peace. Nothing any of you did or didn't do caused my fate. This is on me alone. The world is full of danger.

Peter, my heart breaks to know I'll never again feel the warmth and safety of your loving embrace. I long for it, even now. You are my heart and soul. You always were, even in high school.

Liam and Cassidy, my heart explodes with pride when I think of you both. Continue with your studies. Forget all that has happened. Love and learn and grow into all you're meant to be. Don't be held back by this tragedy.

In the olden days, people who had committed treason died. Even if you blame Gina, it will not help bring you comfort or me back. I'm almost embarrassed that I denied involvement because someone discovered where I'd hidden the notes in my office – and, of course, they then alerted Gina.

Please know that it was never my intention to hurt the three of you – the people I love most in this world. So yes, in my own way, I am sorry.

Your ever-loving wife and mother,
Emily

I fell silent and Caleb sat across from me, pressing his lips together.

For a long while he fidgeted with his fingers before speaking, his words tentative. "Don't get me wrong, but isn't the phrasing in the second to last paragraph strange?"

I swallowed and glared at him. "You never met my mother! How can you say that?"

Caleb tried to reach for my shoulder and I slapped his hand away, tears blurring my vision.

Instead of touching my shoulder, he took my hand. "I'm not trying to upset you, Cassidy."

I snatched it away. "Leave me alone!"

Caleb's brows pulled together in deep furrows as he stood. "I'm sorry... I never meant—" He broke off, slouching his shoulders as he made for the bedroom.

I wasn't even sure it was his words that had me raging or if I was angry with myself. When he'd closed his hand around mine, that stupid tingle had twitched in my belly. For all these weeks, thoughts of Eric and Amanda had made my stomach clench. How fickle was I that the simple touch of another boy's hand might have sent me into his arms—worse still, Eric's twin brother? I imagined arriving home to Eric kissing Amanda and them both smirking at my heartbreak.

That night, a restless, tortured sleep seized my opportunity to rest.

Chapter Forty-Three

Late the next morning, the waterball ordered us to strap in. The movement was less severe than before. It ground and adjusted, bumping us about. Occasionally a metallic clang accompanied the noises.

When the waterball finally came to rest, the masks withdrew from our faces and the cords slithered away. The entrance door released its suction and the stairway folded open toward the floor.

Without a thought for our belongings, I beelined to the door, with Caleb and Jonas behind, forming a triangle. I felt like an astronaut atop the stairs with my companions—about to descend from a spaceship after returning to Earth, victorious and celebrated. A crowd of fifty or more cheering patrons encircled the waterball. From the virtual monitors, keyboards and control panels which edged the room, men and woman got to their feet and swiveled toward us. I peeked back and up at how Caleb's muscles stiffened while he scanned the room.

Front and center, Austin's bulk towered over everyone. No wonder he'd terrified me before. With his legs spread and enormous fists propped on his hips, he looked every bit the gorilla I remembered. But he wasn't looking at me or Jonas. He cocked his head, focused on Caleb. Finally, he turned his gaze to Jonas and me.

He gestured with a palm at Caleb, scrutinizing him. "Does your *boyfriend* know about this? What about your brother and those two skinny blokes? They told us nothing."

"Not yet, I hope." With a shrug, I descended the stairs with Jonas and Caleb behind.

When we neared the group, Austin hustled four young teens toward the waterball. "Go on. What are you hanging around for? Collect their luggage and be sure it shows up at their homes." He flipped to Caleb. "I'm guessing yours goes to Mr. Porter's house?" He lilted in question.

From beside me, Caleb smirked. "Indeed, it does." Then he flicked his gaze to the four youngsters bounding up the stairs to the waterball. "Gray pack."

I didn't bother telling them mine was the pink one. If they couldn't figure that out…

I looked around the room—the place where our mission had begun. At that moment, a movement at the entrance snared my attention. "Liam!"

He shoved his way through the crowd, panting as he halted before us. He didn't even properly greet us.

Excitement filled his rapid-fire words. "Everyone is in the town square, expecting you guys. When they announced you made it into the chute, I bee-lined for this place. Austin's men tried to stop me at the station entrance, but they couldn't hold me back. I caught the train they sent to fetch you. Everyone is so happy you guys are back. There's a major celebration out there." He waved his hand in the general direction of town.

Then he nodded at Caleb. "Neither of them knows a thing. You're going to give the old man a heart attack."

Finally, Liam hauled me into a hug. "So, Cass, these idiots got you home after all."

With a chuckle, I heaved him away. "You're squishing me, Li. Anyone would swear you hadn't seen me for a year."

"The way Dad's been fretting, he guilt-tripped me into thinking I'd done the wrong thing in leaving you."

He turned back to Jonas, face solemn. "Before you ask, Harriet's okay. But…" —he gulped.

Jonas' eyes shot wide, voice a growl. "But what?"

Liam drew a ragged breath. "Some people have been in the medical facility. But Harriet is tougher and fitter than most." His voice grated. "We're going to fix this, and she'll be back to herself in no time." It sounded as if he was trying to convince himself as much as Jonas.

Jonas lowered his gaze, his sigh weighted and bleak. "Bro…we need to talk."

Liam angled his face away. "And judging by your expression, I'm not going to like what you have to say, so what the hell is this?"

I slammed a hand to my hip. "Can't you see Jonas is exhausted? Give him a break! You'll know everything soon enough!" My annoyance quickly faded. "Where is Harriet now?"

Liam swallowed. "In the town square with Graham and our parents."

I glanced at Austin as he saluted. "Right! Let's get you kids to Susan." He spread his gorilla arms and swatted a path through the crowd to the door like Moses parting the water. "The party's over, you lot. Get back to work."

We pursued him through the doorway and up, up, up the spiral staircase. By the time we reached the top, I was gasping for breath. The silver bullet train rested at the platform, extending down the tunnel like a glinting, metallic worm.

Caleb shook his head. "Nice to see how the other half existed for the past 'hundred and ten' years." He emphasized the length of time and accompanied us into the train. I didn't bother sitting. A minute later, the youths boarded with our luggage and the doors glided shut.

As the train moved out the station toward town, I laid a hand on Caleb's forearm. "I'll show you the zoo one day." I thrust a thumb behind us. "It's kind of cool how she created a kind of Noah's ark for the animals—regardless of how awful she is to humans."

When the train stopped and opened its doors at the main station, I grabbed Caleb's arm, sped past Austin and leaped to the platform.

With a frown, Austin followed. "What's the rush?"

Caleb stared down at me with a confused grimace.

I squared up to Austin. "Since Eric wasn't with my brother, I'm assuming he's still in prison." It wasn't a question, but my voice rose in pitch. And," —I thrust out my chin—"I'm not leaving until Susan opens that door."

Austin puffed an exasperated sigh. "Very well. A deal is a deal."

After a moment's hesitation, he held his hand out toward the stairs, leading down to the prison cells. "After you."

I burst into a sprint, calling over my shoulder. "Caleb, wait here."

While racing down the silver stairs and taking them two at a time, I gripped the rail so as not to fall. All but swinging around the corners, I skidded into the side-tunnel then burst down the final staircase. My feet hit the lower tunnel in a run, Eric's cell etched in my head.

As I raised my focus and glimpsed who waited outside, my muscles seized and legs slowed. The only strength I could force into them was to muster a numb, wobbly walk.

Chapter Forty-Four

I glared, curling my lip into a snarl as I forced myself to take another step. My words came out in a growl. "What are *you* doing here?"

It wasn't Amanda who answered. She just gawked at me with an open mouth before fixating on her pretty pink sneakers and shuffling her feet.

Instead, from out of sight, a familiar, deep resonant river of sound entered the tunnel. "Cassidy? Cassidy? Is that you? Is it Cassidy? Tell me, Amanda! What's going on?" He snarled his last two sentences.

My throat constricted, energy surging into my muscles. I ran—no, sprinted—the last bit. "It's me, Eric. I'm here."

I skidded to a halt outside the cell, clutching the iron bars of the small window. Amanda backed up.

Eric covered my hands in his, warm and familiar, his voice so soft. "You made it, Cassidy." That single look expressed how I captivated him. Eric was so different from Caleb. Diametric. How could I have missed it?

His words raced through my head. Or at least, what he'd called me. 'Cassidy'. Not 'babe'. Not *my* Cassidy'. Simply 'Cassidy'.

Dread arose, and my stomach clenched. Before I could voice my mind's conjuring, Eric spoke as if reading my thoughts. "Oh, my Cassidy. You're home." He swallowed, his face flushing as he rested his head against the bars.

I laid my forehead on Eric's, his warmth seeping into me as I inhaled his dusky vanilla scent. Tears welled and trickled down my cheeks. Austin's voice echoed at the end of the tunnel. The four entrance guards strode toward us. I gave them space as each prodded a finger on the door.

It clicked and opened, and Eric pushed through. In an instant, he wrapped my body in his powerful arms, lifting me clean off the floor. Gone was his smooth, warm tone. He choked out a hoarse whisper. "Cassidy…Cassidy…Cassidy."

I clung to Eric's neck and settled into his embrace with the ease, the comfort, of a favorite sweater. This was home. My home. My Eric. Although he eased me to the floor, he didn't release his hold around my waist. Rather, he appeared to search my soul with his beautiful aquamarines as he bent forward and our lips met. A fusion of fireworks and heat exploded through me. A tear glided down Eric's cheeks too. If I'd had any lingering doubts about his loyalties, they melted away. A familiar warmth spread through me, pulsing through my veins.

Although our kiss started as a greeting, it didn't stay that way for long, because as Eric tasted my lips before guiding his tongue between, his mouth hardened— demanded. He firmed his grip around my body and a raging inferno grew inside me. I sighed, our heat merging. Eric's raw groan sent a hot thrill through my core. He deepened the kiss, pressing up against me, and when I responded with equal urgency, he shuddered.

But this wasn't our time. Eric seemed to realize it at the same moment as me. I withdrew from him and he looked down at me. "Did you find what Harriet needs?"

At his wording, I bit my lip to hide my grin. He'd said Harriet, not Amanda. And he didn't release me. He laced his fingers behind my back and leaned away, searching my gaze. "Tell me what happened out there, babe?"

"We've got plenty of time for that, Eric. Let's get you out of this hell-hole first, okay?"

"Mm-m." With a low chuckle, he released me, weaving his fingers between mine as we made for the exit.

I'd barely noticed that during our kiss Amanda had slunk away.

When we got to the stairs, she waited a little way up. She propped her palms on her hips, cocking her head and gazing at the ceiling. "What did I tell you, Eric? Of course she meant to return. She beat the odds once before." Amanda sounded impressed. Then she spoke to me. "He couldn't stop reminding me that you're the *love of his life*." Over the last words, sardonicism, bordering on annoyance, slipped into her voice. That was when I knew it. She *did* feel more for Eric than she let on. It was all I could do to stop my lip from curling up into a snarl.

Eric seemed oblivious to Amanda's emotions as he smiled down at me and squeezed my waist. "It's true, what she says. You *are* the love of my life."

I bit my lip. "There's something I need to tell you."

He squinted at me but didn't raise the question — distracted by Amanda, who held out her hand, palm up, for us to ascend the stairs ahead of her. "Can we please get out of here first? You two *love-birds* can catch up when you haven't got an entire town awaiting you."

Eric didn't turn his attention from me once as we climbed each level — as if I'd vanish if he did. I watched him too, absorbing every single nuance of the man I loved. It was as if we both tried to reconcile that we were finally together.

As instructed, halfway to the exit, Caleb waited beside Liam. Eric froze. He dropped his arm from my waist and gaped, his mouth hanging slack. For a moment he cast me a quizzical glance before sliding his focus back to his brother.

After the longest time, Eric managed a gasping choke. "Caleb?" Then again, softer. "Caleb? It can't be." His voice hardened. "Caleb?"

Neither brother sprinted forward — as if afraid to hope, fearful that their vision deceived them.

Instead, Caleb ceased all movement, becoming as still as a statue. It was Eric who moved. With a slow, uncertain gait, he made for his brother. Only when standing before each other did they shoot their arms out, gripping one around the shoulder and the other around the waist. Rough, strangled sobs poured from Eric, his words soft and stumbling. "Caleb. My brother. You found him. You brought my brother home. Does Graham know?"

After a long while, Eric freed an arm and closed his fingers over his eyes. He stepped back, staring at Caleb. For the second time, his arm shot out. This was for no embrace. He balled his fist and slammed it into Caleb's shoulder. His voice turned hard. "What the hell is this? You didn't think to let me know you're okay—or worse, let Graham know? We thought you *died*! You selfish cur."

Caleb slumped in resignation, his voice soothing. "It wasn't like that, Eric. I *did* nearly die with the others. Some guys found me and took me to their refuge. I'd just gotten strong enough again when this lot"—he swiveled a finger between Liam, Jonas and me. He veered his gaze past us and halted. His last word was a numb, distracted murmur—"arrived." I followed Caleb's frozen stare to Amanda. His voice rose as if something truly piqued his interest—not something, someone. "Who is *that*?"

I still stayed at the top of the stairs as Amanda got to my side.

I grinned. "Oh, Caleb. Meet Amanda. You know...the girl I've been telling you about."

He cleared his throat. "You were right. It's not surprising you felt threatened."

Not that I wanted him to blurt it out in front of Eric...or for that matter, Amanda.

I snarled at him, but Caleb didn't even notice. Eric, on the other hand, bit back a grin.

Caleb never once removed his attention from Amanda. He walked—almost floated—around Eric and on toward her, stretching out his hand. "Well, Amanda. It's my great honor to meet you."

Amanda's gulp got me sneering at her. She was too fixated on Caleb to notice, her voice unusually uncertain. "Likewise...Caleb, is it?"

It was as if they had always known each other, the way they drifted into easy banter, as though the rest of us had disappeared.

I headed to Liam, Jonas and Eric. As if my presence once again struck him, Eric reached for me and yanked me against his chest. Brushing a thick strand of dark hair from my face, he grazed his lips over mine. He tilted back, one hand on my waist, the other cupping my cheek. "Full of surprises, aren't you?" He looked at Caleb. As if stunned, he shook his head over and over. "Caleb's alive. My damned brother's alive." He drew in a sharp breath. "Graham is going to"—I finished the sentence with him—"have a heart attack." Then I added, "Yes, I know. I think we should ease him into this one."

"Okay, guys." Liam clapped his hands. "Time to meet your fans. And"—he clapped Jonas on the back—"your sister and parents are going to be beyond happy that you got back in one piece."

Liam raised his brows at Eric. "You and Caleb wait here until Cassidy and Jonas have appeased everyone. I want to see Graham's face when you guys come out. Amanda, I think you'd better wait too, since you were"—he hiked up a questioning eyebrow—"not supposed to be down there?" His voice rose as if in question, and he continued, "We'll fetch you when we're ready."

With that, he turned and traipsed toward the station exit.

I didn't want to extricate myself from Eric and beamed at how he seemed equally reluctant for me to go. With a satisfied chuckle down at me, he tightened his hold. Then, with a deep sigh, he allowed his hands to slip away.

Chapter Forty-Five

As the familiar doors glided open, I stepped from the station. Excitement coursed through me, blood roaring in my ears and goosebumps rushing over my skin. I halted atop the broad stairs overlooking the town square, squinting against the bright sun as I surveyed the enormous crowd. A roar erupted. Across the town square, digital billboards lit up and the Petrivillian Enterprises' bright orange banner pulsed. With the sounding of trumpets, the image burst into fireworks. High above the municipal building, the company flag waved, its flagpole rooted beside the old-style structure's wide Roman stairs.

At the front of the crowd, Jaya and Aaron beamed, flapping their arms in the air. Guilt washed over me. We'd promised to visit the old, now-free slave and Aaron. Under Susan's care, they'd gained weight. They looked healthier, their postures straighter. I returned their greeting and broad smiles.

A little to the side of them, Harriet stepped from the crowd. Before I knew it, I was racing down the stairs with Jonas on my tail. I flung my arms around her small, voluptuous frame as Jonas wrapped us both in his, our three heads making a spiral staircase.

Echoed sobs burst from our throats. "Harriet!" I cried.

As we pulled back, I examined her warm smile and the rounded dents in her cheeks. Harriet's bright blue eyes sparkled as I picked up a strand of her wavy blonde hair. "You look good, Harri. And your hair is glossy."

Jonas cupped her cheek. "Cassidy's right, little sister. You look…well."

Harriet jerked her head back, her speech as emphatic as ever. "What did you expect, Jo? That I'd have gotten old and withered in the weeks you've been away?"

I simpered, taking her hands in mine. "That's the Harriet we know. Damn, girl, it's so good to see you."

My face grew serious. "Have you heard?"

Harriet threw her hair over her shoulder to cascade down her back. "That the VE got corrupted? What do you think?" She tossed her observation skyward. "Of course, I heard! No way could they keep Liam out of the loop. And by extension" — she pointed both index fingers toward herself — "me."

Brows creasing, Jonas croaked, "We don't know if they can fix it."

Harriet threw him a wry smile. "Don't you remember? We didn't think you'd find anything at all. One step at a time, okay?" She sighed and her face slackened. "You guys did great." She glanced up. "Speaking of which, where's that ass-moron who tried to kill you?"

With a finger to my mouth, I looked around before arching my eyebrows in a shocked question. "Liam *told* you?"

Harriet held up her hands. "You didn't think he'd keep it from me? And no, I didn't tell…*anyone*."

Roger and Megan burst from behind Harriet, and Roger gripped Jonas in his thick forearms. "That's my boy. So, you made it home, did you then?"

Megan gave Jonas what looked like a thousand tiny kisses on the cheek. "Oh, my champion son. You've done it. You've saved your sister." Tears streamed down her cheeks.

Neither Jonas nor I had the heart to correct her as Roger and Megan turned equal affection on me.

At that moment, the petite, dark-haired Olivia ran at and leaped onto Jonas. A delighted laugh burst through his lips as he folded her into a hug. After a quick peck, he bent to give her a longer one, and finally a deep and sensuous kiss.

Roger lifted a brow at the two, peered at me and did a double take. With a shrug, I found I gave a contented smile.

A large hand landed on my shoulder, the smooth baritone sending a flood of warmth through me. "You made it, Cassidy."

I spun into a warm embrace and laid my cheek against a familiar chest, my voice a trembling gasp. "Daddy."

I didn't move until Joshua, Caroline, Samantha and Paul bustled from the crowd, immersing me in warm hugs. Joshua wore his familiar soft smile, his Nigerian tone welcoming. "You, young lady, have had enough adventures to last a lifetime, I should think."

The intensity of my sigh surprised even me. "I think I've had enough adventures to last *ten* lifetimes."

The family laughed at my choice of phrase.

Then Graham pushed through, his warm mahogany skin camouflaging the dark freckles on his cheeks. He must recently have had his tight salt-and-pepper curls trimmed short. He hauled me into a tight hug. "Maybe now that woman will release my son."

I beamed up at him, not wanting to give away the surprise — *or outright lie* — so I hedged. "I missed you, Graham."

From behind, Liam touched my arm. "Come, Cass."

He leaned toward Dad and spoke into his ear, and Dad cupped a hand on Graham's shoulder, coaxing him nearer the stairs as I pursued Liam up and toward the station entrance.

Austin erected himself like a sentry at the doorway. Before going through, I caught hold of Liam's arm. "What did you say to Dad?" Without expecting an answer, I scanned the enormous crowd. "It looks like the whole of Petriville is here."

He hiked a brow, commenting on the statement rather than responding to the question. "That's because the entire town *is* here. Everyone got affected in some way — either directly or indirectly." After that, he answered my question. "I told Dad to keep an eye on Graham. Seeing both his sons might prove too much for his ticker. He's a tough old codger, though...so he should be fine. It's just to be safe, you know."

With that, we walked through the glass sliding doors, lingering while they closed behind us.

Out of sight of the entrance, Amanda stayed away from the brothers, perhaps extending them space to reunite.

Eric kept gulping as he rested a hand on Caleb's shoulder. With a hand cupped to his mouth, tears flowed down Caleb's face. I'd never yet seen him this vulnerable—never imagined he could be. As we approached, Caleb half turned away, wiping both palms down his face.

Then he turned back, sucked in a breath and found my gaze. "I'm ready."

"Good, because we're done sticking around." I winked at Caleb but walked to Eric.

As Eric clasped my hands, he tilted his head to the side. He quirked his lip into a naughty smile. "Would you have known me? I mean, if we wore the same color T-shirts, jeans and sneakers."

I huffed a laugh. "But you're not."

Eric deepened his smile. "Obviously…but humor me. What if we were?"

I didn't miss a beat. "You guys don't even look the same. So, what do you think, Eric?"

He chuckled. "Well, that remains to be seen. You can be sure we'll test your assertion."

With a playful whimper, I twisted my mouth into a teasing smile. "More than once, no doubt."

Eric released my hand and fed an arm around my shoulder, yanking me into his side. "Never again am I letting you any farther from me than you are right now, so best you get used to it."

I looked sideways into his beautiful eyes and stretched up on my toes. Eric met me halfway, pressing his full, soft lips to mine. For a moment he pulled back and studied my expression before burying his face into my hair and speaking in a soft whisper, drawing out the first word. "Oh-h, my Cassidy. Don't leave me again. Promise you won't. Please?"

With a swallow, I closed my eyes. "I hope I never have to, Eric. I don't want to."

Liam clapped his hands. "Okay, guys. Let's get this show on the road."

With that, he led the way to the doors. I raised a hand to wave Amanda over, but she beelined for Caleb. Side-by-side, the four of us followed Liam.

As the doors opened, bright sunlight flooded the entrance. Eric blinked once…twice…three times before rubbing his eyes. Liam moved aside and spread his arms toward us, making us the limelight. The square exploded in cheers, amplified through the digital displays. I fixed on Graham.

He looked from Caleb and Amanda to Eric and me before yielding his gaze to his lost son. As if unable to trust his vision, he wiped at his eyes and repeated the process. He stumbled back, and Dad and Joshua balanced him while Eric and Caleb sprinted down the stairs. Olivia wailed, tugging Jonas toward Graham and the twins. When reaching them, she dropped his hand and threw herself at Caleb. As Harriet hustled toward her brother, I grinned uncontrollably. Except, we still had so much to do before we deserved happiness.

As Harriet and Jonas joined us, without so much as a word, Amanda strode down the stairs to Gregory. At that moment, Austin stalked over and patted Liam on the shoulder. "Not to cut your reunion short, but Susan is waiting for you."

He didn't give us the option to refuse. Instead, he ushered us down the stairs and brandished his arm as if to clear a path through the crowd.

I stopped him. "Caleb should go with us. He's the one with the VE."

Graham was still laughing and weeping as Austin looked between the twins. "Which one is he?" He didn't wait for an answer but shrugged and gestured them both over. "It's easier this way."

When they ignored his gesture, I met Eric's gaze but spoke to Austin. "Can't you give them a moment?"

Austin puffed an exasperated breath. "Time awaits no man."

Jonas sided with me, giving a heavy sigh. "Five minutes won't make an ounce of difference."

From behind, Roger walked up and laid a hand on Liam's shoulder. "Hey there, son."

Liam freed Harriet from his side. "This might take hours, babe. I'll come over later and tell you what Susan finds."

The whole incident seemed staged—pre-planned. Harriet clearly noticed too. As Roger enveloped his daughter with a thick forearm, she ripped away, snorting. "I'm not some breakable thing, Dad."

"No, you're most definitely not, my girl. But your mother thinks you are. Do *you* want to argue the point with her then?"

Harriet rolled her eyes and groaned. "Not really. No, I can't say I do."

With a heavy sigh, she surrendered, allowing her father to drag her toward her mother.

Chapter Forty-Six

Austin allowed the promised five minutes before lumbering up to them. He'd barely given the men enough time to reunite, never mind banter and laugh together. Now the initial shock had worn off, warm familiarity circulated between them. Graham did a double take, then turned his head slowly left and right, cupping a hand over his mouth. He swiped at his dark brown eyes, then again enveloped both boys, pulling them to him. He was a tad shorter than Eric and Caleb, though still unusually tall and well-proportioned. Other than that, in appearance at least, they shared no biological trace of similarity. Despite their genetic differences, the old man exhibited every outward appearance of a loving father. No one watching the three of them could have thought differently. Then Austin ushered them over.

Catching my hand mid-stride, Eric laced his fingers through mine. I laid my head against his shoulder as we pursued Austin through the middle of the town square.

Caleb walked as if in a trance, taking in the sights — the grassed areas scattered across the town square, the clock-like design, the large, shiny black numbers fronting the dual conveyors which stretched away into the suburbs, the shady trees and park benches, the cherub-adorned fountain. Then he looked up as we mounted the wide Roman stairs of the old-style stone municipal building and cut through its open-air foyer.

Austin shuffled us into an open elevator when Amanda caught up. She didn't wait for an invitation but bounded inside and squished in next to Caleb. He bit his lower lip and covered his mouth as if trying to hide a smile.

The doors closed, and the elevator glided up. They opened after a short while to reveal the extravagant office I'd called on not long before. My mind drifted to my first time here — minutes after Gina had murdered my mother — and I'd used the venom in Grandma's pen, hoping to end her tyranny.

Susan now stared through the bay windows overlooking the town square.

The snake-like, "Good day, Miss Jones," never came from her, but from a plush leather one-seater armchair that was angled toward the window.

With clasped hands, Eric and I tramped across the lavishly patterned carpet. It felt soft beneath my sneaker-clad feet.

I didn't hide my scowl as Gina popped her head around the edge of the armchair. "My, my... Look who the cat dragged in." Her focus swished from Eric beside me to Caleb beside Amanda. "So, the brother isn't dead after all. What luck. A backup." She hiked her brows and rounded on Amanda. "O-oh. There is yet hope for you, dearie, since batting your pretty eyebrows at the twin proved futile. Naturally, I never meant *that* one for you."

Amanda wasn't so easily put down. "I'd thank you, *Grandmother*, to butt out of my romantic interests. I only visited Eric to give him company, since you and Mother were determined to keep him locked up in there. Besides, we all know Eric insists he's *meant* for Cassidy" — she rolled her eyes — "or the other way around, at least."

Definitely bitter.

Gina lifted a teacup and saucer from a side table, grinning as if she were the Cheshire cat winning a jackpot. "Yes…" Her treacle-smooth snake-like voice oozed out — "of course." She lifted the cup to her lips, blew on the tea and took a sip, pointing her pinky finger.

I ignored her attempt to rile me, but my attention zipped to the decorated wall. The photograph of Gina and Susan again took the focal point — no longer Susan's children at various ages. Those now occupied less important spots. The picture of Susan, Amanda and Gregory was nowhere in sight.

Susan pivoted back to the window. "Welcome home." She gestured toward the crowd in the square. "I dare say our citizens are happy to see you."

A flush of anger flared through me. Strange that I should feel this way on Amanda's behalf. "But not you?"

Susan flapped a dismissive hand, her focus on her daughter. "Naturally, I'm happy, but I have an entire town to consider — not merely my own flesh and blood."

I examined Gina and muttered, "I've seen how important flesh and blood is to *your* family."

Gina ignored my jibe but laid her cup and saucer back on the side table. She got up, crossed to the kingly desk and leaned her stumpy body against it. After slipping her horn-rimmed spectacles down her hooked nose, she peered over the rims, her gaze flat. "So, we understand your quest amounted to nothing but a monumental disaster." She tittered. "A broken virtual experience cube. What, might I ask, ought we do with *that*?"

"Uh, fix it." I was done with politeness.

"Well, for what reason are you delaying? Hand it over." She displayed an open palm, motioning her fingers toward her. "Oh-h, it's in the possession of the brother with whom you gallivanted. No doubt he's withholding his family's prized treasure. Mm-m, I wonder, Miss Jones, did you and the brother at least have some fun?"

Eric flicked a questioning frown at Caleb. It lasted only a second before his forehead smoothed out. Eric trusted his brother.

I ignored her as she focused on Caleb. "Hand it over, then." She again held out her hand.

Although I never thought he'd so willingly offer it up, I stepped forward to block his path. "Uh, I don't think so. That thing goes nowhere without Eric and Caleb."

Susan walked around the desk. She didn't speak to us, but to Gina. "As it happens, Mother, I am in agreement with Miss Jones."

I sidled back to Eric's side as Susan continued. "Our technicians may examine it in your presence. While we wait for someone, I'd very much like to see what we have so far."

Caleb looked to me for confirmation, so I nodded. "You can show them."

He laid the VE at the center of the room, and the memory of his initial reaction sparked in my mind — those moments after he'd first laid his eyes on his parents. I settled my hand on Eric's back as the VE came to life. The light launching from its center sucked us in, and once again the twins' parents showed up.

Eric gasped and stepped back. After shooting me and Caleb quick scowls, he refocused on the VE.

As their parents spoke, Eric's arms fell slack. From the side, I slid both of mine around his waist and placed my head on his shoulder. In something like a numb stupor, he propped an arm on me — a dead weight.

Caleb shifted closer to Eric, a hand on his brother's shoulder. Although I intended to nod my thanks to Caleb when I peeked around Eric, both their eyes were glistening, so I went back to watching the VE.

As before, the cube addressed Caleb.

Their parents' voices and images captivated its audience. Every one of us gawked in dead silence — everyone besides Gina. Her expression looked as identifiable as a robot's.

When the formula showed, Susan picked up her personal digipar from the desk. Instead of writing it like I had, she used the digipar to capture and convert the whiteboard images to text.

Until the VE proceeded, silence reigned. Eric let out a shuddering breath, and I observed his unwavering attention, which was fixed on his parents.

Finally, the VE continued. When it neared the spot of its failure, I stopped breathing, willing it to work its way through and past the dreaded scene. For a moment I thought it might. But, no. At exactly the same point, it again flickered and stopped. Exactly where Eric and Caleb's parents were about to reveal the *Ellen* formula and the one that could end Harriet's suffering.

Numb silence took the group—all, that is, except Gina. I scowled as she broke it. "So, what are we waiting for? Let's get this thing seen to."

"Not so fast, *Gina*!" Liam spat her name, his cheeks red with rage. And something else—agony—as he hugged himself. My brother wouldn't allow her to see the tears he came so close to spilling. "Tell us about these resuscitations... Is *this* what happened to...Harriet?" His voice cracked on her name. No longer could he hold back his emotion, and the saline drops flowed over his lids.

Gina waved a dismissive hand, her voice a scoff. "Of course not. Don't be ridiculous. That is mere speculation."

Liam clearly detected the well-hidden lie in her voice as he spun on Jonas and me. "And you two!" He spat the words, flashing his gaze between us, his voice a cold rasp. "You guys have known this for a *week*! Yet you didn't think it necessary to send me a *message*!" He didn't even glance at Caleb once, not seeming to think he deserved the same rebuke.

Susan seemed at a loss for words as she glared at her mother. Amanda regarded them both, flipping her dark brown eyes between the two older women. Then she slumped the tiniest bit. In the face of discovering she'd once died, Amanda had barely flinched.

While we were distracted, Gina reached down for the VE. Caleb didn't give her the chance. He snatched it from the floor before she got to it, presented it and snarled at Gina. "From what I've heard about you, I don't think so." Then he tucked it into his jeans pocket and faced Susan. "Where do we take it?"

"We'll have it seen to right here." Susan edged behind the desk again and pressed a button beneath its lip. "Send Trevor in."

The man had obviously been expecting the summons, because the elevator doors closed, and not a minute later a vaguely familiar balding man arrived in the office. He wore a short-sleeved white shirt over a paunch, the shirttails shoved into baggy beige pants that ended at too-small brown leather shoes. A tiny pouch was tucked into the belt of his pants. He rubbed his hands together, then extracted it.

I puffed out a derisive laugh. "Are we sure we can trust him?"

Caleb looked around Eric at me. "Can it get any worse?"

Then Caleb paced to Susan's desk and set the VE cube down. While walking, the man unfurled the pouch, then laid it on the desk.

From within, he removed a silver rod. The top half of the front third appeared to have been cut away. The cut-away face emitted a blue light, and he scanned it over the VE cube. After flipping the cube onto all sides, he did the same and finally rotated back to us. His cheeks pinked. "I'm afraid there is no fault."

I bit the inside of my cheek. "You mean you can't *find* the fault."

"No, young lady, I mean there *is* no fault." He wriggled the silver tube between his thumb and middle finger. "This would pick it up if there was. However, this…error"—he phrased it as if unsure—"seems to have been…set up…during recording."

Without so much as a goodbye, he swiveled and stalked toward the open elevator.

Plucking it up from the desk, Caleb followed with Liam, Jonas, Eric and me on his heels.

As we joined the man inside, Caleb twisted around.

I grimaced at him. "How are you so comfortable here when this world is so alien to you?"

Caleb bit his lip and shrugged as if the reason was obvious. "My adoptive dad and brother are here."

He halted his gaze on Eric, who squeezed me in a *possibly* possessive hug. But as I tightened my arm around his waist, I sensed him smiling beside me.

Footsteps whispered on the plush carpet, and I turned.

"I'm coming too." Without lowering her voice, Amanda threw a backward glare. "Right now, I can't stand to be around Mother or Grandmother."

She seemed entirely unabashed from her grandmother's earlier slighting and marched straight-shouldered into the elevator.

As the doors closed, Gina's voice slithered through. "You'll be back…when you learn that without me you can do nothing." She didn't stop there. No, she added something else, her words fading as the elevator descended. "Oh, Amanda… You may find that you and the brother…" The rest of the sentence disappeared into silence.

Chapter Forty-Seven

I looked from Caleb to Amanda to Caleb. Her cheeks pinked, but Caleb remained utterly composed. We were all still gawping at each other when the elevator doors opened at ground level.

As if at any moment we'd pounce on him, the technician raced out and disappeared down a corridor toward the back of the municipal building.

While crossing the open-air foyer, I glanced up. Harriet was waiting at the top of the wide staircase and Liam raced toward her, wrapping her in his arms. He held her with the tenderness of a china doll he needed to protect.

The earlier crowds in the town square had dwindled. Those who remained now turned to face the municipal building and traced our movements as we descended the stairs.

Jonas addressed them in an out-of-character booming voice—as loud as his dad's. "No need to wait around in this baking sun for answers. We have none.

When we do, so will you." Although he couldn't achieve the volume to reach the far end of the square, those who could hear spread his announcement.

We aimed for one of the grassy areas breaking the cobbled paving, and the bright green leaves of the large maple tree made for a cool refuge from the heat. Beneath it, as we formed a circle, Harriet shifted her gaze from me to Eric, then to our clasped hands. Then she whirled on Caleb. She reached up on her tiptoes, pulled her hand back and slapped him hard across the face.

With a frown, Caleb stepped back and stuck a palm to his reddening cheek. After a long moment he lowered his hand, his forehead smoothing. "I guess I deserved that."

Harriet glared at him. "You're damned right you deserved it! In fact, you *deserve* a lot worse than that! You nearly killed three of the people I love most in this world!"

Eric stiffened beside me and I side-looked up into his narrowing eyes. He glared at his brother, spitting the words. "What the hell is Harriet talking about?"

Caleb's responding grimace was all the answer Eric needed. He shot his fist out at his brother, connecting with his nose in a crunch.

I grabbed his arm. "Don't, Eric! He only did it because he thought we'd killed you and Graham."

Eric raised his palms in question, his expression incredulous. "Are you defending him?" He pivoted back to Caleb. "What led you to believe we'd *died*?" He didn't give his brother the chance to respond but lifted a palm. "No, don't answer...jumping to conclusions again, I expect." He scraped a hand through his hair, swiveling his head side-to-side.

Caleb pressed a wrist to the blood pouring from his nose and dipped his gaze to his shuffling feet, his voice resigned. "How was I to know? They were from here. Then we got told about the Cordovas... It was a misunderstanding. I wanted" — he considered his words — "revenge, I guess."

Eric spoke in a rough growl. "Did you not think to verify the facts?" With another angry shake of his head, he went on with his speculations. "Let me guess...*Cassidy*" — he said my name with a sarcastic twist — "somehow manufactured her proof, because I guarantee she wouldn't have kept quiet."

Caleb ground his teeth, his Adam's apple bouncing. "I'm sorry. I didn't realize." He pinched the bridge of his nose and winced. "Ouch. I think you've broken it."

Eric widened his eyes. "If you try anything like that again" — Amanda moved to Caleb's side and Eric frowned but carried on speaking to his brother — "you can bet your bottom dollar I'll make that disfiguration permanent. For now, it looks like Amanda is falling over herself to get you to the medic robots to have it fixed." Eric looked at me, then back at his brother. "You'd best make sure they do a good job, because when I get the full story from Cassidy, I'll probably feel the need to break it again."

Jonas guffawed at the uncharacteristically sheepish Caleb, adding fuel to the fire. "What did Liam tell you, bro — about wishing you were dead?"

Liam apparently hadn't been drawn into Jonas' need to chastise Caleb, his mind elsewhere. He yanked Harriet against his chest, kissing the top of her head. A shudder ran through him. "Can we please stop talking about death?"

Harriet tipped her head back, meeting his hard jawline and anguished expression. "Why so serious, babe? What's wrong?" She swung her head to Jonas, who'd slumped at Liam's mood-shift. "Jo? What's going on?"

As Jonas laid a hand on his sister's shoulder, he swallowed, his Adam's apple bouncing. "Why didn't you go home with Mom and Dad, Harri? You should be resting."

She snorted. "Pah! Seriously? Is that what this is about? Well, I humored them. Since when would I do what they want?"

Liam tightened his hold on her, his tone full of affection. "Or anyone, for that matter."

She squinted, opening her mouth to speak, but Amanda seamlessly distracted her—as if it were the most natural thing in the world. "Sorry to steal your moment, but can I ask a question?"

Eric arched his brows. "You already did."

In a motion that made Caleb slide his gaze down then up her body, Amanda jabbed a fist to her hip and rolled her eyes. "We've all seen how Grandmother enjoys watching me squirm, but doesn't anyone find her parting comment noteworthy?"

Caleb wiped his blood-covered wrist on his jeans and shrugged one shoulder. "Does it matter? It's obvious what she intended to say. Plus, I already knew I found you very attractive."

Amanda's cheeks flushed bright red, and she plunged her gaze to the floor.

Jonas propped his chin in his hand. "You're wrong, bro. What Gina said matters very much. What you *should* ask yourself is, *why* is she so sure you'd be attracted to Amanda when you aren't from Petriville?"

He locked on Eric and me. "That question applies to you two as well."

I fired a glance up toward the office, a hard smile tightening my mouth. "I'm inclined to agree with you, Jonas. We knew Gina calculated DNA matches to pair *couples*. But why did she emphasize the fact that she never *meant* Eric to be with Amanda?"

I probably enjoyed rehashing that snippet of information more than I should have.

A muscle in Jonas' jaw ticked. "I'm so damned done with this woman's secrets. I say we go back up there and demand answers."

"Uh, guys?" Amanda finally looked up, her cheeks still bright red. "I might have overheard a thing or two."

As we focused our attention on her, she drew a deep breath. "I eavesdropped on Mother and Grandmother. Although I didn't hear the beginning of their conversation, I gathered enough to help me draw my own conclusions." Amanda spoke with an air of confidence that bordered on arrogance, belying her younger age.

Caleb met my gaze, bit his lip and lowered his chin, his mouth twitching in a sheepish smile. He *liked* Amanda's dominant personality. I smiled at his uncharacteristic bout of shyness.

Eric appeared to notice our silent communication. He hauled me into his side. *Is he jealous…of Caleb?*

I peered up at Eric, but his focus stayed on Amanda. A less-than-happy grimace creased the normally smooth bronze skin of his forehead.

Amanda phrased her sentence as a question. "So, you know Grandmother matched couples?" She flattened her lips. "Well, it sounds as though it's more complicated than that."

Liam's forearm muscles twitched as he tensed his hold around Harriet. "What the hell are you telling us, Amanda? That I'm not supposed to be with Harriet? Because I'll fight you tooth and nail on that one." He drew Harriet even closer to him, as though Amanda would force them apart.

Harriet squeezed Liam's forearms as Amanda grimaced. "No. No. That's *not* what I'm saying. But don't you think it odd that most pre-planned unions are so very compatible?"

Liam still didn't loosen his arms around Harriet. His mouth dropped open for a second before he shook his head in comprehension. With gritted teeth, he spoke through a snarl. "Gina *changed* our DNA. She *forced* Harriet to be attracted to me." He choked on the word 'forced' then appeared to wait for Amanda to confirm his statement.

Amanda's gaze plummeted, and she concluded in an uncharacteristically soft voice. "Yes…I'm sorry to say that's exactly what Grandmother did…to everyone. At a DNA level she made sure that yours will always be attracted to Harriet's…and vice versa."

Liam's voice exploded out like the firing of a pistol. "Was your *mother* involved with this too?"

"No! Mother was as horrified as I was. It sounded to me like Grandmother was informing Mother for the first time."

I cocked my head and peeked at Jonas, but he beat me to the question, his voice hard. "If that's the case, why didn't things work out between Cassidy and me, then?"

Eric again firmed his hold on me as Amanda replied to Jonas. "That's because she paired your DNA as an afterthought—at least that's what I could make out. Grandmother said a second DNA pairing was less effective than a first. They were discussing me and—" She tossed a quick glance at Eric then looked down, but didn't conclude the sentence.

Eric's voice came out as a sharp growl. "That's why Gina wanted me to touch that silver disk thing. That's why she stopped me from going out there with Cassidy!"

I'd never seen Eric so angry. He softened his voice, but it wasn't sweet. No. It bore pure, bitter hatred, so low I could barely hear him. "When did you find this out, Amanda? When did you know what they planned to do? You also tried to convince me to touch that thing."

Amanda glanced at me. "I'm sorry."

Eric's back went rigid against my arm as he rephrased his question. "*When*? When did you know?"

She dropped her chin. "Just after Cassidy left. I can explain."

Eric didn't let her, spitting the words through his lips. "You misled me! All while you pretended to be my friend! You're the biggest traitor of all. It's a lucky thing I trusted Graham's judgment more."

Caleb stepped forward and stood before Eric, a palm to his shoulder. Eric shrugged it off, and Caleb rotated to Amanda, softening his expression and voice. "Let me guess the answer... She made the DNA alterations a long time before the launch. Stop me if I'm wrong. But in the VE, our parents spoke of how Gina originally offered them a place in Petriville. Now I'm guessing that's when Gina paired Eric with Cassidy and me with you."

Amanda dipped her chin in a slow nod. "When Grandmother learned that you'd died, she knew my attraction to Eric was inevitable because of your similar DNA. She hoped that by changing Eric's DNA, she could make him fall in love with me and forget about Cassidy."

Jonas clenched his fists, his face twisted in fury. "Let me add to that supposition. Since she'd already matched my and Cassidy's DNA, she thought we'd pair up!"

Liam conveyed none of the usual warmth in his speedy voice. "What about your *afterthought* mate, Amanda? The one she paired you up with later?"

"She didn't. Apparently, some families left Petriville before the launch – either not wanting to leave without their extended families or because Grandmother decided they were unsuitable."

Jonas shook his head. "So, my original partner was from one of those families."

"Yes. And since you and Cassidy were friends, Grandmother paired you. She intended to match me up with someone she deemed acceptable after seeing how everyone turned out as young adults."

Caleb cocked his head. "So, if your grandmother profiled your DNA with me – and assuming she cares for you – why did she leave our family behind?"

A blush again colored Amanda's cheeks. "As with everything Grandmother does, I expect it involved her pride. Apparently, she discovered Graham's and your parents' friendship. If she had known the Carters and him were also close, she would most likely have abandoned them too."

I stabbed a fist to my hip. "What exactly did she have against Graham? He supplied her with Kaleidotonium. Without that, our space trip couldn't have happened."

Amanda let out a heavy breath. "His oldest son was an addict, and Grandmother decided it was a genetic flaw."

Liam nodded. "The two most influential people in this project were Graham and Joshua Carter. Without them both, we'd be dead."

As each of us drifted into our own thoughts, the group fell silent. Then Liam, Harriet and Jonas spoke in hushed tones, as did Caleb and Amanda. Eric squeezed my hand and tilted his head toward the sun-kissed cobbled paving. I nodded, and leading me from the shade, he turned to face me.

Chapter Forty-Eight

A pained frown creased his forehead as he bent forward and set his mouth at my ear, ensuring only I could hear his low voice. "You're attracted to Caleb." His statement didn't allow me the option of denying the fact. "The way you looked at him back there...made that obvious."

I scratched my face, hedging. "That exchange was about his attraction to Amanda, not about him and me."

Eric didn't seem convinced. "That may well be. But something happened between you out there. Am I wrong?"

I shrugged. "We became friends, I think." I hauled him toward the fountain—farther from the others—and clasped my hands around his neck. "Eric, I won't lie to you. When I first saw Caleb, I believed he *was* you. Remember, to my understanding, Caleb had died." I scanned from Eric's substantial feet, up his long, muscled legs and thighs, to his lean torso and hard chest, then his strong jawline, full lips and clefts denting his cheeks, right up to his straight nose and prominent forehead. I returned to his large eyes. "Because of that, I kissed him." Eric started, but I didn't let him go. Instead, I tugged myself closer, inhaling his dusky vanilla scent. "That's when I realized he wasn't you."

Eric gave a short, confused frown. "How?" Then his murmur got even softer. "How did you figure he wasn't me?"

My voice emerged steady and sure. "It's because I don't love him, Eric. When we kissed, it hit me."

Eric gulped, fixing on one part of my statement. "You love me?"

"Of course, I love you, Eric. Can't you see that?"

"You hated me after—" Eric cut himself off, probably not wanting to talk about my mother's murder.

I met his frown. "I never hated you. How could I? I was grieving. But out there, when Caleb nearly killed us, I regretted not telling you—not saying the words. Then I convinced myself that Amanda had probably taken my place in your heart."

"Oh-h, Cassidy." Eric firmed his hold around my waist. "Do you seriously think I could feel for Amanda what I do for you? Do you even realize how damned crazy you make me? Every thought of you makes my breath catch. Amanda couldn't have that effect on me. No way. Never."

"You spent so much time together."

Eric emitted a low growl. "I assumed she was my friend—a mistake I won't repeat."

"Didn't you notice she practically threw herself at you?"

He angled backward, cupping his hands to my shoulders as he leveled his gaze on mine. "Cassidy…will you listen to me? Please? There *is* no one else for me. If Amanda was right, Gina matched me with only *your* DNA. But that's not the same with you, is it? She matched you to Jonas…and because we're twins, you'll be drawn to Caleb. How am I supposed to feel about that?"

I recalled the kiss Jonas and I had shared. Guilt surged through me and I squeezed my eyes. "We need to talk, Eric."

He watched me warily for the longest time. Finally, his face sagged, his voice a low croak. "Ah-h…Jonas. I didn't like you going out there with him, and now…hearing you were matched— But nope. Don't tell me. I don't want to hear."

"But I need to tell you, Eric."

He stood back, clenching his fists, voice tight. "Well, I hope it's not as bad as I'm imagining. Best you get out with it."

My brow weighted my eyelids. "After Caleb released us. Jonas wouldn't stop with me, so I asked him what it would take?"

Eric didn't sound angry. Not at all. Rather, his voice cracked. "What…did…you…do?"

No matter how much guilt racked my chest, I wouldn't look away from him. It was fair that I witnessed the pain in Eric's grimace, since I'd caused it. "I kissed him, Eric. I'm sorry."

Eric backed away. "How long did this go on for?"

I reached for his hand, but he pulled it from my grasp. Instead, I searched his gaze. "It didn't *go on*. It was one stupid kiss. I made him promise after that he'd stop."

Eric swallowed. "And did he?"

"He did." I paused. "It was funny in a way, because after that he got quite defensive on your behalf."

"Why?" He wasn't asking about Jonas' defensiveness.

"I don't know. Then afterward, Ethan and Craig told me"—I slipped my eyes shut—"Amanda always visited you, and I assumed—" I broke off and stared up at him.

Eric jerked his head back and sucked in a sharp breath. "You assumed I'd fallen for her. And you didn't trust me—didn't trust my feelings for you?"

"I'm sorry, Eric."

He should have been mad. But it was worse. The color drained from his face and he flinched, holding his hand up as if hovering—undecided between closing the gap or backing away.

After what seemed like forever, I could no longer take it. "Don't just stand there, Eric. Please? Say something. Anything."

Finally, he stepped closer and placed a hand on my face, grazing his fingers down my cheek before lightly pressing my chin up. "Do you love him?"

I shook my head, certain if I spoke, I wouldn't hold back my emotion. Jonas had been my friend for so long. At least I owed them both that, even if Jonas wasn't here to witness it. "I don't love him in the way I love you, Eric. But like I told you once before, he's my friend and he'll always be important to me."

Eric blinked, tilting his head back. Finally, he faced me. "Now it's my turn to forgive you. It's fair I do, since you found it in your heart to forgive me for something much worse. It just hurts like hell." He steeled his jaw. "Regardless, Gina forced that choice on us a long time ago. I can't *not* forgive you because I can't *not* be with you. In truth" — he threaded his arms around me and I sank into him as he kissed the top of my head, his voice an indistinct murmur — "if she hadn't matched our DNA, I'd still have fallen for you. From a crowd of a million girls, I'd have singled you out."

I laid my head on his chest. "We'll never know if you're right. But I think I'm okay with that. It's true, though. We'll always find ourselves forgiving each other. And I think I'm okay with that too."

Eric heaved a cleansing breath, his posture seeming to relax, but he said nothing more.

I put my hand on his cheek. "You have your mother's eyes. Did you know? And your father's dimples."

He puffed a laugh. "Now that, I do recall. Although Graham often told us that, so maybe it's his retelling that I remember." His smile dissolved. "When I saw my mom and dad up there" — he squinted up at the second floor of the municipal building — "it kind of had me feeling happy...and sad...at the same time."

"They loved you, Eric. Everything they did was for you and Caleb."

Eric nodded against my head. "I know. They left us in Graham's care."

I smiled against him. "Do you see, Eric? This is home for me. Right here. In your arms and against your chest. It's exactly where I want to be."

He gripped me against him and let out a huge, weight-freeing sigh. "Oh-h, my Cassidy. You can't imagine how many times I've dreamed of hearing you say that."

I laughed. "Well, now that I'm back and you're out of prison, I'll often be reminding you of the fact. So, brace yourself."

Eric chuckled. "What? Brace myself for a dream-come-true?" He grinned. "Can we get out of here? Go somewhere where we can be alone."

I laughed and cocked a brow at him. "And do what exactly?"

With a cheeky laugh, he raised a brow. "Mm-m... Between us, I'm figuring we can come up with some pretty cool ideas."

Amanda's voice cut into our shared moment. "Hey, you two lovebirds. Get back here. I'm not finished. And I'm afraid it gets worse."

I peeked up at Eric, grimacing, because I knew *exactly* what she was speaking of.

Chapter Forty-Nine

Eric and I rejoined the circle. Like Harriet and Liam, I leaned back against Eric, his arms around my shoulders while I clasped his forearms and he rested his chin lightly on my head.

Since leaving the Morgan home, this possibility had swirled in my mind. My throat clamped and I gazed at my best friend. No one had told her yet. I opened my mouth to remind Amanda to wait with the news, but she beat me. Clearly, she hadn't purposefully distracted Harriet before. "You've probably already realized the VE was right. Grandmother *did* resuscitate us."

For a long while, Harriet stared ahead of her. Then she lashed out. "What are you talking about?" She swiveled her head to look up at Liam. "Resuscitate?"

Liam gave a slow blink, voice fast and soothing and so full of love. "I'll explain, babe. But I think you already know."

Hurt took the place of Harriet's anger, hurt and something like an animal caught in a trap. These were expressions my best friend never wore. "Why didn't you tell me? Jonas? Cassidy? You saw me and yet you chose to tell Susan and Gina first!"

Jonas moved to lay a hand on her shoulder, but she shrugged it off. "Don't touch me!" She again peered up at Liam. "Did you know, Li?" Her voice sounded so small.

He exhaled a shuddering breath and glanced up toward Susan's office. "I found out up there."

When I reached for her, she slapped my hand away. "You're supposed to be my best friend, Cassidy. How could you?"

Jonas wore a frown so deep that a surge of anger twisted my gut on his behalf. "Everything your brother and I did was to help you, Harriet. Everything! How did you expect us to tell you? Do you honestly believe we didn't agonize over it? Maybe you assume it was a simple decision to let Liam see the VE first before breaking the news to you and your parents! Or do you think Jonas felt nothing when he first saw it? And me?"

Harriet's temper never cooled an ounce. "You're cowards! I think you couldn't face me! You're my brother, Jonas. If you couldn't tell me" — she cut off, then continued — "and Cassidy! We grew up together. We shared every secret. Yet you hide the most important thing you discovered from me?"

My gaze plunged to my feet, guilt wrenching my stomach.

Liam kissed the top of Harriet's head. "We all love you, Harri. Once the cure got formulated, we hoped to give you the good news with the bad."

Harriet ignored Liam's comment, not pausing for a beat. "Well, judging by all your expressions...there is no cure."

Caleb looked between Amanda and Harriet. "We *will* fix this. We won't rest until we do."

Harriet ignored Caleb's weak attempt to assuage her anger or her fears. "So, what else are you hiding?"

With her brows drawn together, Amanda cleared her throat. "You and I are in the same boat, Harriet. If anyone is as motivated to find a resolution, it's me."

Harriet pressed her lips together, narrowing her bright blue eyes. "So then out with it, Amanda. I deserve the truth to no less an extent than you do."

As if Harriet intimidated her, Amanda shuffled her feet and sucked in a breath. "Okay... Well, at the time, I believed Grandmother never intended me to overhear these conversations between her and Mother. But honestly...knowing Grandmother...she staged them to make sure I'd hear." For the first time since I'd known Amanda, she swiped at tears.

Caleb laid a comforting hand on her shoulder.

Harriet still looked livid. She yanked from Liam and angled toward Amanda, clenching her fists and seething. "And you didn't think you should tell me? You *knew* it affected me, too!"

Amanda lowered her chin. "I didn't want to scare you or the others. I honestly thought Cassidy would come back with a cure. She's so tough, you know?"

It stunned me that Amanda regarded me so highly. However, her speech never appeased Harriet. She slammed her hands on her hips and snapped, "I may be small, Amanda, but I'm way stronger than you!"

Liam gently encouraged Harriet back against him. I knew what Harriet's temper was like. Liam grounded her. He was good for her. His kind manner seemed to douse those fires that raged inside her.

After a long moment, Amanda went on. "Grandmother manipulated the years they wiped from our memories. She made certain to wipe every resuscitation year, even if it was a tenth. In our memories, she merely left the following year or the one after that. She still eliminated nine out of every ten years. They were just not necessarily sequential."

As if they could block out the possibility, Liam hid behind his eyelids. But Jonas and I had had more time to process the prospect during our home-bound trip.

Eric straightened behind me. "Tell me something. How many people are sick here in Petriville? And are they mostly younger or older people?"

"What does it matter?" Liam shook his head, then replied anyway—deadpan. "Fifty-two." At that moment, as if grasping the full implication of Eric's question, he widened his eyes. "Gina is the oldest person in Petriville, but most of the sick people are around our age."

"Oka-y. In the refuge we had fewer overall disappearances"—Eric air-quoted the last word, then again closed his arms around my shoulders—"but since our population was smaller, I'd guess the per capita stats are about the same. More importantly, older folk disappeared from the refuge more often than our youth."

Caleb took hold of the thread. "So, these robot medics you have here in Petriville can resuscitate pretty much anyone?" His voice rose on the last word, turning his sentence into a question.

Liam tilted his head to the side. "I'm not sure about that. We did have one man die"—he cast a pained glance at me—"before our mother...but we've never known about anyone being brought back to life, only cured of an illness that may have killed them if left untreated. That makes sense, judging from what Amanda is saying about the wiped years."

Eric's voice pulsed a deep vibration against me. "Cassidy said the man who died bled out long before medic robots could get to him. Referring back to the refuge...some people never disappeared but *died*. Now we understand those must have happened in our tenth, non-wiped year. Anyway, regardless... In our experience, most of those either happened from illness or during MAC games. Although Graham was super strict about allowing us to take unnecessary risks during the games."

Caleb clarified the gathered information. "So, you lost more young people, and we lost more elderly. You cured illnesses, but we didn't have the technology. So why in hell did so many of Petriville's youth need to be"—as if reality dawned, he drew out the last word—"resus...ci...tated?"

I contemplated. "We were *never* careful during MAC Challenges. All we cared about was winning." I let everyone absorb my revelation. "And we had a *lot* of MAC injuries—" I didn't conclude the sentence but grimaced.

Jonas cleared his throat. "Listen to what you're saying, Cassidy! You're suggesting that Harriet"—he shivered, then added the dreaded word in a low croak—"'died' in a MAC Challenge?"

Harriet curled a small hand around her brother's. "Jo, if we want confirmation"—she glared up toward Susan's office—"and our assumption is accurate, it might give our argument credibility." Her voice turned uncharacteristically small. "It feels…possible."

I swallowed. *Harriet is right.* An inkling of the chance flitted at the edge of my mind. Like a small flicker…a vague memory of too much agony.

The way Liam gritted his jaw and Jonas' face hung flaccid as he gave slow repeated shakes of his head… All those things told me the same realization was sinking into their minds.

Amanda's voice tore me away from my muddy memory of grief. "If I have any say in the matter, that's what we're doing right now."

Harriet pulled from Liam's grasp. "Hell yes! These are our lives we're talking about. I swear…that woman had better spill."

With that, she stormed toward the municipal building with the rest of us in an inverted V-formation behind her.

Chapter Fifty

Back inside Susan's office, the three hadn't changed position at all. Austin still stood beside the elevator, Susan with her back to the window and Gina leaning against the desk. Both women faced us — like they'd observed our conversation in the square and had expected us to return. Susan observed Caleb's black eye and bloody nose with a cocked head, and she pinched her brows together. She flicked her eyes from Caleb to Eric, who was beside me. Although she didn't know Caleb had tried to kill us, she seemed to wonder why anyone would feel the need to break his nose. She said nothing, and Gina didn't notice. Or if she did, she gave no visual sign of it.

Gina thrust her chin high, exposing her short turkey neck. With a crisp nod, she turned to Susan. "What did I tell you, daughter? You ought to harbor more faith in your mother's instincts." She hiked an eyebrow. "I'm rather pleased you're joining this little gathering, Miss Winters. You'll be wanting answers to the questions my granddaughter's eavesdropping raised. It was quite amusing to watch the silly girl try her utmost to convince Eric he ought to accept the inoculation." Gina sniggered and aimed her next sentence at Amanda. "You are rather the chip off the old block, telling him it would stop the illness from affecting him." Then she was back to addressing us all. "If I'd merely asked the girl, defiant as she is, she would most certainly have refused. Regardless, her attempts were futile" — Gina gave a curt snicker — "and she made an embarrassing amount of those."

Gina regarded Eric, then me, and finally her granddaughter. Amanda cleared her throat, her voice tiny. "How did I die, Grandmother? How did *we* die?"

Gina propped a fist on her hip and cocked her head, considering. "Oh my. I cannot say I recall. You most probably fell off that climbing wall like most of the other fools."

As if her granddaughter's question was a fly to shrug off, she went back to her previous topic, throwing me a dry smirk. "So, Miss Jones, it seems you have the boy rather bewitched."

Eric tensed beside me and I squeezed his hand, silently encouraging him not to give her the satisfaction of challenging her. Gina *loved* the contest. Since her moral compass was flawed, she always came out on top. Almost. Once I'd sent her into a rage. A thrill ran through me at the memory.

A low rumble escaped Eric before he inhaled and spoke in that smooth river of sound. "Well, since you've got it all figured out, may we assume you've established a *cure*?" The sarcasm in his voice was only clear in that one word.

Gina's face reddened, her fists clenching. She drew her stumpy body to its full height. "As it happens, young man, I resolved the puzzle of the cure some time ago. I simply required the *Ellie* formula to complete it — along with your DNA, of course. Why do you think I didn't allow you to leave with your" — Gina dripped syrup into her voice — "*beloved*? I wouldn't lose the only element of my formula that I possessed. Since we've now secured that —"

Harriet cut her off, clearly deciding she wasn't about to let the woman derive more pleasure from the discussion. She spoke as if mid-sentence. "...so, you see...we *have* no questions. But here's an idea. Why don't we tell you what we *know*?" Her voice sounded gleeful.

Gina scoffed, as if trying to maintain control. She drew out the first word — "Yes-s...of course." For the first time, her attempt fell flat.

Harriet launched into the narrative of our hypothesis, making it sound like fact. No one else could have achieved her level of certainty. Gina waited — actually waited — while Harriet outlined the details.

When Harriet concluded, Gina stood upright and clapped — not the impressed, awed cheer of the earlier crowd, but the slow, deliberate clap of mockery. "So, you have it all figured out. Ah-h, yes. The exsanguination — stupid veterinary surgeon of a wife was so intent on trying to stop the bleeding herself — futile as her attempt was. By the time she raised the medic alarm, her" — Gina infused honey into her voice — "*darling* husband was brain dead. Now, since you have this puzzle all solved, let's see how far you get with the cure." She chortled, but I knew better than that. Her voice carried the tiniest bit of tension. We *were* getting to her.

At least this time, I wasn't a young naïve girl. More than that…I wasn't alone. I glared at her.

Of course, Gina's insatiable need to bluster over what she considered her accomplishments stopped her from remaining silent. We didn't need to prompt her. "Rather ingenious — my robots. I had them designed to absorb human bodies into themselves, probe them with tendrils and initiate healing. It was a simple process to keep body functions alive while they regrew or repaired damaged tissue." Gina cackled while she spoke. "I was tempted to awake them to see if they would panic — you know, from being locked inside the robot." She sighed. "Sadly, the robots didn't permit it. Anyway, that was the reason I wiped memories the night before the MAC Challenge, since those were on the last day of the old year. On the night before New Year's Eve, I discharged a sleeping gas with properties which stimulated a state of hypnosis. Then, I simply suggested that citizens head to their own beds. Of course, lightbulb cameras in your homes told me if anyone had moved or changed their bedrooms, so my robots rectified those changes during sleep. I subsequently released the annual memory wipe solution. Thus, if any teens died during the challenge, I had a full year to heal the body and reinstall it in the family home. Naturally, people didn't die every year — or even every second year." She giggled at some probably sick private joke, which I didn't want to know about.

Hot sweat beaded on my forehead. Plummeting headlong into Gina's trap, I raged. "'Reinstall'? And 'it'? You talk as if we're machines."

I should have expected her response, but all I wanted was to launch at her with Eric's snake venom and do it properly this time. If Grandma's wrap-around bracelet pen hadn't still been empty, I might have tried. Regardless, Gina had answered our question. The MAC Challenge *had* caused the high resuscitation rate of youths.

I shook my head at her, my voice soft. "Where does all this come from, Gina? Are you some tortured soul or are you exactly what you seem to be…pure evil?" My next question came out small and weak. "Was it your intention to resuscitate my mom?"

Although I knew it was coming, Gina's chuckle sent an icy shiver down my spine. "Oh, no. Why would I do *that*? Your mother, I fully intended to" — she emphasized the next word, knowing how I'd hate it — "*install* into a cold grave."

Liam bunched his fists and launched at her, and only the combined strength of Jonas, Eric and Caleb held him back.

Liam let out a growl of unadulterated rage. "Let me go!" Then it trembled and cracked, his tone soft and broken. "Why, Gina? Why do you love to torment our family? What did we ever do to you?"

Gina ignored Liam's anguished cry and fluttered her hand in a dismissive wave. "Oh, my dear…didn't you know…? Your darling *mother* brought that on herself." Then she fixed on me. "Oh, now I see it. The apple doesn't fall far from the tree. Perhaps I should have eliminated you both."

Susan put a stop to Gina's obvious enjoyment of brutalizing Liam and me, as well as our own anger flying around the room. She'd been watching from her point of safety while Gina had spoken, as if her daughter weren't present. Susan walked around the desk and closed a hand over Gina's forearm. "Now, that's enough, Mother. You have tormented these kids for far too long. It is time to tell them what you've established." She paused. "Or would you like Austin to help you with that?"

Gina was so arrogant that she *barely* flinched at all as the gorilla of a man took a step forward. Barely. But she *did* flinch. "Very well, traitor of a daughter. I thought, by including you in my deepest secrets, that you'd gain some level of loyalty toward your mother. However, it seems you cannot escape your true and treacherous nature—just like your useless father."

Susan ignored Gina and filled us in herself. "I'm sure you all know Mother obtained, among others, a doctorate in genetic engineering. That is her primary field of expertise. She held back some samples of the Morgans' formulae. While you lot were away, Mother spent some time analyzing these and the smattering of notes the Morgans left, but those predominantly involved dispensing the annual wipe gas. Even though Mother displays no affection for my daughter, it seems she would prefer her project not to fail. The youth dying in a few years would most certainly put a spanner in her works. However, she was unable to identify the exact makeup of these drugs. She believes equal combinations of the following will produce the cure. The *Ellie* formula—or the longevity drug. Also, the *Ellen* formula—or the neutralizer. And finally, *Livvie*, or more specifically, one of the twin's DNA. She tells me the inoculation shall restore balance."

Amanda didn't appear convinced. She thrust her hands on her hips, her dark brown eyes as wide as saucers. "And you *believe* her?"

At least Susan treated her daughter with some decency. She sighed. "Your grandmother has no reason to mislead us, sweetheart. Otherwise, I would not take this chance."

I considered Gina's theory. Yes, she was highly intelligent and no, I wasn't a genetic engineer. Yet the words blurted through my lips before I'd properly formulated the conversation in my mind. "There is no *Ellen*. You destroyed it, Gina! You said so!"

Not that she needed to, but Susan spoke on Gina's behalf. "Mother may have given us...mm-m...inaccurate information regarding that."

My voice came out flat. "You mean she lied. Why am I not surprised?"

Liam had clearly been contemplating the outcome of Gina's formula on the off chance it was possible. "How sure are you this concoction will even work, Gina? You heard what Eric's Dad said in the VE. Any incorrect formula would kill them! How can we even consider taking that *chance*?" His voice cracked on the last word and he pulled Harriet into his arms.

Gina would allow no one to undermine her. She'd fight tooth-and-nail, regardless of whether she was sure. Still, she acknowledged Liam. "I am sure enough. Naturally, we would have no cure without these boys." Even though Gina was so tiny, she managed to glance down her nose at Caleb, then Eric, before addressing the room. "Allow me to be candid for a moment."

I coughed. "That would be a change."

Gina glared at me but continued speaking like I'd said nothing. She directed her conversation to Eric and Caleb, as if they were suddenly the most important people in the room. "When your parents handed me the drugs, I cannot say I appreciated their true value. If

I had, I might have allowed the medic robots to cure your parents' radiation sickness and offered them residency in Petriville. My scientists believed Earth would be ready for re-habitation within ten years. The timing would have been perfect, for the youth would have grown and been ready to mate with their *precisely* matched partners. I originally planned on administering the *Ellie* at that point to ensure they might breed for a protracted period. However, afterward, my scientists informed me the meteorite strike would force us to stay out there for around a hundred years. So, I changed my plans and released the *Ellie* gas. Naturally, I couldn't stop the slaves from inhaling it, so they too received the benefit of long life and wiped years."

I shook my head in disbelief. "Speaking of which… After you murdered my mother, you told me you'd have chosen Eric's family if his twin was a female. But that's not true. You *had* selected and tossed them out!"

Gina scoffed. "What exactly is your point, Miss Jones?"

I never got to continue my interrogation, because at that moment the elevator pinged and a medic robot stepped into the office.

Without moving from her perch on the table, Gina peered between us at the elevator. "Ah. Right on time. Like I said, at least we now have a backup if the one's DNA proves ineffective. So, which of you two will attempt to save these people first?"

Eric dropped my hand and stepped toward the robot, exposing the underside of his forearm and clenching his fist. He directed his snarl at Gina. "You can take my blood, but don't even think of adding anything. I'll rip the damned thing out if you try.

And"—he added deadpan—"no one gets forced into taking this antidote. Got it? Plus, you test it on an older and *willing* person first." He emphasized the words in warning to Gina. "These are people and not mere test subjects."

The robot didn't draw his blood per se. Instead, it extracted the dreaded elongated rod with the small flat, shiny silver disk at its end. After placing it over Eric's inner forearm for a second, it tucked the device inside itself, turned and left.

"Now," Susan concluded, "we wait."

Chapter Fifty-One

After the meeting, while Amanda ushered Caleb to the medical center, Liam and Harriet headed to the municipal building's first-floor library. They said they meant to escape the heat…and they were right. The Petrivillian afternoon reminded me of how humidity dominated the summers in this region of Earth. In space, the Kaleidotonium shell had shielded us from heat and biting insects.

Back in the town square and sitting on the edge of the fountain, Olivia waited for Jonas. With the warmest smile, Jonas waved. Shy as she was, Olivia peered at her feet, her cheeks flushed.

I turned to Eric. "Do you mind if I speak to Jonas for a second?" I didn't have to say the word 'alone'. He seemingly knew what I meant.

After searching my expression for a long moment and without a word, Eric backed away.

I touched Jonas on the forearm. "It's not my place to say this, but that kiss will torment you until you come clean with her."

He did a double take, his voice even softer than mine. "Have you told Eric?"

"How I handled it isn't a factor here." Then I admitted, "Look, Jonas... Obviously, Eric wasn't happy, but I did it anyway. You don't want a lie hanging over your relationship. It's the hard choice, but it's the right thing to do."

For a moment he seemed undecided about whether to tell me what he was considering. Then he inhaled a deep breath. "I'm going to ask Susan to match us...Olivia and me...like how Gina paired your and my DNA."

His words didn't surprise me. "For what it's worth, I think that's wonderful news. Olivia will make you happy. She adores you—even without the forced match."

Jonas went on. "She's so pretty, and it's unfair to her if I'm always looking over my shoulder—"

He didn't need to say the final two words—'at you'. I understood what he meant, and a warm smile tugged my mouth. "It's a kind thing to do, and I'm glad you are."

It was true. Jonas had a kind heart. And it made sense, in some odd way. Why should Jonas only want me when I desired Eric more? He deserved happiness in love as much as the rest of us.

As Jonas raced for the fountain, I went back to Eric, took his hand and grinned up at him, heaving him toward the train station. Eric threw me a skewed look, and I answered before he could ask. "I told him he should be honest with Olivia."

His voice sounded tight. "About the kiss?"

I nodded.

Eric studied my face. "There is a difference between you kissing him and him kissing you. You get that, right? From Olivia's perspective, I mean."

We mounted the stairs into the station, and I looked up at him, my forehead furrowed.

He met my questioning expression, his smile seeming tense. "He doesn't love her—not yet, because he's still besotted with you. And you were never in love with him because you're—" He broke off and bit his lip as if suppressing a grin.

I prodded his ribs. "So, you *did* know how I felt."

Eric curved his body away with a laugh. "Let's call it a hopeful suspicion."

I grinned. "Anyway, his feelings are going to change, because he wants to ask Susan to match their DNA."

Eric chuckled. "Really? Well, call me selfish, but I'm all for it." His smile faded. "Honestly though, I'm glad for Olivia. She's a sweet girl."

A sense of contentment filtered through me as we boarded the silver bullet train. In an instant, the doors made that near-silent whooshing sound as they shut, and the train sailed forward. Eric gazed out of the window as we glided through the suburbs, the ecological factory rings, the farmland rings and the domestic animal rings. He squeezed my fingers. "I'm not sure I'll ever get used to this place."

As a possibility snuck into my thoughts, my mouth went dry. "When this is over, we don't have to stay here. I liked it at Graham's refuge."

He jerked back, brows squishing together. "Really? You'd do that? For me?"

I looked up, drowning in his gaze. "Do you even get what you mean to me? Because I'd do anything for you."

Eric yanked me into a tight embrace and shuddered. "Just so you know, babe…I'd stay here for you without question."

The train pulling into the station near the stables ended our conversation. We disembarked and exited the brick building. As we rounded the corner onto the cobbled road that ran beside the paddock, a swing entered my step. The hedge blocked my view of the horses, but my pulse quickened. *Zenobia is so nearby.* We took the few paces to the end of the hedge before I peered around. The first thing my gaze landed on was Zenobia's liver-chestnut face — and the gleaming white diamond at the center of her forehead. She tossed her head high and nickered, pricking her ears. Warrior grazed beside her. He too picked up his head and watched Eric, his deep black coat glistening in the sun. Then they trotted to us. As soon as they reached us, we launched onto them, bareback and bridle-less.

They simply thrust their heads down into the grass and carried on grazing as if not noticing or caring about our weights on their backs. That sense of familiarity and comfort washed over me as I straddled Zenobia's warm, muscled body — even the twitching movement of her skin and the swatting of her tail against my jeans as she instinctively reacted to flies. I leaned forward and draped my arms around her neck as best as I could without tumbling off. In my peripheral vision, I glimpsed Eric, stretching out his hand to me from Warrior's back. My heart skipped, and I straightened, closing my hand around his. Eric seemed to entertain other ideas and slid his teeth across his lower lip as if suppressing a smile. Then, lifting his leg over the black horse's neck, he slipped down his side. Seconds later, he dragged me from Zenobia and caught me in his arms. "Come here, you famous adventurer, you."

Hard chest against my body, he gripped me, inhaling the scent of my hair as he fed me down him until I was on my feet. "You left me for so long, my Cassidy."

The dusky vanilla of his breath breezed over me in reassuring waves as he sank his face to mine. As if an external force guided my body, I reached up, threaded my arms around his neck and drew myself closer. This was right. It was Eric—not Caleb, and not Jonas. The value of this forgiving, loyal, compassionate man seeped into my soul and the truth of what he meant to me poured out. "You are everything to me, Eric. I'm only half a person when I'm not with you."

He picked up my chin with his finger, and our gazes locked. Then he crushed his soft, moist lips on mine. With desperate coaxing, his tongue parted my lips, and as he slid it through and flickered it against mine, a gasp escaped my throat. My heart stuttered and my body eased into a slow, swaying dance. Eric followed my movements, step for step, heartbeat for heartbeat. As heat grew in my core and drifted down, Eric groaned, tugging me closer and deepening the kiss. An urgent swirl of fire burned through my solar plexus as he sank us into the long grass, clasping his hands behind my head. When he withdrew, he stared into my eyes with a frown raked across his forehead. The blue sky haloed his face, lines slicing into his cheeks. An unfathomable expression passed over his shimmering aquamarines. After a long moment, shaking his head slowly, he ground his teeth then rolled onto his back, squishing his palms into his eye-sockets.

My mouth hung open, throat constricting as I raised to my elbow. "What's wrong, Eric? Why did you stop?"

He raked a hand through his hair, then looked away.

I tried again. "Am I deluding myself? Did my confession dull your emotions?"

Eric turned back, skimming over my face. He drawled the words, sending tingles to the lowest part of my stomach. "Oh…baby. If only you knew. That's not it at all. I do want you. The problem is, I want you too much—every part of you. Don't you see that stopping is taking every bit of my self-control?"

I did a double take. "It is?" I sucked in my lip and settled on his gaze, my words a hoarse whisper. "What if we don't?" He stared at me wide-eyed, so I made myself clear. "Stop, I mean."

"Oh"—he threw a half-laugh—"your meaning didn't escape me. That only makes it worse. Are you trying to drive me completely insane?" He got to his elbow and stroked his thumb down my cheek, his expression as soft as his voice. "About that other matter… Nothing will dull my emotions—not ever—because I have the love of my life at my side. And real, real soon, we'll be together in every sense."

Eric cupped my cheek then pressed his lips to mine in a long, sweet kiss—not hot and passionate like before, but deep and tender, as if he was pouring his entire self into me.

After a long moment, he helped me up and wrapped an arm around my waist, while I threaded my hands around his lean, muscled back. As we crossed the paddock toward the station, Eric kept me firm against him, but even that didn't feel close enough. At the platform, the silver-bullet train waited like a silent chaperone. Before long, it swept us through Petriville then stopped at the town square station.

Sun was tipping the horizon as we crossed the cobbled paving. The water in the cherub-adorned fountain leaped into the air, shimmering. Eric held me just as tight while we rounded the glossy number two and stepped onto the conveyor, when we passed Mamma Candy's with its bright twirling display and as two robot sidewalk-cleaners offered a polite "Good afternoon, fellow Petrivillians." — though we ignored them.

I laughed. "I see you're already adopting our ways."

He smiled down at me. "It's wrong *not* to ignore something so definitely non-organic."

Beneath a dimming orange sky, the conveyor swept us along its revolving journey beneath the familiar transparent, glowing intersection footbridges, past the bright orange Petrivillian Enterprises digital displays and my old school. As we neared the park, the low lantern lights blinked on, ushering their winding pathways toward the playground equipment. Somewhere, a sprinkler system *whoosh-whooshed*. Finally, Eric and I stepped from the conveyor onto the cobbled walkway that passed my home.

I barely noticed my body stiffening as we neared our garden path, but Eric apparently had. He frowned at me. "It's tough. I get it, Cassidy. Let me help you through this, please?"

My heart thumped. I swallowed then balked, unable to reply as tears rolled down my face, catching me off guard.

Eric hauled me into his chest, wrapping his arms around my head and shoulders. "Oh-h, my Cassidy."

Soft music and animated voices leaked through the open windows and door.

"What's wrong with my dad and Liam? How can they have a party when my mother isn't here?"

Eric spoke into my hair. "You've been away. It's understandable that you feel this way. On some level you probably imagined your mom was still here —" He didn't finish the sentence, and the smooth flowing river rumbled in his chest.

Even that couldn't calm me or take away my onslaught of pain, but he continued. "Your dad was on his own for over a month and Liam for a couple of weeks. Try to understand it from their perspective. They had to pick up some shred of life, especially your dad. Liam went through the same thing when he came home. When he and Harriet visited me, we chatted about exactly that. After a while, he accepted your dad needed to move on. He has such a long life ahead of him. He'll always love your mom. But would you *want* him to pine forever?"

Eric lifted his thumbs to my face, stroking tears away from my cheeks. I searched his gaze. "No. Of course not. It just feels too soon, you know?"

As he took my hands in his, Eric gave a slow nod. "For you, Liam and your dad, it will always feel that way."

Then he gave me a light kiss before leading me between the rows of flowers along our garden path.

Chapter Fifty-Two

Lush lawn blanketed our front garden, clear beneath the full moonlight. A robot tended plants beside the house. Since no set hours applied to the machines, they worked at all times of day. Perhaps it was from the naïveté of youth, but I'd never considered these humanoids before now—how Gina had perfectly positioned them to do her bidding. Her spies. These would never lean toward compassion or supply her with false information to keep innocents safe. In fact, they probably submitted actual footage of recorded or filmed data. Spying.

Eric and I mounted the three patio stairs and entered our home. Mom's scent still infused the air—not in a sharp way, but the way going home had always bathed me in her warm comfort.

Achilles and Yvon's claws scraped and clattered across the wooden floor, their sharp ears arousing them and their barks alerting everyone else. Both dogs bounded into me and almost knocked me off my feet. I sank into a crouch and wrapped their squirming necks and heads in a hug. With a raw chuckle bursting from my throat, I teased, "Battering rams! That's what you are...nothing but battering rams."

As if she'd expected us right at that moment, Harriet flew through the door leading from the back yard. "Come on in, you two! We all have cause for a great big celebration." At a leisurely pace, Liam trailed her, observing her rather than greeting us.

It scared me how confident she seemed about the positive efficacy of Gina's concoction.

I wasn't.

Clearly, tears still streaked my cheeks because as Harriet scanned my face, hers fell. "I know it's hard, Cass. It was difficult for Liam too." She lifted his hand.

Eric gripped me around the waist, and I smiled down at Harriet. "Eric told me."

With a slow blink, Liam almost hid the wince, twitching his cheeks, his voice hard. "We don't have a choice but to deal with it, do we?"

As he fixed his bright green eyes on me, I wanted to launch into my brother's embrace and cry into his shoulder. But something between us had changed. Liam no longer played comforter. On some level, he probably still blamed Eric and me for Mom's murder. It struck me that things might never go back to the way they had been between us.

Caleb broke my dire musing when he ducked his head through the back yard door. His nose was now straight, but a black circle still ringed his eye.

He spoke in a nasal cheer. "Brother...come on out here." Then he disappeared back outside.

Eric's smile faded. He combed his fingers through his hair. "Every time I look at Caleb, this horrible flash of grief and anger slams into me. Then it penetrates that he's actually alive, and it wasn't his fault Graham and I suffered through his loss."

I strengthened my grip around Eric's waist, my tone reassuring. "I can't even imagine how that feels."

Eric shrugged. "Well, I guess I have an entire extended lifetime to get used to it."

Then we followed Caleb, Liam and Harriet outdoors.

Everyone was here tonight, talking and laughing in small groups. At the wrought-iron table, Dad sat and, as he glimpsed me, he slid a hand through his wavy blond hair. With the softest expression, he stood and folded me in a tight embrace. "You are too much like your mother. Do you know that?"

He turned to Eric and shook his hand, clapping him on the upper arm. "It's great to see you're out of prison, son." Then he gave me a wink before refocusing on Eric. "And I'm happy to see you two sorted things out."

As Dad returned to his seat, Eric beamed. I cocked a brow, mouthing at him. "Son?"

Eric shrugged one shoulder, a sly smile twisting his mouth as he double-bounced his brows. "Graham, Harriet and Amanda weren't the only ones visiting me in prison."

Joshua Carter and his wife, Caroline, also sat with Dad. Joshua's hair was in an over-grown afro—wilder than I'd ever seen it. They both greeted us with warm hugs. Joshua grinned at me. "So, tell me, has the travel bug left you yet?"

I guffawed. "Travel bug! Us going out there"—I waved my arm around me—"into untold dangers was hardly a draw-card."

As Roger Winters caught my hand and pulled me down, Joshua jested with Caroline. She burst into a feminine laugh and tucked a loose braid behind her ear.

I didn't hear a word, though, as Roger Winters boomed up at me, "Give us a hug then, why don't you, lassie!"

With one thick forearm around Megan's waist, he pulled me down to him, and his one-armed squeeze made me wince.

The same round dimples I knew so well from Harriet dented Megan's cheeks, and she directed one toward me for a kiss. "Oh, Roger. Now don't you go squeezing the young lady so tight that you hurt her. She'll be wanting to run off again."

Samantha and Paul Carter looked up from their game of virtual swing-ball, bright blue lights delineating the bat, ball, rope and pole. "Ouch, Paul!" Samantha growled as a powerful shot from her brother sent the ball smacking the bat from her hand — an electric pulse in the bat created the lifelike physical sensation of the virtual game. While walking toward us, she thrust her hands behind her shoulders and untied the hairband binding her long, glossy black braids into a pony. She snapped the band around her wrist and her hair tumbled loose, cascading down her back.

Paul ignored his sister's scolding and darted across the lawn, abandoning his own bright blue bat, which dissolved on leaving his hand. His pale blue eyes glinted against his dark skin and his curly light-brown hair was as wild as his Dad's dark afro. "So, do you like your welcome-home party? Do you? We're super-excited to have you and Jonas home!"

The beautiful Samantha widened her huge, dark eyes and clipped him over the back of his head. "Don't be rude, Paul. How must that make Eric feel? You know we're also celebrating his release."

It felt strange. Until that moment, I hadn't missed him. "Where is Jonas, by the way?"

Paul pointed behind me and Samantha slapped his hand down as I turned. Jonas walked through the door with Olivia, clasping her petite olive-toned fingers between his. She wore a tight-fitting summer dress. Her frizz of hair, makeup and red nails looked elegant. The scent of expensive perfume wafted off her. Jonas met my gaze, swallowed and smiled, then reached for Eric's outstretched hand. I gave Olivia a squeeze around her slender shoulders.

She had grown into quite the lady. "Thank you for getting Jonas back to me, Cassidy. I hear it was touch and go at one point...thanks to Eric's *brother*."

I shrugged. "We should thank Ethan and Craig for that." Then I changed the subject. "You look truly amazing, Olivia. Jonas must be proud to stand at your side."

It was true, but Jonas flashed me a glance. I guessed he hadn't told her about the kiss, so I laid my hand on his shoulder and pressed my mouth to his ear. "I won't be the one to hurt her, Jonas — and it will hurt. But you know what I think."

As I stepped back, he flattened his lips, then his posture eased as his tension ebbed. Finally, he offered a single nod.

Caleb draped an arm over Eric's shoulder, wedged himself between us and flopped the other over mine. "So...it's great to see you, brother. Although-h...I should probably have kept your woman for myself. She looks pretty good in a shift."

Eric spun me away from his twin, engulfing me in his arms from behind so we both faced Caleb. Despite his quick actions, a smile carried into his voice. "To think I was happy to see you." Then he whispered into my hair, "Is that true? Did he see you in your underwear?"

I closed my hands over Eric's forearms, providing a roundabout answer. "It wasn't *underwear*, exactly. And, in my defense, I was having a hard time staying on my feet. I'd have gotten a night-robe on if the waterball hadn't tossed me from bed in the middle of the night."

He tightened his hold. "What? Why did it do that?"

"Some kind of fault, I think." I didn't elaborate.

Eric relaxed his grip. "So, the bit about the shift was unavoidable..." He crowed. "Well, brother, enjoy the memory, because rest assured you won't be seeing Cassidy like that again. At least, not while I'm alive."

With that, they both fell into an easy laugh and Caleb clapped a hand on Eric's shoulder. "Man, it's good to see you."

Without releasing his hold on me, Eric threw an arm around Caleb's neck and dragged him close. Emotion trimmed his voice, a single soft word grinding its way through his throat. "Yeah."

From behind, Graham broke the short discomfort in his slow, serene baritone. "Eric, my son. It's good to see you out of that hellhole. I can hardly believe I have both my boys back."

As Eric swung away from me, I stepped back. Graham placed a hand on both twins' upper arms, as if unsure who to embrace. Eric blanketed Graham in a firm hug. "Not nearly as good as it is to be out." Then he met the old man's dark eyes. "Thank you for keeping me sane in there."

A warm smile formed on Graham's mouth. "I'd have broken you out if I'd have known how."

Then all three men laughed long and hard.

The party went on into the night before everyone finally left for their homes. Dad and I walked Graham, Eric and Caleb out to the conveyor street, watching as they ambled toward town. Dad weaved an arm around me, and I beamed at their backs — the three tallest men in town.

As we made our way back home, I looked up at Dad. He blinked a few times and firmed his hug. "Oh, my daughter…your mother…it's on occasions like these, when everyone's together, that it gets so difficult."

A brick formed in my throat, and I gulped, half from the ache Dad felt and half from a sense of relief for the same reason. This time, I didn't stop the tears from tumbling down my face as I squished my cheek into my father's chest. While making our way up our garden path, the only comfort I could offer my amazing father was a simple "I know, Dad."

Chapter Fifty-Three

Amanda arrived the next morning like an explosion, bursting through our front door, red-cheeked and grinning. "Is Harriet here?" She grabbed my hand. "Come."

My heart plummeted, but I kept my voice calm. "No, Harriet isn't here. Excuse my trepidation, but you have a tendency not to deliver the best news."

"Well, this time I do. It's done!" As if I needed clarification, Amanda added, "The inoculation. It's ready. Let's get Harriet."

I drew out the first word. "*O-okay-y*. What if we don't want Harriet to have this inoculation?" I considered for a moment. "To be dead honest, I'm not sure I'm comfortable with you having it either."

Amanda placed a flat hand on her chest. "Aw-w, really? I'm touched." She shrugged. "Regardless. I'm not afraid. Grandmother seems convinced it will work."

My eyes stretched wide. "Are you insane? You saw the VE. That thing could kill you. You can't possibly have *that* much faith in Gina!"

She shrank back, and as if her reason justified the action, admitted, "I like Caleb, and" — bitterness coated her next word — "*Grandmother's* DNA manipulation made our feelings mutual. Honestly, I don't want to fall in love with him and die of old age when he's still a young man. I'd rather end it now before any feelings develop."

"I can't say I'd do the same in your place, Amanda, but I'm not standing in your shoes. Harriet and Liam are going through the identical thing. I can tell you now that Liam won't want Harriet to take the chance. Have you asked Caleb what he thinks?"

She didn't skip a beat. "Well, Caleb doesn't love me yet, so he doesn't get a say."

I sighed, just as Liam and Harriet turned up our garden path, hand-in-hand.

Amanda followed my gaze. "Oh, speak of the… Well, not the devil, but you know what I mean. You must come with me, Harriet. The inoculation is ready. Grandmother wants us — you know…the sick ones — to meet in the town square for our inoculations."

Liam wrapped Harriet in a tight hug against his body, his words tumbling out. "Over my dead body. We'll come, but only to stop this insanity."

I faced Amanda, my mouth tugging into a wry smile. "What did I tell you?"

Harriet glanced from Liam to me and back to Liam. "Since when do you guys get to decide what's good for me? You know I won't stand here getting old while you're all young. I'd rather be dead."

I grimaced at the thought. Harriet *dead*! I couldn't bear it.

Amanda threw the same wry twist of her lips back at me. "My sentiments exactly."

Then she clasped Harriet's hand and towed her toward the main conveyor.

Liam didn't release his grasp on Harriet. Neither did he stop her. Instead, he walked with them, trying to convince her not to go ahead.

I pursued two of the people I loved most in this world toward the intersection footbridge. Night lights never dazzled it now, but daylight reflected a transparent kaleidoscope of rainbow colors off its surface. As I crossed and scanned the dual conveyor toward town, I gaped. The lit Petrivillian Enterprises displays broadcast the news of the vaccine for all to see, as if it were a miracle cure — not the death sentence that I expected it was. The consideration shredded my gut into a thousand shards.

My words came out breathless. "Why don't you at least let someone else have it first, Harriet? An adult."

At that moment, running footsteps pounded up from behind and Jonas skidded to a halt at my side.

He spoke to his sister's back, his voice tight with his obvious tension. "I just got news of this, Harriet. You're not considering doing this, are you then?"

Harriet glared over her shoulder, answering both our questions at once. "Of course, I am, Jo. How's that right, girlfriend? How can I let someone else take the risk while I sit back and watch — adult or no? The guilt will kill me. Either we do this together or no one does."

Harriet and Liam stepped onto the conveyor after Amanda. Liam breathed in short bursts, his tone pleading. "Please, babe. We can't have fifty-two people dying on us. If you won't do this for me, think of your parents and Jonas."

As we drifted past the park, Harriet's voice grew softer than I'd ever heard it. "Don't you see, Liam? I *am* thinking of you…you, Jonas, my parents, Cassidy…all of you. Can you imagine the daily guilt you'll suffer if I'm aging and you're not?"

She was right, but as we passed our old school, her confession didn't stop the knot gripping my stomach. My throat constricted. "This is worse, Harriet. You can't do this." My next word was a choked sob. "Please?"

Harriet was done talking. The intersection footbridges were passing too quickly. It was as if the conveyor sped up. Too soon, we passed Mama Candy's and floated toward the large, glossy number two, which signaled the end of our journey. The end of Harriet's journey. The end of Liam's life. Liam, Jonas, Roger, Megan, me. It was wrong, just wrong. With every fiber of my being, I knew it would fail.

People poured from office buildings. A vast crowd already extended across the cobbled town square. Others sat in the grassy areas on benches beneath trees. Yet others hovered around the central fountain. My heart stuttered. My body numbed. I caught Liam's forearm from behind. "Stop her, Li. Don't let her do this." My tears flowed fast and free, joining the silent drops rolling down my brother's cheeks.

Harriet and Amanda ripped away from Liam. In seconds, the two darted into the crowd.

"No," Liam roared while Jonas bellowed, "Harriet! Don't you dare do this!"

But the crowd shut his sister out of view.

Liam jerked me into an embrace, a racked sob bursting from his chest. "How do I stop her, Cass? What does it make me if I force her to do something against her will?"

Jonas slumped, and I stretched out a hand for his. But Olivia emerged through the crowd and flung her feminine arms around his broad frame. I lowered my hand. This was right. Jonas *should* have someone of his own for times like this—someone who loved and comforted him. Someone like Olivia.

While I was pressed against my brother's chest, my mind took me back to when we'd each been fixated on an enormous digital display across the town square— like somebody had activated a replay button. Only, it wasn't Mom on the platform above the town square. It wasn't Mom tumbling to her death. This time, Harriet's life was on the line, as well as Amanda's and so many others.

Her name broke from my throat in a long lament. "Harriet."

Then Graham appeared, draping his arms around us all. I looked up into his warm mahogany face, taking in the electric salt-and-pepper curls. My question came as a sob. "Is Eric here?"

Graham's dark brown eyes were so soft, his voice slow and cadenced. "It's only by chance Olivia and I are. The boys are at home. She and I came into town to purchase clothes for Caleb. The trumpet sounded as we were about to head into a store. So, we looked to see what had happened and noticed the billboards popping up with the...*announcement*." On the last word, sarcasm laced his melodic voice.

I scowled up at the nearest display. Medical robots dressed in white scrubs swarmed the landing of the municipal building. They were assembling gleaming silver hospital cots covered with white bedding — fifty-two of them, to be exact.

As Harriet and Amanda gained the top stair, I glimpsed them on a digital display. Twisting away from it, I faced the building itself as they spun to look directly at us. I stared at them. Side-by-side, the two girls thrust their shoulders back. Harriet fixed Liam with her most resolute gaze before moving to Jonas and me. I couldn't help but shake my head over and over, my forehead wrenched tight as emotion closed my throat.

Graham seemed to hold his breath — clearly weighing whether he should voice his thoughts. He exhaled. "All this has triggered a memory of something the boys' parents said."

He didn't need to say another word to attract our attention. Our full concentration froze on him as he went on. He spoke faster than I'd ever heard him — urgent. "I remembered Matthew and Elena Morgan saying it was important for both boys to survive if all are to remain alive. I don't know if it has something…" He stopped as he met my widening eyes.

It was as if a lightbulb slammed into me. "It's a long shot, but…Liam! Jonas! Whatever you guys do, stop them! Make them give me an hour. One hour!"

Then I bolted through the crowd toward conveyor five.

Chapter Fifty-Four

I ran the usual ten-minute walk along conveyor five toward Graham's home in less than four, and the near-sprint along his arced side street, in one. Barely taking in their lawned front yard, oak tree and shrubs as I raced past them, I attacked the front door, beating on it until it flung wide.

Eric stood with his mouth agape. "What's up, Cassidy? You're out of breath." He tugged me against him, then stretched me to arm's length. "What's wrong?"

When he again drew me to him, I jerked away. "There's no time, Eric. Where's Caleb? Where's the VE? We need it *now*!"

Eric allowed me space to pass. "Well, you'd better come inside."

When Eric didn't immediately call Caleb, irritation bubbled up in my chest. That was when I noticed Eric's cheeks looked flushed. "Are you okay? Where *is* Caleb?"

Eric sighed. "I'm okay." He signaled at the dark-wood upstairs landing. "He's up there. The VE cube is here." He tossed his forehead toward a Kaleidotonium-topped table in their open-plan dining room. He'd pushed the head chair aside and placed the now-dormant virtual experience cube on the table. "And you're wanting the cube for?" His voice rose in question.

"Oh." I dipped my chin in a slow, comprehending nod. "You were using it." I gestured at the VE. My brows tightened, and I gazed up at him with steady compassion. "Was it the same as when Caleb touched it?"

Eric blinked a few times and swallowed. "It was, except they used my name when they spoke."

"Did it play out to the end?"

"It ended seconds before you knocked."

"At the same place?"

Eric dragged out the word, pitch climbing. "Ye-e-s?"

Before I even voiced my hypothesis, Eric whirled toward the upper landing and yelled. "Caleb...Caleb!"

A door opened, and Caleb peered over the banister. "What?"

"Get your ass down here!"

Caleb shrugged but didn't hurry down the stairs as he yawned. "What's the rush?"

Eric turned back to me. "What *is* the rush?"

"It's Harriet!" I halted and met Caleb's bleary-eyed stare as he joined us. "And Amanda."

He straightened. "What's up with Amanda?"

"Gina's about to give them the inoculation."

Caleb clenched his fists, eyes shooting wide. "Now?"

I pinned him with a flat glare. "So, do you see why I'm in a hurry?"

As he hurtled down the remaining steps, he growled. "It's going to kill them! Did you tell Gina, or rather Susan, that?"

"They won't listen. Liam and Jonas are asking them to give us an hour, but I don't know if they will."

Caleb thrust his shoulders back. "Right. What are we doing?"

I didn't need to answer. Eric already seemed to have guessed my intentions. "Cassidy wants us to activate the VE together."

Eric didn't mention *why* I wanted this, but Caleb followed Eric's gaze to the dining-table and stalked toward it. "Well, what are we waiting for?"

He lifted the VE cube and handled it for a few seconds, then handed it to Eric, who examined it for a moment before setting it on the table. Without a second's delay, it burst to life, and the expanding light devoured us—pulled us in to its core. Again Mr. and Mrs. Morgan faced us. They wore different T-shirts. Intertwining my fingers with Eric's, I pressed. *I'm here, Eric. I love you.* Although I didn't say the words, with a deep sigh he returned my squeeze.

Something else was different. Their expressions. They smiled. The familiar scissures marking the man's cheeks while the woman's aquamarine eyes sparkled.

She laughed and cried at the same time, her light, feminine Texan accent filled with love…and warmth…and heartache. "Oh, my boys. My boys. You both made it."

With such affection, she swiveled and looked into the man's blue eyes, which shimmered with unshed tears. "This is the scenario your mother and I desperately hope for" — after a slow blink, he proceeded — "and the one we're creating first."

As he paused, Eric dropped my hand and, winding his arms around me, he half rotated, tugging me against his chest and burying his cheek against the top of my head so we could both watch the VE. I felt rather than saw Caleb resting a hand on Eric's shoulder. Each of us fixed on their parents as they explained the longevity drugs. When they came to the part with the recipe for *Ellie,* my body stiffened. Although we'd already learned this recipe, it was this part I wanted to see. Or at least, I wanted to see what happened next.

It was their mother who continued. Eric's muscled back went as rigid as a board against me, and my hands balled in an involuntary clench.

"Now we will give you the remedy for the people who" — I inhaled and paused, as the VE struck the exact point it had stumbled before. *Dare I hope?* I gritted my teeth. For the longest time, their mother froze. Then — "started aging."

Those two words sent my heart into a soar. I reeled, and in a three-person hug, Eric, Caleb and I jumped up and down. "Yes! It's working!"

Then the VE silenced. Dread again welled in me. Their parents weren't fading in and out like before, and their virtual selves appeared solid. Had the entire thing frozen? Again, my breathing stopped as I observed them. *Are their chests rising and falling and hands moving a fraction?* After the longest time, their mother finally parted her lips. "When recording the individual virtual experiences, we will hold these findings back, because if only one of you survives, we can't save anyone who underwent any form of resuscitation. They need to combine both of your DNA — each of you bears slight variants of the same gene. These are essentially those involved in DNA maintenance, and those that regulate the cell cycle, similar to within the queen ant."

Eric pivoted to his brother. "We should have guessed. Mom and Dad wouldn't have left one of us feeling guilty for not being able to save others. This way we wouldn't have a choice."

Eric's dad cleared his throat. "The ensuing instructions are exigent. At least twenty-four hours before providing this remedy, patients *must* undergo exposure to *Ellen*. This can happen any time from years before up to the preceding twenty-four hours. The *Ellen* won't cause any changes in these patients — neither to halt nor slow their rapid aging nor to re-extend their lives. However, they'll die if they don't receive it in exactly this manner. It won't be a pleasant death. Your DNA will re-extend their lives, but the *Ellie* formulae will kill them, even if administered years later."

I didn't want to think about how they'd established *these* facts, so I blocked the thought. That was the past, and we needed to heal people in the present.

As if expecting my question, their mother cocked her head. "Just so you know, Eric and Caleb, we didn't conduct tests on actual humans. We tested on pseudo-beings — a kind of fleshy blob wrapped in skin with a human chemical makeup. Pharmaceutical labs created these pseudo-beings in a bid to stop animal testing."

I responded as if she'd spoken to me, a sarcastic edge to my voice. "Oh well, that's a relief then."

Eric snorted with a soft laugh, then a deep inhale. "This means we have everything we need."

Almost forgetting our urgency, I nodded. "It does." Then my eyes flew wide. "It also means Susan should *not* give them that inoculation."

Caleb wasted not a second more and snatched up the VE cube. "How much time do we have?"

"I don't know. They may not have listened to Liam and Jonas."

Without delay, Caleb sprinted for the door and out. Even Without delay, Caleb sprinted for the door and out. I couldn't match the twins' long strides, but Eric clutched my hand and boosted my speed as we raced back to the town square.

Chapter Fifty-Five

Graham waited where we'd left him on the cobbled paving of the town square—right near the glossy number two.

Caleb whirled the old man around, but I spoke before he could. "Where are they, Graham? Liam and Jonas? Did they come back?"

"No. They're still up there. They and the girls used the elevator but returned about five minutes ago. But by the boys' body posture, it didn't look promising. They've just headed—"

I didn't wait for Graham to finish. Instead, I towed Eric into a sprint toward the municipal building stairs. Caleb overtook us, but Eric stayed with me, dodging through the spectating crowd. Ahead, Caleb leaped over a man as he bent forward to tie a shoelace. I bumped past several others and my open shoulder ached by the time I ran up the stairs. As we arrived at the top, the medics were readying the inoculation disks.

Caleb produced a voice as loud as a megaphone. "Stop! Don't touch these people! Stop *now*!"

I sprinted at Jonas and Liam. Megan, Roger and Dad encircled Harriet's cot. It was Liam who ripped the rod from the medic robot's hand. Gregory covered his sister with his body, but the robot at the far side of her cot reached the device toward her skin. Caleb dove onto the humanoid, side-tackling it to the paving.

I revolved a full circle, absorbing the chaos. Many ignored us. "Stop!" I shrieked. "You're going to *kill* them."

That was all it took. The families of those lying on the glinting cots sprang into action. I scanned the area as family members and even patients wrestled inoculation disks from medic robots. It was strange, though. The robots fought back. Someone screamed. Then another shriek echoed across the cavernous space. And another. We were *too late*!

When trumpets sounded on the digital billboards across the square, everyone halted. Memories of Mom wrenched at my soul once again and a grimace dragged my mouth down. Gina's snake-like voice came out strong. She wasn't overlooking the square. No. Her and Susan's squat bodies emerged from the elevator bank.

Gina held her chin high. "What is this furor about? Ah-h, yes. Naturally, I'm not surprised that Miss Jones is at the forefront of the upheaval. I should have ended the insolent girl along with her mother, I suppose."

Susan glared at Gina and opened her mouth as if to speak, but the older woman strutted toward Amanda. Not seeming inclined to even try to stop her domineering mother, Susan shuffled after her.

I knew Gina wouldn't listen to me. She hated me. So, I screamed at Susan instead. "The inoculation is going to kill them, Susan. We have proof. We have the cure."

Did she even hear me?

She paused mid-stride, then continued—not casting a single glance in my direction. Instead, she fixed on Caleb and Gregory, who were struggling to restrain the robot, since it possessed the strength of the Kaleidotonium from which it was forged. Dad left Harriet in the capable hands of Liam, Jonas, Eric and Roger to help Caleb and Gregory. Amanda's eyes flew wide with fear. She ducked off the far side of the cot from the battling trio as Dad dove into the fray.

I switched my attention to Harriet. She was still sitting on her cot, but she hunched over and hugged her knees to her chest as if trying to make herself as small as possible. Liam, Jonas, Eric and Roger sat on the robot, which was now flattened to the tiled floor. They were making certain it got nowhere near my friend.

Gina edged around Amanda's cot toward the fighting boys and humanoid. The girl's grandmother would come through for her and instruct the medic to stop.

Although Gina never did what anyone expected, she now bent and snatched the inoculation from the medic's hand. Then she righted herself and straightened the hem of her pink, heavy-fabric top and pressed her horn-rimmed spectacles into the bridge of her nose. "My, my! *Why-oh-why* do I have to deal with such incompetence? Is it beyond anyone's ability to accomplish such a mundanely simple task?"

Regardless of how I loathed her scornful tone, it was over.

Gina rounded the cot, returning to Amanda. She stretched forward as if she meant to pull her granddaughter into a hug—more affection than I'd thought the cruel woman capable of.

Instead of embracing Amanda, though, Gina went on in her sickly-sweet tone. "Well, I suppose if you want something done, you have to do it yourself, now don't you?"

With that, Gina closed her fingers around Amanda's wrist and angled the inoculation device toward her granddaughter's skin. "This shall not kill you—silly bunch of cowards. To prove it, I shall administer the inoculation to my granddaughter first."

My mouth dropped open, and I stumbled backward. A moment later, I was on the move.

Amanda never even got the chance to react—so certain that her grandmother wouldn't hurt her—but I did. I threw myself into Gina, ramming her and knocking the rod and disk from the malicious woman's hand. It skittered beneath the cot to where Susan now stood over Gregory, Caleb, Dad and the robot.

Susan snatched up the inoculation, her voice a ragged scream of fury, heartache and desperation. "You will never lay a finger on my daughter again. How could you? You're *evil*." Susan said the last word like a curse word that she couldn't believe she'd used, let alone on her mother.

Then Susan raised her voice, and it rang out through the displays and over the square. "Medics! Cease what you are doing at once."

She darted around the cot and handed me the device, sobbing as she pulled Amanda into a tight hug. "I am so sorry, my baby girl." She whimpered. "I have failed you. All of you. Did anyone—?"

She seemed unable to complete her sentence. An enormous gorilla-shape mounted the stairs. Austin strode toward Susan, placing one hand on her shoulder and the other on Amanda's, his voice so gentle as he addressed the girl. "You're worthy of so much better than the way your grandmother treats you. Your mom and I will take care of you and Gregory from now on. We'll make sure you're both safe."

So much kindness from the brute who I'd feared not so many months ago.

He nodded at Susan and turned to Gina, who tried to clamber to her feet. Taking her hand, he helped her up. But before she was fully up, he spun her outstretched arm behind her back and grabbed for the other, cuffing her wrists. He grimaced, clearly gleaning no joy from arresting his girlfriend's mother. Still, he managed a snide remark. "So, old woman. Since you're so sure you're a cut above the rest in the intelligence department, no one needs to tell you where you're off to."

Susan tried to repeat her question. "Did anyone —?"

This time she didn't cut off. Nor did she need to. A pained scream drowned her voice. My forehead clenched so hard that it hurt. Tears sprang into my eyes as more screams burst out in patches over the considerable area. Two, three, four, five...

Susan didn't hesitate for a second as she barked an order. "Save them! Oh-h, please? Save them!"

Chapter Fifty-Six

The medic robots had seemingly hibernated. In a split second, they came to life and converged toward the screams nearest them.

Beside Harriet, Megan choked out a ragged sob. "What has that woman done? She's insane! Will her tyranny never end?"

A guttural moan broke from my chest. "I hate her so much!"

Then Eric was behind me, closing his arms around my body, his voice a growl. "You're forgetting it was Susan who allowed Gina to take control, knowing full well what her mother was capable of."

Susan responded to Eric's remark in a strangled whisper. "I cannot deny what you say is the truth. You would not believe how I regret my actions. It is a mistake I shall *never* again make. Regardless, my remorse shall offer no comfort to these poor victims."

I rotated from Eric as another echoed scream erupted beside Amanda. "No-o!" A man, teenage boy and girl wailed, clinging to the figure of a woman on a cot.

She hung limp in their arms, blood oozing from her ears, nose, eyes and mouth. It leaked out red-brown and gelatinous, smearing the faces, necks, shoulders and bodies of her family before dripping to the floor. Four robots whipped her cot away from them.

"Don't take my wife from us." The man sobbed.

But the robots ignored him and raced off with the woman between them. The man and children chased after them, her blood still drenching their clothes and skin.

The robots remaining in the open-air foyer disassembled the cots, though the crowd didn't disperse. Pockets of angry conversation burst out around us. And everywhere, everywhere, expressions were the same—distrust in Susan and unadulterated loathing for Gina. As if seeking their comfort, Susan clung on to Gregory and Amanda.

She greeted my stare with an agonized frown lining her forehead. "I am afraid they are right. I am most definitely not fit to lead them into the future when I cannot even guide them safely past a single threat." With that she sighed, posture slumping. "I suppose you'd better come with me."

I wasn't the only one who followed Susan and her children toward the elevator. Eric, Caleb, Liam, Harriet, Jonas and Olivia joined us.

On reaching the second floor, the elevator doors didn't open. A blue virtual keypad lit up and Susan punched in a series of numbers. Finally, the exit yawned, but Susan didn't step out.

Instead, she dipped her head as if in silent prayer, curling her shoulders forward. "I need to check in with the medics. I hope they're able to stop the bleeding and replace their plasma before it's too late for the poor folks." She gestured her palm toward the plush leather couches. "Please make yourselves comfortable while you wait." She absorbed Amanda's then Gregory's shattered expressions. "I would prefer that you both stay here too."

We didn't sit but paced the floor while Caleb, Eric and I explained to our friends what we'd learned. When Susan came back half an hour later, her face was flushed. The whites of her eyes shimmered pink, and she repeatedly gulped, holding her hand over her stomach — as if she could barely contain her emotions. She leaned against the kingly dark-wood desk but didn't speak, and kept dropping her gaze, trying to hide her trembling chin. Finally, she appeared to force her shoulders back then met our gazes one-by-one.

She took a steeling breath, managing a hoarse, rasping croak. "We couldn't—" Her voice cracked, and she cleared her throat then started again. "We couldn't save them. Six people, we lost." As the hard reality sank in, she reemphasized the number. "*Six!*" She swept her thumb and forefinger together over her eyes and hard lines raked across her forehead. "Two adults and...and *four* teens – *MAC players!*" She paused, then listed the six names, each one a commemoration. "Roger...Hennesy. Melissa...Rutger — the lady near you. Samuel...Jackson. Aretha...George. Clement...Charles. Mary...Anderson. All dead."

Grief washed over me. I didn't know the adults, but Samuel was *fifteen* — barely more than a child. Clement and Mary were my age. And *Aretha*. Aretha was Team Salamander's star player — Amanda's teammate.

Silent tears streamed down Amanda's face, and Caleb pulled her into a tight hug. Although the two barely knew each other, their shared affection was blatantly obvious—the way a moth was drawn to a flame. Caleb would care for Amanda more than her grandmother ever had.

Susan gave a soft, slow blink. Her face slackened as she tilted it back and looked at the ceiling. Without returning her gaze to us, she swallowed and continued, her voice detached and cold. "Present your findings."

Numbness seized my body, and I couldn't open my mouth to speak. Gina had again slaughtered innocent people. Harriet could have been among them. Liam clenched his fists and jaw, and the way he gripped Harriet to him told me he was considering the same thing.

So, instead of telling Susan what we knew, Caleb handed the VE to Eric, who set it on the floor, their touches activating the experience. Rather than watching it, Susan listened until they read off the information about Eric and Caleb's DNA. She didn't lower her expressionless face but lifted the digipar from her desk and let it take notes.

Even as the VE sucked its display in, Susan didn't change her features or position and spoke in the same detached coldness. "Thank you."

Caleb picked up the VE from the floor and Amanda moved to her mother, taking Susan's hands. Tears still made rivulets down Amanda's cheeks, her voice quiet. "This is not your fault, Mother. Grandmother is to blame."

Susan finally lowered her face and rested on her daughter's gaze, her voice flat and resigned. "Oh, but my darling daughter, it is my fault. As Petriville's leader, there is no one else to blame. I should have known better than to allow Mother to manipulate me into doing her bidding. However, I did. And my people are suffering as a result." Finally, she released her unshed tears, and they flowed down her cheeks. "Please leave. All of you." She flashed a glance between Eric and Caleb. "Medics are in the lobby to take your DNA samples. I shall have the new formula produced. It won't take more than a few days. I shall let you know when it's ready."

Susan and even Amanda spoke in the same haughty manner as Gina. Yet they were nothing like their predecessor. Still, their formality highlighted the family trait—punctuating their likeness to the woman everyone hated.

Chapter Fifty-Seven

As the Morgans had instructed, Susan administered Gina's hidden stash of *Ellen* to the ailing — only them. A few days later, her scientists completed the new formula. Again, the medic robots erected cots in the municipal building lobby. In the town square, people lingered with praying hands and bowed heads. The Petrivillian Enterprises banner filled the silent digital displays, wafting in a fictitious electronic breeze. An eerie quiet reigned, fear gripping the waiting crowd. Low rumbled murmurs rippled through across the square and lobby as patients lay on the white bedding of the gleaming silver cots.

On one side of Harriet's cot, Megan clasped her daughter's hand. On the other, Roger stroked his daughter's forehead. Liam stooped over her at the head, cupping her collarbones while Jonas rested a palm on the cusp of her shoulder. At the foot of her cot, Eric, Dad and I rubbed or patted her lower legs — or at least the jeans covering them.

Harriet bit her lip as nervousness slipped into Megan's trembling, too-loud voice. "Now, there's no need to be a martyr. Let them treat an adult first."

Shadows hung dark and heavy beneath Liam's normally bright green eyes. He raised his focus from Harriet's face and blinked. "You're wasting your time, Megan. I've been telling her that ever since the last disaster."

Roger winked at his daughter and swiveled his large head, his broad Scots booming. "Oh, aren't you a cynical bunch? You've got to have some faith in our scientists. Besides, our daughter is going to be quite fine. Aren't you then, Harriet?"

But the way he flexed and clenched the thick forearm nearest me said he was far from relaxed. Harriet managed a feeble nod and a weak smile.

Two cots behind me and one to the left, Susan held her daughter's hand with Gregory at Amanda's head. Austin supported Susan with an arm around her shoulder and a hand on Amanda's forearm. At the end of her cot, Caleb shuffled from one foot to the other but didn't reach out to touch her. Although he'd embraced her a few days before, this was perhaps too personal. Maybe he didn't think he'd earned the right to stand at her side — not yet, anyway.

Although Susan spoke in a soft, steady voice, it reverberated through the digital displays. "If anyone opposes having this, please do not. I've instructed the medics to adhere to your requests." She drew a deep breath. "However, if you are ready, then let us proceed."

In slow, fluid motion, a robot made for Harriet. With steady, human-like hands it carried the shiny silver inoculation rod and disk. Entirely ignoring us, it spoke to Harriet in a gentle melody. "Are you ready, Miss Winters? Would you like me to proceed?"

Harriet nodded, then moved her gaze to Liam before shutting them tight. I firmed my grip on her ankle—not a restraint, a sign of my support.

Complete and utter silence fell—everyone staying their collective breaths.

The robot set the flat disk lightly to Harriet's inner forearm, withdrew it, retreated a single pace and stopped.

Nothing happened. Still, we remained silent. And still nothing happened.

How long did it take before the screaming started the last time? A minute? Two minutes? Five minutes? Too much had happened. I didn't have any real frame of reference. Then, as before, a single scream shattered the silence. Then more and more and more. These weren't the six sporadic cries of a few days ago. These were the screams of every family member and every friend who stood in the municipal building lobby. The violence didn't spare Harriet. She jerked with such ferocity that her cot shook. Megan shrieked as the robot stepped forward and placed a flat silver stick in Harriet's mouth as if to keep her tongue flat. But it did nothing else— nothing to aid her.

"Help her!" Megan wailed, releasing her daughter's hand and hugging herself. "Help my daughter!"

Every cot as far as I could see shuddered and bucked. Caleb closed the gap to Amanda's cot and pressed a hand to her leg while Susan's face twisted as she clung to and chafed her daughter's fingers.

At least no blood poured from her mouth, nose, eyes and ears. Not yet. Nor from Harriet. *How long had it taken for that to happen the last time?* After what felt like an age, my best friend's writhing subsided. Still, ragged, panting gasps followed. Slowly, all around, the screams diminished. The jerking slowed. Before long, quiet descended.

Megan unwound her arms from herself and lifted Harriet's hand, her forehead furrowed. "Are you okay, my child? Are you okay, Harriet? Please speak to me."

Harriet didn't say a word, but she squinted at the surrounding faces. Minutes later, her breathing settled. She gave a tentative smile, her voice a hoarse, slow whisper. "I'm okay, I think."

When Susan again spoke, her voice was neither happy nor sad, nor did it even carry any measure of relief. "Please remain where you are. We will conduct tests to determine if you are indeed okay and whether changes have occurred in your cells."

The robot beside Harriet again came forward and slid a hand into its jacket, extracting a shiny silver rod fixed to the top of a small gold disk. It laid the disk on Harriet's forearm. Without a word of acknowledgment, it returned the rod and disk to its jacket, then retreated with the other robots into the municipal building.

For the next hour, we awaited the outcome. Over that time, the chatting among the crowd grew in volume and in animation. Not too long after that, patients sat up, dangling their legs over the edges of the cots or even getting to their feet. Finally, a lone man emerged from an elevator—a human, at least. Silence dropped over the crowd like a stone. Everyone watched the man. He lowered his gaze, neither hurrying his pace nor dawdling.

When he came to Susan and spoke, his whispered voice didn't reach the digital billboards. A light frown creased his forehead, and I tried to figure out what he was saying—or at least determine what his body-language conveyed. I could make out neither, and Susan offered him a brief nod before he turned and retreated.

She gave nothing away either. Not in stance or voice. She kept her face impassive, her voice level and cool. "Do not forget those who aren't with us today, because they should have been celebrating with us too." Then she took the longest pause and inhaled a slow breath.

Myriad thoughts sped through my mind. *Are we celebrating? If so,* what *are we celebrating? Even if the treatment cured them and they lived...will they live out a normal lifespan...or an extended one, like us?*

Absolute silence hovered over the town square and the lobby. Even along the conveyors, spectators halted, peering up at the digital display boards—at Susan's figure and her unusually cautious voice. I wanted to scream.

Finally, a smile trickled onto her lips. "All who stand in Petriville today will live equally long—more or less."

The roar erupting through the crowd was deafening. Susan spun away, pulling her daughter into her arms as we crowded around Harriet. Tears streamed down every face. But Liam most elicited my attention. He choked and laughed and cried, all at the same time. I wanted to hug him, to tell him how happy I felt for him and Harriet, but this wasn't my time. Instead, I smiled up at Eric, took his hand and led him from the open-air foyer toward the fountain.

Chapter Fifty-Eight

The six deaths marred the celebration in the town square that night. No family members or friends of the deceased attended. Although I wasn't responsible, guilt still raged through me and I often found myself grimacing or biting my lips. That happened in equal parts with joy — a happiness so great that laughter burst from my chest while a sense of warmth infused my body. Most other citizens attended, as well as the outsiders we'd welcomed into our community. Or more precisely Graham, Ethan, Craig, Eric, Caleb and Olivia. Jaya and Aaron arrived too, along with countless friends who now lived in town and received credits for their work. Robots wearing fake tuxedos glided around carrying serving trays of food and drinks.

For the entire time, Caleb and Amanda sat chatting on the fountain's edge. They didn't notice when Eric and I finally left with Graham.

As we strolled with the old man along the conveyor, Eric clasped my hand. I glanced up at Graham's contented smile—as if his world were as good as it could be.

Probably since the mood was so light, Eric broached a potentially uncomfortable subject. He placed his free hand around the nape of Graham's neck, voice tentative and soft. "Graham?"

The old man turned his face toward Eric, a crease moving across his forehead. He waited.

Eric lowered his arm and went on, voice stronger. "The people who disappeared from the refuge... What happened to them?"

He let his voice fade out, but I half peeked around him to see Graham's slow, comprehending nod. He drew his forehead into tight furrows, as if the memory were too unpleasant to contemplate. His voice cracked. "I understand what you're thinking, my son, and you're right. Accident or illness took them from us." Bitterness crept into his tone. "Unlike here, we didn't have the means to bring them back."

"Did we...bury them? Like the others?" *Like the people who died in the tenth year—the year you let us remember*, Eric likely meant but didn't say.

Graham understood. "We did. Everyone attended each of their funerals—like with the people you remember. In fact, I gave them a better send-off, hoping some part of your brains might hold on to the memory. It didn't seem to help." Graham took a long pause, then peered around Eric at me. He straightened as we stepped from the conveyor onto the walkway toward their home and continued talking. "I recall that day I met you in prison, young lady. I hoped to convince Gina to give us her supply of *Ellen*, since she wasn't intending to use it. No one in the refuge would have been any the wiser, so I'd never have had to explain – a coward's way out. Then you handed me Joshua's coded message, and I knew I could never convince her to give us any."

I didn't mean to divert the conversation, but my adrenaline surged, excitement raging through me. "Of course! The coded messages. How could I have forgotten? We drummed those sentences into our heads! But it was a while ago. I'm not sure if I still remember them all. Please tell me you still have the key?"

Graham smiled and pitched his brows together before relaxing his face. "Mm-m, the key to Joshua's codes. Can you tell me the current importance?"

"My mom's letter, Graham. Caleb raised the possibility when we rode in the waterball that she may have used coded words. I didn't think about it when we first read it, but she knew those codes by heart. It makes sense she'd have used them."

Graham questioned my logic. "If she protected her message with your thumbprints, why would she have written the letter in code?"

Eric emerged of a distant stare. "The answer to that is pretty obvious, don't you think? She wrote it with someone looking over her shoulder."

We turned up Graham's garden path, my heart thumping in my throat. "Exactly."

Graham came on board, and his voice lilted in a question. "I suppose you have your letter with you?"

"I do." I patted Mom's final digipar in my jean's pocket. "Right here."

We entered their house and sat at their Kaleidotonium dining table. After extracting the digipar, I thumb-tapped the center and watched while it wriggled itself flat. Then I instructed, "Show me Mom's letter."

A minute later, Graham came out with the coded digipar and Eric set three cups of coffee on the table. "It's going to be a long night, I suspect, so this might help."

I read through Mom's letter slowly while Graham checked for coded words.

To my most adored Peter, Liam and Cassidy,

Of all outcomes, I never thought I'd say goodbye to you like this. Should I apologize? I suppose you won't want that. Please understand that I face my next journey with peace. Nothing any of you did or didn't do caused my fate. This is on me alone. The world is full of danger.

Peter, my heart breaks to know I'll never again feel the warmth and safety of your loving embrace. I long for it, even now. You are my heart and soul. You always were, even in high school.

Liam and Cassidy, my heart explodes with pride when I think of you both. Continue with your studies. Forget all that has happened. Love and learn and grow into all you're meant to be. Don't be held back by this tragedy.

In the olden days, people who had committed treason died. Even if you blame Gina, it will not help bring you comfort or me back. I'm almost embarrassed that I denied involvement because someone discovered where I'd hidden the notes in my office – and, of course, they then alerted Gina.

Please know that it was never my intention to hurt the three of you – the people I love most in this world. So yes, in my own way, I am sorry.

Your ever-loving wife and mother,
Emily

As soon as I'd said Mom's name, I checked. "Did you see any?"

Graham took the longest pause. *What is it with adults?* They seemed to find joy in sustaining the suspense.

Even when he spoke, he didn't answer my question directly. "So, this may well be mere coincidence, but in these sentences—*Please understand that I face my next journey with peace, Don't be held back by this tragedy* and *The world is full of danger.*" He'd emphasized the words *journey*, *tragedy* and *danger*, then stopped and looked back at the digipar.

I could barely contain my irritation at the old man's delay. "What do they translate to?"

"Hold your horses, young lady. I'm getting there. Okay…" Graham seemed to muse. "There is something specific in one paragraph after the word 'tragedy'. There, we need to use every fifth word. Then, the word 'journey' states *The leader is not to be trusted*, so that must refer to Gina. And the word 'full' means Emily herself was in danger."

"So, every fifth word in the"—I scrolled through the letter—"fifth paragraph."

I read it through again and Eric noted the words.

"*People*…died…Gina…bring…back…" Eric looked up. "Well, we already learned that." Then he continued with the remaining fifth words. "I…discovered… notes…of…Gina."

The revelation didn't hit with the force of my adrenaline. Instead, it came as a lethargic realization. "That's why she killed my mom. My mother found out what Gina had done." Tears pricked the corners of my eyes. "Do you think she threatened to expose Gina?

Worse than that, do you think Susan was aware of Mom's discovery?"

Eric hauled me to my feet. "Well, there's one way to find out. What do you say we go wake the old cow up? Heaven knows, when I was in there, they did that to me often enough."

Eric's attempt to lift my spirits had me puffing out a laugh. "What? Now?" I cocked my head and looked up at him.

"Yes, now. There's no time better than the present. And" — Eric pulled his lips into a cheeky smile, tugging the crevassed dimples down his cheeks and bringing a twinkle to his beautiful aquamarines — "I kind of like the idea of making her squirm in the middle of the night."

Chapter Fifty-Nine

The silence of a sleeping night blanketed Petriville as we stepped from the conveyor into the town square. Caleb and Amanda still sat at the edge of the fountain, but the square was otherwise deserted. The two faced each other, Caleb holding Amanda's hands. They were focused so intently on each other that they never noticed us, and we left them to their liaison. Eric and I crossed the cobbled paving to sector four and climbed the stairs to the train station. The glass doors glided open, and the high-tech silver bullet train lay quiet and deserted. But the train station wasn't peaceful — not at all. Or at least the echoing women's voices rising from below were anything but muted. I couldn't make out the content of the vicious, snide remarks, but the tones were clear.

I twisted my mouth into a smirk. "We don't need to guess who that is. It sounds as if they're verbally trying to separate each other's heads from their shoulders."

Eric snorted at my analogy. "Like mother, like daughter. Although,"—he cocked his head as if considering—"I'm not surprised Susan hates her mother after all this."

"Does she though, Eric? Is it even possible to hate your mother?"

"Not for you and me. But neither of us were cursed with a mother like Susan's."

I found a smile forming on my lips—possibly malicious. "Well then, we couldn't have picked a better time to do this. It lends me more than a little satisfaction knowing we're about to add fuel to Gina's temper." My hand in Eric's, we wandered down the silver stairs. "And this time she can do nothing about it."

When we neared the lower level, Susan mounted the stairs. She started. "Are you here to see me?"

I puffed out a heavy breath. "I might as well kill two birds with one stone. So, yes. You *and* Gina."

Susan showed no sign of the raging temper we'd heard from above besides slightly flushed cheeks. "I suppose you heard my argument with Mother." She looked tired.

"Uh...uh." I stuttered an uncertain response, but Eric answered, "No one can blame you for trying to protect your daughter, Susan. She's a nice girl."

My stomach clenched at Eric's affectionate assessment of Amanda. But he was right. She was nice. Just because I was insecure didn't mean she wasn't deserving of his praise.

"Thank you, Eric. I like to assume she is. For my part, I'm sorry for what Mother put you through." She gave a slow blink then added, "No. It's as much my fault. It infuriates me how easily I fell for her manipulations and it makes me wonder if I'm the right leader for this town or not."

Eric squeezed my fingers and laid his free hand over Susan's shoulder. "It's okay, Susan. It's over. You came through for everyone in the end."

I bit my lip. "Well, I still have some questions."

A sneering voice from down the corridor broke our conversation. "Oh…is that Miss Jones I hear? You can't bear to stay away from me, can you?"

With a deep exhale, Susan smiled. "Let's get this over with."

We never spoke as we followed Susan back to Gina's cell. It was the opposite way down the corridor from where Eric had spent his time — and the lighting looked dimmer. It fit.

Gina clapped her stumpy palms to her cheeks when we reached her cell. "Oh, it is you. What a delightful surprise."

I ignored her sarcastic remark. "This isn't a social call, Gina. I found out my mom discovered your papers. She wanted you to confess to what you'd done! She demanded you tell the people you'd discovered the side effects of the resuscitations."

Gina formed a cruel, hard, twisted smile on her lips and leaned back. She clapped in slow mockery. "Oh, my…you have been busy." She laughed. "It took you a rather long time to reach this conclusion, didn't it? Here I presumed you were such a bright girl." Her voice rang cold and hard and bitter. In that moment, I guessed this was the first time in her life she'd felt defeated — and I was the benefactor.

The relief I expected never came. Instead, I felt drained. "Why, Gina? Why do you hate me so much?"

Gina answered my question with one of her own. "You look even more like your aunt than your mother."

I took a step back. "My aunt, Susan?"

"Oh, yes…your Aunt *Susan!*" Gina spat my aunt's name.

I shook my head. "You met her?"

"Met her? She was the bane of my life. I shall tell you a story, little girl. Your despicable grandmother *coerced* my husband into her bed. He *sired* your Aunt Susan. Then when I fell pregnant, unbeknown to me, he had the audacity to suggest we give our daughter the same name — probably so he didn't have to bother memorizing two, the sorry swine."

I glanced at Susan, whose brows were drawn together. "Did you know this?"

"I do not bear grudges, Cassidy. Look at what it has done to Mother."

"Okay, so you did. Then please tell me something else…" I swallowed a lump as it formed in my throat and Eric draped a warm arm around my shoulder and rubbed my arm. "Did Gina tell you she planned to murder my mom?"

Susan didn't need to answer as Gina scoffed. "Oh, my stupid daughter — as if I didn't realize she was the pathetic traitor trying to lead the rebellion. Do you think I would have let her into any of my secrets? Your goody-two-shoes of a mother, however, insisted I inform the people about the…resuscitations. She" — Gina sang the next words out with mock tenderness — "*pleaded* and *pleaded* with me to tell the imbeciles. Then she threatened me, saying that if I did not confess to them, she would."

"Cut the crap, Gina. You didn't resuscitate those people. You pretty much brought them back from the dead. In any other time, they'd have died. No medical doctor could have saved them."

"Semantics, Miss Jones. A resuscitation is a resuscitation. With your mother, however… Well, her brain was rather mushed inside her head — and out." Gina snickered and a wave of nausea washed over me. I swallowed again and barely held my tears back. Gina went on as if none the wiser to my inner torment. "I supposed I could have revived her if I had wanted to, but seeing you writhe in anguish was rather priceless."

"You won't get to me anymore, Gina. I now see your cruelty to me is meant for my aunt. If you hated us so much, why did you bring our family into Petriville?"

With a dismissive wave, she sighed. "Oh, that. You were already here by the time I discovered my husband's treachery." She cackled. "Anyway, I rather hoped your father would abandon your mother in favor of my Susan. That would have provided me immense satisfaction."

Susan looked nothing less than horrified. She'd clearly known nothing of her mother's weak matchmaking efforts.

Gina made another attempt to shock her audience. "My stupid daughter didn't seem to have the foresight to pursue the union. So much like her idiotic father…"

Susan pivoted away. "Think over your life, Mother. Consider for a moment whether this was worth it."

I squeezed Eric's hand. "Wait for us, Susan. I'd like to ask you something."

She slowed but didn't stop, and as we caught up to her, she wiped at her face and blew her nose into a lace-trimmed handkerchief. "I'm sorry that Mother —"

I cut her off in a soft voice. "It's not your responsibility to apologize on behalf of your mother,

Susan. I'm sorry she has treated you and Amanda like she has."

Susan looked surprised at the tenderness in my voice. "Thank you." Then she climbed the stairs. "What is it you want to know?"

"*Did* my mother offer to take the fall?"

Susan's tone became resigned but was soft — gentle even. "Ah…yes. Naturally, you would need clarification on this matter. Mother lied to me. She told me she'd discovered Emily was the rebellion leader. She said she would scare her but assured me she would bring her no harm. Emily was my friend, and I relayed what mother had said. We both held significant roles within the rebellion.

"We considered that the cleaning robots in Emily's office may have discovered some un-shredded rebellion notes. I sat with her — comforted her — while she wrote your digipar letter. The prison cameras most certainly got close-ups of every word she wrote. However, she *was* cautious and took a long time over it. It's possible Emily doubted even me. I wouldn't blame her for that. She disregarded her suspicions, though, and insisted we keep quiet about everything and thus not add fuel to Mother's fire."

Susan sighed as we crossed the glossy flooring of the train station toward the exit. She halted and turned to us. "When Mother murdered Emily, it devastated me. I thought that whatever happened, Emily had conveyed in that letter."

I looked into her steel-gray eyes — so similar to her mother's. "I have a few more questions, if you don't mind?"

Susan nodded. "Go on."

"Did you know the reason she killed my mother before now?"

Susan exhaled a heavy breath. "No. Instead, she told me she knew what ailed everyone. She also claimed to have developed a cure but would only reveal it once you returned with the formulae. I truly believed she had. That was the reason I couldn't put her back in prison and also why I couldn't release Eric."

I shut my eyes for a second, then dipped my chin once. "Before we left Petriville, you said that if I learned the truth behind my mom's murder, I might help everyone. What did you mean by that?"

Susan tilted her head back, her focus moving upward. "Ah-h, yes. I suspect Emily found out things about Mother that she kept to herself. It is possible she hoped to work things out with her. Perhaps she didn't believe Mother would really murder her. During that time, I noticed Amanda becoming weaker. She'd started sleeping during the day. Once Mother slipped, saying she supposed Amanda was not the only person in Petriville who was growing weak. Of course, she always needed to boast, so she added something which made my hairs stand on end. She said she knew exactly who would experience these *symptoms*. When I questioned her on it, she said I ought to stop spreading about silly ravings." Susan drew a deep breath. "What a mess, isn't it?"

Eric nodded in answer to Susan's rhetorical question, but my mind moved to another. I didn't give Susan a chance to rally her thoughts before bringing it up. "When Gina was in prison, she told me my mom never agreed to take the fall as the rebel leader."

Susan frowned, appearing to shrink even more. "Oh, my! Did you *believe* her?"

"Maybe. Although I should know by now that Gina loves saying things she knows will upset me."

"As does she me, my dear…as does she me." Susan wiped at her eyes as the station door slid open.

The enormous Austin ran in. He closed Susan in his arms and she all but disappeared with a soft gasp. He kissed the top of her head, reminding me of a kind of King Kong with his tiny obsession.

As they turned and walked away arm-in-arm, I stopped them. "Susan?"

They dropped their arms from each other and half-turned back to me.

I glanced at Eric, then back at Susan. "Did Jonas speak to you?"

She frowned. "About?"

"Him and Olivia."

"Ah-h, yes. He wants us to match their DNA. It's a request I never expected, but I suppose it's understandable. The girl is besotted with him."

"She is," I agreed.

Susan smiled. "It's already done." Then she turned and walked with Austin, looking up into the big man's face. "As are a few others."

Austin again wrapped an enormous arm around her shoulders and appeared to give it a squeeze as he smiled down at her.

I looked up at Eric and mouthed. "Them?"

With a broadening smile, he shrugged as we watched them go. "It could be their way of committing to each other."

A moment later, we made our way through the glass doors. Dawn called our world to life as Eric and I stopped, gazing out over the town square. Many chirping birds filled the trees while some swooped toward plants. Insects and bees buzzed among flowers while butterflies flitted over the morning dew shimmering off leaves.

Eric drew in a deep breath, sucking in his gut and raising his hands in an upward, back-arcing stretch. On straightening, he lowered them around me, pulling me against him. I looked up. "I wonder where life will take us next."

Eric raised a brow. "Does it matter? Whichever way we go, as long as you're at my side, nothing does."

Eric was right. He *was* by my side in a way neither Jonas nor Caleb could ever be.

He tightened his hold around my body, a shudder running through his. In a hoarse whisper, he spoke into my hair. "Seriously though, do you think this is over, my Cassidy? I mean, really over?"

"I think it is, Eric." My voice came out as a soft whisper. "I think we can move on now."

He beamed, and in a flash, he changed the dire mood of our interaction to a very different one. "So…about our conversation in the paddock the other day—" He broke off and chuckled.

I bit my lip and peered up at him, a laugh bursting from my chest. I'd sounded flirty, even to my own ears. "Yes?"

Eric didn't need to go on. We both knew what this meant—that we could join in every sense of the word.

Elation swept over me. This was our time. We—humanity—would re-surge. And I was truly free to be with the man I loved. No one would ever again dare challenge our union—or, at least, no one would succeed if they tried. Eric was completely mine, and I was utterly his.

His face grew serious. Right there on the stairs into the train station beneath a pinking sky, Eric dropped to one knee. He lifted my hands in his. "My Cassidy... Despite our youthful appearances, we're not that young. And what I know is that you're the girl I love. Irrespective of what Gina said, I don't believe our DNA matching influenced how I feel. And that won't change." Eric pulled a box from his pocket. He flipped it open to reveal a golden ring. "Will you, Cassidy Jones, marry me?"

The Kaleidotonium and diamond setting glinted in the early morning sunlight — bright rainbows shooting upward.

I tugged Eric to his feet, threading my arms around his neck. As he locked me to him, I lifted my feet off the floor, laughing. "Yes, Eric. Yes. Yes. Yes."

He lowered me to the ground and leaned back. With trembling fingers, he slid the ring onto my finger, and when he spoke, he kept his gaze on mine. "A perfect fit for my perfect fit."

Then he yanked me against him and pressed his mouth hard against mine in a kiss that was deep and warm and full of longing. Butterflies fluttered in my stomach and a thought flitted through my mind. *I'm home.*

Want to see more like this?
Here's a taster for you to enjoy!

The Cinder City Embers:
Singularity
Lanne Garrett

Excerpt

My mother, Ezra — *God rest her soul* — was a proud
Chippewa woman and an Ember sympathizer, so they
say. I think she had just gotten tired of sending children
to their deaths. Those who weren't afraid to talk say
that she had been part of an activist group, Free
Embers. They had stood against Cinder City and the
Authority, President Atlas Gold. She and twenty others
had tried to storm City Center. They'd never even made
it to the Golden Gates. All of them had been shot for
treason. Forty bystanders had been killed on that same
day by stray bullets. The City Controllers had opened
fire on a square full of men, women and children. The
Authority's message had been heard by all. No one
stood against President Atlas Gold and lived to talk
about it. He'd sooner kill his own people than allow the
faintest whisper of hope to spread. The Authority saw
hope as a sickness and a bullet was the cure. Hope was
harder to come by than grain outside the Golden City.

I was named after her, my mother, Ezra Larkin. I
was the last person in all the Rings to be of my mother's
people — Chippewa. Even as a young girl, I understood

that the Chippewa people could end with me. My father Cor—an Irish hothead with the temperament of a caged lion—didn't speak much about my mother. Some said he was ashamed of her, but I think he missed her so much that it hurt him to speak her name. The odd times he did talk about her, it was usually about my stubborn nature being much like hers or how my laughter reminded him of her.

I don't remember my mother. A part of me thinks of it as a blessing. The other part sees it as a curse. Not remembering her means I don't miss her in the same gut-wrenching way my father does, but it also picks at my soul that I didn't get to know my own mother. I was six years old when she was killed. I have a single photograph of us together— her, myself and my father, in front of the Golden Gates of Cinder City, but it did nothing to trigger even the faintest of memories. I keep it inside my pillowcase.

Every now and again I have a dream of her and me together. In my dream, she comes to sit with me and listens to me tell her about my life. In my dreams, I knew she was dead. She would always look like she did in her photo. Even in my dreams, the Authority could punish me, reminding me of what he'd taken from my father and me. Some folks in Limits—the ring where we lived—said my father was born and raised in Cinder City and fell in love with the woman who cleaned his family home. As punishment for loving a lower class, he had been sent to live out his days on the edge of the world he'd grown up in. I don't think my father saw that as a punishment, given that he'd gotten the girl in the end.

Cinder City had once been called The Promised Land, or so that was what I'd read in my father's old texts. It was nothing like that now, at least, not unless you were born on the other side of those gates with skin the color of snow and eyes as blue as the sky. The world – or what I knew of it – had been divided into two groups, the promised ones and those of us who scrubbed their toilets. We were called the Solvents and Insolvents – those who mattered and those who didn't. At birth, the Insolvents were tagged with a small GPS chip. They said it was for our own safety, in case we needed help. I didn't buy it and neither did anyone else. All it did was make it easier to hunt us. That tag was how they'd found my mother and killed her.

Every year, Cinder officials opened their Golden Gates and held the Ember Harvest. The Harvest was a test of the potential Embers. It is said that over three hundred years ago the Insolvents had grown tired of their treatment and had developed the ability to awaken deadly parts of their minds then had waged war against Cinder City. Now, as a precaution, every child is tested for the Scoria Singularity – remnants of the genetics from a time the world was almost destroyed overnight.

If someone showed the first signs, detected in a blood test, they were shipped to Ember Gates. They said that each generation burned almost as brightly as the generation that had waged war, and that is why they were called Embers. An Ember burns as hot as the fire which created it. During testing, the genetics of those who were Embers lit up like the Fourth of July, glowing hotter than anyone else.

The auditorium where the Harvest was held was smack dab in the middle of Cinder City. It held over eight hundred people in comfort, but for the Harvest it would be far too packed to consider it anything but sad and hot. That happened during Cinder City's yearly Harvest of the Embers, aka taking children who were potential Embers and carting them off to an unknown location, never to return. I had been attending the Harvest since I could remember. It was mandatory for all citizens to attend. It was the only time I wore anything but torn jeans and sneakers. It was a rare occasion when the Insolvents mixed socially with the Solvents, where the color of our skin didn't matter. Or at least, for one day, they didn't point it out.

This time I'd be there as a potential Ember. It was an odd feeling. I never knew what happened to the Embers. After they had been named, they had been taken away. I only knew that they never came back. And now that I might learn what had happened to them. I would be content never finding out. The night would be a celebration. We would dance, enjoy spirits and foods that we Insolvents never had on the outskirts of Cinder City. Although many parents would be leaving in tears as they understood what was happening, I had always looked forward to the celebration following the Harvest. Aside from the dramatic build-up and muffled screams at the end, it had been a lot of fun. Thinking of it that way was better than facing the truth for most of us. The truth was, children were dying, all in the name of some debt Cinder City said we owed for a war we'd never started.

I would be attending with my best friend and ring neighbor, Zowie Tate. I had been friends with Zow for my entire life. That was how it was in our ring. It was small enough that everyone here knew everyone else and bonds were as long as life. Our parents had grown up together and I was sure our kids would too. Zow and I were only children, as it was for a lot of the families in the rings. There was a birthing cap of two in place for the families who couldn't afford to purchase a license to have more, but most families could just afford one. If ever a son or daughter was taken to Ember Gates, the family could have another child if they wished. Such was the way of life here. We were all replaceable.

There were three belts around the pristine city of Cinder. The first ring was called Fringe. It housed those who worked in Cinder and had enough money to be considered well-off and never struggled for a meal. Those in Fringe could almost pass for Cinder, with lighter skin and hair. As the population grew, it was reshuffled to accommodate a new ring. The second ring was Boundary. It housed the lower middle-class and provided Cinder with their primary source of power from the rivers and falls. It held four hydroelectric power plants. Then there was Limits, last to be created. We were low enough on the pole to not have a class of our own. Limits provided the fruits and vegetables, grains and meats for Cinder.

Limits' residents were all darker skin, like it somehow made us lesser people pushed to the edge of society. My father's textbooks said racism had been abolished in the early twenty-second century, but being on this side of the fence, I called bullshit. Mankind crumbled generations ago in the exact spot where I was standing—segregation, death camps and hate. For every step humanity had taken forward, Cinder City had plunged it back fifty steps into a pit of xenophobia, death squads and armbands. I didn't say it out loud. No one did. Well, no one who was still alive muttered such things.

Each ring of said 'Promised Land' was surrounded by a fence that no one was brave enough to scale, with four gates that opened in the morning and shut at the end of the day. With one exception, Harvest night, when the gates remained open for twenty-four hours.

Being caught outside your zone after the gates had closed was a direct ticket to Cinder Cells. No one risked being tossed in Cells because no family had enough money to ransom their freedom. And on the edge of Limits stood a fence with no gates and no escape, patrolled by Cinder Controllers. There would be no arrest for trying to get out. You were shot and your family would be billed the cost of the bullet used. Genocide was alive and well. I don't think it had ever really gone away – not for us, not for those who stood out like a dark shadow among white daisies.

At the promising age of eighteen, straddling childhood and adulthood, it was my turn for the Harvest, to see if I was an Ember. When I should be planning my future, being courted for marriage and a family, I was preparing for what could be my immediate death. This didn't seem fair to me. My father had tried to prepare me as much as he could. He'd told me not to worry. Since the beginning of the Harvest, my family had always been safe. No one in our line had ever held the Scoria Singularity, but there was always a risk. I prayed to my mother's ancestors for strength and for them to guide me. My father had promised my mother that he would teach me about her people, and every day since I can remember, my father has told me stories and taught me prayers.

My father had gone through the Harvest, just like every other soul in the rings. He said he had been a nervous wreck. But once it was over, it was over for good. After that, once a year it was just another party where someone else worried. Once he'd had me, his fears had come back tenfold. Now, he was scared of each Harvest and awaiting the unknown fate that hung over our family like a storm cloud.

To take my mind off the impending doom, I focused on the potential after-party. For those who weren't named an Ember, it was a grand celebration. Now that I could be named, I realized just how great a celebration it could be. I would dress the part, in case I did get to go home, so if I didn't I wouldn't be dragged away in rags. I stood in front of my mirror, staring at my high cheekbones, and could almost see my mother staring back at me. I was dressed in a hand-me-down from a few houses up. They hadn't needed it anymore. Their daughter had been taken to Ember Gates the past year and had never come back. I didn't dare say it out loud, but this was one of the only perks to finding out someone you knew was an Ember. There weren't many of those to be had around here, either. It was odd, how we'd just gotten used to saying thank you for bags of clothes from families of dead children. It was normal in the rings.

Tomorrow night would be the commencement rituals of the Harvest. We would be carted off to begin the first round of tests that would lead up to the event. Tonight, things in Limits were somber. There were no children playing outside and no screams of laughter. There was nothing. It was as if someone had died but not yet, though I didn't know if Embers were killed or not. I was betting they were. It was said that once they went to Ember Gates, they waited until their maturity had completed and were not just murdered as I had suspected. Cinder doctors had found the age of eighteen to be the perfect age to take us. It was cheaper to do it at the height of puberty. They didn't have to feed and house us for as long. If you didn't display advanced signs of the Scoria Singularity, you were allowed to go home — or that was what we all were told during our Harvest Preparation classes. But no one ever came back. Not once. Never in the history of ever had someone returned.

I pulled off my armband with its patch that said 'Limits' and stared at it for a moment, running my fingertips over the red embroidered lettering. All of who I was had been reduced to a small black and scratchy armband. It told the world around me that I was at the bottom because my mother was Chippewa and my father Irish. My heritage meant I could die, but a possible death was not something I was interested in celebrating. I removed my pale-yellow dress and hung it up over my cracked mirror. Everything I owned was damaged or scratched or stained in some fashion. I had a fleeting moment of wondering what it had been like those many years ago when everyone'd had the same chance in life. My father had said there were no divisions such as this hundreds of years ago. And there had not been one Authority overseeing all. The world once had many leaders and laws that governed them. Not anymore. The Authority was the one and only law.

The first horn of the evening sounded. There were three hours left until the gates between the rings would be locked. Like clockwork, every sixty minutes another horn would sound, the final one being a long warning blast. I pulled my long dark hair into a ponytail, slipped on my ripped jeans and sneakers and climbed out of my window. I didn't have far to drop. We lived in a single-story home, mostly built of rejected wood from Cinder. The windows were broken, and each time a fire broke out, my room turned into a wasteland for the lungs. Because my father was a carpenter, our home was one of the nicer ones in Limits.

Ten yards from the back of my house stood the fence of no return with red and white warning signs that were polite enough to let us know that the sign was the only warning we would get. A single bullet from a Cinder Controller would be the next step in their attempts at keeping us inside our ring. There had been times that children had found a way out of the fence. They had never been seen again. I didn't know what was out there, but it couldn't be good if it was eating up wandering children. The whole thing stunk. How does a person become lost when Cinder Controllers could punch in someone's GPS information and find them in a fraction of a second? I suppose we just weren't important enough to spare the manpower for a search.

Breathing in the evening air, I could almost smell the roses that grew along the metal fence. It mixed with the scent of warm bread cooking in Limits. That bread was not for us. It would be shipped to the Harvest celebration. It was torture, the smells of foods we weren't allowed to touch. My stomach growled. I had eaten dinner but it hadn't been enough. I was always hungry. Limits didn't waste food or overeat, not when Cinder controlled every grain we used. We never risked running out. Cinder had a way of keeping us underfed, always forcing us to submit to their will. To prove this, the Authority would cut the rations in half every so often, as a reminder of who had the real power. I didn't see why they bothered. We all knew who was in charge. No one questioned it.

I stood a foot from the rear fence with my gaze following the steel chain-link to the top. I had never seen a Controller walking the fence, but I was pretty sure they were watching in some way or another. Every twenty feet a metal pole stood cemented into the ground. Fixed to the top of each post were cameras and a walkway that attached to each pole. I had spent almost twenty-four hours watching the fence from my bedroom window and never did Zow or I ever see a Controller. I wasn't brave enough to test out my theory of their nonexistence. To be wrong would mean death. I was curious, not stupid.

"Wait up, Ezra," Zow called out from behind me.

Zow jogged from her house against the fence at the end of my block. Her curly black hair flowed out behind her. Zowie Tate was darker than the midnight sky but much more beautiful. Her silky hair was a froth of shiny curls, wild and free. How I wished she could be that way, too—wild and free and full of choice and life. Each night she and I ran the fence line until our legs shook and our lungs burned. I used to jog it with my father. Eventually, he had grown tired of running in more ways than one. Over the years, he'd become weary of many things, but he had never failed to make sure I was loved and ready for just about anything. He'd taught me how to trap rabbits, how to protect myself, build a fire out of nothing and if I had to, survive on my own. If ever I found myself on the other side of the fence, my father wanted me to be ready.

Zow, on the other hand, was a little slower to catch up. The Tate family had come from a long line of farmers. Not many of the ones in Limits had skills outside raising piglets and collecting eggs from their hens. They didn't have time to be anything more. The Tate family was decent to the bone, as was Zow, but she wouldn't survive ten minutes outside the fence. She didn't have a live-or-die mentality. Her soul was far too pure for that. If love could feed a nation, I'd never starve near her.

Winded, Zoe nudged my shoulder as she jogged beside me. "Honestly, Ezra, do you think we'd ever be lost on the other side of the fence?"

"No, but better safe than sorry."

Zow peered around me, looking out to the tree line on the other side and she shiver, probably at the thought of being out there without protection. Deep down, Zow was braver than she gave herself credit for, but no one knows what they're made of until they're put to the test. I hoped to hell her courage would never be tested.

"My father said that there's nothing out there but the wild. After World War Four had destroyed all but Cinder, the rest of the world became a barren wasteland with wild animals and man-eating people."

I picked up my pace, forcing Zow to breathe more heavily. Part of me did it to make her stop talking. I hated talking about the wars that had helped create Cinder and the rings. The thoughts were more than disturbing. They reminded me of a time long before we were caged animals ourselves. I was jealous. I envied the freedoms people had once had. The war that had started this all… I'd have killed for those freedoms.

After the last war, the fences had been built. Cinder and all their amassed power had created a world within a world. They'd created the rings. I didn't feel safer inside the fences. I felt like a slave. We worked for them, nothing more and nothing less. In return, they protected us, fed us and housed us — or that was what they said. And each year, we sent our children to the Harvest, in hopes they didn't have the Scoria Singularity — the cause of World War Four. The poor and starving waged war against the rich and plump — a history that would repeat time and time again.

"I don't think there are cannibals out there, Zow. Wild animals maybe, but I don't think it's as scary as we're told it is. I mean, where else are the rabbits I catch coming from?"

"Just the same, I'd rather not be unfortunate enough to find out first-hand."

Zow and I were a lot alike, but some things about us were polar opposites. She didn't rock the boat, never asked questions and never argued. She followed the rules and never thought there was a different way of life. She took what was given to her and never questioned it. I, on the other hand, questioned everything. I wasn't content picking up where my father would leave off. I wouldn't be a woodworker or laborer. I wanted more out of life and knew I'd fight tooth and nail to make my way out of Limits. I needed more. I craved knowledge and fact and fulfillment. One day, I knew my life would mean something more than building a house or raising chickens.

I grabbed Zow's arm and lessened her pace. "Hold up."

Zow slowed, following me to the fence.

"What?" Zow asked, her voice shaking from her speeding pulse.

My heart was hammering too hard for me to speak. I pointed to a cherry blossom tree. It was one of our markers. There would be another one in thirty feet, in full bloom. We would run to the fifth cherry blossom then turn back. The pink flowers were brilliant among the stark shadows and rich green foliage. This was my favorite time of year, when Limits looked pretty, even just for a moment. In front of the tree stood a child in a white hospital gown. She stared forward, unafraid.

"Hey!" I screamed at the child and slapped the fence to gain her attention.

"Is that…" Zow whispered. Her fingers gripped the metal fence. "Hey!"

"Go get help, Zow. Run. Get my father," I said, not wanting to take my eyes off the girl.

Zow didn't ask questions. She bolted from my side. I knew she would run flat out, screaming the entire way. The little girl with long black hair turned toward me. Her cheeks were blistering red. Her lips were plumped up, too full for a child. She tilted her head and smiled then turned and walked toward the thick bush.

"Wait! Come back. No, come back," I screamed and pounded my hands against the fence again. "Don't go in there. Come back."

"Step away from the fence."

From above me came the voice. I looked up. There was no one there.

"Step away from the fence. Last warning."

At the top of the pole to my right, a small speaker box hung with a little flashing red light.

Just then my father grabbed my arm and pulled me back with enough force that I stumbled. "Ezra, get away from the fence. I've told you to stay away from the wall. They will kill you. Do you not understand that part?"

My father stood almost a foot taller than I did. He had an extra hundred pounds on me. On a good day, he could create fear so deep that it burned my soul. Today, at that moment, I almost vomited. My father had never yelled at me or handled me in such a way.

I tugged at my arm, pointing at the trees. "There was a child, a small child. She was out there."

My father stopped dragging me from the fence and looked out to the trees. "There's no one there, Ezra. Stop this before you get us all shot."

Zow finally made her way back to us. She was not the runner my father was. "Did you see her, Mr. Larkin?"

"Who?" he asked.

"The little girl," Zow said, looking back to the cherry tree. "Where did she go?"

"Home. Now," my father commanded, giving me a look that said we'd deal with it there.

All three of us jogged back to my house. No one spoke a single word. Once home, my father didn't want to discuss it. He said we were mistaken, that it must have been a trick of the shadows. I asked where the Controllers were and why they used a speaker box. Where were the guns to shoot us down? Where were the Officials to scare us into submission? It was the last of the conversation. My father shut me off and walked Zow home. He'd tell her family the same load of crap he had just said to me.

During dinner, not another word was spoken about the young girl, the Controllers or the fact that we both knew he wasn't being truthful. He was wrong. There had been a child out there. I knew he was wrong and he knew it too. I think there have been many children, wandering around the outskirts of the rings, but someone had to have let them out. If the Controllers had seen me, they also would have seen her. Someone had let her go to her death on purpose. We gripped hands, said a prayer and ate in silence. Our meal wasn't anything special. It was the same thing I'd had for breakfast and lunch—warmed grains and oats with a few berries. It felt like a brick when it hit my stomach, but I wouldn't complain. It was more than most had in Limits.

My father checked on me before he went to bed. I could feel his nervousness in the air, like a hot breeze off a forest fire. I swore it blistered my lungs. I knew he was anxious about tomorrow morning. I'd be heading out and there was a chance it would be the last he would ever see of me, aside from the Harvest

Ceremony itself. We would be picked up in the morning and taken to Cinder. We would remain overnight and meet again at the celebration. We were told that we would be given a checkup and that it was nothing to worry about. It felt as though a loaded gun was pointed at my temple and I was being told to calm down, that I hadn't a need to worry. When my father tucked me in, his hands shook and he gave a muffled cry. He was praying to my mother and all her relations to protect me and bring me home. If he was worried, so was I.

I didn't pray for myself. I prayed for Zow. I prayed she would have the chance to marry and have children of her own. I pleaded with whomever was listening to give Zow a ticket back to Limits. I prayed her children would never see the inside of Ember Gates. I'd like to think my prayers were an unselfish act, but they weren't. If we both ended up at Ember Gates, it would kill me inside to see her there with me. Even if I wasn't certain what happened there, I knew it wouldn't be good. Nothing with the word Ember or Gate ever sounded like a thrilling location. If she were named along with me, my entire world would come crashing down. Then again, if she were named and I wasn't, that would be the end of it for me. So I could only pray she didn't go at all.

FINCH
B O O K S

Sign up for our newsletter and find out about all our romance book releases, eBook sales and promotions, sneak peeks and FREE romance books!

About the Author

Carryn W. Kerr is a young adult fiction author. She has a deep love for all things relating to the English language and considers stories as the rainbows of a sometimes cruel world. Rather than creating characters, she believes they always existed. Hers was the privilege of meeting them. When writing their stories, words flow through her fingertips like a gushing stream. She finds pleasure in escaping to fictitious realms as they develop and grow in her imagination.

Carryn began the adventure of life in a small South African village in the province of Kwa-Zulu Natal. When she isn't writing, she can be found working out in the gym, running, or trying not to fall off her horse as they train and compete in dressage.

For many years she worked in IT. Carryn lives with her husband and son in Johannesburg, South Africa. Her married daughter is on the beautiful island of Zanzibar.

Carryn loves to hear from readers. You can find her contact information, website details and author profile page at https://www.finch-books.com